"Raistli...

Slowly, Amberyl unwound the scarf from her face, letting it fall about her shoulders. She shook out her snow-wet hair, feeling drops of water spatter on her hands.

"So you are not human," Raistlin remarked.

"No, I am not," Amberyl replied. She couldn't bear to look at him. The mage's eyes burned through her, touching something deep inside, filling her with sweet pain.

"Amberyl," he said. "It appears that we will never know what caused this to happen. All that should really concern us is what must be done to rid ourselves of this . . . this *Valin*?"

Shutting her eyes, Amberly licked her lips. Her mouth was dry, the cave was suddenly unbearably cold. Shivering, she tried more than once to speak.

"What?" Raistlin's voice grated.

"I . . . must bear . . . your child," Amberyl said weakly.

For long moments there was silence. Ashamed and afraid, Amberyl buried her face in her arms. But an odd sound made her look up.

Raistlin was lying back on his blankets, laughing. It was almost inaudible laughter, more of a wheeze, but a choking laughter nonetheless—taunting, cutting laughter. And Amberyl saw, with pity in her heart, that its sharp edge was directed against himself.

DragonLance®

❧ Tales Volume 3 ❧

LOVE and WAR

Edited by
Margaret Weis and Tracy Hickman

featuring "Raistlin's Daughter"
by Margaret Weis and Dezra Despain

Cover Art by LARRY ELMORE
Interior Art by STEVE FABIAN

DRAGONLANCE® TALES

Volume Three

LOVE and WAR

©Copyright 1987 TSR, Inc.
All Rights Reserved.

First Printing, October, 1987
Printed in the United States of America.
Library of Congress Catalog Card Number: 86-51589

9 8 7 6

ISBN: 0-88038-519-7

All characters in this book are fictitious. Any resemblance to actual persons, living or dead is purely coincidental.

TSR, Inc.
P.O. Box 756
Lake Geneva, WI 53147
53147 U.S.A.

TSR Ltd.
120 Church End, Cherry Hinton
Cambridge CB1 3LB
United Kingdom

TABLE OF CONTENTS

FOREWORD

*F*itting it is that the many years of creative work on the DRAGONLANCE® saga should come to a provisory culmination with this collection of short stories, the most pleasing and powerful yet. Some of the writers represented in this volume are veterans of *Tales 1* and *2*, and certain of them will continue to write about the world of Krynn in an exciting series of DRAGONLANCE novels in the immediate future.

"A Good Knight's Tale" by Harold Bakst suitably begins this volume that has love and war as its theme. Told by a Knight of Solamnia, it is a tale that involves both love and war—the warring of passions of a selfish father's heart.

Love is painted in a more tender aspect in "A Painter's Vision," by Barbara Siegel and Scott Siegel, but then what can you expect when a dragon gets himself involved?

The story of love as sacrifice is recounted, along with the tale of the undead who haunt Darken Wood, in another of Nick O'Donohoe's revisionist interpretations of a portion of *Dragons of Autumn Twilight*.

"Hide and Go Seek" by Nancy Berberick is the story of the love friends bear each other as Tasslehoff risks his life to save that of a kidnapped child.

"By the Measure" recounts the courage of a Knight of Solamnia fighting impossible odds. Written by Richard A. Knaak, this is the haunting story of a young knight's courage and devotion to his Order.

The adventures of a very young Sturm are recorded in "The Exiles" by Paul Thompson and Tonya Carter. The boy learns his first lessons in courage, facing an evil cleric of the Dark Queen.

A lighter moment is presented in "Heart of Goldmoon" by Laura Hickman and Kate Novak. A tale of romance and adventure, it tells of the first meeting of Riverwind and Goldmoon and how the Que-shu princess came to learn of the existence of the true gods.

Continuing in the romantic vein, "Raistlin's Daughter" written by myself and Dezra Despain, relays a strange legend currently circulating in Krynn. It will end, for the time being, the DRAGONLANCE® saga with—what else—a question mark.

"Silver and Steel" is the legend of Huma's final battle with the Dark Queen. There are many such legends about the valor of Huma, but this one, written by Kevin Randle, is a gritty, moving account of war that will not soon be forgotten.

It is fitting that the book end with "From the Yearning for War and War's End," Michael Williams's poignant reminder for us all that war—though sometimes sadly necessary—is a destroyer of both love and of life.

Margaret Weis and Tracy Hickman

A Good Knight's Tale

Harold Bakst

In those chaotic years just after the Cataclysm, when the frightened citizens of Xak Tsaroth were fleeing their beloved but decimated city, there was among them a certain half-elf by the name of Aril Witherwind, who, while others sought only refuge, took to roaming the countryside, carrying upon his bent back a huge, black tome.

Even without his peculiar burden, which he held by a leather strap thrown across one shoulder, Aril Witherwind was, as far as half-elves went, a strange one. Though he was properly tall and willowy, and he had the fair hair, pale skin, and blue eyes typical of his kind, he seemed not at all interested in his appearance and had, indeed, a slovenliness about him: His shoes were often unbuckled, his shirt hung out of his pants, and his hair was usually in a tangle. He often went days without shaving so that fine, blond hairs covered his jaw like down. In addition to everything else, he wore thick, metal-rimmed eyeglasses.

All this, though, had a simple enough explanation: Aril Witherwind was, by his own definition, an academic. More particularly, he was one of the many itinerant folklorists who appeared on Krynn just after the Cataclysm.

"The Cataclysm threatens to extinguish our rich past," he would explain in his gentle but enthusiastic voice to whoever gave him a moment of time. "And if peace should ever again come to Krynn, we will want to know something of our traditions before everything was destroyed."

"But this is not the time to do it!" often came the curt response from some fleeing traveler, sometimes with everything he owned in a wagon or in a dogcart or even upon his own back, his family often in tow.

"Ah, but this is exactly the time to do it," returned Aril Witherwind automatically, "before too much is forgotten by the current sweep of events."

"Well, good luck to you, then!" would as likely be the answer as the party hurried off to some hopefully safer corner of Krynn.

Undaunted, Aril Witherwind criss-crossed the countryside, traversing shadowy valleys, sun-lit fields, and sombre forests. He stopped at the occasional surviving inn, passed through refugee encampments, and even marched along with armies, all the time asking whomever he met if he or she knew a story that he could put into his big black book.

In time, it became clear to Aril that he usually had the best luck with the older folks—indeed, the older the better. These grayhairs were not only the most likely to remember a story or two, but they were the ones most likely to be interested in relating it. Perhaps it was because they welcomed the opportunity to slow down and reminisce awhile. Or perhaps it was because they had not much of a future to give to Krynn, only their pasts.

In any case, Aril Witherwind soon learned to seek them out almost exclusively, and his book slowly began to fill with stories from before the Cataclysm, when Krynn had been in what he considered its Golden Age.

He gave each story an appropriate title, and then he gave due credit to the source by adding: ". . . as told by Henrik Hellendale, a dwarven baker" or ". . . as told by Verial Stargazer, an elven shepherd" or ". . . as told by Frick Ashfell, a human woodchopper" and so forth.

People often asked Aril what his favorite story was, but, with the professional objectivity proper to an academic, he'd say only, "I like them all."

But, really, if you could read his mind, there was a favorite, and that was one ". . . as told by Barryn Warrex, a Solamnic Knight."

It had been on a particularly lovely spring day—a day, indeed, when all of nature seemed happy and unconcerned with the political upheaval miles away—when Aril, while traversing the length of a grassy and flower-dotted valley, espied a knight, kneeling at the base of the valley wall. The knight, as luck would have it, was an old one.

"Perfect," murmured Aril to himself as he strode toward the grand man, stopping several paces away.

At first, the old knight didn't seem to realize he had an audience. He simply continued his kneeling, his head bowed in either deep meditation or perhaps even in respectful prayer to the recently deposed gods of Krynn. Behind him was a low, rocky overhang, almost a cave really, which was apparently serving as his humble, if temporary, shelter—The Order of the Solamnic Knights, you see, had been destroyed in the Cataclysm and fallen into disrepute, its few remaining members scattered by the four winds.

It seemed to Aril Witherwind that such events must have taken a truly terrible toll on this fellow, maybe making him look even older than he was, for he had a drawn, haggard face; his hair, though thick, was totally white; and his hands, clenched before him, were gnarly, almost arthritic.

Still, Aril could see much in the man that boasted of the old grandeur of his order. He was dressed in his full plate armor, a great sword hanging at his side, his visorless helmet and shield resting nearby on a flat rock. And though he was kneeling, he did seem to be quite tall—that is, long of limb. But what impressed Aril Witherwind the most was his truly copious moustache, a long white one that drooped with a poignant flourish so that its tips nearly brushed the ground as he knelt there.

A lot of pride must go into that moustache, mused Aril as he waited patiently for the knight to finish whatever he was doing.

Now, all that time, the itinerant folklorist thought he was unobserved, so he was startled when the knight, not so much as lifting his head or moving a muscle, spoke up in a deep, though tired, voice: "What do you want?"

"Oh! Pardon me," said Aril Witherwind, stepping ahead, bent forward as if he were bowing, though, in fact, he was merely carrying his heavy tome. "I didn't mean to interrupt anything. Only, if you are done, I would like to speak with you."

"I am in meditation."

"So you are. But perhaps you could return to it in a moment," suggested Aril. "This will not take long."

The old knight sighed deeply. "Actually, you're not interrupting much," he said, his body slumping from its disciplined pose. "I no longer have the concentration I once did."

"Then we can talk?"

The knight began to rise to his feet, though it clearly

took some effort. "Ach, it's getting so I can't distinguish between the creaking in my armor and the creaking in my bones."

"I believe it was your armor that time," said Aril with a smile.

At his full height, the knight indeed proved to be a very tall man, as tall as Aril, who himself, when he did not carry his book, was a gangly fellow. And when the knight faced him fully, Aril got goosebumps because engraved upon the knight's tarnished breastplate was a faint rose, the famous symbol of his order.

"On the other hand, I do not feel much like talking," said the knight sullenly, walking right past the half-elf and seating himself upon a large rock where he leaned back against another and gazed languidly up at the blue sky and white clouds bracketed by the opposing walls of the valley. "I am a man of action only."

"I quite understand," said Aril, following. "But it does seem to me you are at the moment—um—between actions. The thing is, I am a folklorist—"

"Aril Witherwind."

"Yes, that's right. You've heard of me? I'm flattered."

The knight squinted at the gangly blond person with the large book upon his back. "You are indeed a strange one."

"It takes all kinds," said Aril Witherwind, again with a smile. "In any case, you know why I'm here."

"I do not wish to talk."

"Oh, but you must make yourself. A knight such as you surely has many wonderful tales of derring-do, bravery. Why, this may be one of your few opportunities to set the record straight about your order before the world forgets."

The knight appeared unmoved at first. But then, despite himself, he tugged contemplatively at the tip of his long moustache. "Perhaps," he said slowly, "if I do think about it—"

"Yes, do think about it!" said Aril Witherwind as he hurried to another, smaller rock, where he sat down, his bony knees pulled up. He brought forth his book and propped it open on his legs. He then took from his pouch a quill and inkwell, placing the inkwell on the ground.

"You're a pushy one," said the knight, arching an imperious eyebrow.

"These days, a folklorist must be," said Aril. "Now then, first thing's first: What is your name?"

"Warrex," said the knight growing ever more interested. He even sat up. "Barryn Warrex."

"Is Warrex spelled with one 'r' or two?"

"Two."

"Fine. Now what do you have for me? Some tale, I bet, of epic battles and falling castles, of heroic missions—"

"No," said the knight thoughtfully, again pulling on his moustache, "no, I don't think so."

"Oh? Then perhaps a tale of minotaur slaying or a duel with some fierce ogre—"

"No, no, not those either, though I've done both."

"Then, by all means, you must tell of them! People one day will want to read such knightly adventures—"

"Please!" snapped Barryn Warrex, his old milky eyes flashing in anger. "I have no patience for this unless you will listen to the story that I *want* to tell!"

"Of course, of course," said Aril, closing his eyes in contrition. "Forgive me. That is, of course, just what I want you to do."

"To a Solamnic Knight—at least to this old Solmanic Knight—there is one thing as important—more important—than even bravery, duty, and honor."

"More important? My, and what would that be?"

"Love."

"A tale of love? Well, that's good, too," said Aril Witherwind, nodding his approval and dipping his quill into the inkwell. "A knight's tale of chivalry—"

"I did not say 'chivalry,' " snarled Barryn Warrex.

"Pardon me, I just assumed—"

"Stop assuming, will you? This is a tale told to me when I was a mere child, long before I ever thought of becoming a knight. And though much has happened to me since, this tale has stayed with me all these years. Indeed, these days, it aches my heart more than ever."

Aril was already scribbling in his book. ". . . more—than—ever," he repeated as he wrote.

Barryn Warrex settled back once more, calming himself. "It is about two entwined trees in the Forest of Wayreth—"

"The Entwining Trees?" interrupted Aril, lifting his pert nose from his book and pushing his slipping glasses back up with a forefinger. "I've heard of them! You know their story?"

"I do," returned Warrex, trying to stay calmer. "Indeed, my garrulous friend, I intend to tell it you if you would but be quiet long enough."

"Forgive me, forgive me, it's just that this is exactly the sort of story I look for. The Entwining Trees, yes, do go ahead, please. I won't say another word."

The knight looked at Aril Witherwind in disbelief. But, sure enough, as he had promised, the bespectacled half-elf said nothing further. He only hunched over his book, quill at the ready.

Satisfied, Barryn Warrex rested his head back. Then an odd change came over him: His eyes glassed over with a distant look, as if they were seeing something many years ago; his ears perked as if they were likewise hearing a voice from that long ago; and when he

spoke, it seemed to be in the voice of someone else—
so very long ago. . . .

Once, when the world was younger, there lived in a
small, thatched cottage on the outskirts of Gateway—
where cottages were a stone's throw from each
other—a certain widower by the name of Aron
Dewweb, a weaver by trade, and his young daughter,
Petal, who was considered, if not *the* most beautiful,
then certainly among the most beautiful human girls
for miles in any direction. Petal was slender and delicate, with a long, elegant neck, large brown eyes, and
long fair hair that reached her narrow waist.

It came as no surprise, then, that when Petal
reached marriageable age, she found at her doorstep
every young bachelor who was looking for a wife.
These fellows would wander by the front fence, sometimes pretending to be going on a stroll, when they'd
"by chance" notice the young girl gardening in her
front yard, and they'd begin chatting with her.

"Why, hello," they'd say, for instance, "what lovely
roses you have."

Naturally, Petal was very flattered to receive so
much attention, and she'd leave her gardening and go
flirt with the young men, which only encouraged
them.

Now, Aron, though he had always been the kindest
and happiest of fathers when Petal was growing up,
turned stern and dark of expression. He stopped smiling. He grumbled a lot. He became, in a word, jeal-
ous.

True, he tried, at first, to view the situation with
pleasure. After all, the attention she was receiving was
that due a young, beautiful, marriageable girl, and he
tried to pretend that he was prepared for it.

But he couldn't help himself. Whenever one of

Petal's would-be suitors came calling at the front fence, offering Aron a wave and a "hello," Aron Dewweb could only grunt back, or more likely, ignore the young man and stalk into his cottage.

Several neighbors told him, "Look, Aron, you can't keep nature from taking its course."

Aron listened politely, but that was because his neighbors were also customers for his weaving. Really, he didn't give a damn about nature or its course or their opinions. He just couldn't bear the thought of some swain taking away his only, precious daughter. As far as he was concerned, no matter how old she got, Petal would always be that little girl who laughed and squealed when he bounced her lightly on his knee.

So he said, "Dash it all, I don't care what anyone thinks! I don't like what's happening!" And he took to chasing off the young men with a knobby walking stick he kept handy near his loom. "Stay away!" he would cry as he came running out of his cottage toward the fence. The young man of the moment, startled by the attack, would leave Petal standing by the gate and flee. "And tell your boorish friends to stay clear, too!"

Petal was always very embarrassed by this display. "Daddy, why can't they visit me?" she'd ask, near tears. "I'm old enough!"

"Because!" answered Aron, his face red, his knuckles white as he clenched his walking stick. "Just—just because!" And then he'd storm back into the cottage.

Well, "because" wasn't good enough for Petal, and she continued to encourage her suitors. A wink from her was enough to draw them back like bees to a bright, fragrant flower—though none of them dared actually enter the gate.

From his loom—which, incidentally, was a clever, if

noisy, contraption operated by various levers and pedals—the stern weaver could look out his window and see the way his daughter was behaving. And he saw the effect it had on her callers, who were growing ever bolder, some even venturing to open the gate. Apparently, waving a stick at them was no longer enough to drive them away (which was just as well since Aron was getting tired of running out every other moment). So, finally, he decided there was only one thing left to do: He would have to take Petal away from Gateway.

This he did. He piled his loom and other possessions high on a wagon, put Petal on the seat next to him, and off they went, pulled by a tired, old ox, which he borrowed from a neighbor. Petal sighed deeply as she waved farewell to all her would-be lovers, who lined up along the road in front of their own cottages to see her off. They waved back, their hearts heavy.

Aron took Petal far away. The road became unpaved and overgrown, and eventually it led to the Forest of Wayreth. There, Aron had to leave behind most of his possessions for the time being because there was no path between the trees wide enough to allow the wagon to pass. He would have to make several trips, but he loaded up his goods on his back, took Petal by her slender hand, and off they went through the sunless forest.

When he had gone far enough—that is to say, when he became too exhausted to continue—Aron put down his load and said, "Here! Here is where we shall live!" And right on that bosky spot, he built a new cottage of sticks and thatch. He included a small room for Petal, a larger one for himself, and a still bigger one for the cooking hearth, table, chairs, and, of course, his loom, which he had the ox drag through the forest before he returned the beast to its owner.

———

Convinced at last that his daughter was now where no young man would find her, or at least where she'd be too far away to be worth the bother, Aron resumed his weaving. Such a location among the reputedly magical woods was inconvenient for him, for he had to make long trips to his customers in Gateway, but it was worth the peace of mind that came from knowing that his daughter was safe from anyone who would dare try to take her from him.

As for Petal, she cried for days and days. She wanted to go back to Gateway. She wanted to flirt with her suitors.

But Aron said, "You'll get used to it here. Soon, things will be back the way they were before all this foolishness started."

Petal did, in fact, stop crying, but things never quite went back to the way they were. Petal was lonely, and she never looked happy.

"What's the matter?" Aron finally snapped one day from his loom while Petal, long-faced, was sprinkling fragrant pine needles on the floor. "I was good enough company all these years!"

"Oh, Father," said Petal, pausing in her work, her eyes watering, "I still love you but as *my father*. Now it's time I loved another, as my husband."

"Nonsense!" said Aron with a wave of his hand. "There'll be plenty of time for that when I'm dead!"

"Don't talk that way!" said Petal, stepping toward her father, dropping the rest of the pine needles.

"What way? One day I'll be gone, and then you'll be able to entertain all the young men you want!" And, with that, Aron turned his back on his daughter and continued his weaving.

The arguments usually went that way, and they always broke Petal's heart. Finally, she stopped bringing up the subject, which was what Aron wanted, anyway.

The days settled into a routine. Aron worked methodically and constantly at his loom, and Petal tended the cottage and the garden. Neither said much to the other. Petal continued to look sad, and Aron, even way out in the forest, continued to feel uneasy: What if one of those tom cats should sniff his way to the cottage, after all? What if a whole gang of them should arrive and start wailing at his door?

Or, worse yet: What if Petal sneaked away?

This last thought truly began to worry Aron. He kept a constant eye on his daughter, which caused many uneven threads in his weaving. He became so nervous that if Petal were out of his sight for any length of time—and he did not hear her, either—he'd jump up from his loom, knocking over his chair, and cry out, "Petal! Come here!"

"What is it, Father?" she'd call, hurrying into the cottage, with, say, a basket of mushrooms she had been gathering.

Aron never answered. He was just glad to see his daughter, and, relieved, he'd pick up his chair and resume his weaving.

Nights, though, proved even worse for Aron than the days. It was then he had to sleep, and so it was then he could keep neither eye nor ear on his daughter. He kept waking at the slightest sound, thinking Petal might be sneaking away, and he kept checking up on her in her room. She was always there, curled up beneath her blanket on a mattress filled with her fragrant pine needles.

But then, on one warm summer night, shortly after midnight, Aron peeked into her room and found her bed empty.

"Petal!" he bellowed, stepping from her door back into the large room. "Petal!"

She didn't answer.

Aron ran outside into the benighted woods, where only sprinkles of silver moonlight fell through the canopy and broke up the dark forest floor, the way Petal's pine needles broke up the cottage floor.

"Petal! Petal!"

There was no answer except for the hoot of a lone, unseen owl.

All the rest of that night, Aron scrambled about the dark woods, calling his daughter's name and bruising himself as he hit his head on low limbs and banged fully into unseen tree trunks.

By the time the sun rose, sending its early morning rays to light the misty air and awaken the birds, who promptly began their warbling, Aron was ready to faint from exhaustion. He had been searching and calling all night. Defeated and heartbroken, but determined to march to Gateway to fetch his daughter if need be, he trudged to his cottage to get his stick.

Yet, when he got there, whom did he find, sleeping curled up in her bed as innocently as a doe, but Petal.

Aron rubbed his swollen eyes. His heart soared with joy. Was it possible, in his great concern, that he had missed her sleeping there the night before? Everything was as it was supposed to be—except, Aron noted, that there were little puddles of water, footprints really, leading up to Petal's bed. This was curious, but Aron didn't give it much thought. He was happy to have his daughter back. He told himself he would try to be nicer to her from then on, for the last thing he wanted was to drive her away.

That morning, when his daughter awoke, Aron acted more chipper at the breakfast table. Petal was surprised by his new demeanor, but she welcomed it. She, too, was happier.

"You see?" said Aron as he sipped his tea. "Do you

see how easy it is for us to be friends?"

"Yes, Father," said Petal as she nibbled at a muffin. "Forgive me for my pouting."

"No, no, it is I who must ask for forgiveness. I've been an ogre."

"Only because you love me. I know that, now."

Aron reached over and patted his daughter's soft, fair hair, which felt, strangely, a little damp. Again, he gave this little thought. For the rest of the day, he whistled at his loom while Petal hummed in her front garden—which, actually, wasn't growing as well in the constant shade of the woods as it had in Gateway.

In any case, for all his outward pleasantness, Aron, that very night, tossed and turned uncomfortably in his bed, certain once more that his daughter had indeed disappeared the previous night. And those puddles popped into his mind, perplexing him.

It was no use. Aron jumped out of bed. He had to check up on his daughter. But he didn't want her to know, for then she'd be truly angry at him. So he tiptoed ever so quietly to her room.

She was gone.

Aron grew frantic. He bolted out of the cottage. But before he could call his daughter's name, he saw in the moonlight that sprinkled through the tree cover Petal herself, dressed in her flowing white gown, just disappearing silently between two enormous tulip trees.

Again, Aron was about to call to her, but he stopped himself. Was she meeting someone? He had to know. He decided to follow and catch her in the act. He rushed back into his cottage, grabbed his stick, and hurried out to catch up to his daughter.

He passed between the two tulip trees and found himself on a path, one that he had not even known existed. It was narrow, virtually covered with fern fronds, but it was illuminated clearly by the full moon, for there was a slit in the tree canopy that followed the path exactly.

Aron failed to see his daughter, but he walked along the bending path, confident it would take him to her. Using his walking stick for its intended purpose, he proceeded as quickly as he could without making too much noise. All around him, just a step away to his right or left, was the gloomy forest. Only those trees nearest the path were partly lit, their dark and gray trunks marking his way. Behind them, the trees were cast in shadow. And farther from the path still, the trees were in total blackness.

The croaking of frogs grew louder, and soon he came to a small glade, in the middle of which was a pond. Petal was standing on its bank near an old beaver dam, her long white gown bathed in the sky's ghostly light. For several moments she did nothing but gaze at the black water, upon whose surface floated many lily pads, their white blossoms open to the moonshine.

Then she softly called, "My love, my love, take me to your home."

At that, some of the lily pads were jostled from beneath. Petal then slipped off her gown and stepped into the water. She waded toward the center of the pond, pressing past some lily pads. The water rose steadily up her slender legs, reaching her narrow waist, and continued to rise as she went forward.

Aron was confused as to what was happening. But when he saw his daughter in the pond up to her delicate neck, her fair hair floating behind her, he burst from his hiding place.

It was too late. Petal's head dipped below the surface, her hair floating momentarily, then it, too, vanished below.

"Petal! What are you doing?" cried Aron. "Petal!"

He ran back and forth along the shore as he squinted and tried to peer into the inky water. But he saw only the round, white moon above and his own dark silhouette gazing up at him. Finally, he jumped in.

The water was cold and black, and he couldn't see a thing. He came up for air, then dove even deeper, grabbing blindly at the water, ripping at lily pad stems and smacking a few startled fish. But after becoming so tired that he nearly drowned, Aron finally pulled himself onto the bank and collapsed. There he slept, his legs and arms twitching as if he were still diving, until he was awakened by the morning sun and the warbling of birds.

Convinced that his daughter had drowned, Aron mulled over the idea of taking his own life as he returned to his cottage. But, lo and behold, who did he find there, once more curled up in her bed as if nothing had happened, but Petal!

Aron shook his head. He was almost ready to believe he had dreamed the whole adventure, except that, once more, he saw puddles on the floor leading to his daughter's bed.

Though he was overjoyed, Aron was also furious. He was about to shake his daughter awake and demand an explanation when he decided, No, let her confess to me on her own. It would be better that way.

But confess what exactly? That she had gone for a midnight swim? Surely that's all there was to it. Surely there was nothing—no one—in the pond waiting for her.

Still, in the Forest of Wayreth, you never know.

So all that day, Aron waited for his daughter to tell him what happened. From his loom he kept eyeing her, but all she did was go happily about her duties.

Fine! thought Aron in frustration. Let her think she's fooled the old man! I will just have to catch her in the act!

For the rest of the day, Aron played the innocent, too. He smiled at his daughter, engaged her in polite conversation during lunch and dinner, and generally acted as if nothing were on his mind—except that, while at his loom, he was busy weaving a plot.

Then, in the evening, earlier than usual, he said, "I'm tired. I think I'll turn in."

Petal, darning in a rocking chair near the fire, said, "All right, Father. I'll put out the fire."

Aron stretched a phony stretch and went to his room. But he had never been more awake. He crouched by his bedroom window and peered out into the night air, waiting for his daughter to leave the cottage.

He waited so long, though, that he nodded off for a moment. When he stirred himself, he hurried into Petal's room and saw that she had left. Nearly panic-stricken that he had lost an opportunity, Aron grabbed his stick, a lantern, and a net, and he hurried outside and passed between the two tulip trees.

By the time he reached the pond, Petal was already standing on its banks and calling toward the abandoned beaver dam, "My love, my love, take me to your home." Then she slipped off her gown and stepped into the water.

Aron waited. He wanted to catch both Petal and whoever came to her. When the water reached Petal's neck, her long fair hair floating behind her, Aron sprang out and tossed the net across the water. But Petal dropped below too quickly, and Aron pulled in only a turtle and two frogs. He quickly lit his lantern and held it over the water. What he saw below horrified him.

Just beneath the surface, but sinking ever deeper, was the pale form of Petal, hand-in-hand with another being, a shadowy creature made indistinct by both night and water. Aron pressed so close to the water to see that his nose and lantern went under, the flame extinguishing with a hiss. The two forms disappeared.

Aron pulled back and sat on the bank near his daughter's gown, which he took in his hand. His heart was pounding, but this time he would remain calm. He fully expected Petal to return. And this time he would be waiting for her.

Alas, lulled by the croaking of the frogs, he fell asleep.

In the morning when he awoke, the gown was gone from his hands. He dashed straight back to his cottage where he found, sure enough, Petal curled up in her bed, the puddles of water on the floor.

"How innocently you sleep there," muttered Aron, his eyes asquint, "just like the little girl I once knew, eh? But look here, these puddles belie that innocence. Well, sleep soundly, my daughter, for you will be deceitful no more."

Aron left the room, knowing what he had to do. For one more day, he would play the innocent. For one more day, he would pretend he had nothing burdensome on his mind. He even whistled again at his loom, which had the intended effect of reassuring Petal.

But as soon as night fell and Petal went to bed, Aron dropped his pose. He quietly secured both her window shutter and door with braces of wood. Taking up his lantern and stick, he hurried to the pond.

When he got there, he placed himself near the old beaver dam. There, in a high voice, he called out, "My love, my love, take me to your home." Then, his lantern lit, he crouched down and waited for the creature to rise to the surface.

It didn't do so, either because it was fearful of the light, or because it knew that it was not Petal who

---

called.

No matter, thought Aron. He stood up. "You shall reveal yourself whether you like it or not." And, with that, he gripped his walking stick with two hands and started to break apart the beaver dam.

He stabbed at the dam repeatedly, prying it, pulling out the limbs, branches, and mud. The water rushed out of each break, swelling the stream on the other side. The pond itself slowly began to shrink, leaving behind a widening shore of mud that was laced with stranded lily pads and their limp stems. Several frogs left high and dry began burrowing by backing into the mud, their bulbous eyes disappearing last with a blink.

His heart pounding ever faster, Aron worked all the harder. "Come, come!" he called out over the increasingly loud rush of water. "Don't be shy! Let me see your fishy face!" He put down his stick and eagerly held his lantern over the surface.

He was rewarded for his efforts. He saw, swimming among an ever thicker riot of fish, a large, human-shaped something—no, two human-shaped some-things, both still vague in the muddy, benighted water.

For a moment, one of them seemed to be the pale form of Petal, and Aron had to remind himself that he had secured her in her room. He was tempted to run back to the cottage just to make sure, but the water was very low now, and he would see everything soon enough.

Finally, though, as the water dropped to a depth of a mere hand's span and the fish were bumping into each other, many of them forced out and flopping about the muddy shore, the two creatures began joining the frogs and burrowing into the mud.

"No! Where are you going?" cried Aron, stepping forward, his foot sinking in the mud with a slurp.

But the two forms burrowed deeper, even as the pond became only a mud hole, leaving behind a mere trickle of a stream that meandered among the stranded lily pads, flopping fish, and stunned turtles, which just stood there stupidly, not knowing which way to go. In the center of all that was the writhing mud, as the two creatures dug down to escape the lantern light, or the air, or Aron himself.

Eventually, the writhing slowed, the mounds flattened, and the ground was still. All was quiet. Even the fish lay exhausted, their gills opening and closing uselessly. Aron felt cheated not to see the face of the creature whom Petal had called "My love, my love," but he was satisfied that it would be a problem no more.

But who was that second creature?

Aron returned quickly to his cottage and, first thing, checked Petal's room. He saw, to his relief, that she was indeed there, curled up in her bed. So he went to bed himself and slept more peacefully than he had in a long time.

The next morning he awoke and went directly to his loom, waiting for Petal to rise and make him some breakfast. But she slept late that morning. Finally, his stomach rumbling, Aron called out, "Petal! Come on! Make your old father some breakfast."

She didn't answer.

Perhaps she knows what I did and is being spiteful, thought Aron. "Come on, girl! Up!"

She didn't answer.

Aron went to her room and found her still lying in her bed, curled up. Naturally, there were no puddles this morning, a fact that gave Aron much satisfaction.

"Up, my girl!" he called, walking over to her and brashly pulling away the covers.

His eyes nearly popped out of his head. It was not

Petal at all but pillows set up to mimic her form.

Without a moment's hesitation, Aron dashed from the room, grabbed one of Petal's large gardening shovels, and ran to the dried pond.

When he got there, he saw what, in his eagerness, he had missed the night before: his daughter's gown, lying rumpled on the bank. He immediately stepped into the mud to get to the center, but the farther he went, the deeper his legs went into the mud. At one point the mud came nearly up to his knees, and he could hardly walk. But he pressed on, thinking only of his darling Petal lying buried in the mud.

Then, as he neared the center of the pond, Aron noticed something odd. There, right where he meant to dig, was a tiny green plant shoot. Or rather two tiny green plant shoots. They were entwined delicately about each other. And before Aron could pull his right leg from the mud, those two green shoots, right before his eyes, began to grow.

In a matter of moments, they transformed into long, elegant tree saplings, both still entwined about each other. But they didn't stop there.

They continued to grow toward the sun, their trunks thickening as they grew. And as they did so, they encircled each other. They put out ever more branches, tiny leaves, and even some reddish fruit that hung in clusters.

Soon, what had been two delicate shoots only moments before were now two sturdy trees in full-grown glory, their thick, nearly merged trunks coiled around each other, their roots bulging from the mud, their lofty crowns meshed and arching over the entire width of what had been the pond.

Aron pulled himself out of the mud by one of the roots. He gazed at the two entwining trunks and at the leaves overhead, which now filtered out the sun.

"Petal," he whimpered, "forgive me. I believed my love was enough."

And there, in the shade of the two trees, Aron Dewweb sat and wept. By the time the sun had set and the moon had risen, sending its sprinkles of silver light through the two trees' crowns, Aron died of a broken heart, and little green leaves fell gently to cover him. . . .

So ended Barryn Warrex's tale.

When Aril Witherwind looked up from his book, he detected in one of the old man's eyes a solitary tear. The half-elf himself sighed from sadness and had to brush away from his page a teardrop or two that threatened to make his ink run. "Well, I must say, that is not a story I expected from a knight," he said.

Barryn Warrex stirred, his eyes and ears once more seeing and hearing what was before him. And when he spoke, it was once more with his own deep but tired voice. "I warned you," he said. "It is what has been in my heart." With a creaking of his armor and bones, he slowly rose to his feet.

"Well, now it's in my book, as well," said the half-elf, blotting the page and shaking off his own sadness. "But as to the title. How about, 'A Tale of Eternal Love'?—no, no, too corny. How about, 'A Tale of Two Loves'? You see, it's about two kinds of love, get it?"

Barryn Warrex, not much caring what title the folklorist gave the story, trudged over to the flat rock where his helmet and shield were lying.

"Well, I'll have to give that some thought," continued Aril, tapping his quill feather against his downy chin. "By the way, this is most important: Should I put this story down as fact or as fable?"

The knight put on his visorless helmet, his grand white moustaches flowing well out from it on both sides like two elegant handles. "The story is true enough as far as I'm concerned."

"Well, I don't know," said Aril, squinting at the page through his spectacles. "It seems pretty incredible—even for the Forest of Wayreth. Perhaps if you had seen those Entwining Trees yourself, it would lend credibility—"

With some effort, Barryn Warrex stooped and lifted his heavy, dull shield. "My friend, all I know is that I, too, once had a beautiful daughter, and that one day, she, too, reached marriageable age. I behaved no better than this Aron Dewweb."

"Oh—I'm so sorry," said Aril Witherwind awkwardly, not sure how to respond to such a confession. "Uh, I myself have never had children—"

The old knight slung the shield across his back, and he became as stooped under its weight as Aril was under his tome. Even as he spoke, Barryn Warrex started off down into the grassy, flower-dotted valley, where butterflies flitted about him as if to cheer him up. "It is many years since my own daughter ran away with her lover."

Aril remained perched on his rock, and, trying to hear the retreating knight, he started a new page and began scribbling once more in his book.

"Now this old knight has but one last mission in his life," said Warrex, walking ever farther off, his voice growing fainter, "and that is to find my daughter and this husband of hers—"

"—and," murmured Aril, repeating the knight's words exactly as he wrote them down, "—give—them—my—blessing."

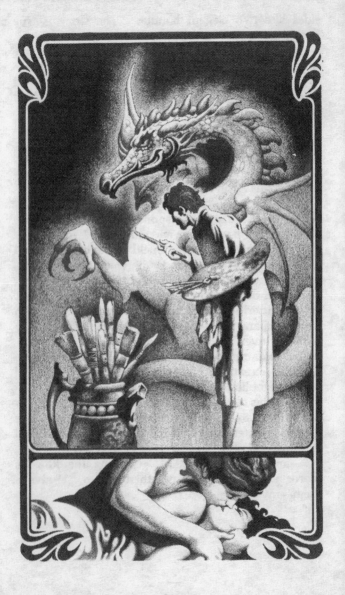

A Painter's Vision

Barbara Siegel and Scott Siegel

"It looks so real," said Curly Kyra with awe. She brushed long ringlets of black hair away from her eyes and stared at the painting, ignoring calls from down the bar for another round of ale. "It's a beautiful boat." Softly, with wonder in her voice, she added, "It seems as if it could almost sail right off the canvas."

"Almost, but not quite," replied Sad-Eye Seron, the painter. He was a skinny man with a gentle face. His eyebrows drooped at the edges, giving him the perpetually sad expression that had earned him his nickname. But he smiled now, enjoying the effect his new painting was having on the lovely, young barmaid he had courted all summer long.

"Will it make a lot of money?" asked Kyra hopefully.

Seron's smile vanished. "I sometimes think that you're the only one who likes my work. Everybody else in Flotsam says, 'Why buy pictures of things that I can see whenever I look out my window?'"

"Hey, Kyra," bellowed a patron with an empty mug. "Am I going to get a refill, or should I just come back there and pour my own?"

The tavern owner stuck his head out of the kitchen. "Tend to business," he warned his barmaid.

"All right, I'm going," Kyra said. But she didn't move. Instead, she shook her head at the magnificent sailing scene and stood there in admiration of Seron's artistry.

If Seron was an underappreciated painter, the same could not be said of the pretty picture known as Curly Kyra. Every unmarried man—and plenty of the married ones—had hopes of bedding her. She had alabaster skin, bright brown eyes, and full lips that seemed created expressly for kissing. Even more inviting than her lips, however, was the purely feminine shape of her figure; since coming of age this summer, she had to slap men's hands more often than she had to slap at bugs.

It was different, though, with Seron. Oh, he wanted to bed her and made no pretense about it, but he truly cared for her and made that clear in a thousand different ways. He helped patch the roof of her family's cottage without asking for so much as a cup of water in return. He gave her painting lessons, teaching her everything from mixing colors to the techniques of his brushstroke. And when she was terribly sick with an unknown disease—and looked like a particularly ugly dwarf he had once painted—Seron risked his own health to help care for her.

The two of them leaned over the bar near each other, the sea-faring picture between them. "You're wasting your time working in this tavern," Seron said earnestly. "I've said it from the very beginning— you're smart, talented, perceptive; you can do more with your life than just serve ale."

"You're only saying I'm smart," teased Kyra, "because I like your work."

He smiled, but shook his head. "I really mean it," he

insisted.

Involved in their intimate discussion, Kyra paid no attention to the growing clamor of angry voices calling out for service.

As for Seron, he hadn't yet tried to sell his latest painting, but he saw that Kyra was so enamored of the picture (and he was so enamored of her) that he suddenly blurted, "I want you to have it. It's a gift."

Kyra was stunned by his offer. Her face turned red, and it looked as if she couldn't breathe.

"Are you all right?" he asked worriedly.

She answered by throwing her arms around him and kissing him on the lips.

That night Kyra lost her job but found a husband.

Her belief in Seron's talents was not misplaced; soon after they were married, he finally began to sell some of his paintings. He didn't receive much for them, but at least it was a beginning. He supplemented their meager income by painting family portraits for the local tradesmen. Still, it wasn't enough.

"Why don't you give art lessons?" asked Kyra one late afternoon as she took down the wash that had dried on the line.

"What? And create my own competition?" he said, laughing as he folded the clothes she handed him.

"You have a wonderful talent," she continued, ignoring him. "You could give classes. I know the kender would love it; they couldn't possibly pass up a chance to try their hand at drawing."

"What makes you think I'd be any good as a teacher?" he asked.

"Because you were so good at teaching me."

"I was good at teaching you," he said, "because you were an excellent student. You could do anything you set your mind to," he continued. "You settle for too little from yourself. If only you—"

"Please! Not that speech again," she complained.

"But you could be so much more if only you tried," he insisted, touching his fingers to the palm of her hand.

"Isn't that the same thing your brother always says to *you*?" she countered. "Doesn't he always say that you're wasting yourself on all these pictures?"

He scowled. "Don't change the subject. We're talking about you—and you know I'm right. You're capable of doing all sorts of things; you're too easily content."

"Content? Me?" she laughed seductively. "Never." And with that, she dropped the sheet she had been holding and began unbuttoning her blouse.

"No one stops an argument like you," he chuckled, removing his own shirt.

Their bed was a sheet on the soft grass, their roof was the afternoon sky, and their souls were one soul long after their passion was spent.

As the afternoon light faded, Kyra felt a chill. She snuggled up close to her husband, who tenderly embraced her. She felt safe in his arms, protected. When he held her like that, she knew both the strength and the tenderness of his love. For her, there was nothing in all of Krynn to match that feeling. Nothing.

Dutifully, Seron gave art lessons to the kender, and anyone else who was willing to pay. Not that anything valuable ever changed hands. Despite their enthusiasm, the kender were inattentive students, and they generally walked off with the paint, the brushes, and half of tomorrow's lunch.

To better provide for his wife, Seron took a job during the evenings as a cook at the Sea Master Inn. Kyra didn't want him to take the time away from his art, but he couldn't bear to see her go hungry. He promised her he would work at the inn only until his paintings brought in more money.

He hoped that would happen soon, for he had chanced upon an entirely new and exciting subject when he met his very first dragon. . . .

"Do you have a red blanket?" asked the young male brass dragon standing at the edge of a clearing in the forest.

Seron could hardly believe his eyes, let alone his ears; the dragon was talking to him!

"Are . . . are you real?" stammered the painter.

"That doesn't seem like an appropriate answer to the question, 'Do you have a red blanket?' Would you like to try again?"

Seron's curiosity was greater than his fear. He stepped closer and touched the dragon's wing. "You are real," he mumbled, astonished. He quickly stepped back again.

"I seem to have this effect on everybody," the dragon said, shaking his head sadly. "Have you never seen or heard of my kind before?"

"Only—only in legends," replied Seron as he carefully examined the tall, majestic dragon standing before him. He didn't want to forget any detail for the picture that he knew he must paint. Finally, he thought, I'll be able to succeed for Kyra. This painting will be worth a fortune!

"It's terrible," complained the dragon. "Wherever I go, people stop and gawk at me. And really," he continued, "I don't understand it. It's not as if I'm wearing flashy colors. Which, by the way, brings me back to the question of the red blanket. Do you have one or not?"

Seron didn't want the dragon to leave. Not yet. He

needed more time to study this wonderful creature. "I'll get you a red blanket," he promised. "Just wait right here."

The painter raced to the hut.

"Kyra, where are you?" he cried when he found their home empty.

"I'm in the back . . . in the vegetable garden."

Not wanting to waste any time, he quickly looked through their trunk and closet. He was sure they had some sort of red blanket—a strange request, come to think of it—but he couldn't find it.

"Any luck?" called out the dragon, who was now standing at the front door.

"You were supposed to stay where you were," said Seron nervously, stepping out to meet the creature. He was afraid the dragon might harm his wife.

"Is someone there?" Kyra called out gaily, walking around the side of the hut. "I thought I heard another voice and—"

She stopped in her tracks with a look of wonder on her face.

"A red blanket!" cried the animal happily, gesturing toward the red shawl Kyra wore around her shoulders.

Seron blinked. That's what he had been looking for.

Kyra smiled at the dragon. She had grown up on tales of these magical beasts. To Seron's surprise, she wasn't afraid of the creature. "Do you like this?" she asked, sweeping the shawl off her shoulders and holding it before her.

"Very much," replied the dragon.

"Then it's yours," she said. "I think you'll look wonderful in it. Much better than I."

"Now, you're a human I could grow to like," the dragon said. "What's your name?"

"Kyra," she replied with a warm smile. "What's

yours?"

"Tosch. And may I say," said the dragon with a bow, "I am very pleased to meet *you*. Him," he added, pointing at Seron, "I must ponder."

"You must not offend me," Kyra reproached gently. "Seron is my husband, and if you like me, you must also like him."

The dragon made a frown. "Is this a rule of the humans?"

"It's *my* rule," said Kyra.

The dragon nodded.

"Good. Now come, let me give you your new cape."

Tosch lowered his head, and Kyra tied the red cloth around the dragon's neck. It was a pitifully small splash of red against the creature's massive body, but Tosch didn't seem to care. He was thrilled with his new appearance and he revelled in it—posturing every which way and asking how he looked in every pose.

To Seron, it was all rather silly, but Kyra took the dragon seriously, giving him her best advice on how to wear the cape to his best advantage.

Finally, Tosch stood still and turned to Seron. "Your wife gave me a wonderful gift," stated the dragon. "What are *you* going to give me?"

"I'm going to paint your picture," he calmly replied. "Once humans have seen your portrait, they won't be so surprised when they see you in the flesh. Isn't that what you want?"

Tosch looked at Kyra. "Can he draw?" he asked.

"Raise your right wing just a little higher," said Seron, as he painted Tosch's picture in the forest clearing where they had first met. "Just a bit higher. Yes. Good. Don't move."

"I think I look better with my wings lower and my head higher," complained Tosch. "And I've got a great profile from the left side. You said so, yourself."

"My purpose is to create a dramatic effect," the painter reminded him, "not necessarily to make you look your best."

"I don't understand the difference," sniffed the dragon. "If I look good, the picture looks good, right?"

"It's the other way around, my friend," laughed Seron. "If the picture looks good, you'll look good."

"Hmmph."

No one else was offering to paint pictures of Tosch, so he remained a willing model despite differences with Seron. The peacemaker was Kyra. She often joined them in the forest clearing, stroking the dragon's head when her husband released him from a long, torturous pose.

Tosch, however, was not the easiest model to paint. The brass dragon would often arrive late for sittings; sometimes he wouldn't come at all. Often, he would quietly mutter a magical incantation, slap his tail against the ground three times, and make Seron's brushes disappear. The dragon seemed bent on driving the artist to distraction.

But Kyra always soothed Seron's anger by explaining yet again that the dragon tales of her youth told of the creatures' freewheeling nature. "A brass dragon," she said, "comes and goes as he pleases and likes to play tricks. It's his nature; don't blame him."

And so the painting continued. At least for a short while . . .

Tosch might have stayed for years instead of a few short months, but when the Highlord and her forces invaded Flotsam, the young dragon fled to the mountains.

Seron and Kyra might have done the same, but Flotsam was all they had ever known; they had both been born there, and neither of them had ever been anywhere else.

The truth was they were afraid to leave.

Times were hard after the dragonarmy took over. But even so, Seron eked out a living. He managed to sell his pictures of Tosch, despite the fact that dragons were now far more commonplace. One of Seron's portraits went to the owner of the inn where he worked as a cook. He sold another to a fierce female ship captain who said she would hang it in her cabin. Yet another was bought by a traveling peddler. All of the buyers admired how skillfully the artist had, at once, captured both the youthful innocence and the natural arrogance of the dragon.

With each sale, Kyra became ever more proud of her husband. His reputation as a painter was growing, yet nothing really changed. They still lived in the same small hut, their clothes were still second-hand rags skillfully repaired by Kyra, and Seron still had to work at the inn to supplement their income.

"You won't believe it!" exclaimed Seron in a rush of words as he burst into their one-room home. "I was up on Cold Rock Point," he explained, "and I saw the Highlord atop her blue dragon. She was leading a whole phalanx of soldiers riding their own dragons. The entire sky was filled with them. Everywhere you looked there were dragons! Their wings were flapping with a power that nearly blew me off the cliff, and their great mouths were screaming in cries that nearly deafened me. But the sight of it, Kyra! I've got to paint it!"

For days, then weeks, he worked on the image he had seen. It consumed him. He had to finish it before he forgot how it looked, how it felt, what it meant.

Kyra watched him work. At first she saw only dark outlines, then the dragons appeared, one at a time. And each of the dragons was more malevolent than the last. There was danger in the picture. The Highlord and her dragonarmy soldiers took shape with menacing faces, and the sky was dark and forbidding. Kyra could feel the cold wind from the wings of the huge beasts, sense the hot breath from their snarling jaws, and she knew—all at once—that the painting had captured the ineffable horror of their conquerors.

Of course, they couldn't sell the painting. If the Highlord or any of her soldiers ever saw it, they'd cut off Seron's hands. Nonetheless, he wasn't sorry that he had done it. And neither was Kyra. They both hoped that eventually the dark days would pass, and his picture would be a valued—and valuable—reminder of this evil time. More than that, they both hoped it would forever establish Seron as Krynn's preeminent artist.

They kept the bleak masterpiece hidden in a wooden crate under their bed. However, it soon began to rankle them both that Seron's greatest work had no audience. What was the point of having painted the picture if no one ever saw it?

It was then that they conceived their daring plan to smuggle the painting to Palanthas where it might be prominently displayed in a gallery. But they would need help.

"Let's send word to Tosch," suggested Kyra. "He could fly here one dark night and take the painting away with him."

"Do you think Tosch would really do it; would he risk his life for a painting?"

"We have nothing to lose by asking," she said.

Two days later, the peddler who had bought a Seron

painting of Tosch carried a coded note out of the city and into the mountain warrens. The note asked their friend to come to them after sunset during the night when the two moons were at their smallest. It was a great favor, and they didn't ask it lightly. And they said as much in the note. If Tosch felt it was too dangerous, they said, he shouldn't come; they would understand.

But still they hoped he would glide down to them out of the dark sky.

The nights passed as slowly as a gnome builds a machine. The days were even longer. Eventually, though, the moons went through their glowing phases. It was almost time.

As the sun descended, sending long shadows across a sad, beleaguered city, Kyra and Seron grew anxious. Tonight was the night.

"Do you think the note actually reached Tosch?" wondered Kyra.

"I don't know."

"What if the peddler were intercepted? If the Highlord deciphered our message—"

Suddenly a loud knock sounded at their door. Instinctively, they both reached for each other. Neither of them uttered a word. The worst, it seemed, had happened. They had been found out.

The pounding on the door continued, matched only by the pounding of their hearts. Seron took a deep breath and kissed his wife lightly on the forehead. "Let's try to be brave," he said in a voice that nonetheless betrayed his fear.

She nodded.

Seron got to his feet and opened the door.

"What did I do, roust you two out of bed?" roared Seron's brother, Long-Chin Cheb. "What took you so long to open up? It's not as if you had so far to go to reach the door," he added, glancing disdainfully at the walls of the tiny hut.

"We . . . we didn't expect to see you," said Seron, catching his breath. "This is quite a surprise. What brings you to Flotsam? Is—is anything wrong?"

"Must something be wrong for me to visit my only family?"

"Seron didn't mean that," piped up Kyra in her husband's defense. "He's glad to see you, just as I am."

Cheb smiled at his sister-in-law. "That's nice of you to say. And let me tell you, you're still a pleasure to look at," he added. "I've always said, my brother's done an awful lot of foolish things in his life, but marrying you wasn't one of them."

To accept the compliment was also to accept the slap at her husband, and that Kyra would not do. She simply nodded curtly and offered her brother-in-law a chair at the table.

He was dressed like a prince, but his clothes looked better than he did. His face was long and sallow, with deep-set green eyes that gave him a cadaverous, if mesmerizing, appearance.

As Cheb strutted through the doorway, Seron nervously glanced out the window into the deepening twilight. Tosch would not show himself if he saw a third person in the hut; they had to get rid of Cheb. Assuming, that is, that Tosch was actually coming.

"You'll be glad I made this surprise visit," Seron's brother announced grandly, "when you hear what I have to say. But first—" he dropped his satchel to the floor and plopped down into the most comfortable chair in the house—"pour me some ale, girl."

When she returned with a full mug, he winked and said, "A barmaid never forgets her craft."

Kyra stepped across the room to stand with her husband. "You said you had news," she said coolly.

The older man downed the mug of ale in one long draught. "Good for what ails you," he said. Then he laughed. "Hey, I made a joke. 'Good for what *ale's* you.' Get it?"

"The news?" asked Seron.

"Of course. You must be anxious to hear it. It's obviously clear," he added gesturing at their home, "that you're in need of glad tidings. Well," he continued, "one day, lo and behold, I received a request for twenty paintings from a wealthy man who wanted to decorate his new home with an artistic touch. Naturally, he didn't want to pay very much, but we managed to settle on a fair price. Of course, I never told him that I had a brother who was a painter. Nor did I tell him that this brother of mine had a hut overflowing with his unsold works of art."

"At what price did you propose this sale of my paintings?" asked Seron.

"Never mind the price," Cheb said with a wave of his hand. "It isn't important. All you need to know is that I will take twenty of your paintings—of my choosing—and give you five percent of everything I make."

Seron physically flinched at his brother's words. Though he could almost feel the knife wound of betrayal, he fought his temper and quietly said, "Forgive me if I choose to ignore this opportunity. I know how you made your fortune—buying unsold goods at a fraction of their cost in one city and then selling them at a generous markup somewhere else. You're entitled to your profits, but five percent of twenty paintings means I'm giving nineteen away for free. No, thank you."

"Come now," said Cheb. "Don't be foolish. This is money in your pocket. Why hesitate? You can't sell this stuff, anyway. Might as well let me take it off your hands."

Seron was silent. He had turned away to look out the window, then glanced back at Kyra. "What do you think?" he asked.

"I say no," she said with firm resolution. "Someday soon," she added pointedly, following his gaze into the dark sky, "your paintings—all of them—will be worth a great deal more."

"You have your answer," said Seron to his brother.

"This is ridiculous," insisted Cheb. "I found a willing buyer and you turn me down. But I'll be magnanimous. I'll raise the offer to a full ten percent. Now what do you say?"

"No," Seron answered emphatically. "You'd best be on your way," he added, afraid that his rage was beginning to break through his calm exterior.

The two brothers glared at each other. Cheb could not understand such an empty-headed artist, while Seron knew, from sad experience, that he could never explain himself to such a money-hungry man.

"Here, take a candle," offered Kyra. "You can light one of our torches outside and use it to find your way along the path."

Seron led the grumbling Cheb to the door. "If you hurry," he said, "you'll still find a bed at the Sea Master Inn. Tell the owner that I sent you. He knows me."

Cheb was already out the door, lighting his torch, when he realized he'd left his satchel in the hut. He rushed back in with the torch aflame and reached for the bag on the floor by the chair.

At the same time, Kyra said, "Here, let me help you."

They accidentally collided while both reached for the satchel, and Cheb lost his balance. Falling over backward, the torch went flying out of his grasp.

The burning torch landed in the corner of the hut, right in the middle of Seron's paints. They exploded in a ball of bright orange flame!

Cheb quickly scrambled to his feet. "Run for your lives!" he cried. He snatched up his satchel and ran out the door without ever looking back.

"Get out! Save yourself!" Seron shouted to his wife, who was trying to drag the heavy wooden crate out from beneath the bed.

"I'm not leaving without your painting," she cried.

The fire quickly spread far beyond the corner of the hut. Soon, the bed and all the rest of their furniture were burning. Two of the walls were aflame, as was part of the roof; a heavy, deadly smoke filled their one-room home.

Seron grabbed his wife around the waist and hauled her to her feet. Both of them were coughing, their eyes were tearing, and their skin was beginning to blister. The fire snapped at the edges of their clothing as he carried his wife to the door of the hut and threw her onto the soft grass outside the door.

But he didn't follow her out into the safety of the night. Instead, he rushed back into the burning hut, diving to the floor next to the bed. The wooden crate was beginning to char, but he knew there was still time; the painting inside had not yet been damaged. He hauled the crate out from beneath the bed and lifted it. The door was just a few yards away. . . .

Though the doorway was open, the smoke and flames were too thick for Kyra to see inside the hut. "Forget the painting!" she screamed. "Seron! Get out of there! Hurry!" she begged.

The roof caved in. The hut collapsed. Seron was buried in an avalanche of fire, and Kyra gave out an anguished cry of pain that stretched on for minutes.

When there was nothing left inside her, she crumpled to the dew-wet grass.

Kyra didn't move. There was no reason. Much later, in the darkest hour of the night, a voice whispered in her ear. . . .

"Am I late?"

At first, Kyra was startled. She lifted her head and saw Tosch. The familiar sight of the brass dragon set Kyra crying all over again. He did his best to comfort her, nestling her frail, shivering frame between his right wing and his body. But he couldn't see what was so upsetting.

As best she could, she told Tosch what had happened. Then she wept throughout the rest of the night. Finally, just before dawn, Kyra fell into an exhausted sleep. The dragon sighed. The sun would be coming up soon—and he supposed he had better take her with him. There was nothing for Kyra here. He lifted her onto his back and then gently took wing.

Tosch watched a female brass dragon sailing in small, lazy circles overhead. Without thinking, he turned his good profile in her direction.

"I don't think I ever told you, but I do like Palanthas," Kyra announced from her seat on a nearby tree stump.

Tosch nodded absently, glancing down at the blue, yellow, and orange clothes Kyra was sewing together for him. "When will my new cape be finished?" he asked.

"I told you it would take six months," she said. "It's only been four."

"You know only humans count time," he replied with a shrug of his gigantic shoulders. "Has it really been four months?"

"I can't quite believe it, either," she said in an aching,

hollow voice.

"Ah, you seem so . . . lonely, Kyra. Perhaps you should marry again."

"No!" she said emphatically. A moment later, a sad smile washed over her face. "I know you mean well," she said, "but I could never love another man after Seron. We were best friends as well as lovers. We finished each other's thoughts, laughed at each other's jokes." She closed her eyes. "I can't sleep without him. I reach for him at night," she softly admitted, and then rubbed her eyes open. "I saw you preening for that female up there," she gestured with a wan smile on her face, "and my first thought was that I wanted to tell Seron that you hadn't changed a bit."

"Please don't point," he said, embarrassed. "She'll know that we're talking about her."

Kyra lowered her hand. "Sorry," she said.

"Apology accepted," he said indulgently.

She reached out and stroked his head the way she used to back in the old days. He smiled.

Kyra had spent all her waking hours—and many of her sleeping hours, as well—reliving her life with Seron. Over and over again, every conversation, every hug, every night of passion played in her mind. She remembered he had always wanted her to do something more with her life. He had said she was capable of doing anything she set her mind to. The only thing she had set her mind to, though, was loving him. Shouldn't that have been enough?

He had tried so hard for her. He never brought home a pocketful of money, but he always brought home kindness, laughter, and a sweetness of spirit. If he had wanted her to accomplish more with her life, why couldn't she try to do that for him now?

She laughed at herself. He would have said, 'Don't do it for *me*, do it for *you!*"

Was it too late now to do it for either of them?

She glanced down at her hands. Tentatively, she allowed herself to ask the question, If I can do anything I set my mind to, what should I do?

Her mind was blank.

"So, what do you think of the way I'm wearing my scales?" asked Tosch, interrupting her reverie.

"What?"

"My scales . . . on my back," said the dragon, turning to give her a better look. "I've forced the edges up just a bit. Pretty stylish, huh?"

"It looks very modern. You might start a trend."

"You think so?"

"If anyone can," she laughed, "it's you."

"Well, the only way I can start a trend is if I am seen by everyone," Tosch said thoughtfully. "So I guess I'd better be on my way."

He flapped his wings and slowly rose off the ground. "I'll be back soon to pick up my new cape. Bye, now."

She went back to the only trade she knew—serving ale. She worked long hours at a new tavern where the owner favored her and the customers appreciated her diligence. But the years of hard work and scraping by had taken a toll on her. Now, the younger barmaids had to fend off the pinches and the propositions, and only the regulars took notice of the pale, disheveled Kyra. She did not care—she did not care about much.

Six years passed before Tosch returned. Kyra understood that to a brass dragon, six years was hardly more than a week; she wasn't angry with him. Besides, in her great and enduring sadness, there was precious little happiness. Seeing her old friend was a welcome relief from her neverending sense of loss.

They sat on a sandy beach at the edge of the bay.

She glanced up and smiled, slightly averting her eyes. It was self-preservation. Tosch was covered with every imaginable color of cloth; it nearly blinded her whenever she tried to gaze at him. He obviously was not interested in the three-color cape that she had painstakingly made.

"Look," he said, insisting that she focus her eyes on him, "I've had my teeth chiseled. What do you think? Good and straight now, right?"

She shielded her eyes and glanced at his mouth. "Every time I see you, you're different," she said. "I can hardly remember what you looked like six years ago."

A tear suddenly ran down her cheek. Her chin trembled.

"Now what's wrong?" asked Tosch, perturbed.

"I'm sorry. It's just that I sometimes forget what Seron used to look like, too."

The dragon lowered his plummaged head and sighed with exasperation. "You still think of him?"

"I never stop."

"Well, I still can't understand what you saw in him. I grant you, he was a passable painter, but after all, he had a wonderful subject. You know," Tosch added, "he was never very nice to me."

"He liked you very much," Kyra said defiantly. "And I don't want you to say another bad word about Seron. Not ever."

"Sorry," apologized Tosch, shrinking just a bit under her wrath. He thought it wise, just then, to say something nice about her late husband. "It's too bad he never did a self-portrait," offered the dragon. "He would have done a fine job. And then you would have had a picture of him always."

Kyra nodded sorrowfully.

"Listen, let me take you for a ride," suggested the

dragon, trying to change the subject. "It'll lift your spirits. Where would you like to go?"

"Home," she said sadly. "I'm not very good company when I'm feeling like this."

She lay in bed for hours, unable to keep from crying. It's been six years, she thought to herself. Why am I still grieving? Why can't I stop?

The answer was as plain as the tears on her face: Her love did not die in that fire. Yes, her memory was fading, but her feelings were as strong as ever.

Finally, late that afternoon, she climbed wearily out of bed and built a fire in order to make herself a light meal. Later, after sitting down at her rickety wooden table to eat, she noticed that her hands were smeared with charcoal. Without thinking, she absently cleaned her fingers by etching an image of her husband in charcoal on her faded white tablecloth.

When she realized what she had done, she stopped and stared at her work. The picture stared back at her. It wasn't a very good likeness of Seron, but it was still undeniably him. More than that, though, while she had been sketching, she had sensed—for the first time in more than six years—the peace and security she had felt in her husband's arms.

After all this time, Kyra finally knew what she could do with her life besides serving ale. Still staring at the sketch, she whispered, "I'm going to paint you, Seron. I may not be the artist that you once were, but I'll do my best to be as good as I can be. I won't settle for less; I can't settle for less, because it's the only way I can have you close to me."

With paints, brushes, and a canvas bought out of her meager savings, Kyra started the memory portrait of her husband that very night. Painting by firelight, she worked until dawn. Her body ached, her eyes were strained, and she was thoroughly exhausted. And when the sun came up, she was also thoroughly disgusted. She hurled the canvas to the floor, where it landed face down. "Terrible," she muttered. "He didn't look anything like that."

It was then that Tosch flew to her door, calling out, "Come look at my new wings!"

Kyra stuck her head out the window and saw gold sparkles on Tosch's wings, dancing in the dawn light.

"You've outdone yourself," she declared.

"And so have you," Tosch cried happily, seeing the paint smears on her face. "Are you coloring your body now, too?"

"No," she sighed wearily. "But I have decided to do some painting."

"Ooh, let me see. I want to see." Tosch bubbled with excitement.

"There's nothing for you to look at yet," she explained. But she knew deep in her heart that even if there had been, she would not have shown it to anyone, not even Tosch. Her painting was too private, too personal. Later, when she improved her craft, when she had captured Seron the way she remembered him, only then would she let the world see her work. Not before.

Tosch was disappointed that he couldn't see her pictures, but the color on her face buoyed him up nonetheless. "I'll fly you over to the tavern," he offered cheerfully. "Let's go."

"Not today," she said. "I want to keep working."

Her old friend shrugged and said, "Okay. I'll see you later."

Tosch did, indeed, see her later . . . fourteen years later. By then, Kyra was an aging barmaid, working only to earn enough money to keep her in paints, brushes, and canvas. She had never stopped painting her beloved Seron.

"Notice anything different?" the dragon said easily, as if he were just picking up yesterday's conversation.

Kyra was used to it, though, and happily beamed with joy at his appearance in front of her crumbling shack. "It's your nose," she said, after looking him over. "It's changed . . . it's smaller!"

"That's right!" he exclaimed. "I knew you'd notice."

"But what happened to it? It looks, well, sort of pinched and turned-up."

"Isn't it cute?"

"Well . . ."

"I asked a bunch of gnomes to do it for me. I just had to have a smaller nose. I don't know exactly what they did. They built a strange contraption, but I think it worked. Look at me. Isn't it darling?"

"Can you breathe all right?"

"Not too bad. You do like it, don't you?" he asked, suddenly concerned that he had made a mistake.

"I'll show you what I think of it," she said. "Lean down close to me."

The great brass dragon lowered its head close to Kyra, and she gave him a loving kiss on the nose. "You'll always be the handsomest, cutest, most adorable dragon to me," she said.

Tosch blushed, though it was hard to tell against the multi-colored cape he wore. To hide his embarrassment, he cleared his throat and asked, "How is your painting coming along? Can I see your pictures now?"

"I'm sorry," she replied evasively. "They're really not good enough yet. Someday," she promised.

"Soon?"

A smile creased her worn, but still lovely face. "By your standards, yes. Soon."

---

* * * * *

Highlords came and went. Great cities rose and fell. Wars were fought, lost, and won. But Tosch, in his fashion, was ever constant. Throughout the years, he visited his aging friend, coming to see her eleven years later, then nine years, then finally twelve years after that. But during none of those visits, did she ever show him her paintings.

It was beginning to annoy him. While the dragon was as young and vibrant as the day he had met Kyra and Seron, she had reached an age where it seemed she was always cranky. Especially on his latest visit. He had seen her earlier in the day and found her to be strangely unimpressed with his new purple hat. All she wanted to do was get back to her painting. She said she was finally getting close to achieving what she'd been after all these years. That was just fine with him, but why couldn't she pay more attention to his hat? After all, everyone else thought it was boldly original. There was no doubt in his mind; he had to talk with her about her moods. He resolved to go see her that very night.

Kyra always felt a sweet melancholy after Tosch's visits ended; it was only then that she was truly aware of her loneliness. This time it was no different, but after a hectic evening of waiting tables she was anxious to pick up her brushes and paint while she still had some strength.

She had no idea how many pictures she had painted of Seron; she had long ago forgotten the count. In fact, she had forgotten many things—but not the face of her husband.

Her husband's image, with all of its sweetness, hung above her bed.

Seron's likeness, with all of its ambition and drive,

hung in the alcove that she called her studio.

Even where she cooked and ate, his face looked down upon her with all of its childish charm and humor.

Everywhere there were pictures of Seron. They were piled one upon another, and hung in every corner of her shack. She was surrounded by his image. And yet she was not finished with her work.

Frail and sickly, she had continued to paint. With eyesight fading, her joints aching, her fingers shaking, she kept on dabbing at the canvas with her brush, hoping to finally capture the perfect image of the man she still loved.

On this late night, painting by the light of red coals in a dying fire, Kyra's breath came in short gasps. She was tired. But she didn't want to stop—not before she completed her latest work.

In this picture of Seron, he was lying on a sheet that was spread out on the grass behind their hut. A pile of neatly folded laundry was off to the left. There was a look of longing on his sad-eyed face. He was alone in the picture, facing forward, with his arms outstretched, reaching.

Was that the way it really was? she wondered.

She gazed at the image of Seron. The sad eyes of her husband stared back at her. Slowly, just as the red mist on the Blood Sea would disappear when the sun reached its zenith, so did the fog lift away from Kyra's memory.

That was exactly how it was. It was Seron in every detail. His hands, with their long, shapely fingers, his prominent cheekbones, his jutting chin, the shoulders she so often lain her head upon—it was all just right.

Or was it?

Kyra's heart began to beat wildly in her chest. Was there something wrong with the painting? Something missing? The picture seemed to cry out to her for its final perfection. But, somehow, she had left something vital out, and she didn't know what it was.

In that moment, she felt so unworthy of her Seron that she turned her back to the wet canvas. Except there was no escaping her husband's sad eyes; he looked down upon her from every wall.

She lifted her arms to him and wailed, "I wanted all of Krynn to stand before you and look up lovingly, just like I did. I wanted them to feel something of what I felt. But look," she sobbed, her arms sweeping in a wide arc, "I never captured your love in a single painting. Not one!"

Kyra fell to her knees and wept with as much anguish as the night the fire took her husband away from her. Against a deep crushing pain in her chest, she cried out, "Did I fail you all these years? Are you ashamed of me? Oh, Seron, am I even half the woman you hoped I would be?"

When Tosch arrived at Kyra's shack, he called out to his old friend . . . but he heard no answer. Again he sang her name out. And again there was silence. Finally, in exasperation, he roared, "Kyra!" as loudly as he could.

Half the inhabitants of Palanthas were stirred out of their beds by the frightful sound.

But Kyra didn't answer him.

Tosch had no patience left. He slammed one of his huge feet against the door and it flew wide open.

The brass dragon's anger instantly turned to pity when he saw the crumpled form of Kyra lying on the floor at the foot of a painting.

Tosch let out a deep, mournful sigh. As old as Kyra was, he never really thought she would act like just another human and die. She was always there to tell

him how he looked, to tell him what he should wear—
to be his friend. And now she was gone.

She had died all alone in this old, dilapidated shack.

He peered inside and, for the first time, focused on
the picture that loomed over Kyra's body. Tosch's eyes
opened wide. It was Seron, just the way he used to be.
It was a magnificent likeness that caught every bit of
character, every nuance of emotion, in the long-dead
painter's face.

The dragon stuck his head farther inside and saw
scores upon scores of Seron's image. Seron in every
imaginable pose and activity. But Tosch's gaze kept
coming back to the picture on the easel. The paint on
that one was still wet. He knew that this had been
Kyra's last, impassioned work.

He had never known, never guessed, what she had
been painting all these years. Even now, staring at the
evidence of Kyra's lifelong devotion to Seron, Tosch
could only shake his head in wonder. He couldn't
quite understand how she could have loved Seron so
much. But then again, maybe he could. After all,
didn't he love her in his own way, too?

He felt his wings quivering and he knew he was
going to do a rare thing—he was going to cry. Kyra
had meant so much to him, and he had done so little
for her. He felt suddenly ashamed, realizing that he
had been selfish, always taking. Why didn't he give
her gold dust for her clothes? Why didn't he chisel her
teeth, too? He could have done all sorts of things for
her. But he hadn't. And what could he give her now?

He stared at her limp, cold body and then lifted his
gaze to the painting of Seron. Then he looked a bit
closer . . .

Something was missing. The picture didn't seem
quite right. He studied it for a long, quiet moment,
trying to discover what was overlooked.

———

Ah, I know what it is, Tosch said to himself. It's so obvious! He spoke a magical incantation and then slapped his tail against the ground three times.

Kyra was in the picture with Seron. Now it was right.

They were laughing and crying in each other's arms, alive in their art. Within the bounds of the canvas, Seron and Kyra were living, breathing, loving souls.

Tosch flapped his wings with joy. He had made Kyra happy. When he turned to fly away, he heard Seron say to his beloved, "You are *all* the woman I had hoped you would be."

"Now *that's* a good painting," said the dragon as he flew off into the night. "Then again," he mused as he soared among the clouds, "a little more color wouldn't have hurt."

Hunting Destiny

Nick O'Donohoe

*B*y daylight, the stag, with an effort of will,
appeared to the knight. The knight's enthusiasm was
gratifying, if anything could please in Darken Wood.
The knight even mentioned Huma's having followed
the stag. The stag moved forward on Prayer's Eye
Peak, knowing the knight and his companions would
follow. If it was his destiny to lead, it was others' to
follow him.

But they did not follow immediately. With one ear
he heard the company debating behind him. The half-
elf said, "Though I have not seen the white stag
myself, I have been with one who has and I have followed it, as in the story the old man told at the Inn of
the Last Home."

The stag, turning to look, saw the half-elf fingering
a ring of twisted ivy leaves, presumably because it
reminded him of his former companion who had seen
the stag. Neither half-elf nor ring brought any memory to the stag.

The mage among them, a robed figure with hourglass eyes, spoke more of the story they had heard,
apparently a few nights ago, at an inn. An old man

had told how Huma, lost in a forest, prayed to Paladine. A white stag had appeared and led him home. "That I remember," the stag thought, "but I had thought no other living being did. Whatever man they met was old indeed, though if he were older, he would remember it as song, not story." A pang of regret for simpler days and easier faith swept over the stag, much as it sweeps over old men for times gone by. He shook his rack of antlers fiercely and kept listening.

The dwarf with the company snorted, almost like an animal himself. "You believe old stories? Here's another, then: Once there was a stag who caused Shadow Wood to turn to Darken Wood."

Another companion squatted on the trail, his ears pricked forward. "Nothing like a good story. When was this, Flint?"

The dwarf scowled at the other—a kender, the stag remembered now. It had been long since he had seen one. The dwarf went on, "Before the Cataclysm. And it's not a good story, not any way at all. The stag chose to betray the Forestmaster—the ruler of this wood, whoever that is. So he—"

"Why?" the kender interrupted. The stag put his ears forward, straining to hear.

The dwarf admitted, "I don't know why." The stag relaxed. "But he wanted to. So he—"

"It doesn't make sense if we don't know why." The kender clearly enjoyed interrupting.

"Nothing makes sense to you; let me go on. The stag went to the king who was pledged to guard the wood—"

"Guard it against what?"

The dwarf reached for the kender. "I'll tie back those foolish ears and make you listen—"

The half-elf stepped between them. "Let him be, Flint. Tas, let Flint tell his story."

———

"That's better." The dwarf took a deep breath, as much to calm himself as to launch the tale. "Why this stag wanted to betray the Forestmaster, whatever a Forestmaster is, I don't know. It's an old story, and parts of it are all muddled by now. The point is, he did betray the Forestmaster, back in the days when Darken Wood was only Shadow Wood."

"That's not the point at all," the stag murmured, knowing he could not be heard. "I've always thought the why of it more important than the sorrows that followed. Still, I am glad that the why is forgotten."

The dwarf went on: "There was a human king in the woods in those days, as well as living soldiers who guarded the woods. They were pledged to hold the borders against invaders, or robbers, but especially against the Dark Army."

"Who?" That was all that the kender said.

Flint swallowed his annoyance. "The Dark Army. An army of the dead raised by dark clerics. In exchange for the dead helping the clerics take the wood from the Forestmaster and make it a fit place for the Queen of Darkness."

All, including the stag, shivered.

"The clerics would cast a spell that made the forest a place where the dead would live again. That's why the Forestmaster set guards on the border, to keep the wood free of evil—but mostly to ward off the Dark Army."

"But the guards failed," the half-elf said softly.

Flint snorted again. "Failed? Failed? They broke their vows. The stag offered the king and his men a chance to hunt in the woods—the story's messy there; I can't tell whether they hunted the stag or something else—and the king leaped at it. He was rebellious, or untrustworthy, or wanted some time away from his job. That's another missing detail. Anyway, the king and his men left their posts at the edge of Shadow Wood, for only one day."

"But that was time enough." The knight who had first seen the stag sounded grim. Clearly, the stag thought, this one took oaths seriously. The stag shifted from hoof to hoof uncomfortably.

The dwarf went on, "Time enough and more. While King Whoever and his oath-breaking guards hunted, the clerics led the dead into Shadow Wood. Once inside, the dead formed a circle, and inside it the dark clerics did something, it has a name like the Song of Dead Land or the Chant—"

The hooded mage in the company said abruptly, "The Curse of Carrion Land. If it is spoken over a place, all shadows deepen into darkness, and all the buried dead rise again." He smiled at his own knowledge. "It's quite easy to do, once you are inside the borders of a land."

After an uncomfortable silence, Flint said, "Right. And then the dead hunted down the traitor king and his men as if they were animals, and killed them and buried them.

"But the dark clerics had made a mistake. The Dark Army hadn't been buried in Shadow Wood, which was now Darken Wood, but the traitor king and his men had been. So at sunset of the first day, the Dark Army died again, this time for good. And that night the buried king and his men rose again and chased the clerics out." Flint looked around uneasily. "But the Curse of Carrion Land stayed. That's why Darken Wood is evil. And every night, the traitor king and his men go hunting, with no rest for them until they redeem their pledge somehow."

The kender sighed loudly in the silence, making the company jump. "But what about the stag? And doesn't the story have an end?"

Forget the stag, the listening animal thought. And no: there is no end. There will never be an end.

"The stag. Right." The dwarf thought a moment. "There was something—"

The listening stag was relieved when the dwarf admitted, "I don't know exactly what happened to the stag. He died, too, and he had some kind of punishment for his betrayal. He and the king are tied together, but the story is all twisted up by now; in some versions the king and his men hunt the stag, in some they hunt a unicorn, and in some they hunt the Forestmaster, whatever the Forestmaster is. But I know that the stag is like the king; he's punished every night for being a traitor. He has to repeat the betrayal over and over, and he and the king can break out of it only if they fulfill their vows of service and loyalty to the Forestmaster. Only they can't. Somebody else is pledged to guard Darken Wood now, and the story says that the stag is too proud or angry or something to renew his vow of service. So there isn't an end. Yet," he finished uncertainly.

"Not a good story," the kender said firmly. "I've heard better."

"So have I," Flint said. "The point is, which kind of stag are we following? The one Huma saw, or the traitor in Darken Wood?"

The stag barely listened to the argument. "Perhaps," he said to himself, "they are the same stag, servant and betrayer. Have any of these fools considered that?" He was relieved when the company, done debating his past and intentions, chose to follow him. He led silently, thoughtfully.

By night he watched the company discuss with the king of the dead. "They are greatly afraid," the stag observed. "That must please the very-late King Peris no end."

Later still, the stag watched them mount on centaurs, who were the Forestmaster's pledged guards, and ride to the Central Glade. Two centaurs remained behind, guarding the way. The stag, freed of his duties as guide, was about to follow the riding company when he heard one of the sentries sing, in a rough and uncouth voice:

> There was a proud and noble stag,
> In Shadow Wood was born,
> And there he grew, and there he met
> And loved a unicorn.

The stag froze, listening.

"There now," the sentry said to his companion with satisfaction, "years it's been since I've sung that, but I can still put it to the tune."

The other centaur answered dubiously, "It rubs against the tune, some places. Are the words right? I wouldn't know, it being new to me."

"New?" the first one questioned. "New? Why, that's the oldest song I know. It was old when our folk fled to the wood, in the time—what's the name? When the seas shook and rocks charged downhill like wild beasts—"

"Cataclysm," the other said.

"Cataclysm," the singer said carefully. "Right. And that's when we were pledged to guard this place. The Forestmaster, she had no living guard then, her own guards being dead and a lot of traitors."

"Traitors? Why?" the other asked.

The stag held his breath, thinking quietly, "Let them not remember. Let it be lost in time. If I know, and if she knows—and if the king knows—that is more than enough."

The first centaur slapped his own bristly side.

"Why? The song tells why. Let me see if I can put more of it in mind. Somewhat about the stag serving the unicorn—"

He sang more hesitantly:

> *He served her long, he served her well,*
> *He served her, whole and part*
> *Until one night in Shadow Glade*
> *He told her all his heart.*

The other said firmly, "If this song turns filthy, I'll hear none of it."

"No, no. She turns him down. 'She did not laugh—' No, that's not it. 'She told him no'—I have the matter of it there, but not the music."

The centaur guards moved off on their rounds. The stag remained, then sang softly, to himself:

> *She did not mock, she did not laugh,*
> *But softly told him nay;*
> *He did not grieve, but chose to leave*
> *And plotted to betray.*

> *He sought out then King Peris's men;*
> *His words were cold and blunt,*
> *"Oh, sentry hosts, desert your posts:*
> *I offer you a hunt."*

The stag stopped and said bitterly, "Ill-rhymed, ill-metered common trash. The song about my leading Huma is doubtless long gone, but this wretched lyric—" His own ears pricked up at the rancor in his voice, and he bounded after the riding company.

He watched them look up at the rock and stare in awe at the Forestmaster. The stag, remembering his own first meeting with the Forestmaster, nursed his dark heart and said nothing as the unicorn met the companions, fed them, advised them.

Finally they were away, born aloft by pegasi. The stag looked at the ridiculous bipeds, particularly the dwarf, and felt contempt for the vileness of the winged horses' servitude. (Cloven-hooved animals feel naturally superior to those with unsplit hooves: the horses, the centaurs, even the pegasi.) "How typical," the stag said to himself, "that they would degrade themselves in that obedience, as close to the stars as they are."

Even after a long and often painful history, the stag was quite sensitive of his honor.

He entered the glade and called, as much command as request: "Master."

"I am here." The unicorn had returned to the rock above the glade.

Forestmaster and stag stood poised, as though pausing before re-entering an old ritual. Each knew what the other would say.

Still they looked, as though they could not help themselves. The stag stood proud and erect, as though posing for a statue. Every hard muscle and taut sinew, every sharp line of limb and deadly point of antler, was etched in shadows. As with all shadows in Darken Wood, they seemed deep and full of death.

The Forestmaster herself seemed all light, as though the curse that held the Wood could never touch her. Her mane shone and half-floated, and the arch and curve of her neck seemed to draw all the way down her flanks and stop only at the ground. Only her eyes were dark, and those not the tainted shadows of Darken Wood but the liquid blackness of a wild thing's eyes, pure and powerful nature.

The stag spoke first. "I have served you this night."

"I know."

"Did I not serve you well?"

"You did."

"Have I not always served you well?"

"You have often served me well."

The stag seemed not to notice the distinction. "And I have asked little in return."

"It was service freely given, gladly accepted." She stared down at him, her horn pointing into the night. "You have more to ask now."

"No. More to offer."

"It is the same thing."

That nearly silenced him. Finally, however, he went on:

"I offer my love. I give it freely, generously; since there is none like me, a gift without parallel."

"I know."

After a silence, the stag finished angrily, "Yet you refuse."

"I must." The Forestmaster broke the feeling of ritual by saying, "Humans say of my kind that only a virgin may catch me."

"It is an old legend. That is not why you refuse me."

"It is old, and it is exactly why." She spoke less firmly, more sadly. "And like most old legends, it is twisted and half true. It is not the humans who must be chaste. To be who I am, to serve whom I must—"

"Enough," the stag said harshly. "Noble vows aside, you have refused my love."

The Forestmaster stared into his death-laden, proud eyes and closed her own. "I have."

"Why?" The word came out hard and sharp, as fresh and painful as it had been the first time it was spoken. "Why, when I have told you my own weakness and admitted that I love you?" For a moment the stag's proud pose was gone, and he looked almost alive in his hurt and desire.

The Forestmaster said quietly, "Because I must."

The stag had regained his poise. "Because you choose. That choice is not without consequence."

"For you? For myself?"

"For both. How do you dare refuse me?" He tried to sound dignified, arrogant. His voice barely shook.

"I have refused others."

"None like me. There are none like me."

"And that, you feel, obliges me to yield the needs of a world to you. Go then." She added, "But know I never wished you to."

He snorted, derisive even in a deer. "Naturally not. Service without debt is more pleasant than solitude."

As the Forestmaster watched him stride off, she murmured, "Anything is more pleasant than solitude." He did not hear her.

"One thing more." He turned back to her, and she bent her head to listen. "You said something about destiny to the strangers."

She nodded, her mane rippling. "I said it to the warrior, though I was thinking of the knight. 'We do not mourn the loss of those who die fulfilling their destinies.' "

"Coldly put. Whom do you mourn? Those who die unfulfilled? Those with no destinies at all?"

"All have destinies." She looked up at the sky. From where he watched, her horn drew a line from him to the north star. "As all have stars. As you have a star."

"What of those who refuse their own star and would choose another?"

She held the point of her horn unwavering. "Stars last. We do not. Refuse it as long as you must; it will still wait for you."

"But I may refuse it as long as I wish."

When she did not respond, he said, "If I cannot shape my own destiny, I still refuse the destiny shaped for me. Farewell—again."

He barely heard her say, "I know—again." He wondered if she were mourning.

Near dawn the stag came to a dark and cheerless spot. When he arrived at the point near which the sedge was withered from the lake and no birds sang, he gazed around.

Ahead of him a shadowy spirit in armor stood, waving his sword restlessly among the weeds. He bent forward, his lips moving in curses too old to mean much to any but the stag.

The king jerked upright, startled, as the stag sang loudly:

> *King Peris's men were duty bound,*
> *To guard the wood from fear.*
> *The king, in pride, set sword aside,*
> *To bargain with the deer.*

King Peris responded, waving his sword in time to the music:

> *"There is no hunt for me," said he,*
> *Of any creature born,*
> *Unless I could in Shadow Wood*
> *Hunt down the unicorn."*

After a moment's hesitation, the stag responded:

> *"None knows so well where she may dwell*
> *As I who did her will,*
> *If you will heed, then I will lead,*
> *And you may have your kill."*

The king resumed his search in the weeds. "Imagine hearing that old thing again, clumsy meter and all. What made you think of it?"

The stag made no move to help the king. "I heard parts of it being sung last night."

"Well, well. Folk art endures amazingly, wouldn't you say? I wouldn't have thought anyone alive would remember it." He looked sharply at the stag. "It was, I assume, someone alive."

"It was. One of the centaurs—you remember them; they replaced you as guardians?—still knows some of the song. But you shouldn't be surprised; scandal always outlives honor."

"True. For example, look at us—though we can hardly be said to be outliving anything."

Presently the spirit grunted in satisfaction and raised a timeworn crown on his sword-point. He put it on with a bony hand, adjusting it carefully and standing straight. For barely a moment he looked like some mockery of a real monarch.

The stag said deliberately, "Long live the king."

"The king lived long enough." The dead king sat a moment, looking much like a tired man, for the dead who may not rest know more weariness than any of us. "Tell me, did you see anyone this night?"

"You know I did. A knight, a mage, a half-elf, assorted two-legged shortlings. They are important to you?"

"They are important, I think." The king said absently, "You seem curious. I had thought you indifferent to everything."

"To everything beneath me, which is much of the world. And you, great and loyal Peris?"

"Much the same. Of course, more is beneath a dead king."

The stag said drily, "Long though we have endured, our standards are still better preserved than we are. May they last forever. What is their importance?"

"The standards?"

72

"Their importance is self-evident, or it is none. I mean the strangers; how are they important?"

"To the future of our wood and world."

"Ah. Politics." The stag nodded wisely. "I try to avoid politics."

"I understand completely," the king said casually. "I tried to avoid politics—once."

"A question of permission to enter, and of forced entry, wasn't it?"

"It was." He added with uncustomary frankness, "A question of entry by evil, and into these woods—which at that time were not called Darken. Perhaps you remember the stanzas—"

"I do." The stag sang, a little too eagerly for the king's liking:

> But one lone guard forewarned the king:
> "This hunt is evil-starred;
> For those with arms and potent charms
> Against whom we must guard
>
> No more will wait with eyes of hate
> And souls and hearts of gall,
> But purge the wood of light and good,
> And gods forgive us all."

He looked expectantly at King Peris, who sighed hollowly and sang with as full a voice as a spirit could muster:

> Still Peris boasts, "step down, my hosts,
> And hear the hunting-horn,
> Let men invade both wood and glade,
> We hunt the unicorn."

He lowered his sword, which he had raised for

emphasis. "It wasn't that way at all, of course. And it wasn't rebellion, or wilful treason, or any of those things. My men were bored; I was bored. A hint or two from their commanding officer—" he made a mock bow "—was all it took." He looked around himself. "Imagine thinking anything in a short life and a merry one could be boring. I threw away a kingdom for a day's amusement and an afterlife of painful tedium."

"I am surprised to hear you admit it."

"I am surprised also. Perhaps something is troubling me. Let us change the subject."

"I shall. Did you speak to any of the strangers?" As the king shook his head, the stag nodded, "For I thought I saw one address you."

"Ah. That one was a mage. He spoke first." The king looked as though he had never even tried to evade answering.

"What did he say to you? I could not hear."

King Peris said with difficulty, "He knew that we were the spirits of men who had failed a pledge, that we were doomed to perform that same task endlessly until we somehow earned final peace."

"Knowledgeable man."

"Mages often are. I think he meant to remind me that I could earn final peace."

"And what did you say to him of your present state, O King? For if I may be truthful, you do not appear in full majesty. Empty majesty is more like it."

"I told him that we were called to fulfill our oath, one day."

"When you say we," the stag said carefully, "I assume that you meant 'my men and I.'"

"I was not specific. I did not mention you by name, but that does not mean he did not know you also were called to fulfill your oath."

"Did you tell him," the stag inquired, "How long it has been since we first heard that call?"

The king shifted, a move of discomfort in the living. "Discussing these things is not easy. Have you no understanding of how shameful it feels to rehearse a long-broken pledge?"

"I have more feelings than I commonly show. Let us change the subject."

"I shall. Something troubles you."

"Of course. I am in love." Even now the admission came hard.

"That is always trouble. Unrequited, I assume."

"Strangely, yes. Can you imagine my love not being returned?"

"By now, it is easier to imagine than it once was; habit and repetition make all realities seem more real." Seeing the stag tense, the king added hastily, "But because it was true long ago, and for your feelings now, let us say it seems unimaginable."

"It does." The stag tossed his head. "I will, of course, want revenge for my hurt feelings."

"Feelings?" The king struck one shadowy arm with another. The blow left no mark, and the king's expression did not change. "You can still speak of feelings?"

"I can." The stag looked away. "I prefer to speak of them, though I still have them."

"Time changes feelings. Time may change all things, even us."

"Time has not changed what we do, nightly." The stag turned his head, briefly, to look at the north star. "I do not think it can change what I am, nor will it change what I do. I choose, again, to betray the one whom I—the one whom I should obey."

"Another might not so choose. Even you, after some consideration, might not."

When the stag did not respond, the king continued,

75

"Tell me, though you have told me often before: is this a lover one could betray to hunters?"

"One could. Does that surprise you?"

"No more than it surprises me that you would."

Without warning the stag lashed out at a sapling with one of his front hooves. The kick left a sharp imprint in the wood. "How could she have refused me? How can she refuse me?" He kicked again, splintering the small tree. "How *dare* she refuse me?"

He stood trembling with anger, then mastered himself. "Excuse me," he said to the king. "I'm not myself today."

The king said heavily, "I rather fear that even after ages of punishment, you are still yourself."

"Perhaps you are right. Still, I like to think I would not burst out so, except that I had rather a long night last night."

Peris nodded. "Your feelings have always been hard to contain; long ages of irony and veiled illusion cannot hide them. As for your night, all of our nights are long." He added more slowly, "I have news that may interest you. A second band of strangers, seeking to kill the first, has entered Darken Wood. They are on the same path as the first were."

"And no sentries have stopped them? History repeats itself."

"It does, as we do. I am inclined to make an end to repetition."

The stag paid no attention to the king's last remark. "If these strangers are not invaders, might they be hunters?" the stag asked indifferently.

"Hunters of men and of other bipeds. They might be lured to other hunts." He added, "And as for invading, this band, too, is politically important, though they are—" he hesitated.

"Yes?"

"Evil. One would not have thought more evil could be done to Darken Wood, but apparently so."

"After what you have received at the hands of Darken Wood, does that disturb you?"

"It should," Peris said with assumed indifference. He gave up the pose. "It does. The peace of a world is more important than my petty grievances."

The stag pointed out, "Once, long ago, the fate of a wood wasn't."

"Now it is."

The stag was too stunned to respond. The king added, "I am no longer the sworn guard of Darken Wood, but I choose to return to my post. I will not hunt you this night."

"You have hunted at my request—have hunted me, as my punishment—every night for—" The stag stopped. How, in this endless cycle, could he measure time?

The king nodded. "Granted. But a king may change his mind. Once you have seen these strangers, you will understand."

"Will I? You seem sure of that; what are these strangers like?"

The king hesitated. "Complete strangers, let us say." He said nothing more. "Go see them. Perhaps they will change their mind."

"Or perhaps they will hunt at my request."

The king said simply, with more emotion than he had shown before, "Look on them for yourself, and think what they mean. The hunt must end."

"The hunt will end when I choose it—which means that the hunt will never end," the stag finished bitterly, "oh, great and loyal king."

King Peris dropped his hands silently. "Then go and ask them if they will hunt you. Let them slay you, let them listen to the same bitter words, the same old pain, over and over. I also can choose—and I choose never to hunt again. If you have ever loved these woods, this world—if you have ever loved at all—see what these strangers mean for our world, and choose to break the cycle." He fell silent again.

The stag ruminated—as befits a thoughtful ruminant. Finally he said, "Evidently, you have business with those who enter Darken Wood. Might you be persuaded to leave that business—"

"—for a later time? Yes. After all, as you point out, I have left my post before; I could postpone returning to it for a while. At my time of life—" he gave a grisly and meaningless smile— "one day or night is as good as the next."

"I gather you find it easy to postpone duty. A matter of habit, perhaps?"

The king scratched his ghostly beard with a ghostly finger. "Or else I am betraying my current habits. One is inclined to hope that you, too, could betray your current habits, as easily as you once, and ever thereafter, betrayed the For—"

"Now who is tactless?"

"Granted. You will consider all that I said? You may still choose—"

"I may. I will consider." The stag bounded off, knowing he did not need to agree on a later meeting-place with the dead king. Some meetings are all but foreordained.

Near the edge of the wood, the trail stopped abruptly, leaving only brush and a dense wall of plants. On the outside were false vallenwood, which looked like the great trees but grew no taller than a dwarf, some berry bushes, thorned and unthorned, and bright wildflowers.

On the inside were stands of twisted nightroot, the

bane of all animal life; guantvine, dense enough to bind the unwary; and Paladine's Tears, the tiny blue flowers that grew and wove into an upright mat between tree trunks. Though the wall kept curious folk out, the stag knew how many reckless souls it had kept in.

As he watched, the brush swayed and shivered under the pressure of hands.

Hands—of a sort. The stag stared at the first clawed fingers that emerged, waving in the air blindly to push more branches aside, finding none. The scaled man-thing that followed them out, blinking, into the sunlight stretched batlike wings in the open space.

"Kin to dragons." There was no question in the stag's mind, though the stag had never seen these creatures before. He knew also how few would know that: if the stag's appearance to Huma was barely legend now, the dragons were less than that.

More armored figures followed the first. The stag backed a few steps, more for his world than for himself. There were only a few creatures, if ugly ones, but their presence in this wood, in this world, meant unthinkable things.

He shook himself and murmured aloud, "The Royal Peris has a gift for understatement. 'Strangers' indeed." He tensed his muscles for flight, but stepped forward. "I greet you."

Nothing happened. The dragon-men stared in all directions, unhearing and unseeing.

He concentrated and said more loudly, "I greet you."

The leader leapt into the air, his wings holding him aloft a moment. Where the pegasi in flight looked graceful, this thing looked foul as it sank back, half-rejected by ground and air alike.

It watched the stag suspiciously. "Where did you

79

come from?"

The stag shuddered at the hollow, awkward voice that sounded like a dried man, but he answered it bravely. "From Darken Wood, where you are. Where have you come from?"

The dragon-thing ignored the question. "Darken Wood?" He held his sword at guard. "This is an evil place." He lisped slightly.

The stag wondered, none too happily, if the thing's tongue were forked.

"Evil only to those who bring evil with them." He added to the ritual response, "Many have. They do not leave again." He thought, briefly, of King Peris, of the Forestmaster, and of betrayal. "But there is much to be gained here, as well as risk."

"Name the gain." The dragon-man signaled behind him. The arriving troops moved to the very edges of the trail, not beyond, and formed twin lines, guarding each others' backs without a word. They were well-trained for war.

The stag considered what that meant, but went ahead. "There is one who watches over this wood." He hesitated, then amended, "Who rules this wood. All in it, living and . . . human and animal, serve her." He took a deep breath and finished, "To take this wood, it is only needed to slay her."

Treachery neither surprised nor impressed the dragon-man. "And she is?"

"The Forestmaster. The ruler here. A white unicorn."

Several of the company hissed involuntarily. The leader started. "A unicorn? You suggest a blood-force of draconians could—"

"Hunt her and slay her, yes." The stag added drily, "It appears the moral requirements for such a hunt were exaggerated. That seems sensible, since there is no morality to such a hunt." He added more plainly, "You need not be virgins."

The dragon-man waved a claw. "We have no capacity for desire." He made a face that could have been a smile. "Or for love."

"You are happier than you know," the stag said, mainly to himself. Aloud he repeated, "I have offered you a unicorn hunt. Will you take my offer?"

The dragon-man considered. "How would we find her?"

"You would not. I would, and you would follow. For the rest—" The stag shrugged, his shoulders rippling the motion up his well-muscled neck. "Surely you need not ask me how to hunt and slay animals." An old ache reminded him what this betrayal meant, to the lover as well as to the loved. For one moment he had a vision of those teeth, those claws, tearing at the shadowless white flesh of the Forestmaster.

The dragon—draconian—had not moved for some time. "We would do this for conquest, as well as for reasons we will not share." He smiled, after his kind, with a great many teeth. "Why would you do this?"

"For reasons I will not share." He finished more softly. "For reasons which, apparently, would mean little to you." More and more, the stag was wondering why scorned love and thwarted desire meant much to himself. "I was not aware that soldiers needed excuses, or perhaps you do not feel up to your quarry."

The draconian answered without anger, "Look in our faces. We could hunt any creature alive to its death."

"I see. And beyond?" the stag asked politely, but the joke was lost on them. "Follow, then. Not too closely."

As he turned and bounded away, he heard a single command, a word or a language he did not know. Once again he was afraid—for his world, and not for himself.

"Perhaps I grow sentimental. Next I will write bad songs and carry noisy bipeds on my back," he said aloud. But the joke was flat, and he realized that sarcasm and self-parody could no longer protect him from his own feelings. Behind him he heard the rasp of strange and wicked claws, tearing at the wood that was his whole world.

He was more than halfway to the clearing when bulky shapes, half-hidden in leaves, blocked his way. He froze in place, hoping the draconians behind him would do the same.

A voice called, "Halt."

"Remarkably alert," the stag observed, "if unnecessary."

"Don't be giving rudeness to those who keep faith." The deep voice, unbothered at the stag's sarcasm, went on, "Where does tha go?"

"I have an errand." He spoke coldly, hoping the sentry would take offense and turn away. "Is it habitual in this wood to question duty?"

"Not my habit, nor that of my kind." The figure emerged from the undergrowth. It was, as he had known from the size and voice, a centaur.

Nonetheless, he peered at it curiously.

"Ah," he said as if in recognition. "A draft human. Tell me, how is life in harness?"

The centaur regarded him, as always, with the easy contempt that the hooved and human show the merely human or the merely hooved.

"We are not in harness but in service—as others should be," the centaur said heavily. He tossed his head restlessly. "I have heard rumors and smelled scents this day, as well. Are more strangers in Darken Wood?"

The stag would not look in the centaur's large, dark eyes. "Perhaps you smell the strangers from last night. Is there any reason that their smell would cling to you?"

"We bore them on our backs," he said with dignity. "As all in this wood know. Are more strangers in Darken Wood?" he repeated.

"Why ask me? Surely you think you know more than I; your breed studies stars as well as any beast of burden could."

"Mockery. It's all tha has." He snorted, horselike. "Try to hide the truth from us both, if tha wishes. I study little, but I know stars. These past nights they tell of battle, and of life and death for a stag. It's a' there—for them as looks close." He added, "Maybe tha has not seen these strangers—but tha will." He turned to go.

The stag watched him. "I have a retort," he called, "timed and well framed, laden with irony and literary allusion—but I refuse to favor you with it. I have my dignity."

The centaur said nothing, and in the stag's heart he knew that was the best retort of all. The centaur waited a moment longer, then went his way.

A moment later the lead draconian appeared, sword ready, behind the stag. "He is gone?"

"He is." The stag was looking where the centaur had been, thinking hard. He tried to imagine the centaurs dead and defeated, bleeding as the wood fell again to strangers. He could not imagine that any centaurs would run, or would turn traitor, or would think at all of themselves.

"Then we remain undiscovered."

The stag thought over the centaur's words. "Let us say you remain unseen. Remain so a while longer, by moving behind me again."

The draconian looked at the stag without love and withdrew. The stag moved slowly, thoughtfully, toward the center of Darken Wood.

He caught himself humming. "It's that damned song," he muttered. "Crude and folkish, but the tune sticks in the mind."

Actually, it was the words which stuck in his mind. He found himself singing, half-unwillingly:

> The stag led on from night to dawn,
> From sunrise into morn,
> And in the shade of Shadow Glade
> Betrayed the unicorn.
>
> She spoke to him; her voice was grim:
> "What have you done for pride?
> You know and see your destiny
> And yet you turn aside.
>
> You would betray me to my death
> And quite forsake your vow?
> Then service lent without consent
> Is all you do me now."
>
> She touched him once, she touched him twice,
> And three times with her horn;
> And there he fell, and where he fell,
> He rose a unicorn.

He heard reptilian muttering behind him and stopped singing. If those behind him were truly to kill the Forestmaster, all music here—perhaps, eventually, all the music in the world—would cease, and all for the stag's petty revenge.

A winged shadow drifted overhead. He ducked automatically, but it was only one of the pegasi, circling and diving above the wood.

The stag could picture something larger, something with wings like the draconians', stooping onto the pegasi. He could hear them shrieking, flapping frantically, tumbling from the sky—

"Not them," he murmured. "Not by my doing, surely. But what can I do against these invaders?"

And a moment later, he thought, startled, "And could I give up my revenge, my vengeance for being scorned, after treasuring it for so long? In this cycle of sorrow, vengeance is all that sustains me."

It was something to consider on a long walk.

At mid-day the stag entered the Central Glade alone, well ahead of the draconians. "Master!" The woods took his cry in, draining it, not echoing.

"I am here," came the voice from the rock softly. "I am always here." The woods echoed *always*.

"I have a question."

"You have often had questions. You may ask."

"There are many and diverse beings who l-live—" he stumbled over the word "—inhabit this wood. Some hooved, some human, some both; some living, some dead, some a mix of living and dead."

"That much is true." She waited.

"How do they think of me? Do they think of me as one of them?" The loneliness in his own voice startled him.

"You are regarded differently by different beings. Do you wish to be thought one of them?"

The stag thought of those he knew and taunted, then thought of the draconians. "I had not thought so. But recently I discovered a threat which I do not want to harm creatures here, as though they were mine and I cared for them."

"Then by that care, they are yours and you theirs.

———

Does that please you?"

After a long silence, the stag said quietly, "I had not thought it would."

"I am glad." The Forestmaster added, "But that is not why you came, this night, as you have come all the others."

"True." The stag came forward to the rock. "I have come to you a final time. Will you not have me?"

"In service, yes. In love, no." She leapt from the rocks, landing in a cascade of light like stars, even by day. Like the king, like the stag himself, she did not seem surprised by events.

But she was astonished when the stag bent his forelegs and knelt awkwardly in the dust before her. He swayed, unaccustomed to kneeling. "Then I will serve you, a final time. This last thing I do of my own choosing."

The unicorn stared at his lowered head. "May I ask why?"

The stag answered, not moving. "Do not think me inconstant."

"That is the last thing I would think you."

"Good. All that I felt, all that I wish for and desire—" his voice wavered "—are unchanged. But in all the endless times that I have left here, returned here, betrayed here, I never saw the simplest reality of this place: That the wood is larger than I am. It is larger than my need. In the end, it will be larger, and last longer, than even my love could. I offer that love, to it and you, freely and without asking in return—since without asking, you and the wood itself and all in it have always given what you could. I offer my service, and," he finished humbly, "I hope it is well done enough to be of use."

The unicorn looked at him for a long time, seeing every detail of him, every hair and horn and eyelash.

At last she said gently, "Most well done, beloved. And remember that I have only said that I *could* not love you—never that I *did* not. Go with the hunt."

She touched his forehead with her horn three times.

He fell sideways, legs jerking and twitching. Terrible cries came from him, most loudly when the antlers broke off. His coat grew paler with each moment, and where the Forestmaster had touched him a single spiral horn emerged, blood-tipped, pulling itself through his splintered forehead.

When the draconians emerged, they saw a rock peak and only one unicorn, tottering unsteadily on its hooves. With shouts of triumph they leaped into the air, gliding in pursuit of the unicorn, with their swords swinging and their fanged mouths wide.

The stag moved, stumblingly at first, into Darken Wood. One by one the draconians alit and stalked him on foot.

Through the long afternoon, the stag learned again the old lesson: some hunters one may outrun, but not outlast. Whenever he entered the slightest clearing, the draconians covered more ground than he, gaining rest from the time spent gliding. He wondered if they could fly at all, but soon he was too tired to wonder. While he stayed in the densest forest they could not fly, but he could not run easily, either.

Moreover, in the forest he had to break his own trail, but they could follow in the way he left behind; he was doing their trailbreaking as well as his own. If he stopped to rest even a moment, he heard the snap of brush and swish of branches closer behind him than they had been when last he rested.

"I would not," he observed to himself as he raced after one such pause, "have thought they could be so patient. It is like being pursued by the dead, as I above all have cause to know."

———

They had swords and daggers, and perhaps other weapons as well, but the animal in the stag thought most of those pointed teeth, the cold eyes, the hissing breath. He had been pursued—how many times?—for sport, for the challenge, even for his antlers or for a vow, but being chased as meat—

His heart went sick within him and pounded every beat as hard as his hooves pounded the rock-strewn ground.

Behind him came the cold cries of the hunting draconians. To the rhythm of his own rock-chipped hooves, he could not choose but hear the darkest verse of the song touching on himself and on King Peris:

> *The guards have fled; their trusting land*
> *All undefended lies;*
> *And through the wood invaders ride*
> *With darkness in their eyes.*
>
> *Without alarms they practice charms*
> *That drive away that light*
> *And Shadow into Darken Wood*
> *Is made that evil night.*
>
> *And afterward, with sword and spear*
> *And horse and horn and hound*
> *They hunted down King Peris's men*
> *And ran them all to ground.*
>
> *The king was slain, his body lain*
> *Among his dying men,*
> *But they were told ere they were cold*
> *To rise and hunt again.*

He ran over the green and sunlit hill called Huma's

Breast, and found no peace there. Within sight of Prayer's Eye Peak he raced along the river called Night, and took no sleep by it.

He passed the Vale of Sorrow. He passed the Cliffs of Anger. He passed the Slough of Betrayal. Always the draconians grew closer.

"I had not thought Darken Wood so large," he thought once. "Surely I should never have chided the king for a single lapse in guarding so large a trust." He thought briefly of all the scorn he had shown the king, and more fleetingly of how he had originally tempted the king into betraying his trust, but there was little time for apology.

Twice, in the late afternoon, they encircled him and began closing. The first time, he leaped contemptuously over a startled draconian, in full view of the company. The soldier jerked his sword upright hastily, but barely managed to leave a furrow along the stag's flank.

"A scratch, nothing more," he told himself as he limped away. He considered tossing a stinging retort over his shoulder, but thought better. "I would only be lowering myself." And he might, he admitted silently, need the breath.

The second time, panting and exhausted in the Glen of Thorns, he had lain frozen under a branch of blooming sorrow's end, waiting until the draconians had plodded past him to slip quietly away, unmissed until a soldier looked back and saw the white mane as the transformed stag scuttled, head lowered, through the thorn bushes.

"A fawn's trick," he panted, ashamed. "I got away by hiding like a fawn."

He stared at his own side, mottled with thorn scratches and rock scrapes. "No wonder it worked. Still, perhaps these creatures don't see well by day."

But he looked at the sun, already sunk below treetop level, and he knew that there would be no third escape.

By dusk he was tottering, barely ahead of the draconians, barely able to move his legs. His eyes showed white all around the edges, and he smelled his own blood in his nostrils. Each step brought a new ache, each breath another side-stitch.

There was no question but that they would kill him. All that mattered was when and where.

Once he nearly sank down on a patch of deathwort, ready to let it end appropriately. If this were but one more death in an endless series, what did it matter whether he died well or badly?

But he heard them coming and struggled wearily to his feet. "I have," he gasped, "an appointment. With a friend, and with—others. I will fail no one this time."

The sun was no more than a blood-red sliver in the brush when he lurched across the trail and into the small glade. He looked around dazedly, though he knew the place well. Even where there were no trees, there seemed to be shadows, and the grass itself seemed tainted with death.

The stag nodded. "Here." His voice was rasping, half choked.

As the draconians arrived in the clearing, he half-fell off the trail and sank down on the grass a few lengths away.

A draconian saw him and called, "Captain."

The lead draconian shouted in triumph and leaped off the trail. The others followed.

The draconian cried, "Pride of kill belongs to Captain Zerkaz."

The stag reared up. "Pride, it seems, is universal, Captain. So is kill."

He punched forward with a hoof. Zerkaz had time

to screech with pain before his heart ruptured and his body turned to stone. It wavered once, but remained standing.

While the soldiers gaped, the stag charged another, head lowered.

He had forgotten that he had but a single horn, not antlers. As he pierced the draconian, the dying soldier brought his sword down as hard as he could at close quarters. The horn cracked all the way into the stag's skull.

He staggered back with closed eyes, barely noticing as the second soldier turned to stone. A third, sword out, was facing him, but the others had closed behind him and stood almost touching each other, staring into the field. Their blades wavered, almost trembled.

Around them, dead human warriors, Darken Wood's best guard, were rising, at last ready to fulfill an old promise. Beside them stood King Peris in full battle gear a thousand years old.

The king's armor was white silver over steel, decorated in rubies, for the blood of enemies, and emeralds and sapphires, for an archer's clear eyes. It was, as the stag had often noted, largely ornamental. Perhaps that was why the king and his body of men had once failed to guard against a real menace.

The soldiers of the dead king writhed up from the grass, unbraiding from it as though their bodies were recomposing. Swords in hand and no shields, they fell into a battle line; their empty eyes showed no mercy, no hatred, and no hope.

The stag cried in what voice it had, "Forward!" It leaped awkwardly and took a sword full in the chest as it punched a third draconian. As the sword withdrew, the stag made no sound at all.

Peris the King leaped over the falling animal. "I, not you, lead my men, beast. Forward!" The troops of the dead advanced, and the draconian ranks, weakened already, wavered.

The battle was like some deadly mime. The dead's weapons made no noise—yet their attackers fell, bleeding green liquid and turning stony in anguished poses. Blows against the dead passed through—yet many dead spiraled back into the carrion-tainted earth, and their lightless eyes glowed with an odd relief as they sank.

Forces were in disorder, yet few commands were needed; the dead fought as they had for so long, and the draconians fought for their lives. Except for a few cries of anger and pain from the draconians, the only other sound was the slow fall of stone bodies as, one by one, the draconians fell to earth clutching unseen wounds and half-twisting scaley faces in agony. Starlight flickered off real and ghostly weapons; bodies twisted or toppled into grassy shadows and were bodies no longer.

To an onlooker it might have seemed some strange dance without music. It was a war with little sound and no corpses, a battle for nightmares.

Through it all walked the king, his sword flashing right and left at arm's length. By himself, in the brief fight, he accounted for three draconians, and his heart seemed to beat again with his own pride as they dropped to the right and left. His arms felt, not the endless weariness of the accursed dead, but the growing soreness and strain of a living warrior. His eyes flicked back and forth alertly, noting even how a sweet night wind ruffled the grass into which allies and enemies were falling.

Ahead of him a draconian crouched over the prone stag, bringing a sword down with all the force he could above the near-motionless neck. The stag had not even looked up, dust and chaff barely moving in its nostrils.

The king dove forward, sword aimed at the draconian's heart. He made no attempt to parry the descending sword as it passed through his ornamental armor and into him.

His own blow took effect a moment later; the draconian doubled over, gasping, and froze that way, a corpse carved from a boulder. The king, carried by his own momentum, rolled against the stone body and winced with the pain. "I'll have a bruise tomorrow," he thought vaguely, unsure after all these years what a bruise felt or looked like.

He lay still and listened, hearing nothing but the stag's labored breathing. He struggled to his feet, barely able to hold his sword but aware of triumph and of great pain.

The stag opened his eyes. "Peris. The draconians?"

"Dead." Never, in Darken Wood, had the word been said with such satisfaction.

"An unusual way to end a hunt, with dead hunters."

"You have said so before." The king knelt, taking the stag's head on his lap. The stag's chest wound, pulled free of the ground, re-opened, but the king paid no attention. "You have often said that at a hunt's end the hunter should be alive, the quarry dead."

"I have often been insulting." His eyes blurred; with great effort he shook his head and cleared them angrily. "What will happen now?"

"If I know soldiers, the commanders who ordered the search of Darken Wood will decide to delay another search until they feel they can risk further loss. They will also hope that their quarry, the questing party of the other night, appears elsewhere, as someone else's responsibility." He shuddered. "At any rate, we will have saved this part of the world for a while—if, as they say, I know soldiers."

———

"You know soldiers well. You lead them still better."

"Thank you." The king sat down heavily by the bleeding stag. "A satisfying night, but not an easy one. I have been wounded."

"Recently?" The stag grunted as its forehead horn, cracked by the sword-blow, split all the way to the skull.

"Tonight, in fact."

"At any other time, I enjoy a joke—"

"Seriously." Red leaked through the holes in the king's armor, as though the rubies were melting. "I had forgotten how painful this was."

"You could have asked me." The stag raised its pain-wracked head. Now the split horn sagged apart, its cleft gaping, and exposed bone at its root.

"I could have," the king agreed. "It seemed rude." He spoke with difficulty. "It seems I have fulfilled a pledge and will die in service."

The stag said, "I also." He added, "Could you help me over to the last standing draconian? I would not mind dying with such memorial."

The king, gasping, carried the shuddering body of the stag to the foot of the standing draconian. "He has—" He coughed.

"Can you speak no more clearly than that? I seem not to hear well just now." The rumble of the moving horns covered all sound.

The king braced himself and said distinctly, "This one has a hoof-print on his chest. Yours?"

"I would nod, but I have a headache." Blood ran from his split forehead. As though watered, the twin horn-shards sprouted buds of antlers.

"Then he will wear my marks as well." Holding the stag with one arm, the king removed his own crown and placed it on the stone figure before sliding wetly down its side to the grass.

The stag rasped, "Either I am overly sensitive by nature, or this seems harder than usual." Blood was flowing darkly around the dust in his chest wound. "Could you not distract me?"

"I could try." The king tilted his head back in pain as he inhaled, and sang in a quavering voice:

> *"For every wraith who breaks his faith*
> *Must wander without cease*
> *And, cold, perform what he did, warm,*
> *And never rest in peace.*

He coughed, and a hairline of blood ran from the corner of his mouth. The stag, looking up through filmy eyes, took up the song for him:

> *So, every night the stag betrays*
> *The love he could not keep*
> *And king and host desert their post*
> *To hunt and never sleep.*

They finished, singing together. It took them a long time, since one or the other often stopped to gasp for air, and it seemed important to them that they finish as one:

> *And so they shall betray and hunt,*
> *Until the day they show*
> *That they somehow fulfill the vow*
> *They broke so long ago."*

Done, they collapsed against each other. "Not a bad song, really," the king said. "Needs a little tightening here and there, perhaps, fewer cousin-rhymes, but at least it's something of us left behind."

"True. Many have died with less fame and with

worse poetry." The stag's antlers shuddered painfully back into place. The stag, eyes upward, lay his head on the king's lap and stared at the draconian. "Who would have thought that I should be hunted by such as this? Or that you should hunt them?"

The king's voice was low and halting. "True. They are vile, and we were proud. But for once, we both have died for something besides ourselves. And when you have been dead as long as I—" he wavered, and said in a last breath— "a little variety in one's chosen way of dying is not such a bad thing."

And as the stag joined the king in final death, he thought sleepily that after a thousand years of nightly betrayal, transformation, pursuit by the dead, painful death and more painful rebirth, almost any change was pleasant. He cradled his head against King Peris's stomach, and the two accepted death as, long ago, it had accepted them.

No one but Time removed the bodies; eventually they disappeared. The stone draconians became overgrown and powdered under the pressure of weather and vines; time's best warriors. Only the one draconian, wearing an ancient crown and scarred on its breast with a cloven hoof, remains. For reasons no one living knows, it does not crumble. Go to the wood, no longer called Darken, and you may see it yet.

Once, not long ago, the Forestmaster came into the glade and stood before the single draconian. The crown was tarnished, the sword rusted; only the hoofprint was still sharp and clear. The Forestmaster stared at the print, then looked thoughtfully around the glade. There was not so much as a mound to show that anyone had died here, and even the memory of the draconians was fading from those who lived in

Shadow Wood.

The unicorn tipped her head up and quietly sang two stanzas she had heard recently, added onto a very old ballad:

> *"The shadows in the woods are plain*
> *And mingle now with light;*
> *They flow and play with sun by day*
> *And dance with moon by night.*
>
> *From Darken Wood has Shadow Wood*
> *Been granted its release,*
> *Those who were killed in vows fulfilled*
> *Have there been granted peace."*

She strode to the edge of the woods and thrust her horn in among the vines, circling it quickly. Walking back to the statue, she lifted her horn to the stone and slid a floral wreath onto it. It slid down too far; she moved parallel to the sword and adjusted it. For a moment, sword and horn both pointed to the north star, faintly visible in the darkening sky.

She stepped back. "Sleep well, beloved." She turned and was gone.

The wreath of Paladine's Tears stayed fresh a long time.

Hide and Go Seek

Nancy Varian Berberick

---

*F*OR a long time Keli did not know where he was. Sometimes he smelled the forest and the river, sometimes only dirt and rocks. Once the boy thought he heard thunder rumbling far, far away. Then, on the tenuous bridge between darkness and consciousness, he knew with the flashing certainty of lightning's strike that it was not thunder he was hearing.

It was the voice of nightmare: the voice of a goblin.

"Tigo, let's dump the little rat in the river. We have what we want."

Keli expected to feel the goblin's huge gray hands drag him up and cast him into the river.

Far back in his mind he knew about the leather thongs pinioning his arms, binding him at knee and ankle. Too, he felt the hard earth, the fist-sized rock digging into his ribs. Pain, however, was not as immediate as death-fear.

A second voice, sounding like the rattling of old bones, growled, "Bring him over here, Staag; see what he's carrying first."

Someone shouted, then yelped. Keli's eyes flew open, his heart leaped hard against his ribs. He was

---

99

not alone in his captivity!

Bruised, pinioned, and bound as Keli was, his fellow prisoner was in a worse plight, caught hard by the neck in the goblin's iron-fingered grip. He was small, but no child; the cant of his ears as well as his slim build and small stature marked him as a kender. Several pouches of varying sizes and materials bounced at the kender's belt each time Staag shook him. And Staag, that slope-shouldered, gray-skinned nightmare, shook him often and hard simply because it amused him to do so.

The kender, a game little fellow, hitched up his knees and drove them into the goblin's belly. Had a mouse attacked a mountain the result would have been the same. Laughing, Staag loosed his grip on the kender's neck and dropped him.

The kender writhed against his bonds. "Swamp-breathed, slime-brained bull," he croaked.

Keli's heart sank. So much for the kender, he thought. Staag's going to kill him now!

But the goblin didn't. Tigo stopped him with a command.

If Staag, his arms too long, his legs too short, his skin the color of something a week dead, was the nightmare, his human companion Tigo was reality gone twisted. Tall and lean, bony-shouldered, with limbs that might have been stolen from a scarecrow, Tigo bore a four-pronged grapnel where his right hand should have been. His eyes, muddy and brown, held little sanity in them.

"I said bring him over here, Staag." Tigo glanced at Keli, who shivered despite the close heat of the summer morning. "And the boy, too."

A bull, the kender had called the goblin, and bull-strong he was. He tossed the kender over one shoulder, Keli over the other and, with no thought, he dropped them next to Tigo.

Breathless, Keli lay still where he fell. The kender, his face in the dirt, snarled another insult.

"Let's just kill the kender and get it over with," Staag grunted. "We should have slit his throat at the tavern and got done with it."

"Aye," Tigo drawled. "And left him bleeding all over the place for anyone to find. I don't think this one traveled alone."

Staag snorted. "Since when do these little vermin travel in company? Tigo, we waste time." He peered up through the forest's brooding green canopy. "It's almost noon and we're still too close to that village. Let's just kill him and the boy and get *out* of here!"

Keli clamped his teeth down on a whimper and prayed to every god his mother had told him was real.

"Be patient, you'll have your fun. But we're not going to kill the boy yet." Tigo, his hands thief-light, slipped a finely tooled leather map case from the kender's shoulder. He laughed, a sound that reminded Keli of rusty hinges creaking. "Nice collection of maps, kender."

The kender hitched himself onto his back, spat dirt, and looked at Tigo with the expression of a guileless child. "Used to clean middens for a living, did you? I can tell by the smell."

Keli groaned again, hoping the kender's blood wouldn't splatter all over him. Yet, though he paled, Tigo didn't reply. Staag kicked the kender.

"Please, kender," Keli breathed. "Be quiet!"

Sometimes a bad dream, steeped in terror and warped perspective, turns funny. Keli felt he was in one of those odd turns now: the kender winked.

Before Keli could be certain he'd seen the wink, Tigo cuffed the kender hard.

"These maps! How recent, how dependable?"

With a speed that left Keli confused, the kender became the spirit of helpful affability. "Some are very old—I've been collecting them for years, you know. It's kind of a hobby of mine. I like the drawings, especially the things the mappers sketch when they don't know who or what lives in the land. And I like the little legends and poems in the borders of the larger ones. That one, the one drawn on hide, is my oldest and the one I think I like the best. I got it in Schallsea; an old man gave it to me and he said—"

Tigo's hook-hand flashed silver in a shaft of sunlight, dancing threateningly before the kender's eyes.

"Right. Some of them are old, some are new. I guess it depends on where you want to go," the kender added hastily.

"Away from here," Staag growled, "and fast."

The kender did not give the goblin a glance, but spoke to Tigo. "Then you're really lucky you brought me along. I've been all around these parts, many times, and I know them nearly as well as I know the inside of my own eyelids. That's why I don't have any maps of this area in the case. Who needs one? Not me. Where do you want to go?"

Tigo hissed a snake's warning. "What makes you think we need a guide?"

"You said so." The kender was all innocence now. Keli marveled at his composure. "Not in so many words, of course, but I can tell. Otherwise why would you be so interested in my maps?"

"You make a large guess, kender."

Keli thought so, too, but held his breath now, waiting.

The kender shrugged as best he could. "Maybe I was wrong. But if you *did* need a guide—and I'm not saying that you do—I'd be the one you'd need. As I said, I know—"

"Aye," Staag snarled, "all the lands about here."

"That's right, I do. What do you think? Do you need a guide?" The kender lowered his voice in a confidential manner. "If you want to kill someone, for example—"

Staag rumbled threateningly, loosed the dagger at his belt.

"Whoa! Wait! I'm not saying you do. I'm not saying you don't. But I can take you to a place I know where you can do whatever you need to do and no one will be the wiser."

"In exchange for what?" Tigo asked.

The kender snorted. "For my life!"

Keli's heart sank. Whatever that wink had been, it certainly hadn't been an expression of solidarity.

Tigo shook his head, baring his teeth in a deadly smile. "What's your bond, kender? What will keep you from sneaking off in the middle of the night, leaving us with daggers in our backs?"

Staag laughed then, thunder and nightmare. Keli's stomach turned weakly. "The same thing that keeps him here now, Tigo. Loose his feet so he can walk, but keep his hands tied and him on a short rein."

Keli shifted away from the kender. This was no fellow prisoner now, but one in league with these two who, for some reason Keli could not figure out, wanted to kill him. He squeezed his eyes shut against a cold wash of despair and only partly heard the argument between Tigo and the goblin about whether the kender's pouches should be rifled now or later.

It hardly bore listening to anyway: Tigo argued that there was no time, and clearly Tigo was someone whom even the goblin feared. I'm not dead yet, the boy thought, but it's only a matter of time and place now. And I don't even know why!

* * * * *

Tanis had suspected all winter that the real purpose for Flint's journey this year was to attend Runne's wedding. Flint mentioned the occasion only once, when he and Tanis were mapping out the summer's trips, and then only told a brief tale of how the girl was the grandchild of Galan, the man who had been the old dwarf's first customer and who many, many years ago had become a friend.

"Runne's father, Davron, was killed a few years ago in a hunting accident. And Galan . . . is gone now. Someone must stand in her father's place at the ceremony and, while there are uncles to spare, the little maid has remembered her grandfather's old friend and asked me to fill that place. I want to do that, Tanis."

Though it was high summer now, the dust of the only street in Seven Wells dancing in the hot breeze like phantoms around his knees, Tanis well remembered how the winter firelight had looked like memories in Flint's eyes when he told that lean little tale. Yet every event of the summer seemed part of a conspiracy to keep Flint from Long Ridge and the wedding.

Hot and too early the summer had come, drying the stream beds and cutting hard into their travel time. Near Gateway one of the few storms of the season sent lightning lancing from the sky to ignite the tinder-dry forest. Two weeks on the fire line there, digging trenches to help defend the town from the burning rage of the forest fire, ate into their travel schedule. A merchant late for their rendezvous at Pine Glen, and another customer who never did meet them at Fawn's Run, left them here in Seven Wells with a two-day journey to Runne's home in Long Ridge which must be reached in one.

Now Tas had vanished.

Caramon would have no part of a search around Seven Wells for Tas. "Who knows where the little bandit's got off to now? *I'm* not spending the cool of the morning looking for him. He knows where we're bound. Let him catch up."

Raistlin removed himself from the discussion altogether. Sturm, who decided it might be profitable to look while the others argued, returned after a time with the news that Tas was not to be found.

"Right," Flint snapped. "Because he probably took off in the middle of the night for who knows what foolish reason." He lifted his pack with one easy swing and settled it on his back. "I'm not waiting around for him to remember where he's supposed to be. Caramon's right, he'll catch us up on the road. And if he doesn't—then he doesn't."

No one was disposed to argue. The road before them would be a long and hot one. Tas had too often romped ahead, lagged behind, or struck out on some kender-quest of his own for anyone to be concerned about him now.

Tanis hefted his own pack and fell in beside Flint. The kender could be as troublesome as a heel-snapping pup, but he was well able to take care of himself. This disappearance, like so many others, would be explained away with some fantastic tale of adventure or discovery. Tas had been looking forward to the celebration at Long Ridge. Likely he would join them there.

Tanis was not concerned.

Keli wasn't walking well. Tethered to Tigo, as the kender was to Staag, he stumbled, fell, and this time did not try to get up. He was too tired, too hot and frightened, and too certain that wherever the kender was leading them would be the place where Tigo would kill them both.

It was the kender, loping back from where he'd been

ranging for trail marks and paths, who helped him. Keli pulled away from his hand and staggered to his feet. "Do you really think they're not going to kill you, too?"

The kender only grinned and shook his head. "They won't. And they won't kill you either."

Staag hauled hard on the kender's line. "Move away, little vermin."

The kender went where he was pulled, but before he resumed his scouting he looked once over his shoulder and again winked. Trust me, the wink seemed to say.

Keli was in the way of trusting no one, and he certainly wasn't going to trust a kender who would bargain with killers. The boy hunched his shoulders against the heat and his fear and trudged on. He ached for home, he who had been so proud to leave it as his father's courier only a week ago.

Ergon, his father, had been almost casual about charging his son with the message to his old friend Carthas.

"Give him the scroll, son, but remember to give him first my regards and personally tender my regrets that I will not be able to accompany him this year on his horse-buying expedition. I must honor my promise to your mother's sister. Your uncle was a long time ill before he died. Though he tended his business as best he could, your aunt will need my help to untangle the mare's nest he left her. "Tell all this to Carthas. He will understand."

Keli had accepted the charge as though entrusted with a message to the High Clerist himself.

The tavern at Seven Wells had been Keli's third stopping place. And, it now seemed, his last. He'd come in late, stabled his horse, and snatched a quick meal. When he tried for a room, he was able to get lodging only in the barn with his horse. A party of horse traders filled the paddocks with their stock and most of the tavern's rooms with themselves.

So tired had Keli been that the straw seemed a princely bed. He'd fallen asleep easily to the stamp and chuff of horses.

And wakened to the nightmare of the goblin and moonlight streaming along Tigo's hook-hand. One of them hit him hard. There had been nothing but pain and darkness, and finally, the woods.

His horse they must have turned out among the stock in the paddocks so that none would wonder in the morning why the young courier had gone and left his mount behind.

And they'd snatched up the kender as well. Keli still didn't understand why, couldn't fasten on a reason. Tigo jerked on the tether again as though calling to heel a wandering dog. Keli tried to pick up his pace.

He could either look at the ground or the kender scouting ahead, and he chose the kender coursing the forest as though leading them through streets of a town he knew well. Bright blue leggings flashing in and out of the underbrush, topknot bouncing, the kender reminded Keli of a blue jay.

Chatters like one, too, Keli thought. The boy didn't mind the kender's chatter very much. Running like the song of the river they'd left behind, it took his mind off what must await him at the journey's end.

That would be death. The kender talked long and often, but he was not the only one who did. In fits and snatches Keli had picked up bits of his captors' guarded conversation.

Staag was pressing for opening ransom negotiations. Tigo had other plans.

"Aye," Tigo snarled once, "we'll send a ransom demand. But it's not only ransom that one will be paying out for his son. He owes me, Ergon does. He'll pay the coin, but all he'll find is a body."

Sweat traced paths in the dust on Keli's face, ran stinging into his eyes. After a moment the kender dropped back, jostled him lightly, and stumbled to cover the move.

"Don't worry," he whispered. "This is just like a game of Hide and Go Seek, only I'm sure my friends will find us. Tanis is the best tracker there is. And Raistlin and Sturm and Caramon learned from him. The place I'm going to take us to is a place Flint showed me a couple of years ago. Once they get on our trail, Flint will know right off where I'm heading. Probably."

Hide and Go Seek? Keli turned away in disgust. "This is not a game, kender. I told you, those two are going to kill me."

As before, the kender grinned and shook his head. "Those two? Flint alone could handle three or four of that sort. Or five, or six, depending on the circumstances . . ."

Tigo booted the kender up ahead again, and Keli was left with something to consider.

His friends, the kender had said. Keli squinted hard at the kender's back. He *did* look familiar. Had he been at the tavern last night? Aye, and, despite what Staag had said about kender not traveling in company, this one had been with a red-haired hunter who had an elven look about him, three young men, and a dwarf. He remembered them because one of the young men, thin and pale-eyed, no warrior like his two companions, had threatened to turn the kender into a mouse and fill the tavern with cats if he so much as looked at his pouches again. A mage, by the sound of that threat. Keli had thought at the time that the others probably traveled with the mage just to keep the kender in line.

Could it be that these companions would be looking for the kender? *I'm making sure that my friends find me. . . .* How? Keli drew a breath, and hope with it.

But the hope was small and too slim to flare. Hide and Go Seek, the boy thought, is played with friends in the streets and alleyways of the town you live in. Not with goblins and thieves in the forest.

The bride was a summer princess, her hair golden wheat, her eyes blue-touched with dawn's mist. Roses blossomed in her cheeks. Her laughter rose and dipped the way a bird's song will.

So she seemed to Tanis. She must have seemed that way to Flint, too, for he gifted Kavan, the miller's son, with her hand as though presenting the boy with jewels. How Karan felt was clear for all to see; all the jewels of Krynn would be but poor stones and rubble when compared with this girl.

"Lucky fellow, this Kavan," Caramon murmured when the ceremony was ended.

Tanis gave him a sidelong look and a grin. "Caught, is what he is, but the jailer is pretty enough, isn't she?"

"Aye, and it won't be bread and water for him. Though it will be some time before he has any interest in kitchen matters—" He did not finish the thought but jerked around when a hard finger caught him between the ribs.

"Keep a civil tongue in your head, youngster," Flint growled.

"I didn't mean—"

"I know what you meant. Now why don't you go off and do what you do best: find yourself something to eat."

It was a suggestion Caramon never found amiss. When he was gone, Tanis grinned again. "Runne is a beauty, isn't she?"

"Aye, she's that. Her grandfather would have been proud this day."

Memories darkened the old dwarf's eyes again, clouds in a clear sky. As though to deny the sudden thread of sadness running through his day, Flint looked around, searched the crowd of family and friends now surging around the new bride and her husband. "That addle-pated kender never turned up."

"I haven't seen him, but Tas isn't one to miss a celebration. He'll be here before long and likely you'll be wishing he wasn't."

Yet through the long summer afternoon and into the hot dark of night the guests at the wedding moved easily, refilling wine goblets or ale pots and plates too soon emptied of the good food. No one cried thief, no one wondered where his purse had got to, no lady missed even the smallest trinket or scarf.

There was no kender in attendance, and by the time red Lunitari reached his zenith and white Solinari left the horizon behind, Sturm came to Tanis wondering.

The forest had thinned near sunset, the oaks and pines were spare now, replaced by stony ground and boulders. Night's dark cloak brought no relief from the day's heat, and Tigo was not bearing the simmering night well at all. His eyes were black pits, his lean, hard jaw jerked from time to time under a tic of which he seemed unaware. His fingered hand stroked the grapnel's hook as though he'd decided to do murder with it.

Beyond a gulp of water, Keli and Tas were granted nothing. The rope tethers were gone, the knee and ankle thongs were back. Above the whine and drone of gnats, the bright song of crickets, Keli heard the kender's low cursing. Twisting so that he faced the fellow, Keli grudgingly whispered, "Are you all right?"

"It's not," the kender grumbled, "so much that I'm nearly starved to death and those two have eaten everything but the bones of that rabbit. It's these thongs. It's not easy to breathe when your hands, your knees, *and* your feet are tied!"

The kender was more actively suffering now, so completely bound, than he had been all day. His breathing was the short, hard gasping Keli had seen once in a dog whose collar was caught in a fence.

"Kender," he whispered, thinking to distract his companion from his troubles, "I'm Keli. What's your name?"

"Tasslehoff Burrfoot. Call me Tas, all my friends do."

"Tas, how did they get you? And why?"

"With a sack over the head, followed quickly, I can tell you, by a big stick of wood. I was in the barn, at the tavern, just looking. Someone had ridden in that night on a big red horse, and Caramon said he'd never seen a bay with a mane and tail that color before. They were all gold, you see, and I just wanted a look. Nasty beast, too. Nearly took off all my fingers when I went to touch his mane. It was like gold, though, soft and yellow." Tas hitched himself up so that the small of his back rested against a boulder. In restless preoccupation, he worked his wrists against the binding leather. "I walked in on them just as they were tying you up."

From where he lay Keli saw a thin line of blood, black in the darkness, trickling down Tas's wrists to his fingers. "Stop—" he hissed, "you're bleeding!"

After a moment, Tas sat still. "Why did they take you?"

Keli shook his head. "I—I don't know."

Tigo's shadow, thin as a black knife, cut between them. Keli fell silent, hoping the kender would do the same. For once Tas did.

Tigo's eyes gleamed like dark, hateful stars. "Don't you *know*, boy?"

Keli chewed his lip and shook his head.

"You don't know the tale of the brave knight Ergon who went boldly against a barely armed pickpocket with his sword?"

Keli flared. "My father would *never* fight an opponent who was not equally matched!"

"Wouldn't he?" Slowly Tigo raised his hook-hand. For a moment he seemed lost in the play of Lunitari's blood-red light along the steel. His eyes dimmed as though all their gleam had gone into the grapnel. When he spoke again, his voice was flat. If dead men could speak, Keli thought, his was the voice they would use.

"This hook is a thing I must thank the courageous knight Ergon for. My hand he claimed in payment for an old man's purse."

"You lie," Keli spat.

"Careful, boy. This hand is not flesh and it cuts deep."

"Aye, and you'll kill me anyway. You've said as much. I'd sooner die for the truth than a lie."

Tigo's eyes burned, his jaw twitched. "It is no lie!"

The night's heat was cool when compared with Keli's outrage. It was no easy thing to be a knight in these troubled days. All his life Ergon had followed the rules of his order humbly, honorably, as though they were a code he was born to.

"I remember the tale well—I thought my father would die of the wounds he got at your hands and those of your accomplices. And the old man, he *did* die, thief. He was no match for four daggers. My father barely was. And it was no sword my father used, but his own dagger."

Keli choked on his fury, would have said more, but Tas, under pretense of shifting cramped muscles, fell hard against him. Tigo reacted with a howl of outrage. "You'll die for your twisted truth, boy, soon enough. But not yet. For now," he said, eyeing Tas, "I've an interest in the kender.

"What's in your pouches, little bandit?"

Tas shrugged and grinned. "Nothing."

"Nothing?" Like a hawk diving, Tigo's good hand came down, caught the kender by the front of his shirt and lifted him full off the ground, dangling him in front of Staag. "Why don't I believe that?"

The buzzing of the gnats and the shrilling of the crickets seemed louder to Keli. He hoped with all his heart that the kender wasn't going to do something to get himself killed. And from the look of things, he thought, hunching around so that he could see, it wouldn't take much.

The thief's dark eyes were only narrow slits now. His teeth, gleaming white in the light from the fire, were bared in a snarl. He threw the kender down at the goblin's feet. The snarl turned to a grin the moment Staag began to cut the pouches from Tas's belt and the kender raised his protests.

Keli didn't understand the kender. What seemed a matter of soul-wrenching pain only a short time ago—his bound wrists and knees and feet—was as nothing now compared with the rifling of his pouches, the throwing away of what he called his treasures.

"A line of wicking," Staag grumbled, "a gray feather, two chipped arrowheads, a bundle of fletching—junk! Nothing but junk!" He pawed through first one pouch, then another. Tas's fury only amused him.

A gold earring he kept, stuffing it into his own belt pouch along with a ring set with polished quartz and a small enameled pin. The rest, an assortment of things that could not have been of value to any but a kender, he kicked aside.

Tigo, like some thin, black vulture, leaned over Tas. "Just where are you taking us, kender?" he demanded suspiciously.

"I told you, to a place I know where you can do whatever you have to do and no one will find you."

"Aye? Not on some roundabout trail that will lead us to trouble?"

Keli felt Tigo's fury, banked but still hot, where he lay. He prayed the kender would be careful now.

He wasn't. "Not trouble of my making."

Tigo kicked Tas hard, and the whoosh of air exploding from the kender's lungs made Keli's stomach hurt. The kender jack-knifed over, nearly wrapping himself around the thief's ankle. He was furious, but not so furious that he didn't take good aim when he bit. His teeth clamped on the man's leg above his boot and it took Staag to pull him off.

Tigo roared. "Hold him while I rip the belly out of him!"

Keli screamed protest, struggling against his bonds.

"Go on," Tas taunted. "Where will you be then, you brain-sizzled, hook-handed ass? Stranded, that's where you'll be! You haven't a drunk's idea where you are now!"

Tigo would happily have crimsoned the earth with the kender's blood, but Staag had no appetite for killing their guide. Moving faster than Keli thought any goblin could, he whisked the kender away and threw him down next to Keli.

"Keep your mouth shut, kender," he hissed. "I won't be able to keep him off you next time."

Tas choked, gasped for air, and coughed. Keli shrugged himself closer to the kender and nudged him with his shoulder.

"You all right?"

Tas muttered something into the dirt.

"What?"

"I want my dagger, my hoopak, a rock, anything!"

Keli braced his own shoulder against the kender's, offering companionship, commiseration, comfort. "Maybe," he whispered, more for Tas's sake than because he believed, "maybe your friends will find us soon."

Merciless summer sun glared from the hard blue sky, baked the ground, radiated from the humped clusters of rocks. Tanis wiped sweat from his eyes with the heel of his hand and bent to retrieve the one thing Flint had missed: a fog-colored wing feather from one of the gray swans of Cristyne.

Because a cut through the forest from Long Ridge would take a day off their journey to Karsa, the half-elf and his friends had bidden the bride and her new husband farewell the night before and struck south and east at first light. Runne would have kept them longer, but Flint pleaded business and promised her that he would see her again on his way back north.

"I don't think," he told Tanis wryly, "that she's going to miss me or anyone for a time."

Tanis, remembering the hard poke in the ribs Caramon had earned for himself with a similar remark, had offered only a noncommittal smile. It seemed that where Runne was concerned some things could only be said avuncularly.

Now, the darkness bordering the edges of those memories, the half-elf absently stroked the edge of the large gray feather with his thumb. Tas had been here recently.

Or his pouches had. And those had been ruthlessly emptied, their contents carelessly scattered. The hot breeze carried Caramon's deep voice from up the trail and Sturm's answer. Tanis knew by their tones that they had found no sign of either struggle or a body. He left the underbrush and joined Flint where he knelt in the path.

"One more thing, Flint."

The old dwarf took the feather without looking and added it to the pile of oddly assorted objects to be stuffed with hard, angry motions into Tas's pouches.

A blade-broken dagger, a blue earthenware ink pot, a little carved tinderbox, a copper belt buckle that Caramon had lost somehow and which Tas would swear he'd always meant to return, a soft cloth the color of dawn's rose, a bundle of the stiff green feathers Tanis liked best for fletching his arrows . . . all of these kender-treasures and more had been discarded as so much junk.

Flint's anger might seem, from his tight-lipped muttering, to be directed against a packrat of a kender. Tanis knew the old dwarf better than that.

"We'll find him, Flint."

Flint still did not look up, but drew the thong tight on the last of the kender's pouches. "Did you find his map case?"

"No."

"Good. I wish whoever took it the joy of trying to find his way with those maps! Hardly one of them is worth the parchment it's penned on."

Tanis found a smile. Few of Tas's maps were any good at all without his interpretation and translation. And those were never the same twice.

"We'll not make Karsa any time soon now, Flint."

"Aye," Flint grumbled. "And you can be sure that I'll take it out of that rascally kender's hide when we finally catch up with him, too."

Tanis thought the threat lacked conviction.

Silent as a shadow moving in the breeze, Raistlin came up beside them. "If someone took the map case, and there is nothing to show that the kender was killed here, it would not be amiss to consider that the case, Tas, and whoever waylaid him are still together. The trail is rocky up ahead, Tanis."

"Tracks?"

"None. But there is something else." Raistlin nodded toward a small grouping of boulders. "Camp signs. Perhaps you should see them."

Tanis moved as though to signal Flint to join them, but the young mage shook his head. Fear, like a dark thread of night, crawled through Tanis's belly.

The campfire had been small, ringed by rocks. Several yards beyond them was a flat-sided boulder. On the near side of the boulder, a handspan from the ground, was a mark no larger than a kender's fist. Though it was rough-sketched in blood, Tanis recognized the sign at once: a stylized anvil bisected by a dwarven F rune. Flint's plate mark.

"Tas?"

"Who else would leave that mark?" Raistlin touched the rusty brown blood. "It was fresh not long ago."

Both turned at the sound of an approach. Flint stood at Tanis's elbow.

"Wretched kender!" The old dwarf clenched his fist. "Vanishing out from under our noses and getting himself into Reorx only knows what kind of trouble!" He stared for a long time at the device which had always marked his best and most beautiful work, sketched now in dark blood on the stone. It was as though he'd never seen the mark before and sought now to memorize it.

Tanis said nothing, did not want to speculate at all now. Raistlin it was who spoke, and when he moved his shadow fell between Flint and the mark.

——

"The blood is fresh, Flint, not a day old. He's still alive." The young mage looked from one of his friends to the other. "And, by the look of this, hoping that we're on his trail. We'd best waste no time in wondering now."

Tanis did wonder: He wondered if they were too late.

The sound of the waterfall might have been the angry roar of some outraged god. Racing and tumbling, the river threw itself from the cliff nearly two hundred feet above and slid in foaming white sheets only to vanish a third of the way down. Then, like some conjurer's trick, the falling river reappeared from a spout after twenty-five feet of sheer, burnished cliff face and finished its headlong dash into the narrow lake.

The mist was as thick as rain on the shore and as drenching. Though Keli and Tas were tied to the base of a thin spire of rock, all the thirst and heat of the day seemed to vanish beneath the soothing kiss of the vapor.

Keli sidled as close to Tas as he could. He sent a quick glance over his shoulder, assured himself that Tigo and Staag were well occupied refilling their water flasks, and let a long, gusty breath speak of the almost solemn wonder that filled him at the sight of this wild and glorious falls.

"You knew," he whispered, "you knew this was here."

"Oh, yes. I've been here before." Tas frowned a little, then shrugged. "Although it's not exactly where it's supposed to be."

"What?"

"Well—it isn't the place Flint knows. The trail looked like the one to there. But I guess it wasn't. This must be"—he squinted at the setting sun—"sort of east of it. Or north. Or—"

Keli's heart sank and with it any hope he might have nourished for rescue. "They're not coming," he said bleakly.

"Oh, yes, they are. It—just might take them a little longer to get here. But that's all right. Things will work out if you stick with me." Tas winked, something Keli was beginning to recognize as a sign that more trouble was on the way. "All the way."

"All the way?"

"All the way to the top."

"The top of the *falls?*" Keli's mouth went suddenly drier than it had been all day. "I don't—I'm not sure—"

"Don't worry!" Tas's eyes were bright with expectation. "Really, Keli, you worry more than anyone I've ever met. Except Flint. Now, there's a worrier. How old are you, anyway?"

"Twelve."

"Twelve! Far too young to be worrying as much as you do."

Keli closed his eyes against the sight of the roaring falls. "Tas, I'm sorry you got caught by those two . . ."

"I got caught?!" Tas was indignant. "Why, it's more like they got caught by me! After all, they didn't even know where I was taking them! Ha! Of course, as it turns out, I didn't know either, but that's a small point. By the way, can you swim?"

"Yes," Keli said warily.

"Good! That's the last problem solved."

"The last? But—"

"What are they doing, can you see?"

Again Keli looked over his shoulder. "They're still at the lake. I can see Tigo, but not Staag. I hear him, though."

"Good enough. Now, look."

———

Tas twisted a little so that his back was to Keli. Clutched in the kender's bound hands was a small dagger.

"Tas! Where did you get that?"

Tas shrugged. "Oh, well, you know, sometimes people are a bit careless about where they put things and I . . . just . . . find them. This," he said, grinning again, "I found in Staag's belt this morning. He'll miss it sooner or later. But by then I think we'll be too far away to give it back. Now, turn around and stand very still. I don't want to nick you."

He cut Keli's thongs blind, his back to the boy. The patience to unknot the most tangled puzzle and nimble, firm hands were a kender's gifts. Keli was free before he could worry that Tas would sever a wrist rather than a thong.

"There. Now do mine."

Keli worked carefully, his fingers still numb, his hands aching with the sudden rush of blood in veins. Soon the kender, too, was free.

"Now," Tas whispered, "follow me!"

With one glance backward, swift and silent as a hare on the run, Keli followed the kender. They made distance, angled sharply north and then abruptly west to the stony shore of the lake. When Tas skidded to a halt on the rocks, Keli nearly toppled into him.

"Tas! I don't think—" Keli swallowed his doubt. Tigo had discovered his captives' escape and his cry echoed along the shore. In an instant, the goblin and the thief were in furious pursuit.

"Keli, make straight for the falls, then cut to the north when you begin to feel the force of the cascade. Slip in behind the wall of water. I'll be waiting for you."

Tas's dive was a whirl of arms and legs. He hit the water hard and whipped his hair out of his eyes.

"Come on!"

The inside of Keli's mouth was like sand. He shot a terrified glance over his shoulder and another at the lake and its thundering falls. He knew with certainty that if Tigo caught him now he'd rip the heart out of him with that grapnel hand. There would be no false ransom note to his father, nothing but bloody revenge for a wrong never committed.

There was no reasoning with insanity.

The drop to the lake from the rocky ledge was as deep as a tall man's height. Keli drew in all the air he could and dove, feet first, into water as cold as a newly melted glacier.

"Go!" Tas yelled to the boy. "Go!"

Keli struck out hard and fast, and Tas overtook him a moment later, cutting the lake as smoothly as any sleek otter.

They'd not covered even a quarter of the distance to the falls when two splashes behind them told them they had not lost their pursuers.

"Where are your friends?" Keli wailed.

"I don't know!" Tas shouted back. "They're usually better trackers than this!"

The waning sun twined ribbons of golden fire through the cascading water and ran along the sheer sides of the far cliff face as though etching veins of gold and rubies. The narrow part of the lake was at the western shore. On the eastern side, the churn of the thundering falls turned the lake white and deadly.

For a long moment, squinting through the light and the mist, Tanis forgot to breathe. His breathing was not stilled by the beauty of the place. That he hardly saw at all. It was stilled by horror.

Far out across the lake, small as abandoned nestlings, two swimmers surfaced at the roil's edge. There was something about the dive and play of one to tell him right off that he was Tas. The other, clutching at air and shimmer, looked like a boy.

Behind the two, closing fast even as Tanis watched, were two other swimmers. One, huge-armed and gray-skinned, was clearly a goblin. The other, lean and one-handed, coursed ahead, angling as though he meant to cut in behind the boy.

Flint's groan could have risen straight from the depths of Tanis's own fear. Moving quickly, the half-elf tossed aside his bow and quiver and pulled off his boots. Raistlin's light hand caught his wrist.

"Wait! Tanis, let my brother go, and Sturm. You're the bowman and the longest-sighted of us all. Defend them while they swim."

Though reluctantly, Tanis agreed.

They were fast, the two young men, out of most of their clothes and into the water on smooth, long arcs almost before Tanis could reclaim his bow and quiver. But there was more than half the lake to cover and the goblin was closing fast, his lean companion already cutting in behind the boy.

"They'll never reach them in time," Flint whispered.

Tanis nocked an arrow to his bow's string, drew and sighted. Released, the arrow cut through the sun-jeweled mist and shied its mark, the goblin's neck, by the width of its shaft. It was enough, however, to send the surprised creature diving beneath the water for cover.

Tanis drew again, searched for a target, and found none. The lake was suddenly empty of all but Caramon and Sturm swimming strongly for the falls. Caramon faltered, rose high, shaking his hair out of his eyes.

Both his quarry and their victims were gone.

* * * * *

The water was liquid ice, his limbs as heavy as lead. Keli twisted hard, kicked back once, and then again. He was free of the pull of Tigo's hook-hand! Off to his right, blurred figures wrestled: Staag and Tas. Ahead, close enough to suck at his legs, to draw him farther down, was the roil of the falls.

Thunder roared all around him. The black-watered lake was white as diamonds here. Tigo surged forward and up, wielded his hook and snagged it again on the back of the boy's belt.

Keli rolled and jack-knifed, his lungs afire and screaming for air. He reached down, grabbed Tigo's ears, and pulled as though he would tear them from the man's head. When Tigo opened his mouth to scream, he took in what Keli thought must be a gallon of icy water.

Again the boy kicked, and once more he was free. He surfaced, sucking air in huge, greedy gulps and saw Tas break into the light at the same moment. Behind the kender, rising like a sea drake from the water, Staag roared and then flung himself aside and out of the path of a green-fletched arrow.

"Tas!" Keli waved and pointed back toward shore. "Down! Duck!"

Tas rose, whooping with glee. "It's all right! That's Tanis! Our rescuers! Look!"

Two young men, one broad-chested and brawny, the other slimmer and faster, cut through the water with strong, distance-eating strokes.

"Caramon and Sturm!" Tas threw his head back, laughing. "Ready or not, here they come!" He dove and angled through the water, coming up beside Keli. Staag shot up behind him, grabbed, and missed by a hand's breadth.

"Tas! They're too far away!"

Tas yanked the boy under the water, ignoring his

---

sputtering protest. Staag's thick legs thrashed to the right of them, and Tigo surfaced just behind the goblin.

Tas released Keli, jerked his head to the left, and dove down and around the goblin and Tigo before either could get his bearings. Keli followed gamely, hoping with all his heart that the kender knew where he was going.

Down just didn't seem like the answer to their problems.

Sturm shouted once, then again. He'd lost the hook-handed man or found Tas and the boy—Tanis couldn't be sure which and did not spend a moment's concentration wondering. His hands knew nothing but his bow, his eyes only his arrow's target. That target, the gray-skinned, maddened goblin, had dragged Caramon beneath the lake's surface and held him there now.

His breath held tightly, legs braced wide, Tanis waited the interminable space of five heartbeats for Caramon to surface again, afraid to loose his arrow for fear that Caramon would come up between it and the goblin. Dimly, he was aware of Raistlin's soft intake of breath, of Flint's curse and then his whispered plea.

Caramon did not surface.

Tanis let fly and prayed for the gods' grace, for their favor, for mercy.

Rainbows danced in the air, shimmering along the tumble of the falls. Mercy, and the arrow, were delivered at the same time. The shaft flew true and took the goblin full in the throat. In the veil of the mist, Sturm broke the water, graceful as a dolphin leaping.

Seeing himself alone, he dove again, resurfaced, and filled his lungs with air. He returned to the water twice, and the second time he came up dragging Caramon, gasping, to light and air.

They were alone in the lake, Staag's body gone into the rage of the falls, Tigo vanished. There was no sign of Tas and the boy.

Though they dove and searched for longer than those on the shore knew anyone could survive beneath the water, they did not find Tas or his small companion.

Caramon raised his fists to the thundering falls. The dying sun colored his brawny arms red and gold. His howl of rage echoed for a long time between the shores, so loud and grieved that Tanis did not hear the small clatter of his own bow when it fell from his hands to the rocky shore.

Numb, Tanis watched as Caramon and Sturm made their way back to land. He joined Raistlin and Flint to help them, awkward and earth-bound again, onto the shore. For a long time he felt vacant, emptied. The feeling well matched what he saw in Caramon's eyes, in Sturm's, in Flint's stunned disbelief.

Then after a time, when the sun was nearly gone and they were still waiting—for something—he heard the old dwarf draw a sharp, hard breath.

"He's lost his mind." The words hardly matched the breathless awe, the chilled amazement, of Flint's tone. "By Reorx's forge, if that kender ever had a mind to lose, he's lost it now. Tanis! Look!"

Tanis raised his head from his drawn-up knees, looked to where Flint pointed. Impossible, the half-elf thought dully, he's dead, drowned.

"Impossible" was not a word one could apply to a kender's resourcefulness with any hope of accuracy. Tas—topknot flying in the wind from the falls, arms spread for balance—negotiated a natural bridge no wider than the span of two hands across the cascade's spout high above the lake. Even as Tanis watched, the kender turned his head as though speaking to the one who followed him on hands and knees.

Tanis scrambled to his feet and ran out to the edge of the shore. Sturm and Caramon joined him, squinting up into the last light of the day.

"Aye," Sturm muttered. "And there's that hook-handed villain who escaped me in the lake! How did they *get* there?" He looked around wildly as though seeking a way to get to the arch above the falls. There was only the lake, and he would have made that swim again.

Tanis held him back. "You'd never get there in time, Sturm."

"Where does he go after he gets across? There's nothing but cliff and rock!"

Tanis shook his head. "Nowhere," he whispered. He turned away from the lake and saw Raistlin standing above him, looking into the rainbow dance of the falls' mist. The young mage smiled, his light eyes eager and sharp.

"Raistlin, can you help him?"

The mage nodded slowly, thoughtfully, his eyes still on the jeweled mist and the last shafts of sunlight. "I think I can. He has a mountain climber's skill, our little friend, and it is a good thing he does: he's going to need it."

Stone bit sharply into Keli's hands. Stalled and frozen in the middle of the narrow rock span, he dared not look down, could not look back.

Across the arch Tigo crouched, a lean and hungry predator waiting for his prey to realize that it was trapped, caught. There was no need for him to venture on the bridge, no need to pursue farther. At last he would have his murderous revenge!

Across the bridge, his back to the spray-soaked wall, Tas shouted, "Keli! Come on!"

"I—I can't—I can't—" Keli could not move, it was all he could do to speak.

"You have to! You can't stay there! Pretend you're a spider! Spiders don't ever fall! Come on! It'll be fun!"

Fun! Keli swallowed dryly and tried hard to be a spider, wishing all the while he were a bird instead. Hand over hand, he crawled across the slick stone bridge, swearing futile boy's oaths under his breath. Fun!

"That's it!" Tas called. "I told you it would be fun!"

Tigo, across the span, laughed. His laughter was ghostly, only faintly heard above the roar of the water. Keli ignored him, concentrated on Tas and the bridge.

"Come on, Keli, a little more! You've almost got it! Ever do anything as much fun as this?"

Keli groaned and shook his head. He regretted that at once. The bridge seemed to sway and rock under him. "No," he panted, staring at his white knuckles. "Nothing like this!"

Hand to hand, knee to knee, Keli crept, trying not to give in to black-winged vertigo, wishing it weren't so hard to breathe.

After what seemed a lifetime of crawling, Keli's fingers touched the kender's, cold and slick. Tas leaned a little forward to grasp a wrist, then an arm. "Up now, on your feet. I've got you."

Keli gained his feet, wobbled a little, and then straightened.

"That's right. Now just edge over here. We can both fit on this ledge. Probably."

Probably! "Crazy as a kender" was an expression Keli had heard from time to time. He used to think he knew what it meant. Now he was certain. Keli dragged up every bit of strength he had and lurched hard against the wall. He pressed his face to the wet, black stone, shuddering. "Now where?"

Tas attacked the answer obliquely. "We can't go back, but he's not coming on, either."

"What, then?"

"We can always wait."

Out over the lake the jeweled and dazzling mists of sunset were gone. On the far shore twilight's purple shadows gathered, the outriders of the night.

"It would be nice," Keli said tightly, "if we could fly."

"Sure would," Tas agreed, "and a lot better than being stuck up here."

Keli wanted to wail. He clamped his back teeth hard and whispered, "Then—but—why are we out here? I thought you knew a way *out* of this mess!"

Tas shrugged. "I didn't think he'd follow us. I thought he was drowned in the lake. Twice."

Across the arch Tigo sat, his back against the stone, patient as inevitable doom. Keli couldn't look at him without feeling sick, without feeling, in imagination, the rip of his grapnel hand and the long, shattering fall to the water below.

Light, the faint and fading gold of sunset, the silver of approaching twilight, danced up from the black surface of the lake and came together, shining in the gloaming like hope promised.

Far below, the red-haired bowman Tas called Tanis and one of the young men who had been in the lake stood on the shore. The other was in the water again and swimming hard toward the falls. The dwarf and the slim young man moved quickly to the north.

"Tas, what are they doing?"

"Something, they're up to something. Look! Tanis sees us! He's pointing." The kender leaned so far out to see that Keli had to catch him back by his belt.

"Don't *do* that!"

Clearly the fact that he'd almost tumbled to his death didn't bother the kender at all. He laughed, and the sound of his glee skirled high above the roar of the falls.

"Look, Keli! Raistlin's doing something to the air!" Tas thumped the boy's shoulder joyfully, nearly knocking him from his tenuous perch. "I don't know what he's up to, I usually don't, hardly anyone ever does. But it's always magic, and it's always worth waiting for."

Clinging like a soaked bat to the wall, Keli swallowed his nausea. Whether or not what the mage was up to was indeed worth waiting for the boy couldn't say, but he didn't see that they had much choice.

Raistlin's hands moved, deft and certain, in magic's dance. He gathered translucent rainbows and gemmed mist, separated their shimmering strands, and wove them swiftly, one around the other, into a rope of gleaming enchantment.

It grew quickly, the magic rope, and leaped away from the young mage's hands, directed and sped upon its way by will and spell. Out across the black surface of the water it flew, with the grace of a hawk rising, with the certainty of one of Tanis's well-drawn arrows speeding to its mark.

Sturm leaped into the lake, cutting through the icy water with powerful strokes. By the time he reached Caramon, the shining line had passed well over their heads, flying toward the arch and Tas's outstretched hand. On the shore Flint shouted, his voice rising high in triumph, ending on an oddly broken note, a cry of warning.

Tigo was halfway across the bridge, the hook that passed for a hand glittering balefully in the fading

---

light.

Tas stepped in front of Keli and wound the shimmering rope around the boy's hands. "We'll go together. It'll hold, I swear it. Just slide right down. It won't burn your hands—you can hardly feel it."

Keli eyed the water, then Tigo advancing slowly across the arch. "Tas, it's not a rope—it's *light and air!* It can't hold us!"

"Oh, sure it will. It's Raistlin's magic." Tas cocked his head as though he'd had a sudden thought. "You're worrying again, are you?"

"Worrying?" Keli gasped. "Tas, I'm so afraid I can't even think!"

"But it'll hold. I *told* you: it's magic. And Raistlin does the best magic I've ever seen. He'd never let you fall."

"Tas, the rope's not real!"

"It *is* real! But—well—look! Down in the lake. There's Caramon and Sturm— Did I tell you that Sturm wants to be a knight? Like your father. He'll be a good one, too. He knows that solemn old Code and Measure like he made 'em up himself, and—"

"*Tas!*"

"Well, right. So if you do fall—which you won't—they will get you. You'll be all right. Now let's go or we're going to have an appointment with Tigo real soon!"

That last, more than any of Tas's assurances, decided Keli. He grasped the rope, silver and gold, woven of magic and light. He squeezed his eyes tightly shut, sucked in a lungful of air, and left the ledge.

Tas followed.

Behind them Tigo raged, a beast whose prey had flown, wingless, from his reach, abandoning him to his impotent anger.

———

* * * * *

The air was cool and shivery by the night-dark lake. Far over the water's black surface stars reflected and, Keli thought, as he hunched closer to the fire, something else did too. Ghostly light and shimmer, faintly rainbowed and silver. A residue of Raistlin's magic? The boy thought so.

None sat waking now in night's darkest hour but Keli and Tas, the half-elf Tanis, and the dwarf Flint. The young mage had been the first asleep. Keli knew nothing of magic or its tolls, but it was clear to him that Raistlin's light-weaving had left him drained. It seemed to Keli that the thin young man was hardly strong enough to exert such effort often. Or, the boy thought as he stole a covert glance at the sleeping mage, maybe he is. Even in exhaustion something of power and strength had lighted the mage's eyes.

The mage's brother was Caramon, warrior big, with mischief dancing in his brown eyes, a kind of magic of his own. He slept so soon after his brother that the difference could hardly be measured. His snoring was like low thunder.

"Asleep between one bite of rabbit and the next," Flint had growled. "We could be witnessing the dawn of a new age of miracles." Keli had wanted to laugh at that, but he didn't. The old dwarf bore a forbidding look in his eyes, scowled easily and grumbled often. Here was one who would need a wide berth.

For a time it looked as though Sturm would stay awake long enough to make good his claim on the first watch of the night. He didn't. Likely, Keli realized, his friends knew him well enough not to argue the point. And well enough to know that Sturm's exertions in the lake would put him quickly to sleep.

Tanis—his red hair the color of copper in the firelight, his long elven eyes sometimes the gray-green of leaves turned to an approaching storm, more often emerald bright—divided his time between smoothing Flint's grumbling and listening to the endless stream of Tas's chatter. This he did with the air of one who knows that a storm will not end until all the thunder has rolled and all the rain has fallen.

These, then, were Tas's friends of whom he'd been so certain. Of all of them only Tanis and Flint remained awake to hear the tale of capture and escape told in odd tandem by Keli and Tas. Though neither, Keli thought indignantly, seemed to want to credit Tas with the heroics Keli stoutly attributed to him.

His back propped against a rock, his feet as close to the fire as he dared put them, Keli now looked first at Flint, then at Tanis.

"If it hadn't been for Tas, Tigo would have killed me. He's a real hero."

"Hero!" Flint laughed. "That one? Aye, lad, and I'm Reorx's forgemaster!"

"He *is*," Keli declared stoutly.

Tanis tried, for the sake of Keli's rising anger, to swallow his own laughter. He glanced at Tas crouched before the fire. The kender's dignity was not in the least disturbed by Flint's customary derision.

"He saved my life," Keli insisted. "He got those two good and lost, found the caves behind the falls, and the stairs that led up to the top. *I'd* never have known about the caves or the stairs or the bridge."

Flint shook his head. "I don't suppose Tanis's tracking or Raistlin's light-weaving had anything to do with the fact that you're here and safe, lad?"

Keli did not quail before the dwarf's gruff question, but defended his friend. "They did, and I thank you all for what you've done. But—but you were almost too late. And—" Keli foundered, looking from one to the other. They were still amused, and Keli could not understand what was so funny. "And—Tas *did* save my life."

"Risked your neck about a half a dozen more times than you remember or know about is more like it," Flint growled. "It's lucky you are that you're here to tell us the tale.

"Look at you, lad, you're half-starved despite eating a rabbit and a half, and dead tired. Get some sleep now, you'll see the right of the matter in the morning."

"I know the right of it," Keli maintained. He looked to Tas, who only shrugged.

"They're a little slow," the kender drawled. He grinned then, suddenly, and that grin was like the flash of a comet across a midnight sky. "But they always manage to catch up." He stretched and yawned hugely. He shot one quick look at Flint and then winked at Keli. That wink, always trouble for someone, sparked Keli's smile.

Flint started to protest, but Tas only grinned again. He waved an off-hand goodnight and went to find a place to sleep. As tired as he was, Keli knew he wouldn't be able to sleep yet. He settled down more comfortably near the fire and sighed.

After a moment Tanis said, "We'll have to get you home somehow, Keli."

"Just back to Seven Wells would be fine," Keli murmured. "I'm sure my horse is still there and there is the message to be delivered to my father's friend."

"Oh, no," Flint rumbled. "If we let you out of our sight now, who knows what you'll get yourself into next? Home, lad, and the message can be delivered along the way." He reached into his pack, pulled out a block of wood, and applied his dagger's blade silently for a time. Keli would have offered his thanks, but Tanis caught his eye and stilled him with a smile and a shake of his head.

When Flint looked up again, he spoke not to Keli but to Tanis.

"If we've any sense at all, we'll make for home our-selves after we've delivered this lad and his message."

That was not what the half-elf had expected to hear. "Back to Solace this early in the summer?"

Flint was quiet for a long moment. When he spoke at last his voice was rough. Almost cold, Keli thought.

"I thought he was dead," Flint said, and Keli knew it was Tas of whom he spoke. "I really did. I didn't fear it. Fear still allows you to slip hope in behind it. I thought he was dead from the minute I saw my mark on that rock, and I didn't expect to find anything else.

"It is a bad thing to be without hope." He cleared his throat softly and went on. "And Caramon. When he didn't come up from the lake, when Sturm had to dive to find him, I thought, between the first time and the last, that he was dead, too."

Keli felt that fear, and heard it in the dwarf's voice. His eyes were not so hard now, his expression not nearly as forbidding as it had been. An odd look graced his rough features, but Keli could not put a name to it. He'd seen the look before on his father's face.

Tanis poked up the fire and by its flare Keli saw that he, too, had thought his friends dead. When he spoke, though, it was not to reassure himself but Flint. "They're all right now."

The old dwarf drew a long breath and let it out in a heavy sigh. He looked at his young friends sleeping around the fire: Caramon, his scabbarded sword lying near to hand; Sturm, who slept deep and looked as though he could wake fast at need; Raistlin, likely walking in dreams only he could understand; and Tas, curled like an exhausted pup against Caramon's back. When the dwarf spoke again, Keli sensed that some decision was being made. He sat forward and listened.

"Aye, Tanis, they are. But the lands are changing, lad. I feel it in my bones that things are shifting, growing darker. At first it was good to have them along on these trips for their company. Lately, it's been good having them along because I could not ply my trade, such as it is these days, along the old routes without them. Look at what happened to the lad here! Goblins and bandits! And rumors of worse and stranger things haunt the roads now."

Tanis reached out absently to ruffle Keli's hair. "You'll not keep them safe in Solace by wishing it so, old friend."

"No, I know them better than that. And we're partners, you and I, have been for a long time. This isn't a decision I can rightly make for both of us." Flint shook his head. A smile warred with a scowl. The scowl won, but only barely. "And we don't get much done these days chasing that pesty kender from one end of the land to the other, do we? No, home sounds better and better to me."

As hard as the dwarf was to read, that was how easy it was to divine Tanis's thought: plainly he doubted that Solace would keep Tas or any of his friends long for all that it seemed to be home. But aloud he only said, "All right, then, Flint. Home it is, for Keli and for us."

Solace won't keep them long, Keli thought. Hawks may grace your wrist for a time, his father had once told him, but they do not domesticate well at all.

Now, Flint leaned forward and gently roughed the sleepy boy's chin. "Home, aye, lad?"

Keli smiled in the night's shadow. "Oh, aye, home."

By the Measure

Richard A. Knaak

*H*is head was pounding, and his mouth was dry.
He had neither eaten nor slept for two days—not since
burning Standel after a day of mourning. Standel, his
one companion. The only other knight to accompany
him on his flight from an Order that had decayed.
Brave, strong Standel. He had never understood his
own death.

Garrick scanned the terrain as well as his bleary
eyes were able. More of the same. Villagers were coming from the south, away from the advancing army
sent by the Dragon Highlord. They were seeking protection from the garrison at Ironrock. The knight
smiled bitterly through cracked lips. How long did
they think a garrison of one hundred men was going
to hold out against an army one hundred times its
size? Not to mention the added pressure of trying to
feed several hundred refugees.

He steered Auron away from the group. The warhorse turned reluctantly, perhaps sensing the grain the
people carried. The horse had been forced to subsist
on what little it could forage in this bleak area. Garrick sympathized with its plight, his own last meal

having consisted of a handful of berries and some cheese and hardbread bought from the innkeeper who had been indirectly responsible for Standel's death. The lands he had traveled through since offered nothing in the way of sustenance. The inhabitants themselves had long ago spirited away anything edible.

He could not believe what the Order had become. The older knights smiled patronizingly at his plaints; some of the younger ones scoffed. Some understood him, though. Understood that even the Knights of Solamnia had turned away from Paladine more than they admitted. The Knights were no longer an Order that aided the repressed so much as a petty sect living on its past glories and shunning those they believed had turned on them. Never mind that the Order had such black marks as Lord Soth to live down.

In his worn state, he did not notice the second group of villagers until they were almost on him. Like so many before, they spat at him as they passed and cursed him for being what he was. A stocky man with slightly gray hair and a perpetual scowl blocked his path with an open cart drawn by two oxen. Several other villagers stood behind the man.

"What do you want here, oh great and noble knight?" The venom fairly dripped from his mouth.

Garrick sighed. "I have sworn by the Measure that I will defend my fellow men from the evil that is the Queen. I intend to keep that pledge."

They laughed. Laughed loudly. The laughter was magnified a thousand times in Garrick's mind, though he knew it would come. It always had. The loud, bitter laughter.

The stocky leader stepped closer, his eyes shifting back and forth between the knight and the warhorse. It was obvious that he did not trust either of them. Closer now, he studied Garrick's battered armor, the chipped and bent weapons, his pale and sweating face.

"Aye, you look like a terror that will frighten away the dark ones. Frighten them into conquering the world, I'd say!"

There was more laughter, though much more muted than before. The looks the villagers gave Garrick were ugly, full of hate. Hate for his not having been there when it counted. The leader shifted closer, his intentions clear. Pull the knight down into the mud where he belonged. The knight drew his well-worn blade with a speed that belied his weary appearance. He kept the group at bay with the weapon, allowing no one within arm's length.

"For your own sakes, move on."

Muttering, they did so, much more quickly and complacently than Garrick would have thought possible for them. He realized why with a sadness that sank him deeper into the darkness he had ridden in since Standel's death. He was nothing to them. If anything, they were disgusted with him. Disgusted with all the knights.

It hurt Garrick that they had good reasons for their hatred.

The few huts he passed now were stripped of anything worth carrying. Mere shells. Skeletons. It was as if the war had already been through here. In a sense, he realized, perhaps it had. Standel would have been stronger, more able to cope with the shouts, the curses, the looks. Garrick could not understand why he should live while a better knight should die so ignominiously. Not for the first time since his companion's death, he wavered slightly in his belief in the Measure.

The ground reached for him. Garrick steadied himself and wiped his brow. To collapse this close, to leave his task unfinished, would be unforgivable. Paladine would surely condemn him. He waited for exhaustion to overtake him, but something held back the final fall. A warmth in his chest, around his neck. A feeling of guidance and love.

His shaking hand tugged hard on the chain circling his throat. The medallion given to him so long ago gleamed despite the lack of any sunshine. On each side of the medallion were engraved words from the Measure. More important, the medallion carried the face of Paladine as known by the Knights of Solamnia.

The pain in his mind eased. Paladine had not condemned him after all. There was still some purpose to Garrick's life, some reason the god still watched over him. He thanked his lord and allowed the piece to thump against his chest again. Though his body was worn beyond the limits of most men, he smiled gratefully. He would be allowed the chance to fulfill his Oath.

Somewhere to the south lay his objective. Somewhere to the south, perhaps four days, perhaps only two, lay part of the advancing army of the Dragon Highlord—a sizable portion commanded by one of the Highlord's most dangerous generals. Pushing ever closer, its only real obstacle was the tiny garrison four days north from Garrick's present location.

They would be forced to travel through the woods to obtain the pass, he realized. In the woods, they would be vulnerable. In the woods, he stood a chance.

He came across the bodies just after crossing a stream. They had been carelessly stacked to one side. Plague victims. The stench nearly overwhelmed him. The knight shivered. Better to die in battle than waste away in the end. He covered his nose and mouth with tattered, dirty cloth and urged the warhorse to move at a quicker pace. That their loved ones had left these poor shells to rot did not bother him. Now was a time to take care of the living, to help those still with the breath of life within them. The dead were in no hurry.

The light began to fade as the sun, hidden by clouds, plunged closer toward its own death. Garrick eyed the huts in this region. Unlike those he had passed shortly before, these were more or less whole. Knowing them to be contaminated, though, he could not bring himself to rest in one. He dared not rest, anyway. Each moment was as precious to him as if it were his last.

The woods came into view less than an hour later, marking the beginning of the pass even before the great ridges that stood to each side. Garrick blinked, rather surprised that he had made it this far. That in itself was a miracle. He gave thanks to Paladine and suddenly felt warm all over.

The first trees were little more than stumps. This part of the forest had been raped by the desperate villagers. Panic had finally taken over at some point. To one side was a small stack of firewood. A little farther, a tree stood with its trunk chopped half through. Idly, Garrick wondered if the woodsmen had fled because of plague or because of the approaching horde.

Auron was hesitant to enter the woods and would do so only after much persuasion. Garrick frowned. The warhorse was not prone to hesitancy. The knight put one hand on the hilt of his sword, but did not draw it. With more urging, he managed to get the horse to move at a reasonable pace.

The woods were deathly silent. No birds, no ground creatures. Not even the faintest hint of a breeze. Auron snorted. Garrick tightened his hold on the sword. He searched for but did not find any trace of draconian activity in the woods. The feeling of death was in the air, though. It was as if animal life had abandoned this area to the Queen. Even the trees seemed to have given up; many were obviously dying—another sign of things to come should the armies of darkness emerge triumphant.

He rode on. The night air cooled his burning head. He forgot some of his pain. To either side, the ridges grew higher and higher. Garrick pulled his mount to a halt momentarily and picked out a likely spot on one ridge. Auron snorted and would not move. The animal had given more than most and had finally reached its limit. Even its training could not overcome such exhaustion.

Garrick patted the animal gently and dismounted. Leaving the horse to rest, he made his way to the ridge top. It was steep but by no means impassable. Discarding some of his heavier equipment, the knight made progress.

He thanked Paladine that it was not a long climb. The campfires became visible just after he had cleared the tops of the trees. Further in, the pass sank deeply, giving him a much better view of the region than he had hoped. Seeing the vast number of fires, Garrick knew he had located the Queen's forces. They had dared to settle in an area where they could easily have been trapped if there had existed an army to trap them. The northern garrison, of course, was too small. All other resistance had been crushed. The commander of the army had a right to be confident.

Tomorrow they would head through the pass and into the unprotected lands. It would not take them long to reach the garrison then. The battle would be even shorter.

Once more, he wished that Standel had survived rather than he. Standel would have looked at the massed forces and scoffed. He would have organized, would have planned. Garrick had only a few wild ideas and a hope that Paladine would grant him the chance.

His head pounding, Garrick returned to his mount.

The horse was grazing peacefully. He saw no reason to disturb the animal. Auron had already performed miracles for his master. The knight could not honestly ask for anything more. It was up to Garrick alone.

With shaking fingers, he pulled out the medallion. It was still warm to his touch and seemed to shine even in the darkness. He caressed it for a moment and then sank to his knees in prayer.

They came just before dawn.

He had just put out the last of the fires. Now he rested against the side of a tree, sword drawn, shield ready. He had released Auron and sent him away, not wishing so loyal a beast to perish for little reason.

The fires had been easy to build. The forest was dying; branches littered the ground. Most were dry and made good kindling. The fires were strong, though not long in burning themselves out. That they existed was more than sufficient for Garrick's purposes.

By their slowed movements, he knew that scouts had found the remains of more than one of the fires. He had been careful to scatter a few fragments around each fire, junk he had gathered on his way here. Just enough to lend truth to the thoughts of the enemy—that the Queen's foes awaited her army in this forest.

Garrick heard the hiss of an indrawn breath. A leathery, misshapen foot moved into sight.

The knight's sword was a blur. It was into and out of the draconian's neck before the creature had a chance to die. The body solidified to stone and tumbled forward. Garrick glanced around the tree and then darted swiftly away.

He did not stop until he was some distance from the area where he had killed the reptilian warrior. Again, he pushed himself tightly against the tree and waited. This time, the wait was not long. His eyes were already getting blurry; soon he would be unable to see.

These scouts were men. His first blow took out the closest of the two. The scout had time to gasp and no more. Even as he fell, Garrick was already working on his companion. This man had time to ready his weapon, but his skill was far inferior to the training a Knight of Solamnia received. Garrick disarmed him first and then stunned him with a blow to the shoulder. When the man attempted to crawl away, Garrick knocked him out. Sheathing his sword, he dragged his senseless opponent behind a tree. He forced himself to concentrate on necessary actions. There were some things that had to be done.

He stayed as long as he felt was safe and then moved off to what would be his third, and probably final, position. He dared not take any longer. His head was already pounding.

Falling against a tree, he sought desperately to catch his breath. They were ready for him now. The bodies of their fallen comrades had alerted them to the immediate threat. No longer did they attempt to sneak through the brush. Garrick estimated at least five adversaries, two of whom were almost within striking distance. He steadied his hands as best he could and blinked several times in a futile attempt to clear his vision. He could hear the hiss of the draconians as clearly as if they were breathing in his ears.

The first to pass him made the mistake of looking the wrong way as it passed. Garrick nearly sheared its head off. Unfortunately, his speed had slowed considerably. The draconian petrified and fell, pulling the great sword from the knight's weakened grasp even as it dropped.

Weaponless, Garrick's luck nevertheless remained with him. The second draconian had been momentarily stunned by the sudden attack. Before it could react properly, Garrick was already on it. They struggled fiercely, the draconian's awkward build proving a disadvantage in hand-to-hand combat on the ground. Only the knight's exhaustion evened the contest.

There were shouts from all around, both human and draconian. A patrol had arrived. Garrick was torn away from his adversary, who remained on the ground, gasping for breath. He was able to strike one human in the stomach, sending the recipient of the blow back a good four or five steps. Then, his arms were pinned behind his back and he was forced down. A draconian slapped him hard on the face. There was the sound of steel being drawn, but someone muttered something Garrick was unable to understand. The muttering was followed by the sound of the weapon being sheathed once more. As he had surmised, they had been ordered to take him prisoner.

Two of the draconians, their wings fluttering in anger, held him tight while one of the humans bound his hands together behind him. Someone produced chains. Garrick's feet were hooked together so that he stumbled when he tried to take normal steps. His helm was torn from his head and a leather collar with a leash attached to it wrapped around his neck, nearly choking him. He stumbled then and fell to his knees. Determination more than anything else made him stand once more. He could barely feel the blows of his captors anymore.

A human who must have been in charge led the entire group back to camp. They were obviously convinced that a large band of knights was lurking somewhere in the woods. Having faced one knight who, despite his appearance, was readily capable of taking on a good half dozen opponents, they were in no hurry to meet up with a larger force. The various members of the patrol took turns pulling him. Had they not been convinced that he must have information of some sort, they would have gladly killed him in order to speed up their retreat even more.

At some point during the trek, Garrick could hold out no longer. His head felt like it was bursting. The woods became unbearably hot. He was no longer able to coordinate his movements, nor could he even tell what was happening around him.

Mercifully, the entire world chose to go black.

Cold reality struck him in the face and dripped down his neck. Garrick shivered and tried to focus his eyes. The light of midday burned into his very mind, forcing him to close his eyes once more. He tried to stand, but found himself bound tight to some sort of chair. Someone stirred.

"Shall I throw another bucket in his face, General?"

The voice was as cold as it was commanding. "I think not. If our knight is anything of a man, he will open his eyes and face us. Still, if he is a coward, perhaps another bucket of water would be . . ."

Garrick gritted his teeth and forced himself to look into the light, despite the agony it caused him each moment. After seeing nothing but glare for the first few seconds, he was eventually able to make out two figures. One had the slightly stooped look of a draconian. The other was human—so to speak. All Garrick could tell at first was that the human stood a good seven feet in height. Both the knight and his captors were in a large tent. Tables and chairs stood to one side. Numerous piles of armor and equipment lay scattered elsewhere. There seemed to be no one purpose for the tent. For now, it served as his prison.

The giant chuckled softly. "Very good. I see the Knights of Solamnia deserve something of their reputation after all. I was beginning to think it was all myth."

"Untie me." The words escaped the knight's lips as little more than a croak, but the giant caught them nonetheless.

"Oh, I couldn't risk that. You might overwhelm us and crawl to safety—given six or seven hours head start."

The draconian hissed its amusement. Garrick studied the two as they became clearer. The reptilian aide was much like its brethren, save that it was motley-colored compared to those the knight had seen earlier. There was, however, a vicious look in its eyes, one that said that this draconian would readily pull Garrick's fingers from his hands and his arms from his shoulders if given the chance. By all practical consideration, this was the general's torturer.

The general himself was most definitely a giant among his fellow men, and not just in height. He easily outweighed Garrick by almost one-third again his own weight, and none of it could be called fat. Strength alone, though, was not sufficient to coordinate a major army with great success. The knight did not doubt for one minute that the massive frame was matched by an equally impressive mind.

"I am General Krynos of Culthairai, a land I'm sure you've never heard of and which does not deserve any notice whatsoever. When I learned of the Queen's return and the armies being raised, I seized the chance to join and prove my skills. Up until now, though, I've lacked a sufficient challenge."

In truth, even the Knights of Solamnia had been awed by some of the accounts they had heard about Krynos. The armies he had crushed would have turned back a number of Dragon Highlords, much less their various generals. It was even said that the next opening in the ranks of the Highlords would see the addition of Krynos.

Only a garrison stood in his way. A tiny army. A tiny army and Garrick.

Krynos stroked his rich, black beard. He was a handsome, proud man. Proud and stubborn.

"What is your name, Knight of Solamnia?"

"Garrick."

"That's it? Just Garrick? Not Garrick the Great? The Champion? The Draconian Slayer?"

The wings of the torturer spread in anticipation. The draconian bore a huge reptilian smile that told of deadly delights to come when Garrick was its to play with. The knight pointedly ignored the creature.

"Just Garrick."

"Well then, 'Just Garrick,' how many of your comrades lie in wait in the forest? The scouts and patrols count at least three dozen fires. The Knights of Solamnia, whatever their faults, do not run away. Even against impossible odds."

"I am the only one. You can search all you like. You will find no others. I came on my own."

Krynos laughed, and the draconian hissed. The sharp claws of the latter slapped Garrick hard across the mouth. He could feel the blood flowing from his lip. The general put a hand out to halt another blow by the torturer.

"Not yet—and not the mouth. We want to be able to understand him when he talks. And you will talk, Knight. Ssaras is very good at this job, especially with humans. You would do well to give up on such a stupid tale and tell us where your comrades have hidden themselves. I can afford to wait them out for a few days. Nothing lies beyond them that can stop me. Only an already-battered land and a tiny, insignificant garrison. The nearest force of substantial strength is two weeks away and much too busy with problems of its own to bother worrying about me."

It did not surprise Garrick that the general was so well-informed about the region. That was perhaps one thing that had helped the knight. Used to the thoroughness of his information network, Krynos could not accept the solitary presence of Garrick. The fires might be real; they might be fakes. If one knight could wait in hiding, could not others? Everyone knew that the Knights of Solamnia were skilled in all aspects of warfare. Who knew what sort of tricks they might pull? Krynos could not afford a mistake at this time. Even a minor one would cause him a loss of face.

Garrick remained silent. Krynos frowned and then, nodded to Ssaras. The draconian waddled eagerly to a table upon which a number of devices, recognizable and unrecognizable, had been placed. The creature selected one and showed it eagerly to its master. The general eyed it with almost clinical interest before shaking his head. Disappointed, the draconian put down the instrument and waited for further orders. Krynos turned his attention back to his prisoner.

"Where are your companions, Garrick? How do they plan to meet us? In one massive charge on the field? Sounds foolish, but I know your Order. I wanted to become of your kind before I came to my senses and turned to the Queen."

Earlier, such a statement might have stung Garrick. Now, though, he was well beyond such petty things. It was difficult enough just to remain conscious, much less be bothered by meaningless slurs from the tongue of his foe.

The general snapped his fingers. Ssaras scurried over to a pile of odds and ends and picked something up. Garrick gradually identified it as his own shield. The general took it from the draconian and looked at it with some amusement.

"Perhaps I am overestimating the noble Knights of Solamnia. Perhaps they are indeed skulking around in the woods, hiding out of sight, fighting like elves or gully dwarves—with no honor—coming from behind their opponents." He dropped the shield and spat on the front. One heavy boot came down on the wet spot. With little effort, Krynos had put a great dent in the shield.

Garrick's growing madness threatened to burst then, but the warmth around his chest checked it. It occurred to him then that they had removed his armor but not his medallion. He could see no way that they could have possibly missed it in their search.

Ssaras looked hopefully at the general. Krynos was calculating his possibilities.

"Get Thaygan."

The torturer hissed. "Thaygan is a fraud. All clerics are frauds, General."

"Would you like to tell that to the Queen herself, Ssaras? She might beg to differ."

The draconian quieted immediately. Without further ado, it scurried away to seek the cleric. Garrick muttered a prayer to Paladine. Should Thaygan be a strong enough cleric, the knight would have little chance of defending his mind from the psychic onslaught. Unlike many of his brethren, he had a strong respect for the power of clerics.

A strong, gauntleted hand pulled his head up by the hair. Krynos moved close to him, so close that Garrick was able to feel the other's hot breath on his face. "Tell me what I want to know now, and I'll spare you the tender touch of Thaygan. In his own way, he leaves a prisoner much worse off than Ssaras does."

"There is only me."

The general's eyes flared. "Do you swear to that?"

Garrick avoided the binding trap by repeating his statement once more. As he hoped, his refusal to swear only convinced Krynos even more that there were other knights lurking around somewhere near or in the forest ahead.

The general let Garrick's head drop. He paced the width of the tent several times before the sudden presence of the dark cleric brought him to a startled halt. The cleric stared at the general and then at the prisoner, who was struggling feebly with the bonds. Nothing of the cleric was visible save his hands.

"You have need of my services, General Krynos?"

"Regretfully so. I need information from this man, and you know how stubborn Knights of Solamnia can be."

"A Solamnic Knight? Here?"

"Are your ears still stuffed with the chants and incantations of your order? A Knight of Solamnia, found in the woods—and where there's one, there's more. I want the truth from him. Beware, though. He is not in the best of condition. I fear my men must have mussed him up a little bit too hard."

The cleric drew back his hood. Garrick had the brief notion that he was being visited by Death itself. The cleric was emaciated beyond normal tolerances. To the prisoner, it seemed as if Thaygan's face should crack in pieces each time the old man spoke.

As the cleric stepped toward the knight, Krynos actually blanched slightly. Garrick dimly wondered what could frighten a man of the general's reputation. That thought vanished with all others as the cleric reached down and put a hand to each side of the prisoner's head.

The knight fell down an abyss. He screamed all the way. Somewhere, he could hear a commanding voice that demanded things of him. The words meant nothing to him, though, and he kept falling.

A mighty hand came from the darkness. It glowed with a light all its own. With little effort, it caught the plummeting Garrick and held him tight. The pressure of the monstrous grip was not stifling; rather, it reassured the knight. Overwhelmed by a wave of peace and love, Garrick slid off into velvety blackness.

He awoke briefly to see two men arguing. One was incredibly ancient and looked more like an old corpse. The other was a giant who looked capable of breaking the thin man in two without trying. They seemed to be arguing about something. Occasionally, one would point at Garrick. The knight waited patiently for someone to ask him a question. When none was forthcoming, he drifted slowly back to sleep.

The golden-armored man looked down at Garrick with fondness and respect. Garrick found himself unable to look the other straight in the eyes. He did not feel worthy of the audience granted to him.

The other smiled. "It is time, Garrick. Time you joined the ranks. Time you joined Huma and the others."

For the first time, the young knight saw the ranks behind Paladine. Among them stood one he knew well. From his place, Standel nodded gravely to him— and then broke out into a big smile.

Paladine bade him stand. "The time is now, Garrick."

"Time to wake, Knight!" A rough hand shook his head.

Garrick's vision was red, and he realized belatedly that blood was dripping from his forehead. His right foot felt numb, his arms burned with excruciating pain. He spat blood from his mouth.

A draconian stood next to the general. It was Ssaras and what expression was readable on the reptilian face showed that the creature was angry beyond words. The draconian's breathing was haggard, as if it had been laboring hard. Of the cleric, whom Garrick only vaguely remembered, there was no sign.

General Krynos scowled at him. "What are you made of, Knight? For three days, you've endured tortures that have turned other men into screaming maniacs! You've sat there all this time, mumbling to your god! Even Thaygan could get nothing from you!"

Garrick did not answer. There seemed no need for a reply, and his head hurt too much to think, anyway.

"You are useless to me, Knight. Whether or not your allies are out there—and I admit for the first time that you may have fooled me by giving me the truth—I will lead my army come the morrow. We will be through the pass and well on our way to the garrison by the time the day is ended. The Queen will see who among her followers is most valuable to her."

Ssaras swayed unsteadily. The general frowned. With some effort, the draconian stood straight. Its mottled color looked even more splotchy than before.

Krynos wiped the sweat from his forehead. "In all fairness, you've proved a worthy challenge. Any last request before I have Ssaras make an end of you?"

With superhuman effort, Garrick forced himself to sit straight. The glazed look was gone from his eyes. "I demand death in combat."

The general raised an eyebrow. "Combat? You can barely stand, much less fight. I will make Ssaras give you a swift, painless cut across the throat. Yes, that would be much better, much more efficient, I think."

Garrick virtually ground the words out with his teeth. "I demand death in combat—with you, unless you're afraid."

One mailed fist went for a weapon. The general was barely able to restrain himself. He slowly released his grip on the hilt of his sword.

"Very well. I shall grant your request for death."

The torturer looked at him in shock. "Master! Think what you say! This is a trick!"

"It is the request of a dead man, Ssaras! If he wishes to fight me, then so he shall. It will give me some little amusement before I begin final preparations for our departure. Untie him, Ssaras."

"Lord master Krynos, powerful warlord, I beg—"

"Untie him—unless, of course, you think that I am incapable of defeating one such as he."

Ssaras moved over to Garrick and pulled out a knife. For a brief moment, the draconian eyed the knight's unprotected throat. A frown appeared on the reptilian's face as it tried in vain to discern something.

"I'm waiting, Ssaras."

The draconian hurried about its work. The strangling bonds fell away. Slowly, carefully, Garrick rose from the chair he had been tied to for at least four days. His muscles were cramped, but he otherwise felt little pain.

He moved one foot and discovered part of the reason for such little pain. Much of his body was numb, probably permanently. Blood still trickled from a few wounds. Garrick purposely turned his mind to attaining a weapon of some sort.

"Ssaras, present him with an appropriate toy."

Scurrying to a junk pile of Garrick's own equipment, the draconian pulled out the chipped, dirty sword. In a mockery of the knights, the creature held it high and waved it three times, hissing the whole while. Krynos smirked and motioned the torturer to get on with things.

Ssaras dragged the sword over to Garrick and

dropped it by the knight's feet. Garrick bent down slowly and retrieved it, each movement sending shocks through his system. If not for the medallion still hidden under his tunic, he would have given in to his pain. Only the warmth and strength it provided kept him going.

With the shadow of a smile, General Krynos pulled out his own weapon. It was a tremendous broadsword which many men would have had to handle with both hands. The general swung it around easily with only one. He saluted Garrick. "Are you ready?"

In answer, the knight held his sword before him and tested its balance. It was like holding an old friend. Somewhere to the side, by the tent entrance, Ssaras hissed displeasure.

"Ready."

The look of amusement left the face of General Krynos the moment he saw the sword coming toward him. He was barely able to block the blow. Cursing silently, he backed away to regain his balance. Garrick followed through, giving his larger opponent little time to do anything but defend. The draconian jumped up and down, hissing all the time. Sharp claws continually stroked the hilt of the knife that the creature always kept tucked in its belt for when a prisoner broke loose. The draconian's greatest fear was not knowing whether its master would approve of such initiative or cut off his servant's head.

Krynos was bleeding from three minor wounds, but Garrick's attack was slowing. The general was able to breathe and think now. The tide was turning swiftly.

All his strength left Garrick's arm with a suddenness that surprised both fighters. The knight's sword went flying toward the tent entrance, where an alert Ssaras was barely able to leap aside before the blade buried itself in the spot where the draconian had just been standing. Garrick blinked and let his hand fall to his side. Krynos moved in to finish the fight and his opponent with one thrust.

Garrick fell to the ground, untouched by the general's blade.

Krynos stood there, staring at the body. The torturer rushed over and turned the knight face up. The reptilian face moved to within an inch of Garrick's. After a quick examination, the draconian looked up at his lord.

"He is dead. His wounds must have been more than he could stand."

"It's a wonder he lived through what he did." The general sheathed his weapon. "He was half-dead when the patrol brought him in. I wonder why."

"What shall I do with him, master?"

"Bury him. He deserves that much—fool that he was."

"As you command." The draconian left the tent.

General Krynos, late of Culthairai, studied the figure sprawled before him and sighed. He had been hoping for much more from the knight. The war had grown dull.

The four soldiers that buried Garrick, Knight of Solamnia, were half-asleep. Most of them were sweating profusely, despite the cool breeze blowing. One had to be excused to seek out a cleric after he nearly fell into the hole. The remaining three continued their work, trying to finish the job quickly and get back to more important things, like their card game. In their haste, not one of them happened to notice the medallion which slipped out of hiding when the corpse was tossed in. Even as they buried it with the body, the medallion seemed to glow brighter and brighter, despite the lack of any real light.

* * * * *

On the following morning, the army did not move. A great number of soldiers complained about heat and great thirst. Most of them had become bedridden. The number of ill grew quickly.

The clerics were of no help whatsoever. They had been the first to be stricken and, oddly, the worst cases. Most of them died within a day.

General Krynos attempted to organize the remainder of his troops. He had the healthy separated from their fallen comrades. Yet more and more men collapsed, a total of one-quarter of the army's strength in only one day.

Confusion reigned. Some soldiers attempted to sneak away. Many were caught and executed, and the rest were tracked down. Each time, they were found dead no more than a few hours from the main camp.

It was General Krynos who first understood what had happened. He had let the bait of the trap lure him into a battle with the one foe he could not defeat. Even as he himself fell victim to the plague, which by that time had claimed almost half his army, he could not understand how he and the others, especially the late cleric Thaygan, could have missed the signs.

Four days later, the plague, which Garrick had fought to a stalemate for more than a week, had wiped out all but a few scattered remnants of the once-powerful army. The tales told by the survivors would prevent any other army from coming through that way for the rest of the war. Even the clerics of the Queen refused to go near, for they could feel that the power of Paladine was involved somehow.

With time, the villagers would return, the garrison would be reinforced for an enemy that would never come. No one would remember the single knight who had kept his vow the only way he knew how.

The Exiles

Paul B. Thompson and Tonya R. Carter

---

*H*e dreamed of battle. The small bed shook with the shock of phantom cavalry and the tramp of spectral men-at-arms. In the midst of this dream melee a deep voice said, "Sturm, wake up. Get up, boy."

Sturm Brightblade opened his eyes. A tall, burly man, dark of eye and fiercely moustached, towered over him. The torch he carried cast smoky highlights on his steel breastplate and wolf-fur mantle.

"Father?" said the boy groggily.

"Get up, son," Lord Brightblade said. "It's time to go."

"Go? Where, Father?"

Lord Brightblade didn't answer. He turned quickly to the door. "Dress warmly," he said before going out. "Snow is flying. Hurry, boy." The door thumped shut behind him.

Sturm sat up and rubbed his eyes. The tapers in his room were lit, but the ashes in the grate were cold. He pulled on a heavy robe, wincing when his feet touched the bare stone floor. As he stood, unsure of what to do next, he heard a knock on the door.

"Enter," he said.

Mistress Carin, handmaid to his mother, the Lady Ilys, bustled in. Her usually cheery face was pale under a close flannel hood.

"Are you not yet dressed, Master?" she asked. "Your mother sent me to speed your packing. Do hurry!"

Sturm rubbed his nose in confusion. "Hurry, Mistress? Why? What's happening?"

"It's not for me to tell you, young lord." She hastened across the narrow room to a black wooden chest and began tossing clothing out of it. "This, and this. Not that. This, yes," she muttered. She glanced at the puzzled boy and said, "Well, get your bag!"

Sturm pulled a long leather bag from under the bed. He was big for his eleven years, but the bag was nearly as long as he was tall. As clothing rained on his bed, Sturm gathered each item and folded it neatly into the bag.

"No time for that," Carin declared. "Just fill the bag, Sturm."

He threw a single woolen stocking aside. "Where are we going, Mistress?" he demanded. "And why are we going?"

Carin looked away. "The peasants," she said.

"The people of Avrinet? I don't understand. Father said they were suffering from the hard winter, but—"

"There's no time for talk, young lord. We must hurry." Carin shook her head and dug into the half-empty chest again. "It's a terrible thing when people forget their place. . . ."

Sturm was still methodically folding every article of clothing when the maid took it away from him and stuffed in the last few remaining items.

"There," she said. "All done." She dragged the bag to the door. "Someone will come for that. In the meantime, finish dressing. Wear your heaviest cloak—the one with the fur hood."

"Mistress Carin?" Sturm's lost tone halted the woman. "Are you coming with us?"

She drew her short, round body up proudly. "Where my lady goes, so go I." And then she was gone.

The main hall of Castle Brightblade was in a hushed tumult. Only a few candles burned in the wall sconces, but by their troubled light Sturm saw that the entire household was astir. In recent days, many of the servants had fled, taking tools and petty valuables with them. Sturm had only the vaguest notion of how things were beyond the castle walls.

Armed men stood at every door, pikes at the ready. Sturm fell into a stream of rushing servants and was carried with them to the door of the guardroom. His father was there, with another large man who lifted his head when the boy entered. Sturm recognized his father's good friend and fellow knight, Lord Gunthar Uth Wistan.

"I'm packed, Father," Sturm said.

"Eh? Good, good. Go to your mother, boy. You'll find her in the north corridor." He looked back to the map spread on the table before him. Sturm bowed his head and withdrew, his heart heavy. He leaned against the outside of the guardroom door.

"He's only a boy, Angriff," he heard Lord Gunthar say. "Not yet a man, much less a knight."

Lord Brightblade replied, "Sturm is the son and grandson of Solamnic Knights. Our blood goes back to Berthal the Swordsman. He must learn to cope with hardship."

Sturm lifted his chin and strode away. Following the line of burning torches along the corridor, he ran a finger in a joint of mortared stones, as he had every day since becoming tall enough to do so. This might be the last time Sturm would trace the crack. He slowed his pace to make the feeling linger.

Overhead, a loophole shutter banged loose in the wind. Sturm mounted the narrow steps to the loophole and reached out into the cold to catch the wayward shutter. Through the silently falling snow he saw a red glow on the horizon. It was too early for dawn.

"Close that shutter!"

Sturm whirled. Soren Vardis, sergeant of the household guard, was striding toward him. He took the steps two at a time. Soren reached easily over Sturm's head and closed the shutter, letting the bolt fall in its slot with a loud clank.

He smiled at the boy. "There are bowmen in the woods," he said. "A face in a lighted window makes an excellent target."

"Sergeant, what will the villagers do?"

A crack in the shutter let in the red glow. It striped Soren's face with a streak of blood. He looked at Sturm, standing so straight and proper. "I suppose you have a right to know," he said. "The peasants are in arms. They've set fire to the north wood and burned the fallow pastures east and south. Your father's cattle have been stolen and slaughtered. Some of my men were killed in Avrinet, but not before reporting that the villagers were preparing to attack."

"They can't get in the castle," Sturm said in a pleading tone.

"Alas, young lord, they can. I have less than a hundred men to defend all of the wall, and of those I trust not twenty."

Sturm could not fathom these revelations. "Why are they doing this, Soren? Why? My father never used them harshly."

"The common folk, here as throughout Krynn, blame the knights for not calling down the aid of Paladine in the dark times." Soren shook his head in sorrow. "In their mad anger they have forgotten all that the knights have done for them."

They descended the steps. "So Father will fight our way out?" asked Sturm.

Soren cleared his throat. "My Lord Brightblade will remain behind to defend his home and lands."

"Then I shall stay, too!"

The sergeant paused and rested a battle-hardened hand on the boy's shoulder. "No, young lord. Your father has given orders that you and the Lady Ilys be sent to far Solace for safety. Our duty is to obey." He knelt in front of Sturm and scrubbed away the tears with his rough thumbs. "None of that now, lad. Your mother will need all your strength to make this journey. It will fall to you to be the Brightblade man of the party, you know."

Wind sighed through the north corridor. The double doors to the courtyard were open. A two-wheel cart waited in the calf-deep snow. Lady Ilys, splendid in a cape of white rabbit, was bidding farewell to her husband.

"May the gods go with you," Lord Brightblade said, clasping her hands between his own. "You will always be my lady."

Their cheeks touched. "And you, my lord," said Lady Ilys.

The sniffling from the front of the cart was Mistress Carin. Sturm and Soren halted before Lord Brightblade. The sergeant saluted. The master of Brightblade Castle clapped the guardsman on his ironclad shoulders.

"My best man-at-arms," he said. "Keep them safe, Soren Vardis."

"Aye, my lord."

He faced his son. "Sturm, heed what your mother and the sergeant tell you."

"Yes, sir." How he ached for just one embrace! But that was not his father's way, not even at a time of parting.

Soren lifted him into the back of the cart, then mounted his own horse. Mistress Carin snapped the reins, and the cart jerked forward. Sturm buried his face in his sleeve. He couldn't bear to leave. In spite of Soren's admonition, the bitter tears returned.

At the west gate, torches were doused before the portal opened. The guardsman and the cart moved into the night. The castle was quickly lost from sight in the swirling snow.

The road west was high-centered and paved with stone, a relic of the great days before the Cataclysm.

Sturm and his mother were nestled among the soft heaps of baggage. Though warmed and rocked by the easy motion of the cart, neither could find sleep. The boy could hear the sharp clat-clat of the war-shod hooves of Nuitari, Soren's black gelding. The sergeant kept to a measured pace as he watched the road ahead for trouble. As soon as was practical, they would leave the well-marked, well-paved track for a less conspicuous route. If the peasants had a mind to pursue them, they would be harder to find that way.

Soren reined up short. He snagged the carthorse's bridle and pulled the beast off the road. No sooner was the party screened by a stand of cedars than Sturm heard a low rumble of voices. His heart beat quickly as he peeked through the slatted side of the cart.

A band of rough-looking men came slogging through the snow. Some wore fresh, hairy hides over their backs, hides with the Brightblade brand.

"I'm cold!" one declared loudly.

"Shut your gob, Bron. We'll all be warm enough when we put the torch to the knights' hall!" Ugly laughter greeted the boast. Sturm heard his mother praying quietly to Paladine.

Soren led them back onto the road. They reached the fork the sergeant wanted. Mistress Carin hauled back the reins, and the cart slipped off the stones into a narrow, muddy rut. The naked, black arms of leafless trees closed over their heads. At last Sturm dropped into a light and troubled sleep.

He awoke to the sound of weeping. "Mother?" he said.

She put a hand over his mouth. "Quiet, child." He saw the tracks of tears on her face. He sat up and saw what was making her cry.

Below, across a snow-gilt field, three houses burned. Against the curtain of flame dark figures moved. Cows and calves bawled in pain as cudgels beat them to the ground. Angry, starving men tore them to pieces with billhooks and hand scythes.

"They would do the same to us," said Lady Ilys.

Sturm looked to the sergeant in helpless anger. Soren was afoot, his back to Nuitari, sword drawn. The fire displayed his blue eyes burning under the brim of his helmet. There was nothing he could do against twenty. And there were the women and boy to protect.

They slipped away as if they were the brigands. The snow continued until dawn, when the sun split the dense gray clouds. Their hearts did not lighten with the sky. They ate cold bread and cheese, and sipped tepid melted snow from the sergeant's pigskin waterbag.

Sturm spelled Mistress Carin on the reins. He simply kept them clear of the traces, as the old carthorse was content to follow the rutted path without guidance. Carin fussed over Lady Ilys, trying to screen her from the new sun and cold wind. Sturm knew the woman was exhausted. He wondered why his mother let her carry on with needless niceties of castle protocol.

Sturm stayed at the reins until midday, when Soren halted again for food and a consultation.

"As I recall," he said, chewing on a strip of dried beef, "the way forks again not far ahead. If we go straight, we'll end up in the mountains along the coast. Should we bear south, we'll reach the coast in a day's steady ride."

"Where on the coast?" asked Lady Ilys.

"Near the port of Thel, where ships on the Inland Sea often call."

"Ships, yes . . . a sea voyage would be more comfortable than rolling in this cart," she said. "Could we find passage to Abanasinia in Thel?"

"Easily, my lady. 'Tis a thickly traveled route."

"Then we shall proceed to Thel, then take ship."

The carthorse wheezed and shivered. "I pray the beast holds out till then," said Soren.

The beast did not. By the time they reached the fork, the poor carthorse collapsed in harness, never to rise again.

"Oh, lady, what shall we do?" Carin wailed.

"Nuitari will have to serve," said Lady Ilys. Soren could only obey in silence. He loosed the tracings from the dead animal and dragged the carcass aside. Then he backed the black, straight-limbed Nuitari between the poles of the over-burdened cart. Soren patted the horse's nose consolingly.

"There's no shame in it," he said in a low voice, though Sturm was near and heard him. "We all must serve beneath our worth sometime, my friend."

Day passed and night came. The two bright moons rose, shone their faces on Krynn, and set again. Mistress Carin drove all night, and Sturm noticed that his mother parted with one of her fine scarves so that her maid might have some protection from the facing wind.

The air warmed with day, and the ice on the track changed to mud. It gripped the cart wheels and the sergeant's boots with fervor, but neither Soren nor the brave Nuitari complained. They climbed a long, grassy hill to an ancient ring of standing stones. Strange images were graven on the triliths. Sturm knew dark forces were abroad in the land. He held close to his mother when they stopped amid the ruined circle.

Soren advanced to the crest of the hill. He pointed down to a vista Sturm could not see. "It is Thel," he said.

Thel was a modest town of five-hundred souls, but to Sturm's eye, it was a complete city. Some of the half-timbered houses had three stories—not so tall as the towers of Castle Brightblade, but so full of people! Sturm was fascinated.

Soren walked the cart along the high street. The toll of four days and nights on the road was obvious. Even Lady Ilys was bedraggled, her fair face chapped by raw wind and her soul weighed down with bitterness and hurt.

The Thelites paid them no large attention as they passed. Strangers and refugees were common in the town. Lady Ilys, for her part, ignored them in turn.

"Rabble. Riff-raff," she said through pursed lips. "Remember, Sturm, you are the son of a knight. Do not speak to these people unless they address you properly, with the deference due us."

Soren found an inn off the waterfront. He went in to dicker with the owner, leaving the women and boy in the cart. Sturm climbed atop the baggage and watched the passing crowds with total absorption.

One fellow in particular caught Sturm's eye: he was short and slender, a green mantle draped over his shoulders. His ears drew back in sharp points, and his eyes slanted down at the corners. He walked with smooth, unconscious grace.

"There's elf blood in him," Mistress Carin said knowingly.

Across the street, a hulking figure loafed in an open doorway. A shaggy mane of hair did little to conceal his ugliness, and his lips could not hide the jagged teeth protruding from his outthrust jaw.

"Half-orc," said Carin.

Soren returned. "My lady," he said. "The innkeeper has a small private room for you and Master Sturm. Mistress Carin may have a place by the kitchen hearth, and I a bench in the beerhall. All this for four silver pieces."

"Four! That's outrageous!"

"I chaffered him down from seven."

"Very well," she said. "If it is the best we can do." She sniffed the moist, salty air. "I suppose there are *elves* and things in there?"

"No, lady. In the cold season, such folk generally go to warmer climes."

"Let us be thankful for that, at least." Lady Ilys took four coins from her purse. Soren helped her down from the cart and escorted her and Sturm into the inn.

The innkeeper was a fat, bald man who grinned through rotten teeth. He bobbed his head and waved Lady Ilys to the stairs. Before Sturm reached the steps, the innkeeper let out a howl.

"Put that back, you two-legged rat! Don't tell me you found it; I know you stole it!" he cried. A diminutive manlike creature, a head shorter than Sturm, silverware poking out of his pockets, stood by a beer keg. When the innkeeper yelled again, the little man put his fingers in his ears and stuck out his tongue. Spoons, coins, and buttons cascaded from his clothes onto the floor.

"I'll swat you good, you roach!" the innkeeper bawled. He reached for a stout broom. The tiny fellow—a kender, according to Carin—stooped to retrieve his booty. The broom's first swipe was a miss, but the innkeeper caught the kender by the seat of his pants and swept him out the door.

"My 'pologies, ma'am," the fat man said. "I never allow them kender in here, but they slip in sometimes when I'm not watchful."

Lady Ilys gave the man a glacial look and dropped only three silver coins in his palm. The man was too flustered to protest. He bowed and backed away. Soren hoisted two bags on his shoulders and went up the steps, chuckling.

The room was small, and the beds were stacked one above the other. Sturm was delighted and climbed nimbly up the ladder to the top bunk.

"We will need more money for the voyage," Soren said. "May I have my lady's approval to sell the cart for what it will bring?"

"Nuitari too?" asked Sturm, aghast. Soren nodded curtly.

"See to it, Sergeant. We shall not stir till your return," said Lady Ilys.

It was long dark before Soren came back. He thumped on the door. Mistress Carin admitted him. Soren bore a wide trencher of food. He'd intercepted the innkeeper's wife on the stair and taken the heavy platter off her hands. Soren set the trencher down on the lone table and announced, "We have a ship."

Sturm stabbed a slab of boiled mutton with his knife. A stern look from his mother froze him at once.

"What ship? And where bound?" asked Lady Ilys.

"The good ship *Skelter* is bound directly for Abanasinia and the Hartshorn River," said Soren. "From there we can go upriver to Solace itself."

"Who is master of this *Skelter*?"

"One Graff, a mariner of many years' experience on these seas."

"Very good, Sergeant. And when do we sail?"

"With the morning tide, my lady."

With the morning tide. Sturm repeated those words over and over in his head. Since leaving the castle, he had imagined their quick deliverance. He would hear a sharp tattoo of hoofbeats behind, and Lord Brightblade would gallop over the hill at the head of a troop of horsemen. "Come back! All is well!" he would shout. How would his father ride to them across the sea? The answer was clear, and Sturm did not like it.

The good ship *Skelter* lay fast against a long wooden pier. Short and round, she was freshly caulked and painted. Sturm wondered what exotic cargoes had been carried under the green planking of her hull.

Dark-skinned sailors clung to the rigging, doing mysterious things with lengths of rope and bundles of sailcloth. Sturm never took his eyes off them as he trailed after his mother and Soren down the pier. The captain of the *Skelter* greeted them at the foot of the gangplank. He clasped his own hands across his belly and bowed shortly to Lady Ilys.

"Captain Graff, at yer service, ma'am," he said. His beard was plaited in intricate braids, and a dull gold bead hung from one earlobe. "We'll be weighing anchor ere the sun strikes the housetops of Thel. Will ye board now?"

She made only the slightest nod of assent. Mistress Carin went ahead, and two husky sailors fell upon their baggage. Soren stood aside, one hand on the pommel of his sword. Sturm stayed by him, taking in the busy spectacle of a ship being readied for sea.

"Will it be a long voyage, Sergeant?" asked the boy.

"Depends on the sea and the wind, young lord. And the skill of the mariners."

"Couldn't we wait a while longer? For news from Father?" asked Sturm.

Soren did not reply. He stared at the housetops of the town, waiting for the pink sky beyond them to blaze yellow, then blue. Vapor steamed from his nostrils in the chill air.

"Sergeant, I shall board now," Lady Ilys said. Soren offered his arm. "Come along, Sturm," she said. The boy responded with a sigh. He dragged his feet up the worn plank, looking back often to the barren hills east of town.

Lines fell from the ship to the water. Gangs of sailors manned two broad sweeps and rowed *Skelter* out of Thel harbor. Open pilot boats guided them past the bar into the Inland Sea. Sturm watched them turn back as *Skelter*'s single sail was raised.

Captain Graff rigged a screen of hides below the sterncastle for Lady Ilys and Carin. Barrels and crates of trade goods were pushed aside to create a space for the women under the castle platform. A smoky oil lamp was lit, and Mistress Carin set to making pallets for her lady and Sturm.

The ship rolled with a steady motion to which Sturm quickly adapted. He wanted to go on deck and watch the sailors at their work, but Lady Ilys forbade him. The strain of recent days was bearing on her hard, and she wanted most of all to rest.

"Stay by me, Sturm," she said. "I need a strong man at my side while I rest. I won't feel safe otherwise."

She took off her fur cape and lay down, pulling the

soft wrap around her as a blanket. Sturm lay down, his back to hers, vigilant as a knight and wary as a Brightblade—for all of ten minutes. Then he, too, lapsed into heavy slumber.

He sensed a change. The ship's motion had lessened. The air in the hide enclosure was close and hot. Sturm rolled to his feet, tightened the drawstring of his pants, and went out on deck.

A cold, thick, white fog had settled on the warmer sea. The *Skelter* glided under a feeble following wind. They were far out in the midst of the Inland Sea. No land was visible; indeed, nothing could be seen ten paces beyond the ship's rail.

Sturm prowled the waist of the ship, scampering out of the way of the sailors as they tightened the mainsail tackle. The big square of canvas hung limply in the misty air, flopping only rarely when a stray gust struck it.

Soren was on the poop. The steersman leaned on one leg behind the sergeant, shifting the thick black staff of the rudder with practiced ease. Timbers and rigging creaked as *Skelter* eased across the flat, languid water.

The weather was no fairer the second day at sea. Captain Graff and his first mate—a squat, dwarvish fellow with yellow eyes—put their heads together by the mast. Naturally, Sturm was on hand to listen.

"Do ye think it's for the wind cord?" asked the mate. Sturm was fascinated by the brass tooth in the front of the man's mouth.

"Nay, 'tis not the time. This cursed mist may rise soon, and the natural wind will spring up," said Graff.

Sturm asked Soren what the mate meant by 'wind cord.'

"Magic," he said. "Mariners often buy wind from

seaside warlocks. They keep the wind bound in knots of magical cord. When the ship's master needs a breeze, he unknots as much of a blow as he dares."

"Is there much magic on the sea?" Sturm asked, wide-eyed.

Soren wiped mist from his helmet brim before it could drip off. "Far too much to suit me, young lord. This fog seems too clinging to be nature's work."

Midday was no brighter than dawn. The sea flattened out like the puddled wax around Sturm's study candle in Castle Brightblade. The lapping waves fell silent, and the sail stayed slack against the mast. Captain Graff emerged from below deck with a length of rawhide two spans long. Sturm peered through the sterncastle rail as the captain crossed the waist and mounted the steps to the poop.

"Sargo," he said to the helmsman. "I'm loosing a knot."

"Aye, aye, sir."

Graff put one end of the cord in his teeth. There were a dozen knots along its length. The idea of a magic cord intrigued and repelled Sturm at the same time. Such power was forbidden to the knightly orders.

Graff picked at the first knot with his blunt fingernails. In the stagnant air, each of his mutters was clear.

"Come loose, you son of a snake," he said.

Soren moved suddenly off the rail to the sternpost. He gazed into the fog. "Captain Graff," he said calmly. The master of the *Skelter* cursed some more at the tough loop in the cord. "Captain!" Soren barked, using the parade-ground voice that Sturm had heard so often from the training yard. The old seaman looked up.

"Don't bother me, lad; I'm engaged," he said.

"There's a ship out there," Soren said. "It's coming

toward us."

"What? Eh? Do ye have the second sight?"

"No, just two good ears. Listen!"

Graff put a hand to his ear. Sturm came up on Soren's left and listened, too.

There . . . a faint knocking sound . . . like two blocks of wood slapping together.

"By the gods, yer right!" Graff said. "Those are oars beating, or I'm a thieving kender!"

Idle sailors collected in the stern to hear the approaching ship. Soren backed out of the press, drawing Sturm with him.

"You must go and tell your mother what is happening," he said.

"What *is* happening, Soren?"

"A galley, a ship rowed by many men, is close upon us. I fear they mean us mischief."

"Pirates?" asked the boy, half-fearful, half-delighted.

"Mayhap, or rogues of a darker stripe. Run to your mother and tell her this."

Sturm slipped down a stayrope, as he'd often seen the sailors do, and dropped to the deck outside his mother's enclosure. He pulled back the flap. It was dim and smoky inside, but he spied Mistress Carin tending a small fire in a copper pan.

"Mother! Mother!" he called.

"What is it?" Lady Ilys said from the shadows.

"Sergeant Soren says a rowing ship is coming for us. It may be pirates!"

Mistress Carin gasped. Lady Ilys's face appeared out of the darkness. She was very pale, and her expression was grim.

"Why would pirates bother so small a ship as this?" she asked.

"It's so foggy, my lady, Paladine wouldn't know us

for who we are," Carin said.

"Sturm, fetch the sergeant to me. I want a soldier's view of the matter." The boy bowed hastily to his mother and ran out to find Soren.

The thump and swish of oars was clearer now, even to Sturm's young ears. The fog swallowed the sound, dispersing it, making it hard to tell from what quarter the galley approached. Definitely astern; that was certain.

"Sergeant! Sergeant!" Sturm shouted. He found the guardsman on the poop deck, whetting the blade of his broadsword. The *Skelter*'s crew of lean, raffish seamen nervously shifted hatchets and cutlasses from hand to hand. Only Captain Graff and Sargo, the aged helmsman, were calm.

"Sergeant, my mother wishes to speak to you," Sturm said.

"I honor your noble mother, but I regret I cannot leave the deck just now," Soren said. "The enemy, if enemy they be, is near."

"Where? Where?"

"Treading on our heels."

Sturm strained to see. The oars pounded ceaselessly. . . .

"Ship on the port stern!" sang out a man in the rigging. Out of the white murk came a massive object wrought in bronze. To Sturm it looked like the head of a mace.

"The galley's ram," Soren told him.

"Hard a-starboard!" cried the captain. Sargo put the tiller over, but the becalmed *Skelter* scarcely noticed. Graff ordered the helm kept over. He held the wind cord aloft and undid the knot he'd worked so hard to loosen. "Elementals of the air, I release you!" he exclaimed.

The sail snapped out with a crack, and the deck

dropped from under Sturm's feet. *Skelter* heeled sharply to starboard just as the phantom galley charged through the dead water where the roundship once plodded.

Wind freed from the cord sang in the rigging. "How long will it last?" Soren asked the captain. Graff rubbed his ears and shrugged, a confession of total ignorance.

Skelter bounded over the waveless sea, tearing the fog apart like rotted cheesecloth. The galley trailed them, trying to draw nearer. Sturm held on the port rail, the wind in his eyes, as the galley swept clear of the mist. The bronze ram gave way to a black timber hull that cut the water in spurts with each dip of the oars. The galley's upperworks were daubed blood red. Movement on the deck suggested men behind the red planking, and a hedgehog of spears bristled in the air. Below them, blending back into the fog, were the oars, black with water, rising and falling in time with a muffled drum.

"Keep back from the rail, lad," the captain told Sturm. "They may have archers."

The boy forgot his mother's request and stood with Sergeant Soren on the port quarterdeck. The magic wind pushed the roundship without falter for one notch of the candle. At one notch and a half, the galley ran its oars in.

The *Skelter's* crew cheered. Sturm said, "Have we bested them, Captain?"

"Not yet, lad, not yet."

Sturm saw dark triangles billow from the galley's masts. Their pursuers were taking to sail, using *Skelter's* own wind to keep up with them.

The sun burned a hole in the clouds. Details of the black galley stood out at once. A pennant whipped from the foremast. Sargo squinted his good eye at it.

"That be no pirate," he said. "That be a ship of Kernaf."

"Who is Kernaf?" asked Sturm.

" 'What' be more like it—the isle of Kernaf. That's a ship of their navy," Graff said.

As Sturm watched, the magic wind diminished, and the *Skelter* slowed. The galley wallowed in the press of sail and drew along their port side.

"Hail, ship of Kernaf!" Graff shouted through his hands. "What would ye want with us?"

"Heave to! We mean to board!" was the reply. Sturm could see men massing on the forecastle.

"We're a free trader out of Solamnia. What business have ye with us?" bawled Graff.

"You are sailing in waters claimed by our great Sea Lord," the Kernaf spokesman said. "Heave to, or we'll take you by force."

Oars sprouted from the galley's sides like legs on a centipede. "Go, young lord. Go to your mother," said Soren. He plucked a dagger two spans long from his belt. "You must defend her when all else is lost."

Sturm accepted the iron blade. It was heavy and keen, and in the guardsman's hand it could easily pierce a single thickness of mail. Sturm darted across the deck to the hide enclosure. Mistress Carin and Lady Ilys stood together by the starboard bulwark, amid the wine casks and clay pots of oil.

"Mother, I am here to defend you!" he said, brandishing the dagger.

"Come here," she said. She gathered Sturm in her arms and hugged him tightly. "My brave boy," she said. "Carin and I heard all."

Shouts from the deck: "The ram! The ram!" *Skelter* leaped sideways in the sea, rolling far to starboard. Lady Ilys and Carin fell back on the pots and casks. Sturm's head banged onto the deck, and the dagger flew from his hand.

Above came the sounds of fighting—heavy thuds, the ring of metal on metal, the screams of the wounded and dying. Men fell overboard with loud splashes.

A shaft of sunlight slashed into the enclosure. Kernaffi marines had cut down the hides. Sturm groped dazedly for the lost dagger. The boarders charged in. Mistress Carin bravely faced them, but the nearest man grabbed her by the hair and dragged her out on deck. Lady Ilys called for her son. By then Sturm was crawling about, searching for Soren's weapon. The Kernaffi approached Lady Ilys, but she walked out on her own and stood regally in a circle of poised javelins.

Sturm saw his mother confront the rough, kilt-wearing Kernaffi. His throat tightened when the ring of spearpoints closed in. He cast around desperately for the dagger. Back among the crates of cloth the braided handle gleamed. Sturm reached for it. . . .

A rough hand grasped the hood of his cloak and hauled him to his feet. *"Koy esk ta?"* said the Kernaffi, laughing in the boy's frightened face.

By the time Sturm was drag-marched to deck, the battle was over. The Thelite sailors were bunched together by the mast, on their knees and begging for mercy. Sheer numbers of javelin-armed Kernaffi had forced Soren back to the starboard rail. They pinned him there, spearpoints at his throat. Soren's broken sword lay at his feet, as did a good number of wounded Kernaffi.

Carin was weeping. Lady Ilys comforted her. There was a scuffle on the poop deck. Two marines in conical leather hats shoved old Captain Graff down to the main deck.

"Who commands here? I demand to see yer captain!" Graff said, rising to his feet.

"Polo kamay!" said the Kernaffi holding Sturm. All eyes followed his glance.

Down a narrow boarding bridge came two extraordinary figures. The first, in a gilded breastplate and plumed helmet, was obviously the commander of the galley. Behind him, and taller by half a head, came a woman in mail and black leather armor. A corona of copper-colored hair shone around her conical cap.

"Which one is the ship's master?" said the woman, stepping down onto the *Skelter.*

"I am Graff."

"Captain, this ship is ours. Yield your cargo manifest."

"Demons take you!" he said, spitting at her feet. The woman backhanded him with one mailed fist. Graff's head snapped back, and blood ran from his split lip.

"I am Artavash, lieutenant to our great Sea Lord," said the woman in a loud, ringing voice. "You people are now his prisoners."

The plumed commander went to Lady Ilys and Carin. "What's this? Passengers?" he said. "Lady Artavash, look here!"

The tall warrior woman looked down at Lady Ilys. She ran a finger over the nap of the fine velvet dress Sturm's mother wore. "Wealthy, highborn, or both?" she said. When Lady Ilys failed to answer, Artavash drew a knife and put the point to Carin's stomach.

"It would cost me not a moment's rest to gut this lady like a chicken," she said. "Who are you?"

"Lady Ilys, wife to Lord Brightblade of Solamnia."

"And why is a great knight's lady traveling the open sea without her noble husband?"

Lady Ilys's lips set firmly until Artavesh pushed the knife tip through the first layer of Carin's dress. The maid inhaled sharply.

"We are traveling—for our health," Lady Ilys said.

Artavash laughed and translated the remark for the Kernaffi. They joined her in mocking laughter.

"*Mujat!* Enough!" She turned to the galley's commander and said, "Well, Sir Radiz, how shall we treat this poor company?"

"They have nothing we want, lady. Why not let them sail on?" the beplumed Kernaffi said.

Just then, Sturm managed to slip his arms out of his cloak. He dropped on his heels and left the marine holding an empty bundle of cloth. Sturm ran to the women. He pushed the knife away from Carin and interposed himself between Artavash and his mother.

Artavash turned her strangely burning eyes on him. "Well!" said the red-haired warrior. "Here's a young hero. Another Brightblade, I'll wager."

"Sturm, Angriff's son," the boy said.

Artavash smiled. "How old are you, boy?"

Sturm was put off balance by this ordinary question. That, and the smile of one who was in fact quite beautiful.

"E-eleven years," he said.

She unlaced the mitt from her right hand and ran tapered fingers through his long brown hair. "Ah, yes. Our master will be pleased to meet you."

"Lady, I do not think—" began Radiz.

"That I know," Artavash snapped. "Take the boy and the women to the *Sea Raven.*"

Radiz glared at Artavash, but held his temper in check. A quartet of Kernaffi shepherded the women and Sturm toward the boarding bridge. Soren started to struggle against his captors despite the naked blade at his throat. A sharp exclamation from one of the soldiers brought Artavash and Radiz up short.

"What about him?" asked Radiz.

"Kill him," said Artavash with a shrug.

"No!" cried Sturm. He ducked under a hedge of javelins and dashed to the sergeant. "Please do not harm him!"

"And why not?" demanded Artavash. "He is a man-at-arms, and dangerous. I cannot take him aboard the *Sea Raven* as a guest."

"He is my f-friend," Sturm pleaded.

Artavash went to where the five Kernaffi held the far bigger Soren immobilized. The sergeant was the only man present tall enough to look her in the eye.

"Give me your oath," she said, "that you will be peaceful, and I will let you live."

Sturm looked up at him and his eyes said, "Please, Soren!"

"Don't do it, man!" Captain Graff shouted. "Don't trust that bloody sea witch!"

Artavash whirled and flung her knife at the old captain. It buried to the hilt in his chest. The soldier holding him let Graff sag to the deck. Sturm stared in shock at the growing stain of red soaking through the captain's coat.

Artavash stood over the dying man. "Do you think I am to be trifled with, old fool? Mine is the power of life and death here." She flung her unmailed hand at Soren. "Will you give your oath?"

"I cannot," said Soren. "While I live, I cannot willingly allow my lady or my lord to enter anyone's captivity."

Artavash smiled again. The effect on Sturm was near magic, for, in spite of her violent acts, he was charmed.

"Good, good," she said. "That's what I wanted to hear. Sir Radiz! Strip this man of his arms and armor. Set him to an oar on the *Sea Raven*, and mind you, double-chain him. It would not do to have him loose among the other slaves."

The Kernaffi hauled the belligerent sergeant to the bridge. Lady Ilys and Carin waited until the men surged by. Artavash went to Graff and rolled his limp form over with the toe of her boot. She freed her blade and wiped it clean on the captain's sleeve.

Lady Ilys and her maid started for the bridge. Sturm moved in behind his mother. Just as he was about to step up, a hand grabbed his ankle. He almost cried out in surprise, for it was the captain who held him.

"Boy," Graff whispered.

Sturm knelt. He swallowed hard and said, "Yes, sir?"

"Take . . ." Graff's leathery fingers were twined in the wind cord. "Take . . ." he gasped again. "Ver' strong . . ." Dry rasping filled the old man's throat, and the captain breathed his last.

Sturm stared at the dead man until a voice broke his trance.

"What have you got there?" said Radiz. Sturm showed him, his heart pounding for fear he might be punished. Radiz looked uncomprehendingly at the strip of rawhide. He rolled it between his fingers and gave it back to Sturm. "Come along," he said.

From the forecastle of the *Sea Raven*, *Skelter* seemed small and forlorn. The impact of the ram had been a glancing one, and the hull was crushed rather than torn open. The surviving Thelite sailors lined the rail as the galley backed away.

"What will happen to them?" asked Sturm.

"With luck, they can bring her in," said Radiz. "If they sink, it will be the sea god's fault, not ours."

Even at his young age, Sturm found that hard to believe.

The stern of the *Sea Raven* was covered by a luxurious pavilion. Walls of rosewood and cedar rose from the oak deck. Overhead was a cloth of gold canopy, and tinkling brass chimes hung from ivory ridge posts inside.

Artavash swept in and bade Lady Ilys and Sturm to sit. She unbuckled her armor and tossed the segments in an ebony chest whose hasp and hinges were of silver. A steward appeared, dressed in red velvet vest and billowing silk pantaloons.

"Wine, Dubai," Artavash said. She scratched her sides where the armor chafed, just like Sturm's father always had, and settled onto a heap of plush pillows.

Sturm strained his neck taking in the opulence of the pavilion. When Dubai returned with a silver ewer and three goblets, he had to ask, "Is this your ship, Lady?"

"Mine? No. It belongs to the Lord of the Sea. I'm not even its captain; Sir Radiz sees to our progress over the water."

The steward poured three measures of dark red wine. Artavash sipped, nodded, and allowed Dubai to offer the other two goblets to Lady Ilys and Sturm. Sturm's mother refused for the both of them.

"You offend my hospitality," Artavash said darkly.

"I would prefer to be recognized as a prisoner, rather than a guest," Lady Ilys said. Artavash sent the wine to Mistress Carin. She too declined to drink.

"Pah! Why are you northerners so haughty? Could your noble Order of knights prevent the Cataclysm? Has your devotion to Paladine brought you glory? You mystify me. Wealth and power belong to the strong. If you cling to your outdated ideals, you will all vanish like the ancient deities you serve." Artavash took a long drink, then waved for Dubai to refill her cup.

"What is to become of us?" asked Lady Ilys.

"That is for the Lord of the Sea to decide."

———

"We cannot be ransomed. Lord Brightblade will not pay one copper to you."

"Your knight's money means nothing to my master. Gold runs from his fingertips, and his tears are purest silver."

"If not for vulgar money, why did you take us?" Lady Ilys demanded.

Artavash leaned back, reaching out to idly stroke Sturm's hair. "My master will have a use for you, never fear."

Another measure of wine disappeared down Artavash's throat. Dubai filled her goblet automatically.

"If you do not drink with me, I shall finish the wine alone," she said.

"Drunkenness is a common fault of barbarians," said Lady Ilys.

Artavash glared and flung the silver cup at Sturm's mother. Lady Ilys closed her eyes but did not cower. The goblet hit the rosewood panel behind them, and wine splattered over them like scarlet rain. A single drop ran to the corner of Sturm's mouth. It tasted sweet and hot.

"I will not be insulted on my own ship!" Artavash declared. "Guard! Guard!" Two armed Kernaffi entered the front flap. "Escort this *lady* and her servant to a cabin below. Put a watch on the door." She stood, to get the benefit of her commanding height. "Now, begone!"

Lady Ilys rose and put out a hand to her son. Sturm rose also, defiant.

"He will remain," said Artavash. Sturm could feel the tension between the two strong-willed women. This time his mother did not press her point, and instead, drew him close and kissed his forehead.

"Be wise," she said in a confidential voice. "And

remember who and what you are."

Artavash sent the steward out so she and Sturm would be alone. "You are a brave boy," she said. "You might have been killed on the roundship, yet you defended your mother and friends courageously."

"Tomorrow is too late to be brave, my father says," Sturm replied.

"Hmm, just so. Your father is a wise man. Is he a great warrior as well?"

"He is a Solamnic Knight." That said it all.

Artavash held out her hand. "Come, sit by me. I wish to know you better." Sturm half-knelt in the pile of cushions by her right hand. She said, "You are educated, are you not?"

"I know my letters, and have studied the Chronicles of Huma."

"Huma? Who is that?"

"You don't know? Huma was the greatest hero of Krynn." Sturm cleared his throat and recited:

Thus Huma, Knight of Solamnia,
Lightbringer, First Lancer,
Followed his light to the foot of the Khalkist
*   Mountains,*
To the stone feet of the gods,
To the crouched silence of their temple.
He called down the Lancemakers, he took on
Their unspeakable power to crush the unspeakable
*   evil,*
To thrust the coiling darkness
Back down the tunnel of the dragon's throat.

Sturm finished the canto. Artavash was smiling again. Very quietly she said, "And this demigod, this Huma; you are a descendant of his?"

"From olden times, yes," Sturm said with pride.

"I cannot wait to present you to my master," she said.

The fog dispelled and never returned. *Sea Raven's* oars beat day and night.

Sturm worried about Soren. There had been no sign of the sergeant since he disappeared into the dark, fetid hold of the galley two days ago. Artavash was not available, so the boy complained to Radiz.

"You will not like what you see," Radiz told him.

"I want to see Sergeant Soren," Sturm insisted. The commander agreed without any more argument.

"Perhaps it would be instructive for you to visit the benches," he mused.

The boy and the commander descended a steep set of steps into the hold. There, a long wooden walkway ran from forecastle to stern. Below on either side were the rowers' benches. Four men were chained to each oar, and twenty oars were set on each side. Hard, grim-faced men prowled the walk, lashing the rowers at random. The sight and smell of the neglected slaves was fearsome.

Soren was not hard to find. Compared to the skinny wretches around him, he was a giant. Radiz let Sturm on the catwalk to speak with his friend.

"I'm sorry, Soren!" he said, choking on disgust and angry tears. "I didn't know they'd put you in this horrible place!"

The guardsman hauled back his oar. "Don't—worry—young—lord," he panted in time to the sounding drum. "Alive—there is—hope."

"Hope is a good breakfast, but a poor supper," countered Radiz. He led Sturm away. The boy went back to his mother. He sat between Lady Ilys and Carin and said nothing to anyone for a long time.

After four days and three nights, the *Sea Raven*

hove in sight of land. The coast of Abanasinia lay like a low, brown cloud off the port beam. Lady Ilys looked longingly at the far shore.

"So near," she said. Sturm leaned on her arm. "If I knew we were close enough, I'd throw you overboard to swim it and find help."

"I could try," he said eagerly.

She stroked his tangled hair. "No, my son. I fear you would drown."

Abanasinia receded as the *Sea Raven* bore south and west. A plume of smoke followed the wind away from the mountaintop.

"Kernaf is a fire-mountain," explained Artavash. "The natives call it *'Hej Maraf,'*—the Furnace."

"Are you not a native?" asked Sturm.

"Me, a fish-eater? My ancestors laugh at the idea!"

Sturm peeked at Radiz. The swarthy face under the shiny helmet could not conceal annoyance at her insult.

Sea Raven gained steadily against an offshore breeze. The sea was empty of ships, even as she drew in sight of the mouth of the main harbor. From the high forecastle, the city of Kernaf spread in a half-circle around the bowl-shaped bay. Two tall, stone towers flanked the narrow harbor entrance. The tower tops were blackened by fire.

"Has someone attacked your town?" asked Sturm.

Radiz squinted into the morning glare. "No, boy. Those are signal towers. Fires were burned up there to mark the entrance for passing ships," he said.

"Don't they use them anymore?" Sturm asked. Radiz was silent.

Artavash ordered message pennants sent as the galley churned to its haven. They passed large numbers of fishing smacks moored to buoys. They were waterlogged from neglect. In the main dockyard, large merchant ships swung untended at anchor, their rigging ragged and their main yards lying rotten on their decks.

"Strange," said Lady Ilys. "Everything looks abandoned. I thought this would be a teeming port."

"Not a soul in sight," agreed Mistress Carin.

That changed when a light ketch skimmed out to meet the *Sea Raven*. A Kernaffi stood in the boat and called to the galley in his native tongue. Radiz replied at length.

"What do they say?" asked Sturm.

"Merely the greetings of our great lord to his returning ship," said Artavash. The man in the boat did not look so very pleased to Sturm.

Sea Raven dropped anchors fore and aft. The oars were run in. The pilot ketch put about and tacked back to a long stone pier. Radiz shouted orders, and all hands except slaves assembled on the main deck.

A squat barge rowed out to the galley's bow. Sturm, his mother, and Carin followed Artavash to a ramp that led down to the bobbing barge. Sturm stopped short of the ramp's end.

"What about Sergeant Soren?" he said.

"He will come ashore with the other rowers," said Radiz.

Sturm appealed to Artavash. "He must come with us," he said. She seemed willing to accommodate the boy's wishes, so she sent for the sergeant. Soren was half-carried from the hold and dumped on the ramp by Kernaffi sailors.

"You see, my lady, how four days with an oar tames the boldest warrior," Radiz said. Artavash laughed all the way down to the barge.

Sturm helped his friend stand. "Are you well, Soren?" he said.

"Well enough, my lord." His quilted tunic was in tatters, and red welts streaked his back. The rowing master had not spared Soren the whip. The guardsman's hands were also raw from gripping the heavy oar.

The barge glided in to the pier. An honor guard awaited them. Brass horns blared as Artavash led the group up some steps to the street. A parade formed: the warrior woman leading Sturm by the hand, followed by a grim Lady Ilys and Carin. Soren, Radiz, and the Kernaffi guard brought up the rear. Fifes shrilled and drums rumbled as they began to march.

The streets of the city were as empty as the harbor. A few people peered out their windows, and some curious loafers filled open doorways. As soon as they caught sight of Artavash, doors closed and shutters shut.

"Passing strange," Sturm said. "Harbors without ships, streets without people."

"The natives seldom venture out this time of day," Artavash replied. "They think it's too hot."

The parade turned a corner. Ahead rose an imposing facade, a palace of some sort. Before the palace was a high wooden platform covered with a golden canopy. Artavash halted Sturm ten paces from the foot of the platform. The guards ran ahead, forming a double line from Artavash to the bottom of the steps. Javelins clanked on shoulders in salute, and the music stopped.

"Hail, Lord of the Sea!" Artavash cried.

"Kai! Nam kamay durat!" echoed the guards.

Sturm shaded his eyes. How warm it was here! The afternoon sun glared over him, making sweat break out on his face. Maybe the natives had the right idea!

Something stirred on the platform. A thin shape, black against the dazzling light, came to the front of the platform. Two hands rose, spread in greeting.

"Welcome, beloved Artavash. Who have you

---

brought to me?" said a high, reedy voice.

"Noble guests, my lord." She introduced Lady Ilys, Carin, and Soren. Then she pushed Sturm forward. "And this, Master, is Sturm, Angriff's son, of the house of Brightblade."

A thin, gurgling sound emanated from the platform. "So? Come closer, young fellow, that I may see you better."

Sturm cast a glance back at his mother for guidance. Artavash didn't wait; she put a hand to his back and steered him up the wooden steps. When the shade of the gilded canopy fell across his face, he saw the man known as the Lord of the Sea.

He was tall, and so thin his back bowed under the weight of his large head. The black robe he wore hung loosely from his shoulders. Long, smooth fingers were clasped together at the Sea Lord's waist. And his face—Sturm would long remember that face! Two black eyes glittered on either side of a sharp nose. The skin of his beardless face was gray and dry as autumn leaves . . . strange that his hands, though bony, were pink and unwrinkled. The Lord of the Sea had only a few wisps of black hair clinging to his globular skull.

"My name is Mukhari Ras," he said. His voice was like a creaking door. "I am so pleased to meet you." He extended a hand to the boy. Sturm took it uncertainly. It was dry and hot, almost feverish.

"Have I done well?" asked Artavash.

"Oh, very well, far better than I expected," said Mukhari Ras. "And you shall be rewarded. All my loyal subjects will be rewarded."

He picked up a large canvas sack, grunting from the obvious weight. Shuffling to the front of the platform, Mukhari said, "Loyal men of Kernaf! I am pleased with the guests you have brought me. Taste the gratitude of Mukhari Ras!" So saying, he dipped his hand in the sack and flung a handful of the contents into the air. A shower of gold coins fell on the soldiers below. The men broke ranks and scrambled after the money, which rang and rolled on the paving stones.

Sturm blinked. He saw coins hit the ground, but it was sand, common sand, that Mukhari threw by fist-fuls from the sack.

"You—you're a magician!" he said.

"No, boy. I am no crude conjurer, but a humble aco-lyte of the mysteries of cosmic matter. My alchemical art has made me master of this island. Soon I shall command all the Inland Sea." Mukhari threw another handful of sand to the Kernaffi. "More! Take more! All the gold in the world is yours if you serve me!" The men dropped their weapons and crawled on all fours in the dirt. They filled their helmets with gold and laughingly chased each new coin as it struck the ground.

The sack emptied, Mukhari Ras tossed it aside. "That's done," he said, showing blackened teeth in his smile. "Artavash, my dear, bring the boy and his noble companions to the palace. I shall receive them for dinner."

Sturm, Lady Ilys, and Carin were taken to an airy suite of rooms on the east side of the palace. There, amid billowing sheets of gauze, the smell of incense, and the ever-present tinkling of wind chimes, bowls of scented water were brought for their bathing. Vested servants stood by with towels, even presuming to pat dry the Solamnians' faces and hands for them.

"What odd people they are," said Carin.

"That Mukhari Ras is the oddest of them all. Who could imagine a quacksalving alchemist as the ruler of an island? It's—it's contrary to nature, that's what it is," said Lady Ilys.

"Mother, what will become of us?" Sturm said once the towel was taken away from his face.

"I cannot guess," she confessed. "A man who throws gold in the street cannot desire ransom money. In truth, were it not for the violence of our being brought here, I would believe we were honored guests."

Sturm was uneasy. Why had no one else noticed that Mukhari's gold was only sand? He opened his mouth to mention it to his mother, but before he could say a word, Artavash appeared at their door.

"The table of my master is laden. Let us eat," she said.

Dinner in the palace was a major event, presented in an elaborate style. Sturm enjoyed sitting on the floor at the low table, though Lady Ilys provoked a minor crisis by insisting that a proper chair be provided for her. It was not decent, she said, for a well-born lady to squat on her haunches like the family wolfhound.

As the diners—including Sir Radiz, Artavash, and Soren—were busy hacking open their first course of melon, Lady Ilys said, "Lord Mukhari, may I ask how you came to rule this country? Your servant," she gestured to Artavash, "admits not being native to Kernaf."

The alchemist, who sat by a plate heaped with fruit, replied, "I was marooned on the south coast of Kernaf by men of my own land."

"What land is that?" asked Sturm.

"Moranoco, or as you call it, the Plains of Dust."

"You were exiled then?" said Lady Ilys. Without looking, she handed a napkin to Sturm. The boy blotted melon juice from his chin.

"Indeed, lady; as you are now, so was I once a hard-pressed refugee. By my skill in the Art, I won the loyalty and affection of the people of Kernaf. I know the straits you are in, which is why I make you welcome."

"Your servants have not always been so kind," Soren said, giving Artavash a caustic glance. The warrior woman plunged a blunt table knife into her melon and split the fruit in two.

"Ah, well! It has been explained to me that your ship refused the *Sea Raven*'s summons and resisted with blood when boarded. Is it surprising that my good Artavash resorted to stern measures to bring you here? If murder and plunder were our aims, you would not be dining with us now," Mukhari said.

Carin looked confused. Lady Ilys said, "Why do your ships stop free traders on the open sea?"

"Tribute is necessary for the maintenance of Kernaf's position," said Artavash. She popped a sliver of melon in her mouth. Sturm watched her every move with fascination.

There was silence around the table for a moment. Everyone was eating except Mukhari. Sturm wondered why he had the choicest fruit on his plate if he weren't going to eat any of it.

The alchemist fixed his black eyes on Lady Ilys. "Where were you bound, Lady?"

"Solace, in Abanasinia," she replied.

Mukhari wiped his mouth on a linen napkin, though no food had touched his lips. "Shall I put one of my ships at your disposal?"

"That would be wonderful!" said Mistress Carin.

"It is gracious of you to offer," said Lady Ilys.

Radiz interjected, "Only *Sea Raven* is on hand, Lord."

"When can it be ready for sea?"

"Not for nine days, Lord. The hull was strained when we rammed the roundship. The seams should be re-caulked," Artavash said. Radiz opened his mouth to say something but was cut off by her harsh glance. "No other vessel is expected back in less than a fortnight," she said.

"It seems you must be my guests for nine more days," Mukhari said. "So that you will be comfortable, please feel free to roam my palace at will." He stood to leave, though the second course had yet to be served. "And now I retire to my nightly studies. Good health to you, my friends."

He waved a hand through the air. A slim glass vial appeared in his fingers. Mukhari hurled the vial to the floor. It shattered, and a coil of rose-colored smoke snaked out. The smoke enveloped Mukhari Ras. The last thing Sturm saw was the alchemist's face. In a halo of pink smoke he looked quite benign.

The cloud dispersed, and Mukhari was gone.

"Oh!" said Carin.

"Tricks," muttered Radiz.

It was hot. Sturm rolled over and pushed back the slick satin sheets. Currents of air stirred the filmy curtains, but the heat in the room was stifling. He got up, pulled on his Kernaffi-style pants and vest, and checked on his mother. Lady Ilys was sleeping soundly. Her cheek was cool and her forehead dry. So why am I sweating so? wondered Sturm.

He tip-toed through the colonnade to the main room. The cool tiles felt good under his feet. Beyond the columns was an atrium. Stars glittered overhead. As Sturm stood searching for familiar constellations, he heard footsteps and muffled voices. He went to the door and lifted the latch.

Two Kernaffi soldiers flanked a third, taller man. Chains clinked faintly from the middle man's wrists and feet. Sturm cracked the door wider. The men passed a wall torch. The fettered man was Sergeant Soren—and he was gagged, too.

Sturm shut the door quickly. His mind raced in tandem with his heart. Why was Soren in chains? Where were they taking him? When the footsteps faded around the corner, Sturm knew he had to follow.

The massive suite door swung back without a whisper. Sturm saw the hinges were made of ruby. There seemed no limit to the wealth of the alchemist-lord. He slipped down the hall, straining to hear the last word of the Kernaffi guards and Soren. The palace was still.

He kept close to the wall, just as he did when he played 'Storm the Citadel' in Castle Brightblade. His damp palms moved stickily over the glossy wood panels. A strange, irresistible smell came to Sturm's nostrils, an odor of spice such as he had never known before. Where the corridor crossed another he stopped, uncertain which way to go. A fresh waft of spice drew him to the right. Down the hall a high, curving staircase of black marble spiraled up, following the sweep of the palace wall. Midway up, a single torch burned in an iron bracket.

Sturm mounted the steps. The odor was stronger and more compelling with every rising step. As he passed under the torch, Sturm heard a peculiar sound—the gurgle of slow-moving liquid. The steps ended at a black door studded with silver spikes. It was ajar.

Sturm's hand reached out, wavered . . . He could not resist. He touched the door with one finger, and it opened wide for him.

Even yellow light filled the room beyond. It was a workshop of some sort, filled with all sorts of strange things: tables laden with crystals of odd color and shape; stuffed animals with glass-bead eyes that stared knowingly back at Sturm. Shelves lined with fancy canisters and bundles of dried herbs, neatly labeled in some foreign script. And books. More books than

Sturm had ever seen in his life.

He found the source of the gurgling and the spice aroma. An elaborate arrangement of clear tubes and bottles bubbled slowly on a round table in the center of the room. Beside this apparatus was a large red candle, as thick as his wrist. The odor was coming from it.

"Careful, young lord," said Mukhari Ras, appearing ghostlike from a deep alcove. "The essence still is very delicate, and I have need of it soon."

Sturm flinched and stood away from the table. The fluid in the tubes was thick and dark, very like the color of—

"Blood," said the alchemist. "Merely the unwholesome remnants of my last experiment," said the alchemist. He drew nearer even as the boy shrank from him.

"Human blood?" asked Sturm in a small voice.

"Of course," said Mukhari. "No other kind is of any use to me."

Sturm slowly pointed to the red, sweet-smelling candle. "What is this made of? It smells good."

"I am pleased you noticed. It is a very *special* candle. You see, I cannot smell it at all." Sturm couldn't believe that. The spicy aroma was almost overwhelming in the close room. "Only very special people can smell it. The young and pure."

A cold hand came to rest on the back of Sturm's neck. "What does that mean?" he asked.

"It means, my boy, that I needed to know what sort of boy you are, to know if you were suitable for my purposes."

Sturm backed a step. "What purposes?"

"At the command of my Dark Goddess, I seek the true restorative medicine, the elixir of life. My research uncovered the formula, but to make it work,

I need noble blood. Your blood."

"Mine!" cried Sturm. "Why mine?"

"You passed the test. The candle led you here."

Sturm bumped into a table. He cast about wildly for a way out. Mukhari did not seem to notice. He looked far away, musing about his experiments.

"Artavash brought me children from Kernaf, but they were imperfect, unworthy. The elixir made from their blood was only partially effective." He held out an arm and pulled back the loose sleeve to his shoulder. "See? I have the arms of a man of thirty, while the rest of me rots at sixty-six."

Fear and disgust rose sourly in Sturm's throat. "So that's why the town is empty—you murdered the children!"

"Don't be silly, boy. Most families fled, true, but they'll come back once I'm rejuvenated. They will come back and fall to their knees to worship the Goddess of Darkness who grants eternal life!"

"Life purchased at the cost of others! Paladine will not allow this!"

"And who is Paladine's representative? You?" Mukhari grinned evilly at the boy. "No matter. In two days the dark moon will rise, and the celestial conditions for the making of the elixir will be propitious."

"You will not suceed—Sergeant Soren—" Sturm began shrilly.

The alchemist clucked his tongue. "He cannot help you. Even now he lies trussed up in my dungeon. As for you, my young lord, if you give me the slightest difficulty, l shall order harm done to your mother and her maid."

"You will not!"

"Nonsense, boy. You're not in Solamnia. I am master here."

Sturm closed his hand around a smooth, cold

object— a flask. He hurled the flask at Mukhari and turned to run. The aged alchemist dodged awkwardly. Mukhari, reached for a braided bell cord. Hidden chimes rang. A concealed door sprang open, and Artavash came in. Sturm rushed blindly into her grasp.

"Take charge of him, my dear," Mukhari said. "Only don't bruise him. I wouldn't want him less than perfect for processing tomorrow."

"As you command, master," said Artavash. She laid a firm hand on his neck and guided Sturm from the room.

On the stairs Sturm said, "So—so this was your plan all along?"

"Why do you think my master had me scouring the seas?" she said. "Other ships have come and gone, seeking pure blood for Lord Mukhari's work. Noble offspring are hard to find; they're usually well guarded. It was the greatest stroke of luck that I intercepted your ship."

Sturm didn't feel at all lucky. He submitted without a struggle as Artavash took him to her chambers. All the while, even when she bound him to a heavy chair with silken sashes, he was thinking, thinking. He batted the feeling of helpless terror that gnawed at his mind. Soren a captive, his mother and Carin hostages, . . . and himself. To be bled dry, his life drained to further the evil work of the Queen of Darkness . . .

He thought of his father, standing on the battlements of Castle Brightblade with only a few loyal retainers while a mob of madmen howled around them. Lord Brightblade would meet the foe face to face, head to head, to conquer or perish. It was the knightly way. It was the Brightblade way.

The tremors in Sturm's limbs faded. In their place a heat grew in his chest. He was angry. His father had trusted him to take care of his mother, and he had failed! And who would bear the Brightblade name back to their ancestral home if not him?

"Be still, boy," Artavash said. She tipped a clay cup to her lips and drank.

"Lady Artavash?" said Sturm, his voice cracked with emotion.

"What do you want?"

"Would you help me?"

She yawned and kicked off her sandals. "Don't be silly, boy."

"All you need do is untie me. Then I'll get Soren, and together we'll take my mother and Mistress Carin—"

"You're not going anywhere. Mukhari Ras has decreed your fate." Artavash sat on her high couch and leaned back against the wall. She laid the naked blade of a shortsword across her lap.

"How can you serve a man like him? H-he is a monster who kills children!" said Sturm.

"Children die every day," she said flatly. And with that, young Sturm saw Artavash for what she was: a heartless mercenary. Her only loyalty was to her paymaster.

She drained another cupful of wine, the last of many that evening. "Now, go to sleep." Artavash slumped over a pile of pillows. Her hand went slack, and the clay cup rolled out of it.

Sturm waited until her breathing was soft and regular before he tried to shift the chair. The stout seat bumped loudly on the bare stone floor. Sturm froze. Artavash snorted and buried her face deeper in the satin cushions.

He gazed longingly at the sword Artavash had drawn, now lying point out on the couch. If he could only reach it! He strained against the sashes, but the silken knots only tightened further. Sturm relaxed and shook the damp ends of his long hair from his face.

The lamp above Artavash's couch guttered and went out. In the dense darkness, Sturm could feel his pulse throbbing in his hands and feet. He wiggled his fingers under the binding. His hands were crossed over his lap, so his left hand was over his right pocket, and vice-versa. There was a lump in his left pocket he recognized as Captain Graff's wind cord. He counted the knots. Two hands, plus one; eleven fresh gusts of magic were locked in that dirty strip of rawhide.

But it *was* magic. As a knight, he was forbidden by the Measure to make use of it. Still . . . to fight the Dark Queen. . . .

The day dawned bright and hot. Sturm awakened from a tense, shallow sleep with the sun in his eyes. His body ached from being tied all night. Artavash did not stir until a pounding on the door compelled her to rise.

"What in thunder?" she grumbled, her voice husky and dry.

"Where is my son?" demanded Lady Ilys through the door.

"Here, Mother! I'm in here!" he shouted.

Artavash winced. She yanked a bell pull by her couch. By the time she staggered to the door and opened it, eight soldiers were waiting for her outside. Two more stood by with Soren, whose hands were chained together.

Artavash slit Sturm's sashes with the shortsword, and the young Brightblade threw his arms around his mother.

"They're going to kill me!" Sturm cried.

"This can't be true!" Lady Ilys gasped, turning to Artavash, who merely shrugged.

"My lady, your son spoke truly. These people mean to kill young Sturm," said Soren.

Lady Ilys pushed her son behind her skirt. Mistress Carin moved in on Sturm's other side. Lady Ilys declared, "No one shall move from this spot until some explanation is given for the barbarous manner in which we are being treated!"

Artavash rubbed her temples a few times and said, "The explanation is this. My master, Mukhari Ras, has need of your son's life. If you interfer in the slightest way, you, your maid, and your man will be speedily killed."

"Impudent pirate! Do you think my son is a lamb, to be butchered for that walking scarecrow's evil purposes?"

"It matters little what you say, Lady. Mukhari Ras commands it, and it will be done." She gestured to the Kernaffi soldiers. They pulled Lady Ilys and Carin apart. Artavash reached for Sturm.

Chained or not, Soren could not stand idly by as Artavash laid hands on his charges. He gathered the bond links in his hands and lashed out at the nearest man. The guard folded under the blow and bowled over his comrades. Soren lumbered forward. Artavash released Sturm and turned to meet the sergeant.

"No, Soren! Stop!" cried Sturm. Artavash nimbly dodged the guardsman's rush. She brought the flat of her blade in hard on Soren's head. The sergeant buckled and fell face down on the cool marble floor. Carin screamed.

Artavash waved the sword point under Carin's nose. "Don't shout so! My head is splitting!"

"Too much wine," said Lady Ilys coldly.

"Enough! By the gods, your tongue is sharper than a dozen swords," Artavash said. "I have no more time to

---

dally with you. The guards will lock you in your rooms." She gave the orders in Kernaffi. Two men picked up Soren, and the rest formed in close order around the two women.

"Sturm! Sturm!" his mother called. He made a step toward her, but was collared by a grim-faced Artavash.

"The time for indulgences is past," she said. "If you resist, the two women will die."

"Mother!" he cried desperately.

"Come." Artavash seized Sturm by the wrist and dragged him away.

Radiz joined them in the main hall. He was splendid in his fine armor and plume, but his face was expressionless. He and Artavash exchanged a look Sturm could not fathom. Then the Kernaffi gave him a handkerchief.

"Dry your eyes," he said with a strange note of compassion.

Radiz and Artavash stood on either side of him as Sturm faced the steps leading up to the palace roof. Radiz, Sturm noted, kept one hand on his sword hilt all the way to the roof.

Four bearded Kernaffi priests stood to one side, offering up prayers and incense to the Dark Queen. Radiz stopped and bowed to them, but Sturm thought he detected a look of disgust on the man's face when he rose. Artavash shaded her aching eyes from the brilliant sun.

Ten paces away, Mukhari Ras worked to prepare the special table for his great experiment. His gaunt, bent figure scuttled from one side to another, reminding Sturm of the vultures that haunted the southeast tower of Castle Brightblade. The alchemist's wide black robe added to this impression.

The air was still. The sun burned fiercely over them.

Sturm shivered in spite of the heat. *Please, Paladine, please save me!*

"Bring him over. Come, come along," said Mukhari, waving his youthful hands. Sturm rubbed his cold, sweating palms on his pants. He looked to Radiz for some sign of sympathy. The commander of the *Sea Raven* stared straight ahead and said nothing.

Halfway to Mukhari, Sturm stumbled. He heard the snick of a sword being freed from its scabbard. A strong hand grabbed the back of his vest.

"Pick up your feet, boy," said Artavash.

Mukhari was waiting, hands folded deep into his voluminous sleeves. Up close, the table was basically just a copper funnel flat enough to lie on. The legs were heavy columns of marble.

"Put him on the table," instructed Mukhari. The priests chanted louder and began to beat a brass gong.

Shouts and clangs of metal rose from the open stairwell. Radiz drew his weapon out of reflex. Artavash shoved Sturm to Radiz and got her own sword ready. A death-scream cut the air, and a few heartbeats later, Soren bounded up the steps, a bloody sword in his chained hand.

"Sturm Brightblade! I am here!" he roared.

"Stop that man!" quavered Mukhari.

Artavash moved out to meet Soren. His stolen blade thrust in; she parried and beat his sword out of line. Soren was severely hampered by his bonds. Only with his extraordinary strength could he even carry on such a fight. He cut hard at Artavash, one, two, three—right-left-right. She dodged, fox-quick, and struck home in the guardsman's chest. Soren staggered back. Artavash circled, circled; feinting an overhand cut, she changed direction in the wink of an eye and thrust through Soren's weakened guard. The point of her blade grew out his back.

Eye to eye, she said, "You should have stayed on your oar." Artavash recovered, and Soren collapsed.

Sturm broke free from Radiz and ran to his fallen friend. "Soren! Soren!"

His eyes were open. He said, "My lord . . . sound the charge."

"Leave him, boy. He's dead." Radiz was standing over Soren. Nearby, Artavash casually wiped the blood from her blade.

Sturm was numb. With leaden feet, he walked between Radiz and Artavash to the alchemist's killing table. His hope was gone. Four steps to go. Below the neck of the table's funnel was a large iron pot. Three steps. Mukhari was pale and sweating in the heat. Two steps.

He had nothing left, nothing at all but Graff's wind cord. Magic . . . forbidden . . . The last step . . .

Artavash swept Sturm off his feet and laid him on the table. The metal was warm from the sun. "Lie still," she warned. "Remember your mother."

She backed away. Mukhari Ras loomed above him. With both hands, Mukhari clasped a long, wickedly curved dagger. Sturm's heart missed a beat. His jaw tightened, and he said the briefest prayer of his life: "Paladine, help me."

The dagger wavered in the frail alchemist's grasp. Artavash opened Sturm's vest and shirt. Mukhari Ras smiled down at him. "Here, then, is your destiny," he whispered. "I give you to my Queen!" He closed his eyes and raised the dagger high to strike.

Down came the blade. Sturm held out the wind cord taut between his fists. The keen edge of the dagger scraped the briefest instant against the rawhide. Mukhari felt it and opened his eyes. "What—?" was all he could say before the cord parted.

A mighty wall of wind, invisible, irresistible, blasted across the palace roof. The emaciated alchemist, his robes filling with air like black bat's wings, was lifted off his feet. Screeching with terror, Mukhari Ras flew backward to the edge of the roof. An upward gust filled his skirt, lofting him. The Lord of the Sea soared into the sky, borne by the ensorceled wind. On and on he flew, his brittle body spread flat by the torrent of air, until he was lost in the billowing clouds and dust.

Mukhari was gone, but the danger was not yet passed. The wind blew Sturm over the table, but he managed to thrust an arm through the funnel hole. He held on dearly as the tempest howled around him. Retorts and alembics from the spirit still toppled over and were blown away. The Kernaffi priests collapsed in a heap, only to be torn from each other by the brutal wind. One by one they were swept away, the last pair clinging together even as they were carried off.

Sturm cried out in pain as the wind tore at him. He thought his arm would snap off at the shoulder, but he was able to get a relieving grip with his free hand. The table shifted and turned. Sturm pressed his face to the copper top. Dust scoured the roof, stinging the boy's exposed flesh. Just when it seemed he could endure no more, the wild fury abated.

He clung fiercely to the table, the instrument of death that had preserved his life. He heard a faint call for help. Gingerly, Sturm removed his aching arm from the funnel hole. The arm was black and blue from wrist to elbow.

The cry came again: "Help me, help . . ." Sturm shaded his eyes and looked around. He was alone on the roof. Everything, including Soren's body, was gone.

Radiz, his plume bent at an angle and his golden armor dented, hobbled up the steps. He stared around. The groan for help came again. Radiz and Sturm walked converging paths to the edge of the roof.

"At last, we are free!" he murmured.

Dangling from a rain gutter was Artavash. The gaping dragonmouth spout had snagged her long military cape as she fell. Now she was suspended high above the housetops of Kernaf.

"Help me!" she pleaded. The cape tore a little and Artavash begged for quick assistance.

Sturm eyed Radiz. The Kernaffi blinked dazedly. "I leave it to you, boy. If you wish, we'll bring her up. Or I can cut her free and let her fall. What do you wish?"

Her gray eyes appealed for mercy. "She killed Soren," Sturm said.

"True," said Radiz. He pulled the sword from his belt.

"No," said Sturm. "The Measure teaches mercy, even to our enemy."

He dropped on his stomach and reached for her cape. Radiz took hold as well. They hauled Artavash to safety. Once securely on the roof, she rolled over on the tiles and gasped for air. Radiz took her sword and knife away.

He jerked Artavash around on to her stomach and quickly bound her arms and legs tightly. When she cursed too loudly, he drew a brightly colored scarf from his pocket and jammed it into her mouth. At last he stood and faced Sturm.

"Now, what can I do to make amends, young lord?" asked Radiz.

Sturm cradled his bruised arm and frowned with concentration. "I wish to leave," he said. "I want a ship to take my mother, Mistress Carin, and me to Solace. It was my father's wish that we go to Solace, so that is what we shall do."

Radiz nodded. As they walked slowly to the steps, the commander laid a reassuring hand on the boy's shoulder. "Whatever made you think of using the old sailor's magic string?" he asked.

"I didn't plan it," said Sturm, swallowing. "My only thought was to turn Mukhari's knife away."

"You didn't realize cutting the cord would release all the wind?"

Sturm shook his head. "I don't know anything about magic. It's not a fitting subject for knights."

Paladine would forgive him for bending the Measure. . . .

At the top of the stairs Sturm paused. "Radiz?"

"Yes, young Sturm?"

"Would you have your men search for Sergeant Soren? He deserves an honorable burial."

"It shall be done."

They descended the steps together. Radiz remarked, "You know, Mukhari was right about one thing; you are a noble lad."

"I am my father's son," said Sturm.

The voices of the boy and the Kernaffi commander echoed through the palace halls long after the rooftop had returned to the clean air, bright sun, and nature's honest wind.

The road to exile was very long. For Sturm Brightblade, this was only the beginning.

Heart of Goldmoon

Laura Hickman and Kate Novak

*T*he air of excitement was high as the Que-shu tribe milled before the ancient stone platform that was the focus of their village. Everyone was clad in colorful festive raiment. Adding to the delight of the senses was the delectable smell of foods being prepared for the celebration to come.

One by one, however, the exhilarated men, women, and children fell into silence as their attention was caught by a lone young woman, climbing the granite construction before them. Soon, all was still. No child giggled, no babe even cried. Nothing disturbed the faint shuffling sound made by the slippered feet of the holy woman as she ascended to the platform.

The woman was Goldmoon, princess and priestess of the Que-shu. Those who watched knew that upon her death—in the far future—Goldmoon would become a goddess, as had her mother, Tearsong, and all her deceased ancestors. Goldmoon was the tribe's link to their gods. Her father, Chieftain Arrowthorn, would also achieve godhood, but, as revered as he was, the silence and awe of the crowd was reserved for the slender woman who was his only heir.

Goldmoon's long, silken hair was brighter than the golden grasses waving in the fields near the village. Sight of her hair still astonished the dark-haired tribesmen. "It is a mark of her favor with the ancestors," they said. As she reached the platform and bowed to the crowd, the sun glinted from those golden tresses, and no one present witnessing her grace, her beauty, or that bright crown of hair doubted Goldmoon's worth in being honored with this ceremony.

Goldmoon turned from the platform edge and bowed respectfully to her father, who had previously ascended the platform. Though it was her mother's blood that decreed Goldmoon's status as priestess, it was her father's greatness as a warrior that had won him Tearsong's hand in marriage. Only Arrowthorn's cunning and wisdom had kept the reins of power from being torn from their family's hands after the crushing blow of Tearsong's early death, and had held them until she, Goldmoon, was old enough to serve as priestess to her people.

Goldmoon moved to Arrowthorn's right side and fixed her gaze out over the plains to the mountain on the northern horizon. She could not see it from here, but she knew that near the summit was a vast cavern, called the Hall of the Sleeping Spirits, where the mortal remains of Goldmoon's dead ancestors lay, behind a door opened by the rays of Lunitari, the red moon, only once every ten years. On the morrow, Goldmoon would journey to that cavern for the first time to speak with her ancestors, her gods. She found herself excited and perhaps a little anxious.

First, however, must come the games that would decide who her escorts were to be. Only those two warriors who proved to be the best would accompany and protect her on the journey. Twenty young Plainsmen, lean and muscled, all eager for the honor, filed onto a lower tier of the platform and formed a semicircle before their princess. Goldmoon, seemingly transfixed by the heat thermals shimmering in the air before her, appeared not to notice the men.

When the last man took his place, however, Goldmoon turned her gaze to the historian seated on the platform behind her father, writing on a parchment with deliberate strokes. She heard Arrowthorn let out a breath that might have been a subdued snort of annoyance at Loreman. The historian's painstaking slowness was an obvious ploy to demonstrate to the tribe the importance of his own position. Loreman finished writing the names of the contestants with a flourish, then looked up and nodded to the princess.

Goldmoon had already performed hundreds of religious ceremonies. Since her mother's death she had carried all the burdens of priestess—praying for her people, their crops and livestock and weaponry, tending the sick and injured, settling disputes, burying the dead. But because of the infrequency with which the door to the Hall of the Sleeping Spirits opened, she had not been able to perform this most important ceremony, during which she would dedicate her life to her people. Now, this day had arrived. These men seated below her would fight for the privilege of escorting her, and undoubtedly one of them would eventually court her, as her father had courted her mother.

"One of you had better be worthy," she said silently to the men.

Goldmoon unfurled her personal banner; the gold crescent moon emblazoned on the dark cloth shone in the sun as brightly as her hair. She called out, "May the blessings of the Ancient Dead give courage, endurance, and strength to the greatest among you."

Cheering in reply, the Plainsmen held the banners of

their individual houses aloft.

Leaning down, the priestess drew a crystal dagger from her boot scabbard. Cunningly fashioned and hollow within, the dagger doubled as a vial containing a handful of sacred sand. With a twist, Goldmoon slipped the handle from the blade and poured some of the fine, warm, dry contents into her palm. Turning with a flourish, Goldmoon sprinkled the golden powder over the men before her, taking care that no head should escape at least a little dusting.

Resisting the impulse to brush the remaining grains from her palm, the priestess began to touch each head with her fingertips in blessing. Each warrior, as she stood before him, knelt and gazed up at her with admiration and devotion. All but the last one.

He wore well-cared-for but well-dented armor, and his clothing showed equal signs of wear and repair. His was not a familiar face, but Goldmoon recognized his banner as belonging to a poor family that lived in a hut at the edge of the grazing lands the Que-shu shared with bordering tribes. The warrior's name was Riverwind, and there was something about him that Arrowthorn, Goldmoon's father, spoke about with other men, but it was a subject always dropped when she entered the room.

Goldmoon moved into position before Riverwind, wondering idly what emotion she would see in his eyes, but he stepped back with a feline grace. Startled, and annoyed at the break in the smoothness of the ceremony, Goldmoon managed not to show her surprise. Believing the young peasant too simple to understand the ritual, she said softly, "We are not quite finished. If you will kneel before me, I will bless you."

"I need no blessing to pass this day's test, and I will not kneel to you or any other mortal creature," Riverwind replied. He spoke quietly, but his deep voice sounded across the platform.

Goldmoon stiffened with repressed anger. She would not be embarrassed before the tribe, her holiness denied. She gestured for the guards to come from the side of the platform. They stood behind the infidel, prepared to haul him away at her command.

Before she could motion for them to remove Riverwind from her sight, however, Arrowthorn was by her side interceding. "If it please, your grace," he whispered to her, "this one"—he glared icily at Riverwind—"intends no disrespect; he simply does not believe as we do."

The chieftain spoke up so the crowd could hear, "Riverwind, grandson of Wanderer, why are you here at this ceremony? It is not required for you to attend."

Riverwind shifted his eyes from the daughter to the father. Goldmoon's breath caught in her throat at his daring and pride. Yet the warrior's blue eyes showed not a hint of nervousness. Calmly, but with enough volume to carry to the tribe below, he replied, "I am a warrior, and my swordarm will be a strength to my people. Although I do not worship as you do, you have my loyalty. I, too, desire a safe journey for my Chieftain's Daughter. Today's games will prove my worth."

Riverwind glanced away from Arrowthorn, capturing Goldmoon's own reluctant gaze. He smiled ever so slightly. Goldmoon quickly shifted her focus out across the plains. What she had seen in those eyes in that brief instant caused her to shiver despite the golden heat of the sun. It was the look of a hunter stalking his prey.

"Well said," Arrowthorn stated, then he turned to the waiting crowd. "Let the games begin."

Goldmoon stood stunned, not seeing the men before her or the plains spread out around her. She could not believe what she had just heard. How could her father give his approval to this arrogant, rebellious peasant? And how dare he circumvent her will? He might be her father, but *she* was the priestess!

The warriors filed from the altar, Riverwind at the end of the line. Goldmoon followed behind him stiffly. She took each step down the stairs firmly, as though she were trodding on this Riverwind's head.

The chieftain followed his daughter, appearing completely calm. Loreman remained up above, still scratching away at the parchment with his quill, relating his version of the events which had just passed.

Goldmoon entered her lodge, closing the door behind her father. Then she whirled about, free to vent her anger and confusion. "I do not understand how you could allow—"

"Silence!" Arrowthorn said.

Goldmoon bit back her words.

The chieftain surveyed his daughter critically. She wore a formal robe that Tearsong, his dead wife, had also worn, and was, but for her hair, the image of her mother. She performed all the duties of Chieftain's Daughter without trouble or complaint. Goldmoon was, in fact, nearly flawless, yet Arrowthorn could never bring himself to tell her so. Godhood was not earned by the careless.

He suppressed his pride and snapped, "Your circlet is crooked."

Goldmoon felt her face flush crimson as her hands rose to straighten the slender silver band on her head.

"How are young men supposed to see a goddess in you if you do not take better care of your appearance? That won't do. Take it off. Have your women comb your hair again before you replace it."

She was a full-grown woman of power, yet her subjects would be astonished to see how she shook before her father's words.

Still, it was not easy for Arrowthorn to watch his only child tremble with shame. He put his hand on her shoulder and lifted her chin to bring her eyes up to his own. "It would hardly matter in Riverwind's case. His whole family is cursed thus."

"What do you mean?" she asked.

Arrowthorn drew in a long breath. "Wanderer, grandfather of Riverwind, learned too much in his wanderings. He broke pact with our gods and taught his family to do the same."

"Is that why they are so poor?" Goldmoon asked, remembering their shabby hut out on the plains.

"That is not important. Suffice it to say that I do not question their loyalty, despite their peculiar beliefs."

"But, how can you not when they deny us?"

"You remember once we spoke together of those among us who say their faith is strong, or their loyalty is great, and yet the truth is another matter?"

Goldmoon nodded. The priesthood of the Que-shu passed from mother to eldest daughter, but—peculiar among the tribes of the Plains—the position of chieftain went to the man who won the hand of the priestess. Such a man's worthiness was judged both by the priestess herself and the current chieftain, her father. It was a tradition stemming from antiquity, a tradition that had kept the royalty of the Que-shu strong. Yet there were men, especially chieftains' sons and spurned suitors, who rankled that their bids for power were thwarted by one healthy girl-child grown to womanhood. Arrowthorn had warned her once that many argued against this tradition, though none dared do so in the royal family's presence—yet. That was why she must be perfect in her example. The people obeyed their goddess-to-be, but evil men could turn them away from her if they could make her seem no more than a mortal woman.

Arrowthorn continued, "And just as it would not be expedient to probe these false claims of loyalty too deeply, we accept the loyalty of those who claim a different belief."

"But why?"

Arrowthorn sighed. "Because they are only mortals, my child. And though mortals are not infallible, they must be given the freedom to make their own choices. How else are we to choose the truly righteous when it comes our time to judge as gods?"

Goldmoon mused over that for some moments, then argued, "But we must teach them the true path."

"Teach, but not force them to march along it."

"Perhaps Riverwind could be coaxed to follow the path," Goldmoon pointed out.

Secretly, Arrowthorn thought: He might follow quarry down it some ways, but he'd drag it back once he'd shot it. Aloud, he merely warned his daughter, "I would not waste too much time on him, my daughter. Men like Riverwind will take orders, but persuasion only brings out their stubborn streak. More likely he will make you look foolish."

"Is that what you discuss with Loreman and the rest when I am not about, how his family makes us look foolish?"

Arrowthorn would not lie, so he merely shrugged and replied, "Among other things."

"Like what things?"

But Arrowthorn turned about to go, commanding her as he left, "Have your hair done, replace the circlet, and go about your other duties. They are numerous this day, aren't they?"

As the contest time neared, Goldmoon crossed the

challenge ground, her hair and circlet now as perfect as the rest of her appearance. All about the edges of the clearing warriors were warming up and practicing. As they caught sight of her, they stopped their activity and watched her approach. The priestess kept her eyes fixed on her destination, the weapons tent. Thus, while all eyes were on her, it was she alone who saw a man crawl out from beneath the canvas near the rear of the tent.

Goldmoon's brow furrowed upon recognizing the intruder. It was Hollow-sky, son of Loreman. The historian was a man of wealth and influence in the tribe; his family had kept the records of the Que-shu for many generations. Goldmoon knew that he had been one of her mother's suitors, but it was impossible for the priestess to imagine Tearsong choosing him over Arrowthorn. His stature was only average, his frame wiry, and the features of his face—though considered handsome and refined by many women—were so pale and ill-defined that Goldmoon sometimes felt sorry for him. He faded into the background beside her father's strongly masculine and still hearty form. Loreman wasn't half the warrior her father was, he was arrogant and tight with his money, and he lost his temper or brooded when he did not get his way. After Tearsong died, he had argued constantly with her father about the management of the tribe. Yet Loreman's son Hollow-sky was among the few men Arrowthorn had judged fit company for his daughter in her childhood.

The princess had thought once how magnanimous that was of her father, but she came to realize it had been the chieftain's way of bartering for peace with Loreman. The unity of the tribe was of the utmost importance to her father. He would buy it at any price, even if it meant selling his daughter's affection to his enemy's son.

Once, Goldmoon might not have minded, for when she was a child she had loved Hollow-sky dearly. But when Hollow-sky began training as a warrior with his older brother, Hawker, he had changed. For the next few years her former playmate, engrossed in more "manly" pursuits, had practically ignored her. When his attentions to her were finally renewed, it had been all too obvious that he was not interested in her as a friend, but only as a prize.

At first, his attentions had been exceedingly satisfying, for then she had thought Hollow-sky was attractive and powerful; but soon his personality began to irritate her as Loreman's irritated her father. Worse, his courtship was tainted by his persistent conviction that he was the wiser, the stronger, the superior of the two of them. He made decisions for her without her leave, or tried to dissuade her from decisions she had already considered carefully. When they fought, he made a point of reminding her of their youthful games to coax her out of her anger, tainting the only pleasant memories she had of him.

Unfortunately, her father seemed to assume her dwindling feelings of friendship for Hollow-sky would grow into love because of his own need to keep the tribe unified, and others whispered what a perfect match they would be—he so strong, she so beautiful. No one could see how her feelings had changed, and she had no mother to counsel her.

Now Hollow-sky was up to some mischief in the weapons tent, a place he should not even be near. Goldmoon knew she should question him, but she did not want to confront him today. She didn't want to listen to his excuses or even speak with him, so she said nothing as she approached the guards posted at the opening to the weapons tent. Oblivious to their failure, they bowed respectfully to the priestess and held back the flaps of the tent for her to enter.

Left alone inside, Goldmoon found nothing apparently amiss. All weapons were stored here on festival days, ostensibly in acknowledgement of the chieftain's sovereignty, though it coincidentally cut down on injuries in brawls that might develop as the celebration wore into the night. Goldmoon shrugged. Whatever Hollow-sky had been up to she would get out of him later. For now she must put him out of her mind and bless the warriors' weapons.

She took a deep breath to calm herself, but her eyes caught on some feathers that she recognized as marking Riverwind's sparring pole. There was nothing shabby about the rare and precious wood, probably something his grandfather, Wanderer, had harvested on his journeys. Angrily Goldmoon snatched it up and started to toss it to the side. "We'll see what a marvelous weapon this is and what a great warrior he is without my blessing." But then she noticed the thin crack running along the upper third of the pole. She saw at once that it was not a natural crack.

"Hollow-sky!" she whispered.

Knowing that Hollow-sky and his brother, Hawker, were clear favorites to win the contests, Goldmoon immediately assumed he'd done this deed for her. Perhaps he'd even tell her later how he had paid Riverwind back for the unbeliever's insult to herself.

Unsure she wanted this sort of championship, Goldmoon debated what to do. Perhaps ignominious defeat was the fate the ancestors had decided for Riverwind. Yet . . . why would the gods have let her discover the crack, if not to correct the matter?

Her duty was clear to her.

Finding another pole of the same rare wood was not easy. She had to substitute one of her father's old poles, and affixing Riverwind's feathers to the replacement was a nuisance. Finally, when she had finished the work and placed the substitute pole among the blessed weapons, she began to have second thoughts.

Her father's sparring pole was a weapon her mother had undoubtedly blessed, perhaps even the one her father had used when he'd won the right to escort Tearsong to the Hall of the Sleeping Spirits. Stubbornly she tried to recall if there was a way to *unsanctify* the weapon.

"Goldmoon?" Arrowthorn entered the tent and looked quizzically at his daughter. A slight smile crossed his lips. "Still praying? They are only going to fight one another, you know, not our enemies!"

Goldmoon lowered her eyes to hide her worry and confusion. "Father, please. This is serious to me."

"Forgive me. Of course. But everyone waits on you."

Goldmoon followed her father and took her place in the viewing stand. The contests started with a series of wrestling matches. The tribe all gathered about, unreserved in their cheers and boos. Goldmoon watched silently with intense interest. She was the leader of a warrior tribe and was herself a trained fighter, as were all Que-shu women.

A new bout was just starting when she heard Clearwing, one of her female attendants, whisper to the other, "Perhaps it's true what they say of this Riverwind."

Goldmoon's eyes remained on the games, but her attention was drawn to her servants' conversation.

"What?" Starflower, her other attendant, whispered back.

"They say he was raised by leopards," Clearwing replied.

"What nonsense!" Starflower sniffed. "There are no

leopards on the plains."

Clearwing shrugged. "My grandmother says he was raised by leopards and that Wanderer brought him back with him from one of his wanderings."

Goldmoon turned her attention back to the wrestling. Riverwind's bout was just starting. Undeniably powerful and graceful, there *was* something feline in his movements.

"You have to admit he has the grace of a cat," Clearwing added, echoing her mistress's thoughts.

"So true!" Starflower said with a sigh.

Not wishing to listen to any more praises of Riverwind, Goldmoon sent both girls off with some coin to purchase stickycakes to keep their mouths closed. The smell of the sweetened bread set her stomach rumbling, but she bore it stoically. The royal family ate in public only on ceremonial occasions so as not to remind their subjects of their mortality.

The wrestling matches, a footrace, and an archery contest culled the contestants down to eight. The ancestors had yet to bring Riverwind to his knees, and Goldmoon wondered if he attributed his victory to whatever gods he did worship. As he came forward with the others to collect his sparring pole, the priestess watched him deliberately, but he gave no sign at all that he detected the switch she had made. He did, however, look up at her and smile.

The grim hunter's expression disappeared from his eyes. His smile was that of a young man, warm and friendly, and Goldmoon saw there the loyalty her father had not questioned.

The final event was longsticks, a contest fought in a large circle, in which the fighters had to stay armed and within the circle. At the judge's signal, the men engaged each other with dangerous thrusts and parries, and the crack of wood shattered the air.

Two men quickly managed to knock each other out of the ring and roll clumsily into the crowd, instantly disqualifying themselves. Goldmoon saw that Hawker and Hollow-sky were being very aggressive, smashing at their opponents' weapons time and again. Riverwind, with a series of unrelenting, well-timed jabs and blows, wore down his opponent, Treewhistle, until Treewhistle lost his grip on his pole. The weapon clattered to the ground and rolled out of the circle before its owner could retrieve it.

There was a sudden snap of wood, and then another, as Loreman's sons both broke the weapons of those they fought. Goldmoon frowned. This could not be coincidence. The full extent of Hollow-sky's activities in the weapons tent was now clear. This was sacrilege! She would let him know of her displeasure.

Simultaneously, the brothers turned on Riverwind. It seemed a foregone conclusion that they would double-team him and win the contest together, but Riverwind had had a moment to breathe and analyze their movements. He held his pole high, almost inviting them to smash it. Only one of them could strike without getting in the other's way, so Hawker declined in his brother's favor.

Hollow-sky swung, but Riverwind was a blur of color as he dodged, weapon and all, beneath Hollow-sky's arms. The unblessed warrior slammed his pole at the unsuspecting and relaxed Hawker. Hawker's weapon soared from his hands over the heads of the crowd and landed on the viewing stand at Goldmoon's feet.

Hollow-sky, witnessing his brother's defeat, seemed about to smash his weapon down on Riverwind's head, but the judge rushed forward between the two, proclaiming them the winners. Riverwind and

Hollow-sky would be Goldmoon's escorts to the Hall of the Sleeping Spirits.

The crowd cheered, but the priestess eyed both critically as they approached her. Hollow-sky gave Riverwind a vicious glare, then stepped forward as Goldmoon extended her hand to touch his forehead in blessing. But Hollow-sky grasped her fingers and pressed a lingering kiss on them.

Though this was hardly customary, the crowd cheered again, laughing. There was, after all, that other aspect to these games—finding a warrior worthy of courting their priestess/princess. Distressed, however, by the ardor in Hollow-sky's gaze and still angered by the broken poles, the princess was determined to show him no favor. She held her hand out to Riverwind to give him the same advantage.

Riverwind looked startled at the slender, graceful fingers before him. He took the hand as though it were very fragile and turned it over, seeming uncertain as to what he should do.

"Well, Riverwind?" Goldmoon said, arching her eyebrows expectantly. Inside, the sudden fear surged that, for religious reasons, this . . . peasant might refuse to kiss her, and she would be embarrassed before the whole tribe.

"Perhaps he reads your palm, my princess," Hollow-sky joked.

Goldmoon was instantly grateful to Loreman's son for breaking the silence and saving her.

"No," Riverwind replied gravely. "That is not one of my skills."

"What? You don't even see a long journey?" Goldmoon teased, though inwardly she was growing just a little nervous—the warrior's grip on her wrist was now quite firm.

Riverwind's countenance grew more serious,

though his smile never entirely left his lips. "A journey you shall have, no doubt. And with my protection it will be a safe one. I swear."

Without turning her hand over he lifted it to his lips. Goldmoon's heart started pounding as she felt him sniff at the scent on her wrist and then, very gently, kiss her palm. Long after he released it and she lowered it to her side, she could feel Riverwind's warm breath on her hand.

The Princess Goldmoon spent the remainder of the afternoon in the privacy of her lodge while the rest of the tribe began celebrating in earnest—eating, drinking, dancing, arguing, and brawling. The music filtered into her quarters, making the priestess wish that she could join them, like any other young woman. She sat at her loom, but her shuttle lay unmoving in her lap. Riverwind and Hollow-sky would be seated with her at the evening feast, and she was anxious to know what further surprises they had in store for her.

Finally, her father sent a servant, signaling that it was time for the priestess to dine with the tribe.

A flute and a drummer accompanied her entrance to the torchlit feasting grounds, where she sat at her father's right. The two chosen warriors then entered as the tribe sang a victory song in their honor. They sat opposite her. Goldmoon rose and, with a quick wary glance at Riverwind, invoked a blessing over the food. If the shepherd/warrior objected, he gave no sign. Then the feast began.

Goldmoon hadn't eaten more than two bites, however, before Hollow-sky rose and begged leave to speak.

"I have a gift to present to you, Princess, in honor of this day," he announced.

As the young man spoke, his father, Loreman,

walked proudly toward the head table. He wore a ceremonial cloak decorated with feathers, and he was carrying a heavy, ornate leather book.

Loreman lay the book on the table beside Goldmoon, saying, "It has taken me many long hours to complete this work. It is a history of the generations of Que-shu since the great Cataclysm three hundred years ago. I have condensed many old writings and made them into one book. The last page, you will see, describes the events of this very day. It is for all the people of our tribe to read, but we give it into the care of the princess, and hope she is the first to read it."

There were many murmurs of appreciation from the people seated at the tables near the royal family. A book was a rare thing, and the gift was completely unexpected, especially coming, as it did, from Loreman, who was not noted for his generosity. Goldmoon ran her hand along the smooth cover, delighting in its texture.

Hollow-sky leaned over the table, placing his hand over her own. "Read it carefully, Princess," he whispered.

Goldmoon wanted very dearly to see this last page. She wondered if Loreman had anticipated his two sons winning today's contests, and if he had had to rewrite it. Hawker, seated at his father's table, did not accept defeat graciously, and did not bother to hide his scowl. Goldmoon was suddenly very pleased that Riverwind had defeated him.

"We had best keep it from harm by storing it in your lodge right away," her father suggested, and he abruptly whisked the book out of her possession.

"Perhaps she would prefer to leave it on display or to look at it further," Loreman argued.

"Forgive my haste, Loreman, but it may rain, and we would not want it damaged," Arrowthorn replied in a tight, sharp voice.

The two men stared at each other in an obvious contest of wills, but a moment later the historian deferred with a bow and returned to his own table.

Arrowthorn summoned some of his own men to convey the book to his daughter's lodge.

Goldmoon, anxious to cover the moment's strain, called for the musicians to play. Her father, too, recognized the need for distraction and bid them, "Play a merry tune, to whet the people's appetite for dancing so that they might not overeat."

Laughing at the chieftain's joke, the people began to feast in earnest. Goldmoon noted that Riverwind had a hearty appetite, if not the most dainty table manners. Hollow-sky, on the other hand, though well-trained in what passed for courtly graces among the Que-shu, picked sulkily at his meal.

Less than half an hour into the meal, young people began to rise from their tables to dance. Goldmoon felt a momentary twinge of envy at their freedom and knew that the emotion had shown on her face when Riverwind asked, "Would you like to dance?" Once again he gave her that warm smile.

Hollow-sky quickly interjected, "Chieftain's Daughter does not dance. But then an infidel shepherd could not be expected to know her as well as a long-time family friend. Perhaps a short walk would suit better," he added, holding out his arm for her to take.

Goldmoon gritted her teeth. It was true that she did not dance. If she were to grow winded, it would be another reminder to her subjects of her mortality, something her father objected to. But Arrowthorn had left the meal early to throw the bones with his generals, and since he was free to indulge in the vice of gambling, Goldmoon could not see what harm there could be in one little dance. There was another reason, as well. She was determined to show Hollow-sky that he could not make her decisions for her.

"Chieftain's Daughter does dance, she just does not always choose to do so," Goldmoon replied coldly. "She chooses to dance now with Riverwind. Later she chooses to walk with Hollow-sky, for she has a few things to say to him."

"Alas, lady, but I must rest early tonight if I'm to be a good guardian in the morning," Hollow-sky objected.

"Then rest well, Hollow-sky," Goldmoon remarked, shrugging. Abruptly, she took Riverwind's arm and moved toward the dancers.

Actually, Goldmoon had *never* danced in public before. Humming the music, she had practiced in the privacy of her lodge, doing as many of the steps as she could recall seeing. But *really* dancing was quite different. As Riverwind led her away from the tables, she began to stiffen.

A calloused but gentle finger ran down the inside of her forearm, startling her into looking up at her partner. "The musicians want to know what dance you choose," Riverwind said softly.

"Please, choose for me," Goldmoon whispered back urgently.

"Something simple enough for my great, clumsy feet," he joked.

Goldmoon looked up into his blue eyes. He knows, she thought, that at this I am not infallible, yet he is kind enough to cover for me.

Riverwind untied the long, burgundy sash at his waist and held it above his head with a great flourish. "The princess chooses 'Tiger-hunt,'" he announced loudly.

Goldmoon relaxed. Tiger-hunt was a reel. Very simple. She noted Hollow-sky's sister, Ravenhair, smiling weakly at her, obviously vexed. But for Goldmoon, Ravenhair had the highest standing among the women of the tribe. She would have led the dance if the princess had remembered her place and stayed off the dance ground.

The high staccato notes of the flutes pierced the air as Goldmoon took her place a few paces behind Riverwind. Riverwind stamped his foot and tossed one end of the sash behind him. Goldmoon echoed the stamp with a lighter patting of her foot, just short of the sash's end. Riverwind walked a few steps forward, pulling the sash in a teasing manner, a hunter baiting a tigress.

Goldmoon pounced forward and scooped up the end of the sash in one graceful motion. She gave it a tug and Riverwind spun on his heel to face her. The hunter's look was in his eyes again, and the torchlight glittering in his blue irises made them appear red. Holding the sash between them, the shepherd and the princess circled one another, Goldmoon entranced by those eyes.

She had always found this dance a little silly, and never understood its popularity. It seemed better suited to children's play. Yet, as Riverwind fell to one knee and she spun about him at the end of the sash, she suddenly understood the dance's true meaning.

Riverwind gave a tug, and Goldmoon began spinning toward him, winding herself into the sash. As soon as she was within his reach, Riverwind caught hold of her and pulled her self-tied form down to his knee. With his arm wrapped about her, it seemed to Goldmoon that Riverwind was not as large as her father, but there was no doubt he was powerful, at the height of his manhood.

There was a pause in the music, and Goldmoon became aware that all about them young men were taking the opportunity to snatch kisses from their "helpless" partners. Her heart beat with anticipation. With a flick of her tongue, Goldmoon moistened her lips, but Riverwind held her stiffly, his eyes averted from her face, staring out into the starlit night.

Though his face was stern, Goldmoon could tell that he was breathing more heavily than the dancing's pace warranted, and with her arm pressed against his naked chest, she could feel his heart pounding.

Goldmoon leaned closer. Riverwind's breathing quickened. He started to turn his face directly to hers when the flute trilled without warning and the dance resumed.

Riverwind and all the other "hunters" gave a tug on their sashes, sending the "tigresses" spinning outward like tops. In a flurry of laughter and bright-colored clothes, each woman shifted around the next man.

"I'll have that flute player flogged!" Goldmoon muttered to herself as she smiled politely at her new partner, Hartbow, Watcher's son. They repeated the same silly pantomime with his blue sash. Hartbow's eyes were blue, too, but the light did not catch them the way it had Riverwind's, and Hartbow's look was not very predatory. He, too, took no liberty with her as she sat, bound up, on his knee, but smiled shyly at her.

It was the same with all the rest of her partners. Some, she sensed, would have kissed her if they'd had more nerve. Hollow-sky would certainly not have hesitated, but he had not stayed for the dance. Still, she found herself irritated that no other Que-shu warrior had the courage to touch his lips to her own. No one had even held her as closely as Riverwind had.

"Is Riverwind kissing his other partners?" she wondered curiously. "Does he watch them with the same hunter's look?" It was impossible to sneak a peek at him, though, and still pay attention to what she was doing. The pauses in the music and the uneasiness of her partners became more unbearable. Embarrassed and frustrated, she vowed silently not to wait until her wedding night for a kiss. . . .

Then Goldmoon was once again only one partner away from Riverwind. He danced with Ravenhair. They held each other as aloofly as possible. Goldmoon understood that Ravenhair resented Riverwind's defeat of her brother, Hawker. But whether her escort had been so distant with all his other partners, the princess could not know.

The last repeat to the dance came with all the original couples together. Goldmoon studied the lines of Riverwind's back and legs, not truly paying much attention to the sash he snaked in front of her, so she was a little late diving for it. But when he tugged, she had a firm grip and tugged back with equal ferocity.

He looked just a little surprised, which made her smile, and if she could have seen herself, she would have recognized the tigress in her eyes. She spun about him, pulling hard, watching his muscles strain to hold onto the sash. Then she twirled herself into his arms. Bound, sitting on his knee with his arms about her, she realized that he was as much a prisoner as she, hardly able to dump his princess on the ground before the whole tribe. The tigress had won.

Placing her arms around Riverwind's neck, Goldmoon pulled his head toward her and pressed her soft lips against his, just as she'd seen the others do but as she'd never done herself.

Riverwind's arms tightened about her, and he kissed her back with a passion that sent an unexpected thrill of pleasure through her body. His mouth tasted of the sweet fruit they'd eaten at dinner, and his bare arms were warm against her sweat-cooled flesh. Suddenly he pulled his head away from hers, as though he had just realized he was kissing Chieftain's Daughter before the entire tribe. His face flushed darkly as he heard murmurs and giggles.

Goldmoon, breathing hard, spun out of his sash without his help. She turned abruptly and walked from the dance ground, leaving her partner behind as the music diminished.

Her father, standing at the edge of the crowd, watched her approach. But before he could begin to chide her, Goldmoon raised her chin and announced, "I go now to my lodge to pray for a safe journey to the resting place of my ancestors. Good night, my chieftain." She kissed him gently on his cheek and walked past him. Suddenly he didn't seem so very much larger than Riverwind. For that matter, Riverwind did not seem quite so overpowering either.

Arrowthorn came to Goldmoon's lodge before dawn, before even the night owls ceased their hunting. He sat beside her on the edge of her cot. "We must speak."

Goldmoon sat up with a yawn. She thought the lecture on dancing was coming. But when she looked at Arrowthorn, she knew something much more serious was wrong. Her father looked tired, as though he had not slept.

"It's about Riverwind, isn't it?" She sighed.

Arrowthorn snorted derisively. "Among other things," he answered. "Since he is still the least of our worries, we will start with him. You know you can never marry him?"

"Oh? Why not?"

"Because our tribe has enough trouble remaining stable without you adding the killing blow. Riverwind is an unbeliever. The man you marry will become chieftain when I die, and the chieftain cannot be an unbeliever. If a chieftain denies your authority, he denies his own, leaving a wedge for another power to drive into the tribe, destroying it."

Goldmoon shrugged. "Riverwind is taking me to the Hall of the Sleeping Spirits. There, when I speak with the gods, he will learn his error."

"More likely the gods will speak with you and not allow their words to be heard by the heretic," Arrowthorn argued.

"But for his disbelief, he would make a good chieftain," Goldmoon countered. "Even you were impressed with him—I could tell. I will beg the gods to give him a sign. Surely Mother will not deny me that."

At the mention of Tearsong, Arrowthorn's warrior's frame shuddered. The years since his wife had died of fever and slipped into godhood had been too long and too lonely. He had carried all the responsibility for raising their daughter, ruling and protecting the tribe, and keeping the likes of Loreman from tearing it apart. But the joy that should have been his reward— lying beside Tearsong every night—was denied him. His leadership and strength had suffered from her absence, and he knew it better than any other. Whenever he let Loreman get his way without an argument, whenever he wasted entire evenings gambling, whenever some battle scar ached or a coughing fit seized him (as they did more and more often these days), Arrowthorn was full of self-loathing. He cursed his unworthiness and lived in despair that he would ever join Tearsong as a god.

The only thing he had to feel proud of was Goldmoon, but if she continued with this stubborn championing of the heretic Riverwind, she, too, would be lost.

There were more immediate dangers than Riverwind, however. "We waste time on this," Arrowthorn declared. "We must speak of the book."

"Hollow-sky's gift? I was wondering about that. I could not find it last night. I wanted to read the last page."

"It is in my lodge. If I could, I would burn it before I would let it defile your eyes."

"Father! Why?"

"It is full of slanders, vile insinuations against the line of priestesses and all the warriors they have married and made chieftains. At the same time it praises Loreman's line. One who reads this book would think the tribe survived only because of the wisdom and generosity of Loreman's ancestors."

"But how can that be? Loreman said he condensed it from ancient writings?"

"If I could get my hands on those writings . . . but Loreman's grandfather hid them away from the tribe. 'For safekeeping,' he said, in anticipation, no doubt, of the day his jackal heirs would gain the daring to threaten us."

"They've given it to me in public, for the whole tribe to read, so we could not burn it," Goldmoon reasoned.

Arrowthorn nodded. "Loreman must have hoped that you would believe it, be shamed by it, and marry one of his sons to gain some semblance of respectability."

"That is exceedingly unlikely." Goldmoon sniffed.

"There was a time you cared very much for Hollow-sky," he said quietly.

Goldmoon's eyes narrowed.

Arrowthorn looked away from his daughter, his eyes misted with tears she must not see. The chieftain had hoped Goldmoon could love whatever man she must marry, but her disgust for Hollow-sky was clear. He spoke softly, "This matter has weighed heavily on me for many years. I do not want you to be unhappy, Goldmoon, and I can understand that your feelings for Hollow-sky have cooled now that you are older and your judgment more sound. But if no other powerful warrior of worthy family can be found, you must consider Hollow-sky your only suitor. Your marriage to him would keep our tribe together." He paused and added, "That is your duty."

Goldmoon breathed deeply, controlling her turbulent feelings. It was rare that her father expressed his concern for her happiness, and she was touched that he did so now. But that did little to soften her anger. Now any accusations she made against Hollow-sky for sabotaging his opponents' poles yesterday would look like a weak counter-attack; Hollow-sky's character did not enter into this, only his skill as a warrior and his family's position in the tribe. The injustice galled her.

"Why must my duty to the tribe always come first?" she asked. "Why can't I choose with my heart as other women may?"

"You are not as other women." Arrowthorn raised his hands as though they were the trays of a balancing scale. "Weigh carefully which is more important, your heart or your duty. Consider—Loreman is powerful, Hollow-sky may become even more so. Unless you wed a strong leader whom all the people will follow, you will never be able to fend off the historian's or his son's lust for the office of chieftain. They will divide and splinter the tribe. Then there will be no priestess, no Book of the Gods, no faith. We must prevent this at all costs, even if it means sacrificing our happiness." He rose and gently stroked her hair as he had when she was a child. Then he left without another word.

Goldmoon's head remained bowed in humility at her father's words and the tears she had seen gleaming in his eyes. Arrowthorn was right. The tribe must be kept together at any price. She could not leave her people without her guidance as a priestess. And the Book of the Gods must be preserved, for in that volume the names of those who were to become gods at death were written down. The faith that had bound her people since the time of darkness must remain intact. She resolved to put her father's worries to rest. She would bear the burden for these responsibilities, but on her own terms.

It was now imperative that Tearsong help her bring Riverwind to the true religion of the Que-shu. If the warrior became a believer, her father could have no strong objection to their union. She was confident that Loreman and Hollow-sky would be no match for her with Riverwind by her side.

The princess was dressed in her riding leathers of doeskin when Clearwing and Starflower finally came in to attend her. She had already packed up her own bedroll for travel.

"Forgive us for keeping you waiting, mistress," Clearwing begged.

"It is of no matter, Clearwing," Goldmoon said softly. "I rose very early. Just do my hair quickly. I'm anxious to be off."

The very first golden rays of morning lit the grasslands as Chieftain's Daughter stepped from her lodge to begin her journey to speak with her gods. Many villagers had turned out to see her off, despite the early hour. Riverwind held her horse's reins and stroked the animal's forehead. Hollow-sky stepped forward.

"Allow me to help you up, Princess."

Goldmoon paused. Her father watched them, looking older and more tired than she had ever seen him look before. She could make his life and her own

Laura Hickman and Kate Novak

much simpler. Hollow-sky's hand reached out for her own.

What kind of goddess has no pride? she thought. She turned a withering look on Hollow-sky and said in a frigid tone, "I've been riding horses since before I could walk! Do I look as if I need help, Hollow-sky, son of Loreman?" She grabbed her horse's mane and pulled herself onto its back.

Hollow-sky and Riverwind mounted their own beasts while Clearwing and Starflower climbed into a small cart driven by Clearwing's younger brother.

Without warning, a flutter of dark wings swooped down on the princess. Goldmoon felt a pinch at her scalp. She cried out more from surprise than pain. Glancing up, she saw a huge raven circling overhead, cawing fiercely, waiting for another opportunity to strike.

"It is an evil omen!" Loreman cried.

"Nonsense," Riverwind countered. The bird plunged again at the princess, but a twang of a bow put an arrow through its breast, and it dropped to the ground with a thud. A boy in the crowd retrieved it and handed it up to Riverwind, for it had been the shepherd's arrow that felled the creature.

"You are a very quick notch and aim," Goldmoon complimented him.

Riverwind smiled at her.

"It is an omen," Loreman repeated more loudly, "of war!"

"Just a crow"—Riverwind laughed—"that wanted to steal the princess's shiny treasure." Carefully he drew out several strands of long, golden hair clenched in the bird's claws. He held them up for the crowd to see. "Wealth beyond any man's dreams," he called out. "Who can blame the poor crow?"

The crowd laughed, and as the sun shone even

brighter, the evil feeling was dispelled. The crowd cheered as the party left, Goldmoon in the lead.

When the near-silent party crossed into lands the Que-shu shared with other tribes—sometimes disputed over—Hollow-sky took the point, which he considered his by his superior rank, while Riverwind rode behind the princess.

As they settled into their new positions, Goldmoon held her horse back from Hollow-sky's and signaled for Riverwind to ride alongside her. She saw that the raven was strapped to his saddlebag.

"What are you going to do with that bird?"

Riverwind grinned. "Later, we will see if it is good eating. Some of them are, you know."

Goldmoon shook her head. It was not a dish she had ever been served. Noticing then that the Plainsman had her strands of stolen hair still wrapped about his fingers, she gave a slight, hastily concealed smile.

Riverwind looked down at his hand to see what made her smile. "Stolen gold," he murmured, flushing. "These are yours, I believe, lady," he said, untangling the golden threads from his fingers and leaning over to hand them to her.

Goldmoon took the hair carefully.

"It is a lovely color." Greatly daring, he reached over to push back a strand of living hair that had fallen across her eyes.

Feeling a thrill at his touch and knowing that her own cheeks must be burning, Goldmoon hastily smoothed her hair over her shoulder. To cover her pleasure, she held up the broken strands. "Thank you for saving these for me," she laughed awkwardly. "I can hardly be Goldmoon without the golden hair."

Riverwind looked back at her. "Of course you can. You were Goldmoon when you were born, and you were quite bald then."

"That's ridiculous!" Goldmoon said, shocked. "How dare you?"

Riverwind shrugged. "It's true. You can ask Hollow-sky, if you like—he must remember. Though he's not likely to tell you the truth if he thinks it will displease you."

Goldmoon closed her mouth on the disparaging comment she had been about to make. Riverwind certainly understood Hollow-sky. She thought for a moment, then argued, "I don't believe there is such a thing as a bald baby. I've never seen one."

"Well, you've never seen anyone with hair like yours, have you?" Riverwind returned. "I was five when I first saw you. I remember asking Wanderer if you'd been sick, because you had only tiny, pale wisps of hair. He told me that you were going to have light hair, and that sometimes light hair comes in more slowly. He said such things were natural among distant tribes. You will see for yourself, no doubt."

"What do you mean?" Goldmoon asked.

"When you have a baby of your own," Riverwind explained.

Goldmoon flushed and looked away, disturbed at the direction the conversation had taken. She lowered her head, allowing her golden hair to fall across her feverish cheeks. The thought of bringing up little Hollow-skys, grandchildren for Loreman, was disgusting! But Riverwind . . .

She was silent for so long that Riverwind asked, "Is something wrong, Princess? Have I offended—"

Goldmoon shook her head. "Tell me about your family," she said, glad to change the subject. "Didn't your father used to be a tanner? Why did he leave the village and become a shepherd?"

Riverwind raised his eyebrows in surprise. "The story is common knowledge," he answered.

"I have not heard it," Goldmoon replied firmly.

Riverwind shrugged and proceeded to explain. "During the summer of drought, the Que-shu battled with the Que-kiri, and my grandfather Wanderer was wounded. Your father went to the village of the Que-kiri to negotiate a peace, and since you were still far too young to sit in judgment, Loreman sat in your place. As Wanderer lay dying, Loreman came to him and offered to write his name in the Book of the Gods—to make him a god for his bravery in battle. But Wanderer refused, saying that men could not make gods of each other."

Goldmoon bit her lip, determined to hear Riverwind's story in full before debating truths with him.

"Loreman was angry and declared that Wanderer had planted a dark seed, meaning, of course, my family's belief in gods more ancient than the gods of the tribe. Loreman decreed that the seed must not spread beyond our family. So he confiscated my father's trade and cast us out. We may live only at the edge of the Que-shu's lands. Therefore, tending sheep and hunting are our only ways of making a livelihood."

"And having granted Loreman the authority, my father could not undo what he had decreed," Goldmoon added. She silently determined that she would do something to reverse Loreman's ban on Riverwind's family when she returned. She had only to prove to Riverwind that her ancestors were the true gods to get him to give up his ridiculous belief in the foreign gods of Wanderer.

Hollow-sky dropped back by the twosome, causing the cart-horse behind them to whinny in annoyance and prance to reposition itself behind the riders' horses. A peevish look marred Hollow-sky's fine-boned face. He gave Riverwind a cursory glance of disdain and then turned his attention on Goldmoon.

"Great Lady," he began, "if you would ride ahead with me, I would enjoy talking with you on such a fine day."

Riverwind's face darkened with hostility, and Goldmoon wished Hollow-sky would vanish.

"Lady?" Hollow-sky queried, impatiently. His hands gripped his reins too tightly.

Riverwind's hand slid smoothly along his longstick in a vaguely threatening manner. In response, Hollow-sky, with seeming casualness, ruffled the feathers atop his own pole.

If I do not separate them, Goldmoon thought, they are likely to continue with yesterday's contest.

"Please excuse me," she said regretfully to Riverwind. "Come, Hollow-sky." She nudged her horse ahead a bit, and Hollow-sky followed.

The party of riders and servants made only a few short stops to stretch their legs. They ate dried meat and fruit on the trail. It was a typical summer afternoon on the open plains—hot and still. Grass insects hummed and swarmed and made a nuisance of themselves. The only excitement of the ride came when their passing flushed birds out of the grass or when snakes or small animals underfoot startled the horses.

At last, just when Goldmoon felt she could no longer bear her own trickling sweat, they began to climb into the hills at the foot of the mountain that held their goal. Cool, pine-scented air reached the travelers, renewing their energy and spirits.

The trail became steeper and narrower. Just when it seemed that the cart could go no farther, a high meadow came into view. Here Goldmoon instructed Clearwing and Starflower to unhitch the cart horse and load it with her belongings. They were then to make camp and await her return, which should be by midday the next day. Her serving women were reluctant to let her go on without them, but she repeated her orders, eyeing them sternly. No one but herself and her two escorts were allowed on the holy ground.

Goldmoon and her escorts continued upward with the cart horse. The trail grew worse; in some spots it became almost vertical. The cart-horse-turned-pack animal balked, and Riverwind had to dismount and coax, tug, and push it along. Hollow-sky watched without offering to help, an amused look on his face. Finally, they came to a spot where the horse refused to be moved no matter what Riverwind did.

Tossing her horse's reins disdainfully to Hollow-sky, Goldmoon slid off her horse and joined Riverwind. She covered the animal's eyes with her hands and murmured softly in its ears. When she sensed the beast relax, she tugged gently and it followed her along the rim.

Riverwind stared at her with admiration, but Goldmoon, failing to acknowledge it, remounted without a word, and they continued on.

The path divided unexpectedly on the lower slopes of the mountain itself, one trail heading up the west slope, the other the east.

"Which way, Princess?" Hollow-sky asked.

Goldmoon's brow furrowed in puzzlement. "I do not know. I thought there was only one trail."

"The shadows are lengthening," Hollow-sky said unnecessarily. "If we take the wrong route and need to turn back, we shall have to travel in the dark to be there when Lunitari's rays open the cavern, and that could be dangerous."

The princess wondered why Arrowthorn had not warned her of this. She looked for signs that one trail was newer than the other, but she really could not tell.

"Why don't you rest, Princess?" Hollow-sky said. "I

will scout down one path and return as quickly as I am able. And you, shepherd, scout the other."

Goldmoon bristled. Riverwind was not an underling for Hollow-sky to command, and worse, the son of Loreman was again making decisions and giving orders on her behalf.

"You will scout the trail, Hollow-sky," she said firmly, "and Riverwind will remain here as guard." Her tone brooked no argument.

Hollow-sky sat stiffly astride his horse as Riverwind dismounted, tossing a tight-lipped smile at his rival. Hollow-sky's fingers strayed to the feathers atop his long stick as they had earlier. Ignoring the subtle challenge, Riverwind defiantly turned his back on Hollow-sky.

The Plainsman stood alertly at the path's divide and watched Hollow-sky depart, as Goldmoon sat down on the ground and leaned against a tree.

"Come sit with me, please," she commanded.

Riverwind lowered himself into a cross-legged position before his Chieftain's Daughter.

"I have something for you. I made it during the ride across the plain," Goldmoon whispered. She held out her hand, displaying a small golden circlet. "You rescued them from the crow," she said, and Riverwind saw that she had woven the strands of her hair which he had rescued into a lacy ring. She laid it in the warrior's palm, where it glistened golden in the sun.

Riverwind was silent for many long moments staring down at the gift. When he finally slipped it around a finger, Goldmoon let out the breath she found she'd been holding for fear he would reject it.

Drawing a chain from his shirt and removing it over his head, Riverwind said, "I would like you to have this."

Goldmoon quickly shook her head. "You don't have

to give me anything in return."

"You must take it," Riverwind insisted. "I have already accepted two gifts from you."

"Two?"

Riverwind reached up and placed a hand over the pole strapped to his back. "This was not Wanderer's weapon."

"Well, I'm afraid his weapon was . . ." Goldmoon paused confusedly—"damaged."

"I thought as much. Why did you replace only mine?"

"It was the only one I knew about. I wanted the contest to be judged by the gods, not by mortals."

Riverwind nodded. "I see."

"But I am not displeased that you were one of the victors," Goldmoon assured him.

Riverwind smiled at her, the smile of a friend. "Then please," he said, "accept this."

Taking the chain from him, Goldmoon saw that it was made of common brass, but the charm hanging at the end—two circles joined together—was of brilliantly polished silver-blue steel, so valued a metal among the Que-shu that it was never used to make jewelry.

"It's called an infinity sign or a forever charm. But it is more than a decoration—it will protect you, keep you from harm."

Looking slightly puzzled, Goldmoon ran her fingers around the steel circles. "This has something to do with the ancient gods, doesn't it?" she asked.

Riverwind nodded. "It is the symbol of a goddess, but her name was lost to the memory of our people as were all the names of the true gods. I suspect Loreman knows them, but he will not say."

On first hearing that the charm was a symbol of a strange goddess, Goldmoon was tempted to reject the gift. However, if Loreman does not like it, she thought, perhaps there is some good to it. She slipped the chain over her head and tucked the amulet into her shirt.

Riverwind, too, let out his held breath and smiled gently at his princess.

They sat quietly, giving in to their fatigue. Goldmoon's eyes closed.

The sound of galloping hooves startled Goldmoon awake. While she slept Riverwind must have tucked her fur cloak around her. He stood alert, his bow at the ready. But it was Hollow-sky who rode up, his face flushed with excitement.

"This must be the right path. It leads to a road like none I have ever seen before. Hurry, the sun is going down."

Goldmoon and Riverwind mounted up and followed Hollow-sky down the path he had scouted. About a quarter of a mile along it suddenly turned into a broad road, at least ten feet wide and paved with huge, flat stones, work never seen among the tribes of the plains. Still, it seemed familiar to Goldmoon, though she could not tell why.

Although the slope was steep, traveling was easier now, for the way was quite smooth and they could let the horses trot. There was still plenty of light in the sky when they arrived at the landmark Arrowthorn had described to Goldmoon—a large stone arch straddling the road.

"I recognize this stonework," the princess said, relieved to know they were on the right road. "It's just like the platform in our village."

Riding underneath the arch, she halted her horse where she could touch the cool rock. Looking up, she saw symbols carved on the underside of the arch. Many were unrecognizable, but the largest, carved at the apex of the arch, consisted of two circles joined together. Goldmoon drew out the amulet Riverwind had given her and gasped softly. The steel charm glowed with a soft blue light in the shadow of the rock.

"Is something wrong, Princess?" Hollow-sky asked, turning to see why she had not passed all the way through.

Instantly Goldmoon cupped her hand about the symbol to hide its light and tucked it back into her shirt. "No, nothing," she said coolly, riding on through the archway.

Beyond the arch was a large, grassy clearing, surrounded by tall, ancient pine trees. The clearing sloped upward to a stairway carved out of the stone of the mountain. Set into the cliff face at the top of the stairs was a pair of huge stone doors. Goldmoon sat motionless on her horse for several minutes, just gazing at those doors. Beyond them, she knew, lay her ancestors who were now gods and goddesses. But most special to Goldmoon was her mother, Tearsong.

Goldmoon remembered her mother alive, laughing and beautiful. She also remembered her ill and dying. And she remembered her dead, encased in the sarcophagus which held her remains until the doors above had opened ten years ago, allowing Arrowthorn to entomb them at last. The princess's dearest and most secret wish was to see her mother again, as a goddess, laughing and beautiful.

A touch on her forearm made Goldmoon turn. Silently, Riverwind made a gesture toward the plains they had crossed. Far below, the sun was setting on the golden fields, painting them a rosy-purple hue. She could pick out a hundred hawks rising on late afternoon thermals, sighting prey, and swooping down on their dinners. Farther off, barely visible, were the thin wisps of smoke which she knew came from her father's village. "It's beautiful," she whispered.

"Shepherd, you cook supper while I tend to the animals," Hollow-sky ordered, tossing a bag of ground grain at Riverwind's feet.

Riverwind nudged the bag with his boot and said flatly, "I will roast the crow instead—after I've cared for my own horse and pitched the princess's tent."

Hollow-sky clenched his jaw, and his eyes narrowed as he inhaled deeply, an angry reply bubbling to his lips.

Assessing the tension, Goldmoon took command. "It is kind of you to raise my tent, Riverwind," she said lightly. Turning to Hollow-sky, she added, "You may make the porridge after you've attended to the pack animals."

"As you command, Princess," Hollow-sky replied coldly.

When Riverwind finished pitching her tent, Goldmoon arranged her things within. She laid out the ceremonial garb she would wear later—a long, sky-blue gown embroidered with gold crescent moons on the hem and sleeves.

Outside, Riverwind roasted the bird that had stolen Goldmoon's hair, while Hollow-sky stirred a pot of boiling cereal, eyeing the bird with apparent disdain. In the brisk mountain air, after the long day's journey, Goldmoon would have found anything delicious. Hollow-sky's well-prepared meal was quite satisfying, but the smell of Riverwind's bird was mouthwatering. So when the warrior declared it done and offered her a portion, Goldmoon could not resist, though Hollow-sky only sneered and would have none of it.

Replete, Goldmoon rose to go to her tent. She

smiled when she saw Riverwind attempt to hide a yawn and fail utterly.

Hollow-sky, on the other hand, seemed to be filled with energy. "If it pleases you, Princess, I will take first watch. Riverwind has worked hard to get us here, he could use some sleep."

Goldmoon looked at Loreman's son, amazed at his sudden thoughtfulness, not to mention the fact that he'd asked her permission before making a decision.

Observing her astonishment, Hollow-sky said lamely, "It is the least I can do."

Wordlessly nodding her assent, Goldmoon hurried off to her tent. The night air was bitter cold. Once wrapped in her warm sleeping furs and rugs, the princess/priestess dropped off to sleep immediately.

She seemed to have slept only a few minutes when Hollow-sky, at the door to her tent, called her name softly. "Dawn is only half an hour off."

Shaking off the temptation to curl up in her warm rugs again, Goldmoon dressed hurriedly in her ceremonial robe and stepped out of the shelter of her cozy tent into the predawn coolness. It was time for the ceremony for which she had waited all these years. She fastened several, small, ancient crystal globes on her belt. In the Hall of the Sleeping Spirits, they would be filled with sacred sand.

"Where is Riverwind?" she whispered to Hollow-sky as he handed her a torch.

"I could not wake him, so I took both watches. The sheep-herder sleeps like a rock," he said, contempt in his voice.

"Try again!" Goldmoon commanded.

Hollow-sky shrugged. "Why bother? The sheep-herder is not a believer. The ceremony will mean nothing to him. He may even spoil it. Let him sleep."

Hollow-sky's refusal to obey her orders angered the priestess.

Goldmoon quickly knelt by Riverwind's bedroll and gave the warrior a shake. But he did not respond.

She spun about and stood to face Hollow-sky. "You've drugged him," she accused.

"Yes," he admitted. "I couldn't let him spoil my plans."

"*Your* plans? What are you talking about?" The princess suddenly felt chilled and even a little frightened in the predawn darkness. She began to search through her saddlebags for something, anything, that might bring Riverwind around.

Hollow-sky shrugged. "I know you will think this presumptuous of me, but I guarantee you will find my plans infinitely preferable to my father's."

"I know about the book, if that's what you mean." She could see nothing of use among her things.

Grabbing her arms, Hollow-sky forcibly turned her back around to face him. "You have no idea, do you?" He grinned and then said, as if explaining to a child, "Goldmoon, my father wants the title of chieftain for himself, but he can't take it as long as Arrowthorn has an heir. If you were out of the way, my sister Ravenhair would be priestess, then my father would be chieftain."

"Out of the way?" she asked in a sharp voice, determined not to reveal the fear spreading through her.

"Yes. Gone. Dead!" He bit off the words as he drew a sharp dagger from his belt and grabbed her roughly around the waist. The knife's edge glinted in the pale light as Hollow-sky held it menacingly near her throat.

"So why didn't you kill me in my sleep?" Goldmoon demanded, feeling the world reel about her. Stubbornly she forced herself to concentrate.

"I told you, I have other plans. I want you for myself, though the gods know why. You really are an arrogant witch sometimes. We'll marry, and then *I'll* be chieftain. Loreman wants the power for himself, but the knowledge that his son, and later his grandchildren, will rule should satisfy him. In the meantime, he'll be content with your dowry." He smiled slightly, a smile that made Goldmoon shudder. "You should thank me for saving your life."

With his free hand, Hollow-sky clenched her hair close to the scalp, forcing her head to tilt back. As tears came to her eyes, Loreman's son kissed her as no man had ever dared to kiss her before. His passion was not an expression of affection, but an assault.

Struggling to wrench her face from him, Goldmoon gasped, "You're dreaming! I'll never marry you." Desperate, she threatened the first thing that came to her: "I'll scream! I'll—"

"There is no one to hear you," he said, sneering.

His crushing grip bruised her shoulders through the silken cloth of her gown. She forced her arms down on the hand holding the dagger and almost succeeded in thrusting him away. He snatched at her and ripped the sleeve from her shoulder. Holding her more firmly than before, his face just inches from hers, the dagger point resting gently against her chin, he said, "Of course, you love the peasant!" He gave Riverwind's unconscious body a sharp kick and smiled cruelly when Goldmoon flinched. "That's why we'll ride down to the Que-kiri this morning. Any woman a man can drag to their priest, they'll declare married. Then, if your father ever wants to see you again, he'll have to agree to my worthiness and accept the vows of the Que-kiri as binding."

He is insane! Goldmoon thought to herself. I will humor him, stall him, until the doors to the hall open.

Then surely the ancestors will aid me!

Goldmoon felt the weight of the forever charm against her breast. Her fingers closed around it. "Please, if this charm truly has a god, then help me now!" she prayed silently. A slow tingling sensation rose in the fingers that held the charm. It was so slight that she wasn't certain she'd felt it. She waited expectantly. Nothing happened. She suddenly felt foolish and angry with herself for even testing the charm.

Forcing herself to relax, she pressed against him, though his hot breath on her face sickened her.

"That's better," Hollow-sky whispered, squeezing her tighter. "Oh, Goldmoon, you'll get used to the idea. You'll discover that I'm more of a man than . . . than that shepherd there." He motioned at the still figure behind his back and moved his face close to hers. "You are so beautiful," he murmured, and then he kissed her again, even more intimately than before.

As Hollow-sky kissed her, she was astonished to detect movement in Riverwind's sleeping-bag. His head poked above the edge, two fingers pressed against his lips in a gesture for silence.

She roughly pushed Hollow-sky back. He scowled and thrust the dagger toward her threateningly, but it never reached the skin. The forever charm gleamed brilliantly, and a single arc of lightning leaped from it and flashed down the dagger, causing Hollow-sky to yelp in pain and drop the weapon. Goldmoon gasped in wonder.

As Hollow-sky stared disbelievingly at his burned hand, Riverwind threw back his bedclothes and stood.

The man reputedly raised by leopards stalked his prey so silently that Hollow-sky was totally unaware of him until Riverwind's two fists landed on his neck. Hollow-sky stumbled forward, stunned, letting go his grip on Goldmoon, who fell back away from him.

The shepherd could have drawn his sword and finished Loreman's son before he ever knew what hit him, but instead Riverwind slid his sparring pole off his back and waited for the other man to recover.

Hollow-sky turned about, his eyes widening with astonishment. "How—?" he started to gasp.

"Draw your pole, carrion crow," Riverwind snarled. "I didn't eat your drug-tainted porridge."

Hollow-sky's hand went for his sword, but Riverwind's pole lashed out. Hollow-sky cradled his injured hand in his other already stinging hand.

"I didn't hurt you badly. Draw your pole before I do," Riverwind warned.

Hollow-sky drew out his sparring pole. The two warriors circled each other warily. Goldmoon crouched on the grass in the pearl-gray of the predawn sky as the echoing crack of wood shattered the silence.

The men thrust and blocked, using jabbing maneuvers that she hadn't seen at the games. With a sharp intake of breath, she realized they weren't sparring but using moves meant only for real combat. Riverwind took a fierce jab under the kneecap, and she heard his gasp of pain. But pain seemed to spur the Plainsman on, for he suddenly whirled his pole aggressively, trying to disarm his opponent. Hollow-sky twisted his pole vertically and stopped the twirling of Riverwind's stick, nearly disarming the princess's champion.

The men were more evenly matched than Goldmoon had thought. Hollow-sky was good. Why he had bothered to sabotage his opponent's poles for the contest, Goldmoon could not understand. Is it possible he did not believe in his own skill, or is he simply so inured to his father's treacheries that he just automatically cheated? she wondered.

Goldmoon bit her lip anxiously.

The sky had taken on a faint reddish light, indicating that the red moon, which would open the doors to the hall, was about to rise. The dawn of the sun was brightening the sky all about her. She could see the combatants' faces clearly now. Riverwind's features were grim and determined. Hollow-sky's eyes were filled with bloodlust and hatred. Goldmoon shivered, but not with cold.

Sweat trickled off the men's bodies despite the cool mountain air. They circled each other again, waiting for an opening in the other's defenses. Goldmoon's fingers dug into the flesh of her arms as the tension rose like the mist in the meadow.

Suddenly, Riverwind snarled like a wild cat. The sound mocked a real wild cat's so accurately that it flushed a small flock of birds from the trees. The noise of their wings diverted Hollow-sky's attention for just an instant, but that was all it took. Riverwind knocked his adversary down, and Hollow-sky lost his grip on his pole. Riverwind closed in to deliver a blow that would knock the traitor senseless—or worse.

But Riverwind's injured knee slowed his attack, and Hollow-sky rolled away, scrambling to his feet. He slipped beneath Riverwind's blocking swing and ran up the stairs that led to the doors of the Hall of the Sleeping Spirits, dragging his pole behind him. Riverwind pursued him, just two steps behind. Goldmoon sprang to her feet and ran across the grass, following the warriors up the stairs.

As she reached the top step, Lunitari, the red moon, made its appearance above the horizon, shedding its light directly across the great stone doors. Very slowly the massive portals began to swing outward, showering gold sparks down on the two men locked in their deadly struggle. The footing on the rock platform outside the doors was slippery with sand, and the sides adjacent to the staircase edge and the door fell off sharply over sheer cliffs.

Goldmoon forgot her desire to gain entrance to the hall as she watched Riverwind, by jabs and blows, push Hollow-sky toward the cliff. Both men teetered dangerously near the edge.

The opening doors nudged Riverwind slightly, breaking his concentration and forcing him to struggle to keep his balance. In that moment, Hollow-sky managed to land a blow across the side of the shepherd's head and face. Dazed, Riverwind raised his staff to block the next attack, but his reactions were slowed. Hollow-sky jabbed wickedly at the shepherd's already injured knee, bringing him crashing down on both knees. Seeing Hollow-sky close in on Riverwind, Goldmoon, consumed by fear for Riverwind's life, drew her crystal dagger.

She lunged forward, holding the dagger high over her head. Hollow-sky, intent on the kill, failed to look up. Goldmoon slammed the dagger down hard, gashing his right arm deeply. Hollow-sky's blood splashed over her dagger and wrist and onto the rock platform.

Startled, Hollow-sky staggered backward—and lost his footing on the sandy precipice. He tumbled over the edge, and his scream echoed up the cliff face, seemingly forever . . . until his body hit the ground below. Bathed in red moonlight, Goldmoon stood staring over the rock's edge, her hair stirred by a gentle thermal rising from below.

"Goldmoon! Come away from there," Riverwind cried, shaken.

As if in a dream, the priestess of the Que-shu turned from the cliff face and moved to the shepherd's side, helping him to his feet. Hollow-sky's scream echoing through her head, she sheathed her dagger without cleaning it.

"I had no choice. He was going to kill you!" she said and suddenly burst into shuddering sobs.

"I know," he answered. "I wanted to protect you this morning, but felt helpless while he held the dagger to your throat. Then the charm . . ." His voice trailed off as Goldmoon softly answered, "Yes, it protected me." Pulling her close to his chest, he stroked her hair in a gentle, calming motion.

Suddenly Goldmoon was very much aware of the man's arms around her. Then, remembering why she was here and how urgent it was that she convince Riverwind of the reality of her gods, she sprang away from him.

"The hall!" she cried. "We must get inside and hold the ceremony quickly before the doors close!"

As though mocking her attempts, the first ray of sunlight shot over the horizon, striking the doorway. The huge stone doors began closing on their own, scraping and rumbling against the stone platform beneath them.

"Hurry!" Goldmoon insisted, tugging Riverwind. With his injured knee, Riverwind had to lean on her to make it through the rapidly narrowing portal.

As they slipped through the opening, it closed with a thunderclap. Beneath the deafening echo, Goldmoon heard Riverwind gasp in pain. "Are you all right?" she asked.

"My injuries are minor," he answered curtly. "How do we open the doors again?"

Goldmoon hesitated. "I'm not sure we can. The ceremony is supposed to be held quickly between the red moon rising and the sunrise, while the doors stand open."

"You mean you risked being trapped in here?" Riverwind hissed angrily. "It's not enough you almost get yourself killed attacking Hollow-sky, you have to also bury yourself alive!"

"I stabbed him to save your life," Goldmoon reminded him with equal curtness.

Riverwind drew away from her. "You should have run," he said coldly, "not tried to save me. After all, I'm supposed to protect you, not the other way around."

"You are no use as a bodyguard if you are dead!" Goldmoon retorted, not understanding her own anger. Remembering those terrible moments when she thought Riverwind was going to die, she began to tremble.

"I suppose not," Riverwind said, chagrined. She could hear him withdraw even further.

Reaching out, Goldmoon found his hands in the darkness and took them in her own. "And, if you had died, I would have died out there, too," she whispered.

Riverwind drew several deep breaths without speaking. Goldmoon could feel his hands quivering in her own. Releasing his hands and moving forward, she wrapped her arms about him and rested her head against his chest. This time she noticed that his leather armor smelled of the spiced oil used to clean it. Riverwind pressed her near, holding her gently. In the cold, damp cavern, he radiated heat like a fire.

"When you first approached womanhood," he whispered, "and I saw then your beauty, I asked my family what age you would have to be before Arrowthorn would allow men to court you." He stroked her hair as he spoke.

Not interrupting him, Goldmoon luxuriated in the feel of his broad back beneath her hands, of his arm about her shoulders.

"My adopted parents tried to make me see that my poverty and faith would always keep us apart," Riverwind continued, "but I would not believe them. You never noticed me when I watched you, but others did, and Loreman himself came to our hut to warn my parents to keep me away from you."

Goldmoon guessed that that must have been the time she'd first heard her father discussing Riverwind with Loreman in hushed tones.

Riverwind continued his story. "My father sent me out to watch sheep in the fields farthest from the village. My mother's skill at weaving is great, so many send their daughters to apprentice under her, even though Loreman has forbidden it. My mother would invite the loveliest of these girls to eat with our family, but the memory of your face stayed with me. Then one night, Wanderer's spirit came to me and told me of the games held to choose escorts for the priestess's pilgrimage to this place. He said that some day you would give your heart to one of those escorts."

"And so I have," Goldmoon whispered. She raised her lips, so that she could kiss him, but Riverwind pulled away from her and held her at arms length.

"I must admit," the warrior said, "I felt certain of myself, seated next to you at the banquet. I could not imagine you with Hollow-sky, though my mother often warned me that the two of you were a likely match. When I saw you watching the dancers and realized you wanted to dance, I thought, 'She is just a woman, like other women.' But I was wrong. You will never be just a woman. You are and always will be Chieftain's Daughter. Now I doubt my worthiness. I am still poor, and our gods remain different."

Goldmoon was silent for many moments, before she said, "If I do not doubt your worthiness, then neither should you. And your fortunes might change."

"And the gods?" Riverwind asked.

"They will show us a way."

"Whose?"

"Yours, mine, both—it makes no difference. My mother used to say that hope is a gift from the gods we must never lose."

"My mother has said that, too," Riverwind replied. "Well, we must find some way out of here, or it will truly make no difference to our corpses!"

Goldmoon felt him take her hand in his and together they edged their way along the wall. They reached the passageway without trouble.

Wondering if her eyes were playing tricks, Goldmoon asked, "Is that a light ahead?"

"I think so." They moved more quickly along the corridor toward the light. Soon it grew bright enough that they could see all about them. Looking for the source of the illumination, Goldmoon saw movement on the smooth cut rock. Looking closer, she realized that the light came from brightly glowing red spots on the insects' backs.

"I think they're fire beetles," Riverwind said.

"Those are only in children's stories."

"I think we are in a children's story," Riverwind said, able to chuckle a little in relief. "Let me have your crystal globe. These little light legends may not live in other passages, so we will need to take them with us."

Goldmoon unfastened the crystal globe from her belt and surrendered it. The other two globes still lay on the grass outside. Riverwind gently scraped several of the beetles into the sphere.

"Here's the lid," she offered.

"I'm afraid they might suffocate."

"Air will get in. There are tiny holes in the lid," the priestess explained. "I've often wondered why. Do you suppose these globes were originally made for this purpose?" she asked.

"This one functions well as a lamp. That is all that is

important." Riverwind held the globe up by its straps, and they made their way safely into the crypts of the Que-shu royalty.

The crypt cavern was so huge that their little light did not illuminate the ceiling or the walls beyond. At the edge of the darkness they could make out the shape of the tombs. The very first they came to bore the inscription, "Tearsong—beloved of Arrowthorn." Goldmoon slid her hand along the words and then snatched it back. The rock was cold. "Cold as death," she thought, shuddering slightly. She moved hurriedly past the memorial to her mother.

The floor sloped down as they passed the remains of three centuries of the princess's ancestors. At the bottom of the slope, Goldmoon could make out a stone altar, carved with the forever sign of her amulet. Realizing that she shouldn't be able to see the carving in the darkness, she became aware that the light around the altar was blue, not red, and that it came from the altar.

The priestess knew that the moment she had awaited had come. She knelt in front of the altar and sang:

> *"The red sun has risen.*
> *The blue doors have opened.*
> *I kneel here before you,*
> *To sing you my song.*
> *You who have left us,*
> *We ask for your blessing."*

Goldmoon waited patiently in prayerful silence for several minutes, but nothing happened, no one answered. Fear crept into her. Was there some part of this ceremony that her father had not known about, something that Tearsong had carried with her to the grave?

Then a voice spoke, "My beloved child! What joy it

is to see you!"

"Mother!" Goldmoon cried out. Her throat constricted in emotion as all the years of loneliness and longing for Tearsong, of quickly suppressed doubt that she would ever actually speak to her again, overwhelmed the young priestess.

Tearsong's laughter rang through the hall like tinkling glass and filled Goldmoon with a pleasure that was also painful. The air shimmered with light as Tearsong's form coalesced in the air behind Goldmoon. Tears of grief and joy welled in the princess's eyes. A harvest of loving memories, which had long lain dormant in sorrow, filled her. Her mother's sculpted features and jet-black hair were even more lovely than she remembered.

"Mother. This is Riverwind," Goldmoon started to say, turning around to summon the warrior forward, but all was darkness behind her.

"I cannot appear to Riverwind."

"But you must! You see, he does not believe that—"

"—that I am a goddess." Tearsong nodded. "He is right. I am a spirit only, and I have only a little time to speak with you—so listen carefully. You are a woman now, Goldmoon, and you must hear the truth and accept it. The gods of the Que-shu, the gods I served all my life, are false. It makes no difference whether or not Loreman has written your name in the tribe's Book of the Gods. Men cannot make gods of each other."

"But I am Chieftain's Daughter!" Goldmoon protested in disbelief.

The spirit of Tearsong smiled at her daughter's arrogance. "Your status in life, whether chieftain or healer, priestess or shepherd, has no influence on the judgment of the true gods. And the true gods will be your final judges, not your tribe, not your father, not myself. The true gods reward each person in the afterlife according to his or her virtues, not some circumstance of birth."

Goldmoon shook her head, stunned. After Loreman's betrayal and Hollow-sky's attack, this was too much to bear. An idea came to her. "This is some kind of test of my faith. Oh, Mother, I will never turn from our gods. I will believe in you always."

A sad expression crossed Tearsong's face. "Your love for me is very great," she said. "That is why I was chosen to tell you of the true gods."

Tears filled Goldmoon's eyes, streaming down her cheeks, dropping onto her robe, leaving dark marks on the blue fabric. "But the spirits of the Que-shu will not obey me after death if I am not a goddess—" the princess argued, feeling cheated.

Her mother's tone sharpened impatiently. "You would do better to be grateful now for the gift of life and all it has to offer you, than to dwell on what power you will have in death." Death, even without godhood, had not robbed Tearsong of her air of authority. Goldmoon was instantly silent and looked down at the ground in shame.

Tearsong's voice softened at the sight of her daughter's confusion and unhappiness. "Time grows short. Will you listen to what I have to tell you, daughter?"

"Yes," Goldmoon nodded, eager to please her mother, lest she leave her.

"This place was really once the temple of one of the true gods, Riverwind's gods, a goddess known as the Great Healer. Long ago, after the Cataclysm, people despaired and abandoned their belief in the true gods. They must believe again, or this world will be conquered by an ancient evil. I have been sent to offer you the first of many tests. If you pass these tests, you will, in time, serve the Great Healer and lead people as her priestess, as a true healer."

"Tell me what this test is, and I will accept it."

"It will not be easy. If you pass this test, harder tests will follow, tests that may break your spirit, others that may destroy your body."

Goldmoon straightened her back and answered proudly, "I accept that."

"Very well, daughter. The first test is this. You must sacrifice these three things:

> *That which hinders healing.*
> *That which hinders loving.*
> *That which hinders daring.*

"Let Riverwind guide you. He will be the leader of a leader. It is foreseen that someday he will bring great power to your hands."

"But he already has, Mother," Goldmoon said excitedly. "He gave me this." The princess removed the forever charm and held it out for her mother to examine.

"That is the symbol of the Great Healer. It is powerful, but only on these sacred grounds." The vision of Tearsong reached out and took the amulet. "When you have passed all the tests set for you and have become a true servant of the Great Healer, this amulet will be returned to you." The vision began to fade. "Farewell, daughter. I know you will prove worthy of the honor bestowed upon you. Remember that my love is with you always." Then the vision was gone.

Goldmoon remained kneeling, still feeling the warmth of her mother's love and puzzling over the test her mother had given her. She did not know how long she had been silent when she heard Riverwind crying out her name. The altar no longer glowed blue, and all about her was darkness. When she turned toward Riverwind's voice, she could see the circular, red glow of their fire-beetle lantern.

"I'm over here," the princess called out.

"Goldmoon! Are you all right?" the warrior asked as he ran, limping, up to her. "Where have you been? Why didn't you answer me?"

"I've been here all along, holding the ceremony I came to perform. I didn't hear you call me."

"I've been shouting your name for a long time now," Riverwind insisted. Goldmoon could see that his face was pale and anxious.

"How strange," the princess whispered. "And I thought *you* had disappeared."

Riverwind's voice grew stern, hiding his fear for her in a show of annoyance. "Don't ever go off without me again! There's no telling what evil creatures inhabit this tomb! And you with nothing to defend yourself but that stupid crystal dagger of yours."

"It isn't a stupid dagger," Goldmoon retorted. "It is a—" The princess stopped in mid-sentence. She had been about to say that it was a sacred relic of the Que-shu, but a sudden insight made her gasp: A dagger *hindered* healing. She drew it from her boot-sheath. She had not wiped off the blade after stabbing Hollow-sky, and the traitor's blood made the crystal appear to be rusted. Shuddering from the memory of his final, long scream, she placed it on the altar.

"Riverwind, hand me your shield," she command-ed.

Puzzlement clearly written on his face, Riverwind unstrapped the wooden disk from his arm. "What are you going to do?" he demanded.

Goldmoon put her fingertips on his lips and said, "Trust me." Riverwind let her take the shield from him. She stepped close to the altar and raised the shield high over her head, but then she paused and lowered it again to her side. If she destroyed the dagger, she would have to explain to her father, probably to the whole tribe, why she had done so. Loreman would find some way to twist her action to make it seem evil. Her father would never forgive her. The tribe would not easily let go of their belief in their false gods.

Stealing a glance at Riverwind, she saw that he looked weary and ill. He limped with each step, and there was a blood-red bruise on his cheek where Hollow-sky's longstick had struck him.

If she earned the amulet back, she could heal all his wounds, make him whole. That was a power unknown in her tribe, a power that could help them all. A power, her mother had said, that might prevent an ancient evil from conquering mankind. She raised the shield quickly and smashed it down upon the crystal weapon.

Goldmoon dropped the shield to the side as the shards of crystal began to glow with a blue light; the light grew brighter until it was painful to look at. The sound of glass chimes tinkling in the wind crescendoed. Goldmoon heard her mother's voice.

"Taste now what you will know in full one day, my child, but think of the healing as a *gift* from the gods, not a power."

The shards of crystal on the altar spun about as though they were sand caught in a dust devil.

Riverwind gasped in fear.

Then, in a flash, the jagged crystalline shards flew at the princess, penetrating her flesh like darts.

"Goldmoon!" Riverwind shouted. He dashed forward to catch her as she fell back from the altar. Her skin glittered with the splintered crystal.

"I'm all right," she whispered calmly.

Riverwind gasped. There was no sign of pain on her face, no sign of blood on her robes. "You should be dead."

"No," she answered hesitantly. "I have never felt so

alive!"

Riverwind lowered her gently to her feet, but he did not let go of her fully.

Placing her hands on his cheeks, Goldmoon wished for him to feel as she did.

The warrior drew a deep breath of surprise. She smiled, feeling the tingling energy flow from her hands into him. The crystal shards faded and disappeared. The weariness left Riverwind's face, and the color returned to it. The wound on his cheek vanished without a trace of a scar, and he stood up straighter, without any sign of pain in his knee.

"What have you done?" he asked in awe.

"I've sacrificed the dagger as my mother told me to do."

Riverwind's eyes narrowed. "I see. You've spoken to your gods." His tone was bitter.

"I've spoken with my mother," Goldmoon corrected. She could tell that the blank look he gave her masked disbelief.

"Oh, Riverwind," she said softly, drawing him near. "Wanderer was right! You are right! My mother told me this and more, much more! But—"

Goldmoon lowered her head, her voice caught in her throat. She hadn't realized how hard this would be to confess. Maybe she wouldn't tell him! Maybe she should let him continue to think of her as a goddess. She had her pride, after all. . . . Suddenly, the feeling of peace began to seep from her. Her love for Riverwind turned into a knot of anger and resentment.

Riverwind, sensing her growing coldness, began to draw away from her. . . .

That which hinders loving!

"Don't! Please don't leave me!" she cried, clinging to him in panic.

"I won't!" he whispered, holding her close. "Not if

you want me! Tell me," he added wistfully. "Did your mother say there was a way for us, even though you are a goddess?"

"That's what I've been trying to tell you," Goldmoon said, ashamed. "I'm *not* a goddess. I am mortal." Half teasing, yet half fearful, she glanced at him through her long lashes. "Can you love an ordinary woman, one who is not a goddess?"

"You—ordinary?" he repeated, his breath coming faster. "You could never be ordinary," he said solemnly.

Sinking into his arms, Goldmoon longed to remain there, wrapped in this blessed happiness forever. But a thought caused her to raise her head and look up at him. "My mother told me that she is not a goddess, nor are any of our ancestors. The true gods are the ones Wanderer taught your family to believe in. I sacrificed the dagger as part of a test so that I might one day become a priestess of the Great Healer, one of the ancient goddesses whose temple this once was. But when I sacrifice my pride and return to the village and tell them what I have learned, denying the old ways, I will be ridiculed. I will be Chieftain's Daughter no longer."

Riverwind smiled down at her. "You will always be Chieftain's Daughter," he said, smoothing the golden hair. "That is not something that depends on false gods, it is something within you. Even if you had not been Arrowthorn's child, you would be a leader. And someday, I know, you will lead people to the true gods. That is something to be proud of. It is only your pride in false things that you need to sacrifice."

Goldmoon entwined her fingers in his hair and pulled his head down so his face was within her reach. The lantern light made his eyes sparkle red, and a grin fluttered across his lips just before their mouths met.

The shepherd's tenderness eased her worries about the future. As Riverwind caressed her lips with his own, he kneaded away all the tension in her shoulders with his fingers.

They both whispered, "I love you," simultaneously. Goldmoon laughed, and Riverwind smiled with a pleasure the priestess had never imagined she could evoke in the man. He put his arms about her shoulders and pulled her a little closer. But Goldmoon was tired of respectful, delicate embraces. She pressed against his warrior's body and wrapped her arms about his waist to keep him from pulling away.

Without witnesses to inhibit him, he let the passion of his kiss match her own. All the while, his hands slid her long hair up and down her back, against the silky fabric of her robe. Goldmoon wanted to bring him the same sensual pleasure he gave her, but his armor covered him like a shell. She wriggled one hand beneath the leather and then inside his shirt, where she could press her fingertips against his back.

Riverwind straightened, and his head jerked up. A low moan rumbled through his chest as Goldmoon ran her fingers along his spine.

"You sound like a cat purring," she teased.

Riverwind gave a little snarl like a wild cat. Though she'd heard him use it in the battle with Hollow-sky, it startled her now. Riverwind grinned at the look on her face, then bent over and very lightly licked her behind the ear. He drew her hands forward and flicked his tongue over both palms.

Goldmoon shivered with delight. She caught the ends of the ceremonial sash about his waist and wound them once about his wrists. "Now I am the tiger hunter," she joked and pressed against him harder, kissing his mouth, then his chin, his throat.

Goldmoon had never before sensed so much burning warmth within her body. The dank cavern no longer felt chill, but Riverwind suddenly struggled free of the sash and held her away from him. "This hunt must end," he gasped.

"What's wrong?" she asked, frightened by the way his whole frame shuddered.

The warrior took a deep breath and let it out slowly. Calmer, he stroked her cheek with his forefinger. "We will change many of our people's ways," he explained, "yet there are some customs which we ought still to follow. I have yet to ask your father's permission to court you."

Goldmoon tapped her foot in annoyance. "I suspect that I might change more customs than you, if I have my way," she retorted.

"Is the honor of marriage vows so worthless a thing to wait for?" he asked.

"No, but Father might not agree," Goldmoon said tightly.

"He cannot deny me," Riverwind pointed out, "if I go on a courting quest."

She gave a sly grin. "The look on Arrowthorn's face will be worth seeing." More seriously she added, "I will wait for you, Riverwind, however long it takes." She sighed. "Though I do not think the waiting will be easy."

"And now," Riverwind said firmly, "we must find the way out!"

"What's that?" asked Riverwind, tilting his head to hear as they walked along by the light of the fire-beetle lantern.

"It sounds like water running," Goldmoon replied, listening. She licked her dry lips. "We can fill our waterskins, at least."

"Better yet," said Riverwind, "it is probably an

underground stream that may lead us to the surface and out of here if we follow it!"

Hope rising in their hearts, the two hurried toward the source of the sound and came upon a swiftly flowing, underground river.

"Crow's luck!" Goldmoon snapped with annoyance as the strong current tore her waterskin from her grasp.

"Don't worry, I'll get it," Riverwind offered, stepping into the water to reach after the bag.

"No, Riverwind. The water's too swift. Leave it," Goldmoon ordered.

But Riverwind took another step, then slipped on something underfoot, and plunged forward with a cry. He tried to swim back to the bank, but despite his efforts, the current dragged him off into the darkness.

"Riverwind!" Goldmoon screamed. She stood up and, in her haste, knocked over the lantern. The lid fell off and the fire beetles skittered out and away from the water.

Echoes of her call rang through the cavern, mocking her. Absolutely alone in the pitch-black, unfamiliar cave, Chieftain's Daughter stood frozen with terror.

"I've got to go after Riverwind! What if he's hurt? But do I dare?" she whispered, her fear of drowning pulling her back from the water as strongly as her love for Riverwind pulled her toward it.

Suddenly Goldmoon laughed grimly. "Of course I dare," she cried out. Tearsong had told her to sacrifice that which hindered her daring—her fear.

The princess unfastened the clasp to her fur cloak and let it fall to the ground. Taking a deep breath, she dove into the water toward the spot where Riverwind had disappeared.

The cold of the water was a painful shock. Goldmoon tried to surface immediately, but the weight of her long dress hindered her and the undercurrent held her in its clutches. Her lungs were ready to burst.

That's it, she thought. I'm going to drown. Let it be quick, without pain, she prayed. She began to feel numb all over.

But with a last burst of energy, Goldmoon kicked her legs hard, driving her up into the small pocket of air between the deep water and the top of the cavern.

Her respite was short-lived. A deep thrumming filled the air all about her. A waterfall, she realized, and she was being carried straight toward it!

Light blinded Goldmoon's eyes, and for a moment, as she shot over the edge of the waterfall, she felt as though she were a hawk hanging over the world. Then she plunged. Shooting pains surged from her stomach and heart, and when she hit the water below, she was too disoriented to tell up from down.

Then strong arms grasped her and pulled her gently from the water to the shore. Too weak to do more than turn her head, she smiled sweetly as Riverwind collapsed beside her. They lay dripping and shivering on the sweet-smelling grass in the warm sunshine, taking deep breaths of the fresh air.

They were in a valley beneath the mountain. The waterfall poured out of a cliff face so far above them that their survival seemed a miracle.

"I knew," Goldmoon gasped, "that you would find us a way out."

Riverwind laughed, and Goldmoon laughed with him. She rolled near to him and lay her head on his shoulder. Then she sighed heavily and her eyes became clouded with concerns for the future—now that they had one. "We'll have to explain about Hollow-sky. At least now we know just how far Loreman will go. He won't catch us off guard again."

"I don't understand," Riverwind said. "After he

tried to get Hollow-sky to kill you, won't your father just banish his family?"

"We have no proof—just Hollow-sky's words—and he is dead. Loreman is very powerful; there are too many people who will take his side. Since Hollow-sky failed, Loreman will probably denounce him as a traitor himself."

"And what do we say about us?" Riverwind asked.

"Father won't be pleased," she said. "But I will tell him that I will wed none but you."

"If I ask him for a courting quest, can he deny me?" Riverwind asked tensely.

"No. He'll be forced to follow tradition. But he may send you to find or do something impossible."

"If it will earn me you, the gods will aid me." Riverwind smiled gently and slid his fingers through her wet hair.

Goldmoon shifted her position and sat up on her knees, facing him. "Tearsong told me that one day you would bring great power to my hands. So I know you will return triumphant."

"And quickly," Riverwind added hopefully.

"Do you know what happens at the questing ritual?" Goldmoon asked.

Riverwind shook his head no.

"Well, after you've spoken privately with Father, you'll stand before the whole tribe. Arrowthorn will proclaim that you will go on a quest to prove your worthiness to be my husband. Then, he'll ask me if that is what I want—"

"And you'll say yes," Riverwind added with a smile of certainty.

"Well, yes." She smiled back. "Then he'll announce us betrothed, until such a time as the quest is fulfilled or forsaken."

"It will be fulfilled," he said solemnly, capturing one

of her hands in his own.

"And then," she said, "we'll kiss before the whole tribe. . . ." She placed her free hand on his shoulder and leaned toward him. She heard his swift intake of breath before she kissed him lingeringly. "Well, perhaps not quite like that," she whispered sweetly.

"The servants are probably wondering where we are," Riverwind said huskily. "It's going to be a long way around the mountain to find them."

"I know."

"We should get started," he added.

"If I must wait for you," Goldmoon whispered, once again settling herself in the crook of his arm with her head on his shoulder, "surely you can wait for me— until . . . until . . ." She pondered. "Until the sun dries my hair," she said finally, laughing.

"That may take some time."

"But not long enough." Goldmoon sighed.

"I will enjoy the waiting," Riverwind assured her as he spread locks of the golden strands across his armored chest. "Who knows? Maybe a cloud will pass by."

Raistlin's Daughter

Margaret Weis and Dezra Despain

I first heard the legend of Raistlin's Daughter about
five years after my twin's death. As you can imagine, I
was extremely intrigued and disturbed by the rumors
and did what I could to investigate. In this I was assisted by my friends—the old Companions—who had by
this time scattered over most of Ansalon. We found
versions of the legend in almost every part of the continent. It is being told among the elves of Silvanesti,
the people of Solamnia, and the Plainsmen who have
returned to Que-shu. But we could find no verifica-
tion of it. Even the kender, Tasslehoff Burrfoot, who
goes everywhere and hears everything (as kender do),
could discover no first-hand information regarding it.
The story is always told by a person who heard it from
his aunt who had a cousin who was midwife to the girl
. . . and so forth.

I even went so far as to contact Astinus, the Historian, who records history as it passes before his all-
seeing eyes. In this, my hope to hear anything useful
was slim, for the Historian is notoriously close-
mouthed, especially when something he has seen in
the past might affect the future. Knowing this, I asked

only for him to tell me whether or not the legend was true. Did my twin father a child? Does he or she live still on this world?

His response was typical of that enigmatic man, whom some whisper is the god Gilean, himself. "If it is true, it will become known. If not, it won't."

I have agreed to allow the inclusion of the legend in this volume as a curiosity and because it might, in the distant future, have some bearing upon the history of Krynn. The reader should be forewarned, however, that my friends and I regard it as veritable gossip.

—Caramon Majere

Twilight touched the Wayward Inn with its gentle hand, making even that shabby and ill-reputed place seem a restful haven to those who walked or rode the path that led by its door. Its weather-beaten wood—rotting and worm-ridden when seen in broad daylight—appeared rustic in the golden-tinged evening. Its cracked and broken windowpanes actually sparkled as they caught the last rays of dying light, and the shadows hit the roof just right so that no one could see the patches. Perhaps this was one reason that the inn was so busy this winter night—either that or the masses of gray, lowering clouds gathering in the eastern sky like a ghostly, silent army.

The Wayward Inn was located on the outskirts—if the magical trees deemed it so—of the Forest of Wayreth. If the magical trees chose otherwise, as they frequently did, the inn was located on the outskirts of a barren field where nothing anyone planted grew. Not that any farmer cared to try his luck. Who would want anything from land controlled, so it was believed, by the archmages of the Tower of High Sorcery, by the strange, uncanny forest?

Some thought it peculiar that the Wayward Inn was

built so close to the Forest of Wayreth (when the forest was in appearance), but then the owner—Slegart Havenswood—was a peculiar man. His only care in the world, seemingly, was profit—as he would say to anyone who asked. And there was always profit to be made from those who found themselves on the fringes of wizards' lands when night was closing in.

There were many this evening who found themselves in those straits apparently, for almost every room in the inn was taken. For the most part, the travelers were human, since this was in the days before the War of the Lance when elves and dwarves kept to themselves and rarely walked this world. But there were a few gully dwarves around; Slegart hired them to cook and clean up, and he was not averse to allowing goblins to stay in his place as long as they behaved themselves. There were no goblins this night, however, though there were some humans who might have been taken for goblins—so twisted and crafty were their faces. It was this large party who had taken several of Slegart's rooms (and there weren't many in the small, shabby place), leaving only two empty.

Just about the time when the first evening star appeared in the sky, to be almost immediately overrun by the advancing column of clouds, the door to the inn burst open, letting in a chill blast of air, a warrior in leather armor, and a mage in red robes. From his place behind the dirty bar, Slegart frowned. It was not that he disliked magic-users (rumor had it that his inn existed by the grace of the wizards of the tower), but that he didn't particularly like them staying in his place.

When the big warrior (and he was a remarkably big young man, as both Slegart and the others in the common room noted) tossed down a coin and said, "Dinner," Slegart's frown broadened immediately to a smile. When the big man added, "and a room for the night," however, the smile slipped.

"We're full up," growled Slegart, with a significant glance around the crowded common room. "Hunting moon tonight . . ."

"Bah!" The big warrior snorted. "There'll be no moon tonight, hunting or otherwise. That storm's going to break any moment now and, unless you're partial to hunting snowflakes, you won't shoot anything this night." At this, the big man glanced around the common room to see if any cared to dispute his remark. Noting the size of his shoulders, the well-worn scabbard he wore, and the nonchalant way his hand went to the hilt of his sword, even the rough-appearing humans began to nod their heads at his wisdom, agreeing that there would definitely be no hunting this night.

"At any rate," said the big man, returning his stern gaze to Slegart, "we're spending the night here, if we have to make up our beds by the fire. As you can see"—the warrior's voice softened and his gaze went to the magic-user, who had slumped down at a table as near the fire as possible—"my brother is in no condition to travel farther this day, especially in such weather."

Slegart's glance went to the mage and, indeed, the man appeared to be on the verge of exhaustion. Dressed in red robes, with a hood that covered his head and left his face in shadow, the magic-user leaned upon a wooden staff decorated at the top with a golden dragon's claw holding a faceted crystal. He kept this staff by him always, his hand going to it fondly as if both to caress it and to reassure himself of its presence.

"Bring us your best ale and a pot of hot water for my twin," said the warrior, slapping another steel coin down upon the bar.

At the sight of the money, Slegart's senses came alert. "I just recollect—" he began, his hand closing over the coins and his eyes going to the warrior's leather purse where his ears could detect the chink of metal. Even his nose wrinkled, as though he could smell it as well. "—a room's opened up on t'second floor."

"I thought it might," the warrior said grimly, slapping a third steel piece down on the bar.

"One of my best," Slegart remarked.

The big man grunted, scowling.

"It's goin' to be no fit night for man nor beast," added the innkeeper and, at that moment, a gust of wind hit the inn, whistling through the cracked windows and puffing flakes of snow into the room. At that moment, too, the red-robed mage began to cough—a wracking, choking cough that doubled the man over the table. It was difficult to tell much about the mage—he was cloaked and hooded against the weather. But Slegart knew he must be young, if he and this giant were, indeed, twins. The innkeeper was considerably startled, therefore, to catch a glimpse of ragged, white hair straying out from beneath the hood and to note that the hand holding the staff was thin and wasted.

"We'll take it," the warrior muttered, his worried gaze going to his brother as he laid the coin down.

"What's the matter with 'im?" Slegart asked, eyeing the mage, his fingers twitching near the coin, though not touching it. "It ain't catchin', is it?" He drew back. "Not the plague?"

"Naw!" The warrior scowled. Leaning nearer the innkeeper, the big man said in a low voice, "We've just come from the Tower of High Sorcery." Slegart's eyes grew wide. "He's just taken the Test. . . ."

MARGARET WEIS AND DEZRA DESPAIN

"Ah," the innkeeper said knowingly, his gaze on the young mage not unsympathetic. "I've seen many of 'em in my day. And I've seen many like yourself"—he looked at the big warrior—"who have come here alone, with only a packet of clothes and a battered spellbook or two all that remains. Yer lucky, both of you, to have survived."

The warrior nodded, though it didn't appear—from the haunted expression on his pale face and dark, pain-filled eyes—that he considered his luck phenomenal. Returning to his table, the warrior laid his hand on his brother's heaving shoulder, only to be rebuffed with a bitter snarl.

"Leave me in peace, Caramon!" Slegart heard the mage gasp as the innkeeper came to the table, bearing the ale and a pot of hot water on a tray. "Your worrying will put me in my grave sooner than this cough!"

The warrior, Caramon, did not answer, but sat down in the booth opposite his brother, his eyes still shadowed with unhappiness and concern.

Setting down the tray, Slegart tried his best to see the face covered by the hood, but the mage was huddled near the fire, the red cowl pulled low over his eyes. The mage did not even look up as the innkeeper laid the table with an unusual amount of clattering of plates and knives and mugs. The young man simply reached into a pouch he wore tied to his belt and, taking a handful of leaves, handed them carefully to his brother.

"Fix my drink," the mage ordered in a rasping voice, leaning wearily against the wall.

Slegart, watching all this intently, was considerably startled to note that the skin that covered the mage's slender hand gleamed a bright, metallic gold in the firelight!

The innkeeper tried for another glimpse of the

mage's face, but the young man drew back even farther into the shadows, ducking his head and pulling the cowl lower over his eyes.

"If the skin of 'is face be the same as the skin of 'is hand, no wonder he hides himself," Slegart reflected, wishing he had turned this strange, sick mage away—money or no money.

The warrior took the leaves from the mage and dropped them in a cup. He then filled it with hot water.

Curious in spite of himself, the innkeeper leaned over to catch a glimpse of the mixture, hoping it might be a magic potion of some sort. To his disappointment, it appeared to be nothing more than tea with a few leaves floating on the surface. A bitter smell rose to his nostrils. Sniffing, he started to make some comment when the door blew open, admitting more snow, more wind, and another guest. Motioning one of the slatternly barmaids to finish waiting on the mage and his brother, Slegart turned to greet the new arrival.

It appeared—from its graceful walk and its tall, slender build—to be either a young human male, a human female, or an elf. But so bundled and muffled in clothes was the figure that it was impossible to tell sex or race.

"We're full up," Slegart started to announce, but before he could even open his mouth, the guest had drifted over to him (it was impossible for him to describe its walk any other way) and, leaning out a hand remarkable for its delicate beauty, laid two steel coins in the innkeeper's hand (remarkable only for its dirt).

"A place by the fire this night," said the guest in a low voice.

"I do believe a room's opened up," announced Slegart to the delight of the goblinish humans, who greeted this remark with coarse laughs and guffaws. Even the warrior grinned ruefully and shook his head, reaching across the table to nudge his brother. The mage said nothing, only gestured irritably for his drink.

"I'll take the room," the guest said, reaching into its purse and handing two more coins to the grinning innkeeper.

"Very good. . . ." Noticing the guest's fine clothes, made of rich material, Slegart thought it wise to bow. "Uh, what name . . . ?"

"Do the room and I need an introduction?" the guest asked sharply.

The warrior chuckled appreciatively at this, and it seemed as if even the mage responded, for the hooded head moved slightly as he sipped his steaming, foul-smelling drink.

Somewhat at a loss for words, Slegart was fumbling about in his mind, trying to think of another way to determine his mysterious guest's identity, when the guest turned from him and headed for a table located in a shadowed corner as far from the fire as possible. "Meat and drink." It tossed the words over its shoulder in an imperious tone.

"What would your . . . your lordship like?" Slegart asked, hurrying after the guest, an ear cocked attentively. Though the guest spoke Common, the accent was strange, and the innkeeper still couldn't tell if his guest was male or female.

"Anything," the guest said wearily, turning its back upon Slegart as it walked over to the shadowy booth. On its way, it cast a glance at the table where the warrior, Caramon, and his brother sat. "That. Whatever they're having." The guest gestured to where the barmaid was heaping a wooden bowl full of some gray, coagulating mass and rubbing her body up against

Caramon's at the same time.

Now, perhaps it was the way the mysterious guest walked or perhaps it was the way the person gestured or even perhaps the subtle sneer in the guest's voice when it noticed Caramon's hand reaching around to pat the barmaid on a rounded portion of her anatomy, but Slegart guessed instantly that the muffled guest was female.

It was dangerous journeying through Ansalon in those days some five years before the war. There were few who traveled alone, and it was unusual for women to travel at all. Those women who did were either mercenaries—skilled with sword and shield—or wealthy women with a horde of escorts, armed to the teeth. This woman—if such she was—carried no weapon that Slegart could see and if she had escorts, they must enjoy sleeping in the open in what boded to be one of the worst blizzards ever to hit this part of the country.

Slegart wasn't particularly bright or observant, and he arrived at the conclusion that his guest was a lone, unprotected female about two minutes after everyone else in the place. This was apparent from the warrior's slightly darkening face and the questioning glance he cast at his brother, who shook his head. This was also apparent from the sudden silence that fell over the "hunting" party gathered near the bar and the quick whispers and muffled snickers that followed.

Hearing this, Caramon scowled and glanced around behind him. But a touch on the hand and a softly spoken word from the mage made the big warrior sigh and stolidly resume eating the food in his bowl, though he kept his eyes on the guest, to the disappointment of the barmaid.

Slegart made his way back of the bar again and began wiping out mugs with a filthy rag, his back half-turned but his sharp eyes watching everything. One of the ruffians rose slowly to his feet, stretched, and called for another pint of ale. Taking it from the barmaid, he sauntered slowly over to the guest's table.

"Mind if I sit down?" he said, suiting his action to his words.

"Yes," said the guest sharply.

"Aw, c'mon," the ruffian said, grinning and settling himself comfortably in the booth across from the guest, who sat eating the gray gunk in her bowl. "It's a custom in this part of the country for innfellows to make merry on a night like this. Join our little party . . ."

The guest ignored him, steadily eating her food. Caramon shifted slightly in his seat, but, after a pleading glance at his brother, which was answered with an abrupt shake of the hooded head, the warrior continued eating with a sigh.

The ruffian leaned forward, reaching out his hand to touch the scarf the guest had wound tightly about her face. "You must be awful hot—" the man began.

He didn't complete his sentence, finding it difficult to speak through the bowl of hot stew dripping down his face.

"I've lost my appetite," the guest said. Calmly rising to her feet, she wiped stew from her hands on a greasy napkin and headed for the stairs. "I'll go to my room now, innkeeper. What number?"

"Number sixteen. You can bolt lock it from the inside to keep out the riff-raff," Slegart said, his mug-polishing slowing. Trouble was bad for business, cut into profits. "Serving girl'll be along to turn down the bed."

The "riff-raff," stew dripping off his nose, might have been content to let the mysterious person go her way. There had been a coolness in the voice, and the quick, self-possessed movement indicated that the guest had some experience caring for herself. But the big warrior laughed at the innkeeper's remark—a chuckle of appreciation—and so did the "hunting" party by the fire. Their laughter was the laughter of derision, however.

Casting his comrades an angry glance, the man wiped stew from his eyes and leaped to his feet. Overturning the table, he followed the woman, who was half-way up the stairs.

"*I'll* show you to yer room!" he leered, grabbing hold of her and jerking her backward.

Caught off-balance, the guest fell into the ruffian's arms with a cry that proved beyond a shadow of a doubt that she was, indeed, a female.

"Raistlin?" pleaded Caramon, his hand on the hilt of his sword.

"Very well, my brother," the mage said with a sigh. Reaching out his hand for the staff he had leaned against the wall, he used it to pull himself to his feet.

Caramon was starting to stand up when he saw his brother's eyes go to a point just behind him. Catching the look, Caramon nodded slightly just as a heavy hand closed over his shoulder.

"Good stew, ain't it?" said one of the hunting party. "Shame to interrupt yer dinner over somethin' that ain't none of yer business. Unless, of course, you want to share some of the fun. If so, we'll let you know when it's your tur—"

Caramon's fist thudded into the man's jaw. "Thanks," the warrior said coolly, drawing his sword and twisting around to face the other thugs behind him. "I think I'll take my turn now."

A chair flung from the back of the crowd caught Caramon on the shoulder of his sword arm. Two men in front jumped him, one grabbing his wrist and trying to knock the sword free, the other flailing away with his fists. The mob—seeing the warrior apparently falling—surged forward.

"Get the girl, Raist! I'll take care of these!" Caramon shouted in muffled tones from beneath a sea of bodies. "Everything's . . . under . . . contr—"

"As usual, my brother," said the mage wryly. Ignoring the grunts and yells, the cracking of furniture and bone, Raistlin leaned on his staff and began climbing the stairs.

The girl was fighting her attacker with her fists—she apparently had no other weapon—and it was easy to see she must soon lose. The man's attention was fixed on dragging his struggling victim up the stairs, and he never noticed the red-robed mage moving swiftly behind him. There was a flash of silver, a quick thrust of the mage's hand, and the ruffian, letting loose of the girl, clutched his ribs. Blood welled out from between his fingers. For an instant he stared at Raistlin in astonishment, then tumbled past him, falling headlong down the stairs, the mage's dagger protruding from his side.

"Raist! Help!" Caramon shouted from below. Though he had laid three opponents low, he was locked in a vicious battle with a fourth, his movements decidedly hampered by a gully dwarf, who had crawled up his back and was beating him over the head with a pan.

But Raistlin was not able to go to his brother's rescue. The girl, weak and dizzy from her struggles, missed her step upon the stairs and swayed unsteadily.

Letting go of his staff—which remained perfectly upright, standing next to him as though he were holding it—Raistlin caught the girl before she fell.

"Thank you," she murmured, keeping her head down. Her scarf had come undone in her struggles and she tried to wrap it around her face again. But Raistlin, with a sardonic smile and a deft movement of his skilled hands, snatched the scarf from the girl's head.

"You dropped this," he said coolly, holding the scarf out to her, all the while his keen eyes looking to see why this young woman hid her face from the sun. He gasped.

The girl kept her head down, even after losing the scarf, but, hearing the man's swift intake of breath, she knew it was too late. He had seen her. She checked the movement, therefore, looking up at the mage with a small sigh. What she saw in his face shocked her almost as much as what he saw in hers.

"Who . . . what kind of human are you?" she cried, shrinking away from him.

"What kind are you?" the mage demanded, holding onto the girl with his slender hands that were, nevertheless, unbelievably strong.

"I—I am . . . ordinary," the girl faltered, staring at Raistlin with wide eyes.

"Ordinary!" Raistlin gripped her more tightly as she made a half-hearted attempt to break free. His eyes gazed in disbelief at the fine-boned, delicate face; the mass of hair that was the brilliance and color of silver starlight; the eyes that were dark and soft and velvet-black as the night sky. "Ordinary! In my hands I hold the most beautiful woman I have seen in all my twenty-one years. What is more, I hold in my hands *a woman who does not age!*" He laughed mirthlessly. "And she calls herself 'ordinary!' "

"What about you?" Trembling, the girl's hand reached up to touch Raistlin's golden-skinned face. "And what do you mean—I do not age?"

The mage saw fear in the girl's eyes as she asked this question, and his own eyes narrowed, studying her intently. "My golden skin is my sacrifice for my magic, as is my shattered body. As for you not aging, I mean you do not age in my sight. You see, my eyes are different from the eyes of other men. . . ." He paused, staring at the girl, who began to shiver beneath the unwavering scrutiny. "My eyes see time as it passes, they see the death of all living things. In my vision, human flesh wastes and withers, spring trees lose their leaves, rocks crumble to dust. Only the young among the long-lived elves would appear normal to me, and even then I would see them as flowers about to lose their bloom. But you—"

"Raist!" Caramon boomed from below. There was a crash. Endeavoring to shake off the gully dwarf—who was holding his hands firmly over the big man's eyes, blinding him—Caramon tripped, and fell headlong on a table, smashing it to splinters.

The mage did not move, nor did the girl. "You do not age at all! You are not elven," Raistlin said.

"No," the girl murmured. Her eyes still fixed on the mage, she tried unsuccessfully to free herself from his grasp. "You—you're hurting me. . . ."

"What are you?" he demanded.

She shrugged, squirming and pushing at his hands. "Human, like yourself," she protested, looking up into the strange eyes. "And I thank you for saving me, but—"

Suddenly she froze, her efforts to free herself ceased. Her gaze was locked onto Raistlin's, the mage's gaze was fixed upon her. "No!" she moaned helplessly. "No!" Her moan became a shriek, echoing above the howling of the storm winds outside the inn.

Raistlin reeled backward, slamming into the wall as though she had driven a sword into his body. Yet she had not touched him, she had done nothing but look at him. With a wild cry, the girl scrambled to her feet and ran up the stairs, leaving the mage slumped against the wall, staring with stunned, unseeing eyes at where she had crouched before him on the staircase.

"Well, I took care of the scum. Small thanks to you," Caramon muttered, coming up beside his brother. Wiping blood from a cut on the mouth, the big warrior looked over the railing in satisfaction. Four men lay on the floor, not counting the one his brother had stabbed, whose inert body was huddled at the foot of the staircase in a heap. The gully dwarf was sticking out of a barrel, upside down, its feet waving pathetically in the air, its ear-splittling screams likely to cause serious breakage of the glassware.

"What about damages?" Slegart demanded, coming over to survey the ruin.

"Collect it from them," Caramon growled, gesturing to the groaning members of the hunting party. "Here's your dagger, Raist," the warrior said, holding out a small silver knife. "I cleaned it as best I could. Guess you didn't want to waste your magic on those wretches, huh? Anyway—hey, Raist—you all right?"

"I'm . . . not injured. . . ." Raistlin said softly, reaching out his hand to catch hold of his brother.

"Then what's the matter?" Caramon asked, puzzled. "You look like you've seen a spirit. Say, where's the girl?" He glanced around. "Didn't she even stay to thank us?"

"I—I sent her to her room," Raistlin said, blinking in confusion and looking at Caramon as though wondering who he was. After a moment, he seemed more himself. Taking the dagger from his brother's hand, the mage replaced it on the cunningly made thong he had attached around his wrist. "And we should be going to our rooms, my brother," he said firmly, seeing Caramon's gaze go longingly to the pitcher of ale still on their table. "Lend me your arm," the mage added, taking hold of his staff. "My exertions have exhausted me."

"Oh, uh, sure, Raist," Caramon said, his thirst forgotten in his concern for his brother.

"Number thirteen," grunted Slegart, helping the ruffians drag their wounded comrade off into a corner.

"It figures," Caramon muttered, assisting his brother up the stairs. "Hey, you got a good look at that girl? Was she pretty?"

"Why ask me, my brother?" Raistlin replied softly. Pulling his hood down low over his face again, he evaded his brother's question. "You know what these eyes of mine see!"

"Yeah, sorry, Raist." Caramon flushed. "I keep forgetting. Damn! That one bastard broke a chair over my back end when I was bending over. I know I got splinters. . . ."

"Yes, my brother," Raistlin murmured, not listening. His gaze went to the door at the end of the hall, a door marked with the number 16.

Behind that door, Amberyl paced restlessly, clasping and unclasping her hands and occasionally making that low, moaning cry.

"How could this happen?" she asked feverishly, walking back and forth, back and forth the small chamber. The room was chill and dark. In her preoccupation, Amberyl had allowed the fire to go out. "Why did this happen? How could it happen? Why didn't any of the wise foresee this?" Over and over again she repeated these words, her feet tracing the circular path of her thoughts out upon the grime-encrusted wooden floor.

"I must talk to him," she said to herself suddenly. "He is magi, after all. He may know some way . . . some way to . . . help. . . . Yes! I'll talk to him."

Grabbing up her scarf, she wound it around her face again and cautiously opened the door. The hallway was empty and she started to creep out when she realized she had no idea which room was his.

"Perhaps he isn't even staying the night," she said, sagging against the door frame in despair. "What would I say to him anyway?" Turning, she started back into her room when she stopped. "No, I *must* find him!" she said and closed the door firmly so that she might not be tempted back inside. "If he isn't up here yet, I'll go after him."

Moving down the hall, Amberyl crept near each door, listening. Behind some she heard groans and muttered oaths and hurriedly shied away from these, realizing that her attackers were inside, recovering from their fray with the mage and his brother. At another door there was the shrill giggle of a female and the deeper laughter of a man. Amberyl continued to number 13.

"But, Raist! What am I supposed to say to the girl? 'Come down to our room, my brother wants you'?"

Recognizing the voice, Amberyl pressed closer against the door, listening carefully.

"If that is all you can think of saying, then say that."

The whispering, sneering voice, barely heard above the howling of the storm wind, sent tiny prickles of pain through Amberyl's body. Shivering, she drew closer still. "I don't care what you do, just bring her to me!"

Amberyl heard a shuffling sound and a deprecating cough. "Uh, Raist, I don't know how grateful you think she's gonna be, but from what I've seen of her—"

"Caramon," said the whispering voice, "I am weary and sick, and I have no more patience to cope with your stupidity. I told you to bring the girl to me. Now do so. . . ." The voice trailed off in coughing.

There came the sound of heavy footsteps nearing the door. Fearful of being caught listening, yet unable to leave, Amberyl wondered frantically what to do. She had just decided to run back to her room and hide when the door opened.

"Name of the gods!" Caramon said in astonishment, reaching out and catching hold of Amberyl as she shrank backward. "Here she is, Raist! Standing outside in the hall. Eavesdropping!"

"Is she?" The golden-eyed, golden-skinned mage looked up curiously from where he sat huddled by the fire as his brother half-dragged, half-led Amberyl into the room. "What were you doing out there?" he asked, his eyes narrowing.

For a moment, Amberyl could say nothing. She just stood staring at the mage, twisting the bottom of her scarf in her hands.

"Hold on, Raist," Caramon said gently. "Don't yell at her. The poor thing's freezing. Her hands are like a ghoul's. Here, my lady," the big man said awkwardly, leading her closer to the fire and drawing up a chair for her. "Sit down. You'll catch your death." He put his hand on her scarf. "This is wet from the snow. Let me take—"

"No!" Amberyl cried in a choked voice, her hands going to the scarf. "No," she repeated more softly, flushing to see Raistlin look at her with a grim smile. "I—I'm fine. I . . . never . . . catch cold. Please. . . ."

"Leave us, Caramon," Raistlin said coldly.

"What?" The big man looked startled.

"I said leave us. Go back to your pitcher of ale and the barmaid. She appeared not insensible to your attractions."

"Uh, sure, Raist. If that's what you want. . . ." Caramon hesitated, looking at his brother with such a dumb-founded expression on his face that Amberyl started to laugh, only it came out in a sob. Hiding her face in her scarf, she tried to check her tears.

"Leave us!" Raistlin ordered.

"Sure!" Amberyl heard Caramon backing out the door. "Just . . . just remember, you're not strong, Raistlin. . . ."

The door closed gently.

"I—I'm sorry," Amberyl faltered, raising her face from the scarf, using the hem to dry her eyes. "I didn't mean to cry. I lost control. It—it won't happen again."

Raistlin did not answer her. Comfortably settled in a battered old chair, the mage sat calmly staring at Amberyl, his frail hands clutching a mug of tea that had long ago gone cold. Behind him, near at hand, his staff leaned against the wall. "Remove the scarf," he said finally, after a long silence.

Swallowing her tears, Amberyl slowly reached up and unwound the scarf from her face. The expression in the golden eyes did not change; it was cold and smooth as glass. Amberyl discovered, looking into those eyes, that she could see herself reflected there. She wouldn't be able to enter again, not as she had on the stairs. The mage had put up barriers around his soul.

Too late! she thought in despair. Too late. . . .

"What have you done to me?" Raistlin asked, still not moving. "What spell have you cast upon me? Name it, that I may know how to break it."

Amberyl looked down, unable to stand the gaze of those strange eyes a moment longer. "No—no spell," she murmured, twisting the scarf round and round. "I—I am not . . . not magi . . . as surely you can tell—"

"Damn you!" Raistlin slid out of the chair with the speed of a striking snake. Hurling the mug to the floor, he grabbed hold of Amberyl's wrists and dragged her to her feet. "You're lying! You have done something to me! You invaded my being! You *live* inside me! All I can think of is you. All I see in my mind is your face. I cannot concentrate! My magic eludes me! What have you done, woman?"

"You're hurting me!" Amberyl cried softly, twisting her arms in his grasp. His touch burned. She could feel an unnatural warmth radiate from his body, as though he were being consumed alive by some inner fire.

"I will hurt you much worse than this," Raistlin hissed, drawing her nearer, "if you do not tell me what I ask!"

"I—I can't explain!" Amberyl whispered brokenly, gasping as Raistlin tightened his grip. "Please! You must believe me. I didn't do this to you deliberately! I didn't mean for this to happen—"

"Then why did you come here . . . to my room?"

"You—you are magi. . . . I hoped there might be some way . . . You might know—"

"—how to break the enchantment," Raistlin finished softly, loosening his grip and staring at Amberyl. "So—you are telling the truth. It is happening to you. I see that now. That's the real reason you came here, isn't it? Somehow *I* have invaded your being as well."

Amberyl hung her head. "No. I mean yes. Well, partly." Raising her face, she looked at the mage. "I did truly come here to see if there wasn't some way . . ."

Laughing bitterly, Raistlin dropped her hands. "How can I remove a spell when you won't tell me what you have cast?"

"It isn't a spell!" Amberyl cried despairingly. She could see the marks his fingers had left on her flesh.

"Then what is it?" Raistlin shouted. His voice cracked and, coughing, he fell backward, clutching his chest.

"Here," Amberyl said, reaching out her hands, "let me help—"

"Get out!" Raistlin panted through lips flecked with blood and froth. With his last strength, he shoved

Amberyl away from him, then sank down into his chair. "Get out!" he said again. Though the words were inaudible, his eyes spoke them clearly, the hourglass pupils dilated with rage.

Frightened, Amberyl turned and fled. Opening the door, she plummeted out into the hallway, crashing headlong into Caramon and the barmaid, who were heading for another room.

"Hey!" Caramon cried, catching Amberyl in his arms. "What is it? What's the matter?"

"Your—your brother," Amberyl said in confusion, hiding her face in her long hair. "He . . . he's ill. . . ."

"I warned him. . . ." Caramon said softly, his face crumpling in worry as he heard his brother's rasping cough. Forgetting the barmaid, who was setting up a disappointed cry behind him, the big warrior hurried back into his room.

Amberyl ran blindly down the hall, yanked open her door, and stumbled inside her room to stand, shivering, against the wall in the darkness.

She may have slept. She wasn't certain. Her dreams were too near her waking thoughts. But she'd heard a sound. Yes, there it was again. A door slamming. Though it could have been any one of the rooms in the inn, Amberyl knew instinctively whose door it was.

Rising from the bed on which she'd been lying, fully dressed, the girl opened her door a crack as a voice echoed down the hall.

"Raist! It's a blizzard out there! We'll perish! You can't take this!"

"I am leaving this inn! Now!" came the mage's voice. No longer whispering, it was hoarse with anger and fear. "I am leaving, and I go with or without you. It's up to you!"

The mage started walking down the hall, leaning

upon his staff. Stopping, he cast a piercing glance at Amberyl's room. Panic-stricken, she ducked back into the shadows. The mage headed toward the stairs, his brother standing behind him, hands spread helplessly.

"This has to do with that girl, doesn't it?" Caramon shouted. "Name of the Abyss, answer me! I— He's gone." Left alone in the hall, the big warrior scratched his head. "Well, he won't get far without me. I'll go after him. Women!" he muttered, hurrying back into the room and reappearing, struggling to lift a pack to his back. "Just after we got out of that damn magic forest, too. Now, I suppose we'll end up right back in it."

Amberyl saw Caramon look down the hall toward her room and, once more, ducked back.

"I'd like to know what's going on, my lady," the big man said in her general direction. Then, shaking his head, Caramon shouldered the pack and clumped hastily down the stairs.

Amberyl stood for a moment in the darkness of her room, waiting until her breathing calmed and she could think clearly. Then, grabbing her scarf, she wound it tightly around her face. Pulling a fur cloak from her own pack, she cautiously crept down the hall after Caramon.

Amberyl could recall no worse storm in her life and she had lived many years in the world, though she was young yet by the standards of her kind. The snow was blinding. Blown by a fierce wind, it blotted out all traces of any object from her sight—even her own hands held out before her were swallowed up by the stinging, blinding white darkness. There was no possible way she could have tracked Raistlin and his brother—no way except the way she did it—by the bond that had been accidentally created between herself and the mage.

Accidental. Yes, it must have been accidental, she thought as she trudged along. Though the snow had been falling only a matter of hours, it was already knee-deep. Strong as she was, she was having some difficulty plowing her way through the steep drifts and she could imagine the magic-user . . . in his long robes . . .

Shaking her head, Amberyl sighed. Well, the two humans would stop soon. That much was certain. Wrapping her scarf tighter about her face, covering her skin from the biting snow, she asked herself what she intended to do when they did stop. Would she tell the mage?

What choice do I have? she argued with herself bitterly and, even as she asked the question, she slipped and stumbled. There! she thought, a sickening wave of fear convulsing her. It's beginning already, the weakness that came from the bond. And if it was happening to her, it must be happening to him also! Would it be worse in a human? she wondered in sudden alarm. What if he died!

No, she would tell him tonight, she decided firmly. Then, stopping to lean against a tree and catch her breath, she closed her eyes.

And after you've told—then what?

"I don't know . . ." she murmured to herself brokenly. "The gods help me. I don't know!"

So lost in her fear and inner turmoil was Amberyl that, for a moment, she did not notice that the snow had suddenly ceased falling, the cutting, biting wind had lessened. When she became aware of the fact, she looked around. There were stars, she saw, and even moonlight! Solinari shone brightly, turning the snow silver and the white-covered woods into a wondrous realm of the most fantastic beauty.

The woods. . . . She had crossed the boundary. Amberyl laid her hand gently upon the trunk of the tree against which she leaned. She could feel the life pulsing in the bark, the magic pulsing within that life.

She was in the magical Forest of Wayreth. Though the blizzard might rage unabated not one foot away from her, here, within the shelter of these trees, it could be summer if the wizards commanded it. But it wasn't. The wind, though it had ceased its inhuman howl, still bit the flesh with teeth of ice. The snow was piled thigh-deep in places. But at least the storm was not permitted to vent its full fury inside the forest. Amberyl could see now quite clearly. Solinari's light against the snow was bright as the sun. No longer was she stumbling in the dark, led on only by the burning remembrance of the mage's golden eyes, his touch. . . .

Sighing, Amberyl walked on until she found tracks in the snow. It was the humans. Yes, her instincts had led her unerringly. Not that she had ever doubted her powers. But would they hold true in this forest? Ever since she had come to this land, she had been hearing tales about the strange and magical wood.

Pausing, Amberyl examined the tracks, and her fear grew. There were two sets—one pair of footprints that went through the deepest drifts without stopping. The other, however, was a wide swath cut through the snow, the swath left by a man floundering along in heavy, wet robes. In more than one place, she could see quite clearly the marks of hands, as though the mage had fallen. Hurrying forward, her heart began to beat painfully when she saw that one set of tracks— the mage's—came to an end. His brother must be carrying him! Perhaps he . . . perhaps he was . . .

No! Amberyl caught her breath, shaking her head. The mage might be frail-looking, but there was a strength in him greater than the finest steel blade ever forged. All this meant was that the two must stop and find shelter, and that would work to her advantage.

It wasn't long before she heard voices.

Dodging behind a tree, keeping within its moon-cast shadow, Amberyl saw a tiny bit of light streaming outside what must be a cave in the side of a cliff, a cliff that had apparently appeared out of nowhere, for she could have sworn she had not seen it ahead of her.

"Of course," she whispered to herself in thankfulness, "the mages will take care of one of their own. Do they know *I* am here?" she wondered suddenly. "Would they recognize me? Perhaps not. It has been so long, after all. . . ." Well, it did not matter. There was little they could do. Hopefully, they would not interfere.

"I've got to get help, Raist!" she heard the big warrior saying as she drew near. Caramon's voice sounded tense and anguished. "You've never been this bad! Never!"

There was silence, then Caramon's voice rose again in answer to words Amberyl could not hear.

"I don't know! Back to the inn if I have to! All I know is that this firewood isn't going to last until morning. You yourself tell me not to cut the trees in this forest, and they're wet anyway. It's stopped snowing. I'll only be gone a few hours at most. You'll be safe here. Probably a lot safer in these accursed woods than I will." A pause, then. "No, Raist. This time I'm doing what *I* think best!"

In her mind, Amberyl could almost hear the mage's bitter curse, and she smiled to herself. The light from the cave was obliterated for an instant by a dark shadow—Caramon coming out. It hesitated. Could the man be having second thoughts? The shadow half-turned, going back into the cave.

Quickly murmuring words to herself in a language

—

that none on the continent of Ansalon had heard for countless centuries, Amberyl gestured. Barely visible from where she stood, a glimmer of firelight burst into being far off in another part of the forest.

Catching a glimpse of it from the corner of his eye, Caramon shouted. "Raist! There's—a fire! Someone's close by! You stay wrapped up and . . . and warm. . . . I'll be back soon!"

The shadow merged with the darkness, then Amberyl saw the bright glint of armor in the moonlight and heard the heavy footsteps and labored breathing of the big man slogging through the snow.

Amberyl smiled. "No, you won't be back very soon, my friend," she told him silently as he passed right by the tree where she was hiding. "Not very soon at all."

Waiting until she was certain Caramon was well off on his pursuit of the elusive blaze that would, she knew, keep always just beyond his reach, Amberyl drew a deep breath, said a silent prayer to her god, and crept swiftly through the sparkling silver snow toward the cave.

Pushing aside the blanket Caramon had strung up in a pathetic attempt to block out the elements, Amberyl entered the cave. It was cold, damp, and dark, being lit only by a fire that sputtered feebly near the doorway to allow for ventilation. Glancing at it, Amberyl shook her head. What firewood Caramon had been able to find was wet with snow and ice. It was a tribute to the big man's skill in woodslore that he had been able to coax a flame from it at all. But it wouldn't last long and there was no wood to replace it when it was gone.

Peering into the shadows, Amberyl couldn't find the mage at first, though she could hear his rattling breath and smell the spicy fragrance of his spell components. Then he coughed. A bundle of clothes and blankets near the fire moved, and Amberyl saw a thin hand snake out to clasp hold of a steaming mug that stood near the blaze. The fingers trembled, nearly dropping the mug. Hurriedly kneeling by his side, Amberyl caught hold of it.

"Let me help you," she said. Not waiting for an answer, she lifted the mug in her hand, then assisted Raistlin to sit. "Lean on me," she offered, seeing the mage endeavoring weakly to prop himself up.

"You're not surprised to see me, are you?" she asked.

Raistlin regarded her for a few moments with his flat, golden eyes, then—with a bitter smile—rested his frail body against Amberyl's as she settled down beside him. Chilled as he was, Amberyl could feel that strange warmth emanate from the thin body. He was tense and rigid, his breathing labored. Raistlin lifted the mug to his lips but began to cough again, a cough that Amberyl could feel tear at him.

Taking the mug from him, she set it down and held onto him as he choked and gasped for breath, wrapping her arms around him as though she would hold his body together. Her own heart was torn, both in pity for him and his suffering and with fear for herself. He was so weak! What if he died?

But, finally, the spasm eased. Raistlin was able to draw a shuddering breath and motioned for his drink. Amberyl held it to his lips, her nose wrinkling at the foul smell.

Slowly, Raistlin sipped it. "I wondered if you would find us here," he whispered. "I wondered if the wizards would allow you inside the forest."

"I wondered the same myself," Amberyl said softly. "As for me finding you"—she sighed—"if I hadn't, you would have found me. You would have come back to me. You couldn't help yourself."

"So that's the way it is," Raistlin said, his breathing coming easier.

"That's the way it is. . . ." Amberyl murmured.

"Help me lie down," Raistlin ordered, sinking back among his blankets. Amberyl made him as comfortable as possible, her gaze going to the dying fire. A sudden gust of wind blew the blanket aside. A flurry of snow hissed and danced on the glowing embers.

"I feel myself growing strangely weak, as though my life were being drained off," the mage said, huddling into the wet blankets. "Is that a result of the spell?"

"Yes . . . I feel it, too. And it isn't a spell," Amberyl said, doing what she could to stir up the blaze. Coming around to sit in front of the mage, she clasped her arms around her legs, looking at him as intently as he stared at her.

"Take off your scarf," he whispered.

Slowly, Amberyl unwound the scarf from her face, letting it fall about her shoulders. She shook out her snow-wet hair, feeling drops of water spatter on her hands.

"How beautiful you—" He broke off. "What will happen to me?" Raistlin asked abruptly. "Will I die?"

"I—I don't know," Amberyl answered reluctantly, her gaze going to the fire. She couldn't bear to look at him. The mage's eyes burned through her, touching something deep inside, filling her with sweet pain. "I have . . . never heard of this . . . happening to—to a . . . human before."

"So you are not human," Raistlin remarked.

"No, I am not," Amberyl replied, still unable to face him.

"You are not elven, nor any of the other races that I am familiar with who live upon Krynn—and I tell you— What is your name?"

"Amberyl."

"Amberyl," he said it lingeringly, as though tasting it. She shivered again.

"I tell you, Amberyl," he repeated, "I am familiar with all the races on Krynn."

"Wise you may be, mage," Amberyl murmured, "but the mysteries of this world that have yet to be discovered are as numberless as the snowflakes."

"You will not reveal your secret to me?"

Amberyl shook her glistening hair. "It is not my secret alone."

Raistlin was silent. Amberyl did not speak either. Both sat listening to the hissing and popping of the wood and the whistling of the wind among the trees.

"So . . . I am to die, then," Raistlin said, breaking the silence at last. He didn't sound angry, just weary and resigned.

"No, no, no!" Amberyl cried, her eyes going to the mage. Reaching out impulsively, she took his thin, wasted hand in her own, cradling her cheek against it. "No," she repeated. "Because then I would die."

Raistlin snatched his hand from hers. Propping himself up weakly on his elbow, his golden eyes glittering, he whispered hoarsely, "There is a cure? You can break this . . . this enchantment?"

"Yes," Amberyl answered without a voice, feeling the warm blood suffuse her face.

"How?" Raistlin demanded, his hand clenching.

"First," said Amberyl, swallowing, "I—I must tell you something about . . . about the Valin."

"The what?" Raistlin asked quickly. Amberyl could see his eyes flicker. Even facing death, his mind was working, catching hold eagerly of this new information, storing it away.

"The Valin. That is what it is called in our language.

It means . . ." She paused, frowning, trying to think. "I suppose the closest meaning in your language is *life-mate*."

The startled expression on the mage's face was so funny that Amberyl laughed nervously. "Wait, let me explain," she said, feeling her own face growing more and more flushed. "For reasons of our own, in ages so far back that they are past reckoning, my people fled this land and retreated to one where we could live undisturbed. Our race is, as you were able to detect, long-lived. But we are not immortal. As all others, in order for our race to survive, we must produce children. But there were few of us and fewer still as time went by. The land we chose to live in is a harsh one. We tend to be loners, living by ourselves with little interaction even among our own kind. What you know as families are unknown among us. We saw our race begin to dwindle, and the elders knew that soon it must die out completely. They were able to establish the *Valin* to ensure that our young people . . . that they . . ."

Raistlin's face had not changed expression, his eyes continued to stare at her. But Amberyl could not continue speaking beneath that strange, unblinking gaze.

"You chose to leave your land?" Raistlin asked. "Or were you sent away?"

"I was sent to this land . . . by the elders. There are others here as well. . . ."

"Why? What for?"

Amberyl shook her head. Picking up a stick, she poked at the fire, giving herself an excuse to avoid his eyes.

"But surely your elders knew that something like this must happen if you go out into other lands," Raistlin said bitterly. "Or have they been away *that* long?"

"You have no conception of how long we have been

away," Amberyl said softly, staring at the fire that was flickering out despite her best efforts to keep it going. "And, no, it should *not* have happened. Not with one who is not of our race." Her gaze went back to Raistlin. "And now it is my turn to ask questions. What is there about *you* that is different from other humans? For there is something, something besides your golden skin and eyes that see death in the living. Looking at you, I perceive the shadow of another. You are young, yet there is a timelessness about you. Who are *you*, Raistlin, that this has happened between us?"

To her amazement, Raistlin blanched, his eyes widening in fear, then narrowing in suspicion. "It seems we both have our secrets." He shrugged. "And now, Amberyl, it appears that we will never know what caused this to happen. All that should really concern us is what must be done to rid ourselves of this . . . this *Valin*?"

Shutting her eyes, Amberyl licked her lips. Her mouth was dry, the cave was suddenly unbearably cold. Shivering, she tried more than once to speak.

"What?" Raistlin's voice grated.

"I . . . must bear . . . your child," Amberyl said weakly, her throat constricting.

For long moments there was silence. Amberyl did not dare open her eyes, she did not dare look at the mage. Ashamed and afraid, she buried her face in her arms. But an odd sound made her look up.

Raistlin was lying back on his blankets, laughing. It was almost inaudible laughter, more a wheeze and a choking, but laughter nonetheless—taunting, cutting laughter. And Amberyl saw, with pity in her heart, that its sharp edge was directed against himself.

"Don't, please, don't," Amberyl said, crawling nearer to the mage.

"Look at me, lady!" Raistlin gasped, his laughter

catching in his throat, setting him to coughing. Grinning at her mirthlessly, he gestured outside. "You had best wait for my brother," he said. "Caramon will be back soon. . . ."

"No, he won't," Amberyl said softly, creeping closer still to Raistlin. "Your brother will not be back before morning."

Raistlin's lips parted. His eyes—filled with a sudden hunger—devoured Amberyl's face. "Morning," he repeated.

"Morning," she said.

Reaching up a trembling hand, Raistlin brushed back the beautiful hair from her delicate face. "The fire will be out long before morning."

"Yes," said Amberyl softly, blushing, resting her cheek against the mage's hand. "It—it's already growing cold in here. We will have to do something to keep warm . . . or we will perish. . . ."

Raistlin drew his hand over her smooth skin, his finger touching her soft lips. Her eyes closed, she leaned toward him. His hand moved to touch her long eyelashes, as fine as elven lace. Her body pressed close to his. He could feel her shivering. Putting his arm around her, he drew her close. As he did so, the fire's last little flame flickered and died. Darkness warmer and softer than the blankets covered them. Outside they could hear the wind laughing, the trees whispering to themselves.

"Or we will perish . . ." Raistlin murmured.

Amberyl woke from a fitful sleep wondering, for a moment, where she was. Stirring slightly, she felt the mage's arm wrapped around her protectively, the warmth of his body lying next to hers. Sighing, she rested her head against his shoulder, listening to the shallow, too rapid breathing. She let herself lie there, surrounded by his warmth, putting off the inevitable for as long as possible.

Outside, she could no longer hear the wind and knew the storm must have ended. The darkness that covered them was giving way to dawn. She could barely make out the blackened remnants of the firewood in the gray half-light. Turning slightly, she could see Raistlin's face.

He was a light sleeper. He stirred and muttered at her movement, coughing, starting to wake. Amberyl touched his eyelids lightly with her fingertips, and he sighed deeply and relaxed back into sleep, the lines of pain smoothing from his face.

How young he looks, she thought to herself. How young and vulnerable. He has been deeply hurt. That is why he wears the armor of arrogance and unfeeling. It chafes him now. He is not used to it. But something tells me he will become all too accustomed to this armor before his brief life ends.

Moving carefully and quietly so as not to disturb him—more by instinct than because she feared she would wake him from his enchanted sleep—Amberyl slid out from his unconscious embrace. Gathering her things, she wrapped the scarf once more about her head. Then, kneeling down beside the sleeping mage, she looked upon Raistlin's face one last time.

"I could stay," she told him softly. "I could stay with you a little while. But then my solitary nature would get the better of me and I would leave you and you would be hurt." A sudden thought made her shudder. Closing her eyes, she shook her head. "Or you might find out the truth about our race. If you ever discovered it, then you would loathe me, despise me! Worse still"—her eyes filled with tears—"you would despise our child."

Gently, Amberyl stroked back the mage's prematurely white hair, her hand caressed the golden skin. "There is something about you that frightens me," she said, her voice trembling. "I don't understand. Perhaps the wise will know. . . ." A tear crept down her face. "Farewell, mage. What I do now will keep pain from us both"—bending down, she kissed the sleeping face—"and from one who should come into this world free of all its burdens."

Amberyl placed her hand upon the mage's temples and, closing her eyes, began reciting words in the ancient language. Then, tracing the name *Caramon* upon the dirt floor, she spoke the same words over it as well. Rising hurriedly to her feet, she started to leave the cave. At the entrance she paused. The cave was damp and chill, she heard the mage cough. Pointing at the fire, she spoke again. A blazing flame leaped up from the cold stone, filling the cave with warmth and light. With a final backward glance, a last, small sigh, Amberyl stepped out of the cave and walked away beneath the watchful, puzzled trees of the magical Forest of Wayreth.

Dawn glistened brightly on the new-fallen snow when Caramon finally made his way back to the cave.

"Raist!" he called out in a frightened voice as he drew nearer. "Raist! I'm sorry! This cursed forest!" He swore, glancing nervously at the trees as he did so. "This . . . blasted place. I spent half the night chasing after some wretched firelight that vanished when the sun came up. Are—are you all right?" Frightened, wet, and exhausted, Caramon stumbled through the snow, listening for his brother's answer, cough . . . anything.

Hearing nothing from within the cave but ominous silence, Caramon hurried forward, tearing the blanket from the entrance in his desperate haste to get inside.

Once there, he stopped, staring about him in astonishment.

A comfortable, cheery fire burned brightly. The cave was as warm—warmer—than a room in the finest inn. His twin lay fast asleep, his face peaceful, as though lost in some sweet dream. The air was filled with a springlike fragrance, as of lilacs and lavendar.

"I'll be a gully dwarf," Caramon breathed in awe, suddenly noticing that the fire was burning solid rock. Shivering, the big man glanced around. "Mages!" he muttered, keeping a safe distance from the strange blaze. "The sooner we're out of this weird forest the better, to my mind. Not that I'm not grateful," he added hastily. "Looks like you wizards saved Raist's life. I just wonder why it was necessary to send me on that wild-swimmingbird chase." Kneeling down, he shook his brother by the shoulder.

"Raist," Caramon whispered gently. "Raist. Wake up!"

Raistlin's eyes opened wide. Starting up, he looked around. "Where is—" he began.

"Where is who? What?" Caramon cried in alarm. Backing up, his hand on the hilt of his sword, he looked frantically around the small cave. "I knew—"

"is . . . is—" Raistlin stopped, frowning.

"No one, I guess," the mage said softly, his hand going to his head. He felt dizzy. "Relax, my brother," he snapped irritably, glancing up at Caramon. "There is no one here but us."

"But . . . this fire . . ." Caramon said, eyeing the blaze suspiciously. "Who—"

"My own work," Raistlin replied. "After you ran off and left me, what else could I do? Help me to my feet." Stretching out his frail hand, the mage caught hold of his brother's strong one and slowly rose up out of the pile of blankets on the stone floor.

———

"I didn't know you could do anything like that!" Caramon said, staring at the fire whose fuel was rock.

"There is much about me you do not know, my brother," Raistlin returned. Wrapping himself up warmly in his cloak, he watched as Caramon hurriedly repacked the blankets.

"They're still a little damp," the big man muttered. "I suppose we ought to stay and dry them out. . . ."

"No," Raistlin said, shivering. He took hold of the Staff of Magius that was leaning against the cavern wall. "I have no desire to spend any more time in the Forest of Wayreth."

"You've got my vote there," Caramon said fervently. "I wonder if there are any good inns around here. I heard that there was one, built near the forest. It's called the Wayward Inn or some such thing." The big man's eyes brightened. "Maybe tonight we'll eat hot food and drink good ale for a change. And sleep in a bed!"

"Perhaps." Raistlin shrugged, as if it didn't much matter.

Still talking of what he had heard about the rumored inn, Caramon picked up the blanket that had hung over the cave entrance, folded it, and added it to the ones in his pack. "I'll go ahead a little way," he said to his brother. "Break a trail through the snow for you."

Raistlin nodded, but said nothing. Walking to the entrance of the cave, he stood in the doorway, watching his strong twin wade through the snow drifts, breaking a path the frail twin could follow. Raistlin's lip curled in bitterness, but the sneer slipped as, turning, he looked back inside the cave. The fire had died almost instantly upon Caramon's leaving. Already, the chill was creeping back.

But there lingered on the air, still, the faint fragrance of lilac, of spring. . . .

Shrugging, Raistlin turned and walked out into the snow-blanketed forest.

The Wayward Inn looked its best in summer, a season that has this happy influence on just about anything and everyone. Great quantities of ivy had been persuaded to cradle the inn in its leafy, green embrace, thus hiding some of the building's worst deficiencies. The roof still needed patching; this occurred to Slegart every time it rained when it was impossible to go out and fix it. During dry weather, of course, it didn't leak and so didn't need fixing. The windows were still cracked, but in the heat of summer, the cool breeze that wafted through the panes was a welcome one.

There were more travelers at the inn during these journeying months. Dwarven smiths, occasionally an elf, many humans, and more kender than anyone cared to think about, generally kept Slegart and his barmaids busy from morning until late, late at night.

But this evening was quiet. It was a soft, fragrant summer.evening. The twilight lingered on in hues of purple and gold. The birds had sung their night songs and were now murmuring sleepily to their young. Even the old trees of Wayreth seemed to have been lulled into forgetting their guardian duties and slumbered drowsily at their posts. On this evening, the inn itself was quiet, too.

It was too quiet, so two strangers thought as they approached the inn. Dressed in rich clothing, their faces were covered with silken scarves—an unusual thing in such warm weather. Only their black eyes were visible and, exchanging grim glances, they quickened their steps, shoving open the wooden plank door and stepping inside.

Slegart sat behind the bar, wiping out a mug with a

dirty rag. He had been wiping out that same mug for an hour now and would probably have gone on wiping it for the next hour had not two incidents occurring simultaneously interrupted him—the entry of the two muffled strangers through the front door and the arrival of the servant girl, running breathlessly down the stairs.

"Your pardon, gentlemen both," Slegart said, rising slowly to his feet and holding up his hand to check one of the strangers in his speech. Turning to the servant, he said gruffly, "Well?"

The girl shook her head.

Slegart's shoulders slumped. "Aye," he muttered. "Well, p'rhaps it's better so."

The two strangers glanced at each other.

"And the babe?" Slegart asked.

At this, the servant girl burst into tears.

"What?" Slegart asked, astonished. "Not the babe, too?"

"No!" the servant girl managed to gasp between sobs. "The baby's fine. Listen—" A faint cry came from overhead. "You can hear 'er now. But . . . büt— oh!" The girl covered her face with her hands. "It's dreadful! I've never seen anything so frightening—"

At this, one of the strangers nodded, and the other stepped forward.

"Pardon me, innkeep," the stranger said in a cultivated voice with an unusual accent. "But some terrible tragedy appears to have happened here. Perhaps it would be better if we continued on—"

"No, no," Slegard said hastily, the thought of losing money bringing him to himself. "There, Lizzie, either dry your tears and help, or go have your cry out in the kitchen."

Burying her face in her apron, Lizzie ran off into the kitchen, setting the door swinging behind her.

Slegart led the two strangers to a table. "A sad thing," said the innkeeper, shaking his head.

"Might we inquire—" ventured the stranger casually, though an astute observer would have noticed he was unusually tense and nervous, as was his companion.

"Nothin' for you gentlemen to concern yourselves with," Slegart said. "Just one of the serving girls died in childbirth."

One of the strangers reached out involuntarily, grasping hold of his companion's arm with a tight grip. The companion gave him a warning glance.

"This is indeed sad news. We're very sorry to hear it," said the stranger in a voice he was obviously keeping under tight control. "Was she—was she kin of yours? Pardon me for asking, but you seem upset—"

"I am that, gentlemen," Slegard said bluntly. "And no, she warn't no kin of mine. Came to me in the dead 'o winter, half-starved, and begging for work. Somethin' familiar about her there was, but just as I start to think on it—" he put his hand to his head—"I get this queer feelin'. . . . 'Cause of that, I was of a mind to turn her away, but"—he glanced upstairs— "you know what women are. Cook took to her right off, fussin' over 'er and such like. I got to admit," Slegart added solemnly, "I'm not one fer gettin' attached to people. But she was as pretty a critter as I've seen in all my born days. A hard worker, too. Never complained. Quite a favorite she was with all of us."

At this, one of the strangers lowered his head. The other put his hand over his companion's.

"Well," said Slegart more briskly, "I can offer you gentlemen cold meat and ale, but you won't get no hot food this night. Cook's that upset. And now"—the innkeeper glanced at the still-swinging kitchen door with a sigh—"from what Lizzie says, it seems like there's somethin' wrong with the babe—"

The stranger made a sudden, swift movement with his hand, and old Slegart froze in place, his mouth open in the act of speaking, his body half-turned, one hand raised. The kitchen door stopped in mid-swing. The servant girl's muffled cries from the kitchen ceased. A drop of ale, falling from the spigot, hung suspended in the air between spigot and floor.

Rising to their feet, the two strangers moved swiftly up the stairs amid the enchanted silence. Hastily, they opened every door in the inn, peering inside every room, searching. Finally, coming to a small room at the very end of the hall, one of the strangers opened the door, looked inside, and beckoned to his companion.

A large, matronly woman—presumably Cook— was halted in the act of brushing out the beautiful hair of a pale, cold figure lying upon the bed. Tears glistened on the cook's kindly face. It had obviously been her work-worn hands that had composed the body for its final rest. The girl's eyes were shut, the cold, dead fingers folded across the breast, a small bunch of roses held in their unfeeling grasp. A candle shed its soft light upon the young face whose incredible beauty was enhanced by a sweet, wistful smile upon the ashen lips.

"Amberyl!" cried one of the strangers brokenly, sinking down upon the bed and taking the cold hands in his. Coming up behind him, the other stranger laid a hand upon his companion's shoulder.

"I'm truly sorry, Keryl."

"We should have come sooner!" Keryl muttered, stroking the girl's hand.

"We came as quickly as we could," his companion said gently. "As quickly as she wanted us."

"She sent us the message—"

"—only when she knew she was dying," said the companion.

"Why?" Keryl cried brokenly, his gaze going to Amberyl's peaceful face. "Why did she choose to die among . . . among these humans?" He gestured toward the cook.

"I don't suppose we will ever know," said his companion softly. "Although I can guess," he added, but it was in an undertone, spoken only to himself and not to his distraught friend. Turning away, he walked over to a cradle that had been hastily constructed out of a wood box. Whispering a word, he lifted the enchantment from the baby, who drew a breath and began whimpering.

"The child?" the stranger said, starting up from the bed. "Is her baby all right? What the servant girl said . . ." There was fear in his voice. "It isn't, it isn't dea-" He couldn't go on.

"No," said his friend in mystified tones. "It is not what you fear. The servant girl said she'd never seen anything more frightening. But the baby seems fine—Ah!" The stranger gasped in awe. Holding the baby in his arms, he turned toward his friend. "Look, Keryl! Look at the child's eyes!"

The young man bent over the crying baby, gently stroking the tiny cheek with his finger. The baby turned its head, opening its large eyes as it searched instinctively for nourishment, love, and warmth.

"The eyes are . . . gold!" Keryl whispered. "Burning gold as the sun! Nothing like this has ever occurred in *our* people. . . . I wonder—"

"A gift from her human father, no doubt. Although I know of no humans with eyes like this. But that secret, too, Amberyl took with her." He sighed, shaking his head. Then he looked back down at the whimpering baby. "Her daughter is as lovely as her mother," the man said, wrapping the baby tightly in its blankets. "And now, my friend, we must go. We have been in this strange and terrible land long enough."

"Yes," Keryl said, but he made no move to leave. "What about Amberyl?" His gaze went back to the pale, unmoving figure upon the bed.

"We will leave her among those she chose to be with at the end," his companion said gravely. "Perhaps one of the gods will accept her now and will guide her wandering spirit home."

"Farewell, my sister," Keryl murmured. Reaching down, he took the roses from the dead hands and, kissing them, put the flowers carefully in the pocket of his tunic. His companion spoke words in an ancient language, lifting the enchantment from the inn. Then the two strangers, holding the baby, vanished from the room like a shower of silver, sparkling rain.

And the baby was beautiful, as beautiful as her mother. For it is said that, in the ancient days before they grew self-centered and seduced by evil, the most beautiful of all races ever created by the gods was the ogre. . . .

Silver and Steel

Kevin D. Randle

---

*I*t had finally come to this. A summer-long campaign that had seen the Dark Queen pushed until the remnants of her tattered army were grouped around her at the base of a massive obsidian obelisk. A few thousand ragged warriors and their tired, dirty families, waiting for the Queen to do something before the final attack.

Huma, his army spread out on the hills overlooking the black tower, climbed from the back of the silver dragon he rode and studied the scene below him, looking for the trap he knew to be there. The Queen's line of retreat had been straight, as if this had been her destination.

Glancing to his right, he could see the movement of his men, the knights on horseback, and the bowmen in front of them but behind the pikemen, as they formed just below the crest of the hills. Long, straight lines, marked by colored flags. The movement of their feet, the pawing of the horses, stirred the dry soil, creating a choking cloud of dust that engulfed them like a thick, morning fog. Slowly, their equipment rattling as the metal pieces struck one another, they fell into a

---

strict military formation. They were a silent group, tense and strained, waiting for Huma to order them forward to the attack.

The scene to the left looked much the same. The men were moving forward. Their weapons, held at the ready, flashed in the afternoon sun. The women and children stayed at the rear of the battle line, setting up their camp and preparing bandages and splints, preparing to clean up the battlefield after the fighting.

The support vehicles, ox carts and wagons, the support men—those who made the weapons, the squires who aspired to be knights, the grooms, and the drivers—stood in the rear, sweating in the hot sun and watching everything, wishing that they could somehow get into the battle.

Near them was the makeshift band. Pipes and drums and flutes that could stir the men with their melodies and inspire them to greater efforts. They choked on the dust that stuck in their throats. Wiped the sweat from their faces as they waited for someone to do something. Waited for Huma to order them forward.

The silver dragon that Huma rode was gone suddenly, and standing next to him was a tall, slender woman with a mane of silver hair. She wore a breastplate of green armor, molded to her, a short, leather skirt, and shin guards that matched the green of her breastplate. In her right hand—a delicate, thin-boned hand with long, slender fingers—she held the hilt of a jeweled broadsword, the silver tip stuck in the dust at her feet. There was a look of grim determination on her face, because she knew what this event meant. She knew what the outcome of the battle had to be, and knew the cost to her and to Huma.

She turned to look at Huma, a huge man with a big,

flaming mustache and long, black hair that brushed his shoulders. He wore armor of silver, a helmet with a plume of crimson on his head, and he held the dragonlance that was nearly twelve feet long. The barbed tip was of pure silver, and the shaft was of polished wood. It was a special weapon, forged by the dwarves with the Hammer of Kharas. The weapon that could destroy the Queen and her army—maybe the only weapon in the whole world that could do the job.

Huma stepped to his right and touched the woman's shoulder, as if assuring himself that she was real flesh and blood and not a mirage created by the enemy. She reached up and took his hand in hers, turning her face, framed by her silver hair, so that she could smile at him.

"We have her trapped now," said the woman, her voice quiet, almost soothing.

"Yes," Huma agreed. "There is nowhere for the Dark Queen to go now. Still . . ." He didn't finish the sentence, feeling an anxiety that he couldn't place. It was almost as if evil were radiating from the obelisk . . . as if the Dark Queen had led them to the spot to be destroyed.

"It will soon be over," she said, quietly, as if speaking to herself. "All over." She stared at Huma, her heart pounding in her chest. Slowly, she reached out and touched his bearded cheek with the tips of her fingers.

"None too soon," he responded gruffly. Yet, he, too, felt a hollowness inside him because he knew what the end of this battle would mean for them personally: a few years of happiness at the very most and then a permanent separation, but that was the price they must pay for the destruction of the Dark Queen.

"You don't regret our decision, do you?" she asked

him quietly.

"Daily. Hourly. Every time I think of what we could have had, I regret it. But it is beyond us. There's nothing we can do about it." He turned to face her, drinking in her beauty, a fine, light beauty, created by illusion, but a perfect illusion that could be preserved for all time if they would pay the price. But they could not.

She nodded, afraid to speak. Afraid of the pain that would creep into her words. She turned away and looked at the army of tired men who sensed that the end was near. Tired, dirty men who had never lost their belief that Huma would lead them to victory. Men who knew Huma would not betray them, and who believed that—one way or another—this day would see the end of the terrible war.

"I wish . . ." she started and found that she was unable to finish the thought. What could she say? She knew from the beginning what the rules were. She knew what it meant for her to take human form, and she knew what the ultimate cost would be for her. And yet, she hadn't realized that it would be as high as it was. And now it was too late.

Huma took her hand, holding it in his own; he squeezed it tightly so that she could not get away from him. There were a hundred things that he wanted to say to her. A thousand, but he didn't have the words. In his heart, he knew that they had made the right decision, but that didn't make it any easier. Rather than telling her that their time together, however short, was worth the sacrifice, he said nothing to her. He knew that she knew, and that was all that was important. The words didn't have to be spoken aloud to be heard.

A silence descended over the valley and the hills around it. The clouds of dust drifting on the light breeze did little to break the heat of the afternoon. The eerie quiet spread outward, as if everybody held their breath, waiting for someone else to take command. Huma pulled the woman closer to him but could not feel her body press his because of the heavy armor he wore. A sweat born of the heat and the anxiety of the moment dripped down his face and ran down his sides; he didn't like the way the Dark Queen had fled to the obelisk. He didn't like the way her army had halted at its base, as if finding protection in its shadow. It smacked of a trap, and that frightened him because he hadn't expected it.

For a moment everything remained static, the two forces separated by one-hundred yards of open, dry, flat ground. No one moved; the only sounds were the flapping of the knight's pennants in the hot breeze and a quiet rattling of the metallic and leather equipment.

And then the woman vanished. A shimmering of light that looked like the heat rising from the plains near him and she was gone. Huma mounted the silver dragon that appeared next to him, holding the dragonlance in his left hand, the butt resting on his thigh. He saw the commanders of his army, the captains of the pikemen, the bowmen, and the knights, watching him, waiting for his orders. He saw the Dark Queen and her army and knew that the wait was over.

Huma leaned forward, his mouth near an ear of the silver dragon, and said, "It's time."

The massive head of the dragon nodded once, and a tear dropped from its left eye.

Huma raised his lance high over his head, then lowered it with a snap of his wrist. At his command, there was shouting in his lines and the bowmen drew the strings of their weapons back. As one, they let their arrows fly, a black cloud of death that arced at the Queen's waiting men, slamming into their ranks. As the second volley was fired, the pikemen began a slow advance on the enemy, their shields held in front of them, the tips of their pikes pointed at the Queen's soldiers.

A shout seemed to rise from one-hundred-thousand throats, a roar that came from both armies. The Dark Queen, a beautiful woman dressed in black armor and mounted on a black horse, waved her men forward. They came on, running across the no-man's land of dried, dead grass, raising a cloud of dust that obscured them and the obsidian obelisk behind them.

Like the sound of the sea smashing onto a beach, the two armies collided. There was the ringing of metal against metal and a grunting of effort as the men of both sides fought with one another. Huma's men momentarily retreated under the heavy onslaught of the Dark Queen's men, but their line finally stabilized.

From his position on the hillside, Huma, astride the silver dragon, could watch the fight. His men waded into the conflict, their swords swinging, chopping at the enemy. Men fell, wounded, screaming in pain and fright. Others dropped, dead before they hit the ground. A few broke and ran, but no one paid attention to them. Even as far from the battle as he was, Huma could see the blood beginning to flow. Puddles of it under the bodies. Streams of it began to form rivers. The dust, churning under the feet of the men, was suddenly wet with blood.

Huma's men forced those of the Queen to retreat. As their line collapsed and her men died, fresh soldiers forced their way into the front ranks. Some, armed with maces, tried to crush the skulls of the attackers. Others, using spears and pikes, thrust into Huma's forces, killing and wounding.

The sight of the battle was almost too much for Huma to bear. It had turned into the bloodiest, goriest affair he'd ever been witness to, as the men killed and were killed. Huma tore his eyes away, unable to stand the sight, but he could still hear the sound of it. He could hear the grunts and cries of the fighting men. Hear the ringing of the metal of their weapons as they slammed into each other. Hear the screams of agony of the wounded and the shrieks of pain from the dying. He realized that there was no glory in war. There was only the bloody and cruel deaths of brave fighting men.

Huma had not been cut out to be a leader. He hated sitting safely on the hillside, watching the battle while his men fought and died on the plain below him. But, from his position, he could see all of it, could see how the Queen was deploying her army and could counter it with his. He could spot his weaknesses and strengthen them, and he could spot hers to exploit them. Flanking him were the knights, the flower of his army, waiting for their orders to attack.

It should have been a quick, easy victory. The Queen had little left in the way of an army. Huma had pursued her all summer, gaining strength as she lost it. He had pushed her, he thought, across the dried plains until her back was against the ominous obsidian obelisk. She lost men in every skirmish. More men than Huma.

And with each loss, her supporters deserted her. Sometimes, using her magic, or that of the black-robed magic-users, she created illusions to frighten Huma's men. Once, believing they were being attacked by a race of tall, raven-haired female warriors who didn't know fear, Huma's men had turned and fled, leaving him alone astride his silver dragon.

Huma had ridden forward, head bowed like a man in a high wind, the dragonlance held point down. He had ridden into the hordes of women, ridden unharmed through the illusion of their arrows and the illusion of their swords. He had ignored all that, attacking into the ranks of the black-robed men behind them, scattering some and killing others. He'd chopped them down so that they could never use their powers for evil again. As the magic-users ran, or died, the illusions they had created vanished.

His army had stopped running then, turning to look at the empty plain. A few men, killed by their own fear or trampled under the feet of their friends, lay dead. Huma and a beautiful woman with silver hair stood alone, the Queen and her army having escaped the onslaught because of the illusions.

Now Huma sat behind his army, watching them pressing the Queen's men, killing them in large numbers. Hacking them to pieces. Pushing the enemy back toward the obsidian obelisk and the Queen.

There came a crack of thunder. Clouds began boiling overhead, coalescing from the clear blue. Crimson clouds that turned brown and black before shooting into yellows and oranges. Lightning flashed as the thunder boomed. Splinters of it struck the top of the obelisk so that it began to glow an iridescent yellow. Sparks flew from the top of it as the wind picked up, swirling down around the shaft of the obelisk, whipping at the clothing, the robes, and the pennants of the Queen's army. The booming grew until it sounded like the dirge of a giant base drum. A crashing sound that rocked the ground, sending vibrations through it.

Suddenly, a formation of soldiers appeared at the base of the obelisk. Each was dressed in glowing black armor matching that worn by the Dark Queen, and each soldier carried a silver broadsword as he fanned outward. Ignoring the coming storm, they hacked their way into Huma's army, killing his troops quickly, forcing them back to retreat.

Around them, the Queen's soldiers who had been

killed earlier seemed to come to life again. Dead men trailing blood, missing limbs, stood, raised their weapons high, and attacked again. Gory horrors on their feet, shrieking with inhuman voices, waving their weapons over their heads. Attacking. Chopping. Killing.

With a cry of rage, of despair, Huma lowered his dragonlance and the silver beast under him leaped forward. With a roar of anger, the knights joined him, urging their horses onward. The line of men, nearly a hundred yards long, swept past their own soldiers to strike the reinforcements issuing from the obelisk and the ground around it.

Now in the thick of the battle, surrounded by his own men, Huma leaped to the ground. He jammed the base of the dragonlance into the dirt, determined that he would not retreat beyond that point. He drew his sword, the blade held upright in front of him, flashing in the bright sunlight as it peeked through the seething clouds over the battlefield; he waited as the black soldiers of the Queen advanced on him.

Beside him, the silver dragon vanished in a shimmering of light. The woman stood on his right, in the place of honor in the battleline. She shook her head, the waves of her silver hair flipping across her shoulders as she drew her own weapon. She lifted it skyward, stepped forward with her right foot, and then she, too, waited for the enemy. There was a smile on her lips as if she knew something that eluded the others.

Huma felt a sudden surge of love for the woman. She had stood beside him in everything—through the bad times when it seemed that the enemy would win momentarily, and through the good, when it seemed he would win easily. She had been there on the dark nights, holding him when he blamed himself for bringing sorrow to hundreds of families. To thousands of families. And she had been there to share in the celebration when the battles went well and the Dark Queen was driven from the field of battle after suffering heavy losses.

He wanted to say all that to her because he felt that time for them was short. The Dark Queen had too much left, had too many soldiers and too much power, and he had too little. In one horrible moment he knew that he would never be able to tell this silver-haired woman anything again.

For a moment, no one moved. The battle had slowed and stopped during the aerial display. Both sides regrouped. Now, without a command from their Queen, the black soldiers advanced, slowly at first, their weapons thrust out before them, forming a deadly steel wall. Huma, forcing the thoughts of his love from his mind, grinned at them in defiance, and his army spread out all around him, waiting.

One man leaped forward, landing directly in front of Huma. The man swung his sword in a wide arc, trying to lop Huma's head from his shoulders. Huma countered by shifting his weight and his sword, blocking the blow. As he did, he twisted his weapon down, forcing the point of the enemy's blade to the ground. When it hit the dirt, Huma stomped on it, shattering the blade like glass. He then swung upward, his weapon knifing through his enemy's breastplate easily, slicing into the soft flesh beneath it with the sound of ripping silk.

The man dropped his sword and grabbed at his stomach, shrieking with pain as he tried to keep his entrails from spilling to the bloody ground. He fell to his knees, his eyes on Huma as he pawed at his intestines, futilely trying to stuff them back into the gaping wound. Then his eyes rolled up into his head and he collapsed on the steaming mass with a whimper.

Almost as if the man's gory death signaled the beginning of a new battle, the black soldiers surged forward, engaging Huma's troops. The ringing of the metal rose again, along with the shouts and grunts and curses of fighting men. The noise increased until it was a din, overpowering all other sound.

Huma pushed his way forward, swinging with his own weapon, cutting into the Queen's forces. Slashing at them, hacking at them, he pressed on, the woman with the silver hair at his side. A huge soldier, his black breastplate slick with the blood of others, thrust a sword at Huma. Using his own weapon, Huma blocked the blow, leaped back, and waited. The soldier advanced, swinging his blade, grunting with the effort. Huma ducked under the blow and, holding his sword in both hands, ripped upward.

The enemy danced to the right, away from the thrust, and came back with one of his own. Huma parried, forcing the blade away from him, and stepped in. With his elbow, he smashed the soldier's jaw with a splintering of bone and teeth. Blood splashed down the front of his armor, but the man ignored it, fighting to keep his balance. He threw an arm out as Huma struck again, severing the limb at the shoulder. A gout of blood washed to the ground. The man roared in pain and fear and anger, but he held onto his weapon with his remaining hand.

Huma stared into the soldier's eyes, seeing the fear clouded in them. The man wanted to retreat but could not. Instead, he attacked with renewed fury, swearing at the top of his voice. But the attack was short as the man, weakened by the loss of blood, almost fell, tripping on his own feet.

Huma dodged to his right, almost colliding with the woman. He turned as the enemy soldier slipped and fell on his side, shrieking with pain. The soldier lost his grip on the sword. With his remaining hand, he clawed at the muddy, bloody ground. Rolling to his back, he stripped the helmet from his head, tossing it to the side. Huma was shocked by the youth in that face. His opponent was a young man who couldn't even grow a beard or a proper moustache; he'd had no chance to live. Now his skin was waxy and unnatural-looking, as the last of his blood pumped itself onto the ground. The young man died, a scream bubbling on his crimson-stained lips.

All around Huma the battle continued to rage. Men hammered each other to the ground, caving in heads and hacking limbs from bodies. Men shouted and screamed and fought. Even the reinforcements the Queen had found in the obelisk were not enough to save her. Slowly, her army shrank as her soldiers died.

And then, again, the sky closed over, the clouds boiled, and the heavens flashed with their anger. Another new army sprang from the remains of the old. Fresh men leaped to fight the exhausted men that Huma had led to this spot. A dozen, two, and then one-hundred more came at them, rising from the bloody ground strewn with the bodies of the slain. The Queen could call on this army, reinforcing it until all of Huma's men were dead.

These new soldiers moved forward with a fury that was impossible to stop. They chopped their way through the ranks of the pikemen, lopping heads from bodies and crushing skulls with the detachment of men clearing vines from a forest trail. The ground was slick with blood and jellied brains.

Huma, seeing his army disintegrating around him, stood his ground. His armor was slimy with the blood of those he had killed. There were patches of splattered gray from the brains of his victims. Sweat from the effort of the fight soaked his underclothes. His feet were wet from standing ankle-deep in the blood of those who had died in the battle.

But there was no more retreat. If the Queen won now, she won for good because too much had happened. Too many had already died. Their bodies were piled around him. These were the men who had trusted him.

The Queen's soldiers came at them with a renewed vengeance. Huma held his ground for a moment, fighting them. Slowly, as more of his men died, he was forced to retreat, selling the bloody ground to the Queen at the high price of the deaths of her own soldiers.

And then he was at the dragonlance, his back against it. There was nowhere for him to go, nowhere for him to retreat to. It was time to make his last stand, because to do less would be a betrayal of the men who had ridden with him. Arms shaking with fatigue, he swung his sword, dripping with gore, and held the enemy at bay.

Two of the enemy came at him, one feinting to the left and moving to the right. That man struck at the woman who was busy fighting another adversary. Huma, sensing the attack on her, dived between her and the man. The enemy's blade slammed into Huma's armor near the shoulder, cleaving it easily. Huma felt white-hot pain wash down his side and into his chest as his blood spilled.

Huma held onto his sword with a super-human effort, and swung it, catching the man in the side. There was a crunch as the metal of the enemy's armor caved in. Drawing on all of his strength, Huma twisted his blade free. But the force caused him to stumble. He went to one knee and began toppling forward. His hand shot out and held him up. Out of the corner of his eye, he saw his opponent raising his sword above his head like an axe. Huma didn't wait for the deadly blade to fall; he rolled to his right, onto his wounded shoulder, screaming in agony. At that same instant, he thrust his own weapon upward into the stomach of the Queen's soldier.

The enemy took a staggering step forward and then dropped his own blade behind his back. He reached with both hands, touching the sword that extended from his stomach. Clumsily, he sat down as blood dripped from his mouth. He tried to grin, his teeth stained crimson, and then toppled to his side with a bubbling croak.

Huma felt cool hands on him and turned. The woman was crouched next to him, her silver hair splattered with blood, her armor covered with it. She had removed her helmet so that he could see her face. Without a word, she helped Huma to his feet. He staggered back a step and reached out, grabbing the dragonlance to steady himself. He leaned on it, using it for support.

Around him were the tattered remains of his army. They had trusted his judgment, and he had led them to annihilation. They had followed him blindly, and he had brought them to destruction. He was sick with the horror that was unfolding around him. But he was powerless to change it. Powerless to stop the carnage. He leaned on the lance and stared at the battlefield. Stared at the dead men lying on it and at the soldiers who still fought on it. The sun, touching the horizon, threw a blood-red glow over the plain that seemed fitting.

Pockets of fighting surrounded the obelisk, but it was clear that the Queen had the upper hand now. Around Huma were the hacked-up bodies of his own dead soldiers. Bodies missing hands and arms and feet and legs. There were bodies without heads and bodies that were little more than chopped-up trunks. Under them, the ground was covered with a thick layer of bloody mud.

The din of battle had dropped off as Huma's men died. He could hear the shouting of his knights, calling encouragement to one another as the Queen's soldiers slowly cut them to ribbons. They were brave men dying bravely in a losing cause. Brave men who wouldn't give up until they were all dead. Brave men who believed that Huma would still, somehow, lead them to victory. Brave men who believed that their loss was their own fault. They hadn't given enough of themselves to win the battle or the war. They believed their sacrifice was somehow less than worthy, so they were not destined to win.

Huma felt the frustration and rage burn through him. It was he who was the failure. If he had been smart enough or strong enough, they would have won. If they failed, it was his fault because his men gave all that they had in them. He stood upright, the pain in his shoulder and chest almost forgotten. He stared at the obelisk. An evil black tower forty feet tall, the top glowing with a golden, malevolent light. At the base, the Queen, the second most beautiful woman he had ever seen, was astride her horse, watching the destruction of Huma's army. She had taken off her helmet and held it tucked under her arm as she studied the progress of the battle. She was grinning because Huma had fallen into her trap.

He could stand the agony of losing no longer. The rage burned in him like a blazing forest because there was nothing more he could do. The battle was lost. The war was lost. And his men had all died in vain. In desperation he jerked the dragonlance free of the ground and aimed it at the tower in a final gesture of defiance. No longer could he beat the Queen. She had drawn him into the battle so that she could destroy his army. She had won the battle, and with the battle . . . the war.

With the strength that remained in him, Huma hurled the lance at the tower. The motion dropped him to his knees, shooting pain through his body. When he looked up, he saw that the lance had buried itself in the obsidian of the obelisk above the Queen's head. The lance, forged over the fires of dwarves, forged with the Hammer of Kharas by dwarves, was more than an ordinary weapon. It had a strength of its own. Designed to kill dragons, it held an internal power that was now directed against the obelisk. A power that could destroy the largest of monsters. A power that was stronger than that of the Dark Queen.

Huma grinned then and saw that the glow had faded from the top of the obelisk. There was a rumbling in the ground, as if the tower were trying to shake the lance from its side like an animal chewing at an arrow in its flank. Cracks, bathed in a cold, blue light appeared, radiating outward from the point where the lance was buried in the obsidian surface. There was a roaring, like a gale through trees, as the cracks expanded up and down the side of the obelisk from top to the bottom.

The Queen turned, saw the damage, and knew what it meant. She knew that the source of her sudden power, of her impossible victory, was being destroyed. She screamed, "No! NO! It's too late!"

But even as she shouted, the cracks widened and chunks of the obsidian broke loose, falling in slow motion. A rumbling, like all the thunder ever heard, washed over the soldiers of both armies, as bigger pieces of the tower fell; the top of the obelisk collapsed inward with a demonic roar.

Huma, unsure of what he had done, struggled to his feet. He was lightheaded, dizzy. He was sick to his stomach and thought that he would pass out. The wound he had suffered pained him greatly, and he felt his blood pumping from his body and dripping down his side. But he ignored the sensation, watching as the obelisk seemed to die before him.

The Queen kicked at the flanks of her horse. It leaped from the base of the structure, but then she turned. She waved her arms, shouting, her words lost in the rumbling, thundering destruction of the ominous black tower. Lightning flashed from it, lancing upward into the clouds that were boiling angrily above them.

A glowing ball of red appeared in front of her, trailing sparks. It flashed upward toward the dragonlance and exploded around it. For a moment, she believed that she had destroyed the dragonlance and that her power would return. But, when the glow had faded, the lance was still there, embedded in the obelisk like an arrow through the heart of a warrior. An arrow through the heart of her power.

The Queen turned her horse again and rode to the foot of the giant black tower. She tried to seize the dragonlance, but her fingers fell far short. Carefully, she slipped her feet under her so that she could stand on the horse's back, but even then she could not reach the lance. Shaking with frustration and rage, she leaped. For a moment, her fingers curled around the shaft of the lance. Suddenly, she screamed in pain and fell to the trembling ground.

As she fell, her horse bolted from her, fleeing from the field, trampling the bodies of the dead. The Queen got to her feet, holding her hands in front of her as if they had been badly burned. She turned and stared into the deepening of the night, her hatred stabbing out toward Huma like a beacon at the edge of the ocean. She stepped back so that she was leaning against the smooth surface of the obelisk, trying to draw power from it.

Wind now swirled around the obelisk as the internal rumbling of it built until the ground vibrated. For a moment, nothing happened, and it seemed that the tower had healed itself. Some of the cracks started to disappear and the icy blue light that wrapped the structure began to fade.

Strangely, abruptly, the rumbling started again, and the cracks reappeared and widened. The obelisk seemed to shrink in on itself and tremble as if fighting with itself. Then suddenly, it exploded, blowing apart in a blinding flash of blue-white light.

The force of the concussion knocked Huma, and those with him, from their feet. Tiny bits of obsidian rained down on them, kicking up dust on the distant hills like the first drops of rain after a summer drought. Stunned by all he had seen, Huma lay staring at the clearing sky as the clouds overhead melted away until he was staring into the deepening of the heavens, studded with thousands of stars.

The Dark Queen, like the obsidian obelisk, was gone. There were bits of the tower scattered all over the plain, but nothing was left of the Queen. She had been banished when the obelisk had exploded in fire and light.

With the silver-haired woman's help, Huma sat up. Before him was a smoking crater where the obelisk had been. Around it were the bodies of his men killed by the Queen's army, but her soldiers, living and dead, were all gone, washed away in the flash of light and smoke and fire that had destroyed the obelisk and the Dark Queen's evil power.

Slowly, those of Huma's men who still lived got to

their feet. They were a tired, bloodstained and mud-splattered lot who stared at the crater. One or two of them started forward slowly, as if they didn't believe what they had seen, as if they couldn't believe that the tower had destroyed itself trying to free itself from the dragonlance.

Huma found that he could no longer move. His hands and feet were cold, as if he had spent the day on a winter outing. Breathing hurt him; his lungs ached as he held his breath, inhaling only when the pain became too much for him.

The woman cradled his head in her arms, her eyes heavy with tears.

"We have won," he told her, the joy in his voice unmistakable.

"Yes," she agreed, her voice hushed. "In the end, it was you who saved the day." She tried to smile and failed. "You saved the day just as your men knew you would."

He tried to nod but found the motion made him sick, made his head swim. His eyesight was failing, and he was no longer sure what was going on around him. He tried to smile and asked, "What happened?"

"It was the dragonlance," she said, blinking rapidly. She looked upward, away from his pale face and added, "It cut to the heart of her power and destroyed it. Destroyed it and her army at once."

"I didn't know," said Huma.

"No way you could," she told him.

"My men? How are my men?"

She looked at the field around her. The womenfolk had lighted fires on the surrounding hills. Many of them, looking for husbands, brothers, and sons, slipped among the dead, searching.

"Your men are fine," she lied to him. "Most have survived." Most had died, killed before the obelisk had been destroyed, but she couldn't tell him that.

Almost as if the words soothed him, he relaxed. "That's good," he told her. "Very good. Now that it's over, I can go to sleep. I'm so tired."

She wanted to scream at him. Wanted to order him not to give in to death so easily now, but knew it would do no good. In the fading light, she could see that he looked peaceful. At ease for the first time since she'd known him, now that the war was over and the Dark Queen finally beaten.

She felt him shudder once and realized that he was gone. Gently, she laid him down and then walked to the edge of the crater to retrieve the dragonlance. She wanted it to mark his grave. For a long time she stood looking at him, silently remembering their sacrifice.

They could have had a few fleeting years together as husband and wife, but the cost to the world would have been too great. They had agreed to forego their pleasure so that others could find happiness.

As the tears filled her eyes again, she realized that they had been cheated. She had expected them to have more time together, but that had been cruelly snatched from them.

Without thinking about it, she began to shimmer and glow.

When the remainder of Huma's army finally found him, he lay at the feet of a silver dragon. The beast had stood over him, guarding his body until he could be properly buried.

FROM the Yearning
For War and
the War's Ending

Michael Williams

ONE

In Hospital, Palanthas
April, 353

Athelard to his brother Bayard, greetings,

I hear in a letter from our mother that you, too,
have chosen the path of a father you do not remember, of the older brother who sends you this. That you
have chosen, if indeed it was ever a choice, to take up
the calling, to enter, as Mother has written, *the
ancient and holy Solamnic Orders, now that the siege
has been lifted, the armies of the enemy driven back
once again from our land and from those things we are
honor bound to defend by the Measure and the Code.*

As always, Mother's words are graceful, high-
sounding. I hear them as I sit by a window that must
face west, for I can feel the warmth on my face most
deeply when the loudest bird song is passing, when the

first crickets of what must be early spring begin that scrape and rattle that brings night to the ear. And since the handwriting in my letter no doubt will surprise you, I must tell you one thing more, that in this room sits a nurse, attentive and kind, who writes down the long words, the longer thoughts from brother to brother. Her voice is soft, muffled. Harder to hear than the sound of the birds or the crickets. I can only imagine she has turned away from me as she writes down what I have to say to you.

She asks me to continue, her voice louder now. As I have said, she is kind. She is attentive.

I wish that when I was younger I had paid more attention to bird song. My nurse has told me that the birds in the evening sing the names of those who will die in the night. I have no itch for prophecy, but I suppose that the song is subtle, that perhaps different birds sing at different times of the day, or that perhaps there is even a language among them—a sort of call and response, some quarrels I might understand had I listened earlier and more intently. It would be good to eavesdrop—something to pass the time in what the surgeons insist on calling *this house of peace and healing*. But it is the land now that is peaceful and healed, the hospital haunted with battle and pain and uneven memory.

Because that story you have heard about the blind is only true in part, that when sight goes, the other senses . . . sharpen? Intensify? Bayard, if this world were all poetry and justice and balance, and beauty no accident—if things took place because they were more beautiful or poetic or just—then the myths regarding the blind would be physical law: what war hath taken away, nature restoreth, or a similar poetry. But it is not like that. What you do in the blackness is pay more attention, and if cardinals and finches and larks all sound the same to you, it reminds you only that long ago there were some things you neglected.

But you cannot blame yourself for the oversights of childhood and of study, because any tale that is entirely and unarguably true, whether of blindness or of birds or of battle, or of something purely noble in any of these things, is the wildest tale of all, for none of these are purely understood until we sink into darkness, until we rise on thin and delicate wings, or until we carry a lance while the fire descends.

Our mother says you are "eager" for news of the siege, for accounts of heroism and high adventure, that you practice your swordplay in the parlor, much to her ill ease and at the mortal peril of her heirloom vases and silver. That you sing of "returning souls to Huma's breast" as your sword dances carelessly near cabinet or candle.

The words of the chant are "Return *this* soul to Huma's breast," Bayard. To be spoken over the fallen body of a comrade, not over the phantom draconians you fight amidst Mother's porcelain. The chant is more individual, more personal than you have imagined. But you were not there at the siege.

Do you know that sometimes the darkness seems more penetrable? That it shifts from a uniform blackness to a muddy or even rust-colored brown? Or it seems to shift to those colors I believe I still remember. Then, perhaps, it is only from the monotony of dark that I imagine the colors arising. Perhaps even dead eyes play tricks, as the living eye plays over the white on white of a blizzard and begins out of boredom or dazzlement to see impossible reds and greens in a snowfall.

For the snow, pure white on white and over white,

began to fall as we were on the road to the tower, as we heard the footmen grumble about *Now snow on top of everything else*, Sir Heros grumbling back to me, *now grumbling on top of snow*, as I set his helmet and sword in front of me on the saddle so that the blanket I had wrapped about my shoulders would cover them, too, would keep them spotless and dry for the battle we knew was coming, inevitable as weather.

It was a mist at first, undecided between snow or rain, though you could guess it would decide as soon as the temperature dropped, the steam rising like mist from the horses, from the breath of the soldiers, until we rode through a fog and I could see no farther than Sir Heros in front of me. I followed his horse and assumed he followed the man in front of him, and he the man in front of him, and somehow I reasoned that whoever led our column had ridden out of the mist by now or at least had the wisdom to know where he was going. And the ground turned to mud beneath us— not that you could see it, but you could hear the hooves of the horses suck and spatter within it. Had I foresight I would have seen this as training for blindness. But foresight in this country was as dim as the horseman ahead of you.

And the footmen sang no songs about Huma's breast, about the kingfisher, crown, sword or rose, or about the high honor of battle, but a new drinking song picked up on the march—a song the knights had hushed before because it was an embarrassment to ladies, a song I suppose they figured was no longer embarrassing because there were no ladies among us. Perhaps you have heard it, the real song of the army:

Your one true love's a sailing ship
That anchors at our pier.

We lift her sails, we man her decks,
We scrub the portholes clear,

And yes, our lighthouse shines for her,
And yes, our shores are warm;
We steer her into harbor—
Any port in a storm.

The sailors stand upon the docks,
The sailors stand in line,
As thirsty as a dwarf for gold
Or centaurs for cheap wine.

For all the sailors love her,
And flock to where she's moored,
Each man hoping that he might
Go down, all hands on board.

I trust you will not show this song to Mother, for I could almost hear the nurse blush as I sang it, she who has bathed me and dressed my wounds over many weeks. As I think further, perhaps it would be best to show none of this to Mother. The story becomes no more pleasant.

We were speaking of snow and the trip to the tower and the indecent singing of footmen. One of the knights—it might even have been Sturm Brightblade, whose name you have no doubt heard in the histories and will hear again and again in this story—took exception to the song, and raised his voice in the Huma chant of which you are, dear Bayard, so fond. It faded into the fog behind us, for few knights took it up, weighted down as they were by the drizzling cold, and the footmen were not about to join in, the only version of that chant I had heard pass their lips an immodest parody in which the breast is no longer Huma's, is a different and softer reward entirely for the warrior.

I keep forgetting that the nurse is here. The Measure is still new to me. And I forget where . . .

The snow, she says.

The snow. It was misery on horseback. I trust it was more miserable on foot, for boots were scarce, and most of the men had wrapped their feet in rags against frostbite and the sharp edges of ice. Breca, an old veteran among the foot soldiers, had bargained, begged, and finally threatened my boots from me on the road to the tower. And though I was angry at first, when I saw the boy to whom he gave the boots, saw the blisters and blackness about his ankles, the blood through the rags bright on the merciless road, the threats were unnecessary.

We passed the first night of the blizzard in marching. Breca returned the boots the next morning. Averted his eyes, said that the boy had no further need, that he rested with Huma now. Breca rejoined his column, and Sir Heros, uncomfortable but safe at least upon horseback, told me I had *seen the dark side of war, that men die, boys die, laying down their lives for justice and for a higher cause*. It was almost inscribed, surely a speech he must have prepared for this moment as a promise to our father, something that smacked of the *Song of Huma* to reassure and hearten his squire, the son of his fallen comrade. As if I had no idea that men die, boys die, from the ambushes that had followed us for a week. Breca, among others, began to claim that we guided our march by ambush—that when we were waylaid, again the knights were assured that we headed in the right direction.

For draconians, Bayard, do not fight in the lists.

The Dragon Highlords may show elegance, breeding, but the war has nothing to do with the Measure, with a stately dance of challenge and courtesy. Often a footman would drop at the rear of the column, a barbed black arrow sprouting in his back, a chorus of catcalls and sometimes hisses from the woods nearby. Indeed they have no love of the cold; their blood thickens and their movements slow. But there are humans among them, and even the draconians can survive such weather, wrapped in furs they do not bother to cure or tan, and they know we have no love of the cold either.

Two days from the tower they struck a final ambush, a flurry of arrows from a stand of vallenwoods, falling harmlessly short. We could see them through the mist and the snow and the bare branches, some recognizably human, all moving like spectres or shadows. A few of our archers returned fire, their arrows falling short, too, which was what the dragonarmies wanted, their own supplies virtually endless.

One of them called out, *Footmen! Listen to the voice of the dragonarmies!* Melodramatic, yes, but effective across the mist and the dead land. Our bowmen ceased fire, glancing at one another nervously.

Footmen! the man shouted again. *How do you like being fodder for the knights?* An old trick, spreading dissension in the ranks, and indeed some of the knights—Lord Derek, Lord Alfred, our own Sir Heros—were outraged, Heros reaching back to me for his sword, Derek preparing to charge the stand of trees, alone if necessary, Sturm and his strange companions bristling in their wet saddles, until the loud voice of Breca stilled the bravery and muttering in the column.

I expect I could explain it better over here.

Perhaps you could, the dragonsoldier shouted

back. *But answer me this: have you ever seen a dead Solamnic Knight?*

It was as though the eyes of the world had refocused. We knew it was a lie, *a base ignoble charge,* as Heros would have said, and I thought of our father returned on his shield. I thought of the centuries since the Cataclysm, of the Code, the Kingfisher, the Crown the Sword and the Rose, of the sacrifices. But all of that meant nothing after such a question, do you understand? For it was Breca's answer, not Sturm's or Hero's or Derek's, we awaited, had to await.

The smell of oil in the room. My nurse has lit a lamp so she may continue to write. Bad for the eyes, my dear. They play tricks enough as it is. We shall continue this in the morning.

TWO

It was Breca's answer we awaited, there on the road to the tower, the landscape white on white and blending into a faraway whiteness, only the thin dark lines of the trees and the shapes among them giving us any idea of distance, of measure. And the answer, though it lay nowhere within the rules set down by chivalry, not a *thee* or a *thou* or an elegant challenge, could not draw complaint from even the most strict of the knights—after all, he was not one of them, and after all, the footmen listened and applauded, their backs to the rising wind.

Every dead Solamnic Knight I've seen, Breca shouted, *had about a dozen of your lizard boys on his dance card. We find them around the bodies, all statued and pretty like a damn rock garden.*

The footmen laughed, but most of the knights sat uneasily atop their uneasy horses, who pawed and snorted as though they had crossed into a country of leopards. Sturm and Lord Alfred smiled. But Sturm had traveled with outlandish folk—he had, after all, served with dwarves.

But what even Sturm and Lord Alfred knew, what most of them knew, and Breca especially, was that the dragonsoldier was not finished with Breca, that this attack was as fierce and as lethal as any with a bow or with those terrible curved swords I still see in sleep until the welcome darkness of morning comes again. For the heart of the battle was at stake before the arrows flew, before the swords clashed, at least in the eyes of the knights, who thought in terms of spirit and morale, of a high game which begins not when the first piece is taken nor even the first pawn moved, but when the players sit before the chessboard.

Breca, on the other hand, was past strategy and morale, safe for now in another world I came to witness in the weeks that followed, in the tower and in the waiting. He was a swordsman, any thrust the same as any other, to be deflected or parried if he were still to call himself a swordsman. The snow settled on his helmet until I feared that soon it would cover him, cover him entirely in the face of his enemies, and then cover all of us—on foot, on horseback, on muleback—until what remained was a pitiful series of drifts in the country of the enemy.

And the dragonsoldier called once more out of the vallenwoods, *You aren't dressed well for such bravery, footman. Even from here I can see the dents in the armor. I can tell where your breastplate is crumpled and useless, where my sword would do the most damage. Your feet are probably wrapped in rags, though the snow is too heavy to tell for certain. Yet I suppose that such is the finery that knights issue their footmen.*

And they retreated into the thick boles and branches of the woods, so that they probably did not hear Breca's retort, which we heard nonetheless, which the footmen heard, which rode in my ears with its flat and furious blessing as we approached the gates of the tower:

You think we dress up to kill hogs?

Inside the tower gates, dismounting, the breathing and steam from the horses misting the air, but not as densely as the snow had misted the air outside, I remember most of all my sense of relief. Of course we were to learn of the frailties later, that in its endurance without change and restoration the tower had become indefensible, but at the time the walls seemed tall and strong, the fortress unbreachable. I would imagine, Bayard, that you have heard the stories, and that in the hearing you have imagined walls of your own, more vividly than the ones I could describe, down to the stone upon stone, to the mortar and to the tightly arranged masonry that permits no mortar, and perhaps your walls are as accurate, as real as the ones I saw, because I knew no more of fortresses and their construction than I did the songs of birds.

Now we fight from defense, I thought. Now we fight at advantage. But more than that, we fight from warmth, on the leeward side of the walls. That warmth, that comfort, was most important then, and the chambers to which Heros and I were escorted, as damp and drafty as an old attic, were a palace, were more than enough. I am spoiled now in the hospital, for there is a fire here and curtains, curtains that for all I can tell may be sackcloth, a plain burlap, but nonetheless do what curtains were intended to do in that time before we saw fit to embroider and adorn them.

If Heros had known what I was thinking, he would have said I thought like a footman. He would have

been right, for they were talking when I went to tend
to the horses, most of them wrapped in blankets and
standing, sitting, lying around the banked fires that
spangled the dark inner courtyards, a few others, the
older veterans, crouched and circled around Breca,
who sat upon his helmet, cupping his enormous red
hands as he lit his pipe, the glow arising from the bowl
spreading over his face in a light both saintly and violent.

I nodded to Breca, receiving a nod in return as he
singled me out from the darkness. He had what Heros
called *the ingrained politeness to his betters*, not as
common as you might imagine among footmen, but a
quality all were urged to adopt and cultivate. Still, I
liked to think—and *do* think—this initial politeness to
me was something more, stood for something. After
all, he remembered the boots on the trail to the tower,
and perhaps in that soldier's mind used to self-
preservation and necessity, small gestures of decency
counted for more than the horse and elaborate armor.
Then again, he may have thought only that I was foolish, or felt sorry for me because of my youth, or he
may have thought all of these things and not have
been wrong in the thinking.

His face glowed above the pipe like a signal fire, or
it could have been from the reflected light of his audience. For there were twenty or thirty men around him,
some of them Lord Alfred's age, several nearly as
young as I, but most in between—as I have said, the
veterans. All of them were like children in the presence of a storyteller, but instead of awaiting the tales
of high deeds and magic we heard and you still hear in
the spacious courts of Solamnia, they were questioning, all questions amounting to one: *What chance do
we have to hold this fort?*

Nor did he coddle them, assure them, as the storytellers do at Mother's—*so it is elves you want, young master? Then you shall hear of elves.* None of that for footmen. Breca was honest, or pretended honesty in a way that came closer to the truth than simple honesty, which sometimes allows for dishonest imaginings.

I expect, he said, *that a centaur designed this tower. I expect he done so after a celebration of victory, on account of the building speaks more of wine than of tactics. I count four gates in the fortress, which is three more than you need, four more than I'd fancy now that we've got inside.*

And what is worse than four gates I will tell you is four wide gates, gates where a half a dozen centaurs might gallop in abreast. The dragonarmies don't mind spending men, and even seem to favor spending draconians, seeing as they have so many of them. What is more, they're liable to send dragons or some terrible machinery right through our doors. And he sat back, the smoke curling like snow or a morning fog, like the mist from the horses, around his enormous, ragged head. The footmen waited, not for the quick and easy answer, the inspiring speech that would tell them that despite all these things, we would win by tactics and by bravery, that one man in the service of Solamnia could defeat a dozen draconians. They awaited his judgment on the walls.

Which are not of your best material or design. I am not a stone mason, nor am I a betting man—this last drawing laughter from some of the older soldiers—*but if I was, I would wager that a fat man at a healthy trot could cause structural damage to this mighty fortress.*

More laughter followed, and I drew nearer the group, curry-comb in hand, the horses forgotten. If what he was saying were indeed true—and I had no cause to doubt him—we were cornered, backed into a shoddy and vulnerable place where the walls stood not between us and the dragonarmies, but between us and our own escape. And the footmen sat here joking and spinning stories.

Look around you, Breca muttered as the laughter died again, as some of the men looked up uneasily, skeptically, looking into the rose embroidered on my doublet as if it were an orb of prophecy, looking at me as though I were a messenger from another planet.

Look around you. Soon enough you'll see the birds no longer light here. The news has a way of spreading amongst the animals, and not just from kind to kind. Soon enough you'll see the rats leaving. The horses have the same instincts, but they're tethered and stabled and—he glanced at me, smiled briefly, and stared at his pipe—*and curried. All that keeps any of us here is the knights, who think they can hold this place with honor alone. Honor is well and good, but it don't stop a spear, boys. Best it can do is leave a cleaner wound.*

But don't fret, boys, he concluded, looking directly at me with those huge gray eyes that the folk tales say are the sign of marksmen or madmen, I forget which. *Don't fret, for at least you've found yourself a warm place to die.*

Not a comforting philosophy to take with you back into the upper chambers, where there were swords and armor to be polished, and wine and a warmer hearth, and where the truth muttered below you, scarcely heard for the crackling of the fire, like a ghost in the stables or the barracks.

Marksmen, she tells me. *Gray eyes for the marksman.* Then was it green for the lunatic or for the poet?

Instead of the legends of eyes let me talk of monotony, of the boredom in waiting for battle. It is no quick thing, no gap between lightning and thunder, but a long waiting in which breastplate and sword shimmer uselessly, in which you worry the horses into a sleek and healthy gloss, in which you watch the sky and speculate on wonders. No time to be slow-witted, this waiting for battle, but a time to attend to tasks, to trivial duties, until the duties become reflex and you return to your thoughts alone.

But even among the thoughtful and the imaginative, there were great dangers. After all, dear brother, there was an enemy approaching, an enemy magnified by his absence. The dragonarmies grew larger, their atrocities greater, as we waited and imagined. A story passed through the ranks that the slaughter of Plainsmen had been even more horrible than first reported, that the draconians had found a way, in the dark recesses of lore and intricate magic, to breed more of their kind upon the Plainswomen—a hardier strain, maturing quickly and able to withstand extremes of climate—and that on the plains these children grew, feeding first upon what little provision the country offered, then turning upon themselves in a frenzy like sharks, until only the largest and most hardy of the brood survived. Survived to be armed with the black bow and the terrible curved knife, which they would carry over the miles and the snow to the Tower of the High Clerist.

And in addition to the rumors of war, a nightmare closer to home, for the second night in the tower the wine ceased to flow in the quarters of the knights, and we turned to water and to mare's milk, knowing that those, too, would dry in the long weeks of waiting. We were fortunate, then, that it was cold, for the food did not spoil as readily, but even the youngest eye could pass over the stores in the larders and see there was less today, would be less tomorrow. Soon it would be biscuit, parched corn. Then horses, and some of the older footmen talked ironically of rats, providing they are stupid enough to still be here when the time comes down to them.

So you occupied your time upon other thoughts, in other pursuits. The footmen wagered, exchanging coins over the strange, many-sided dice from the east. None wagered against Sturm's friend the kender, who eagerly sought to join each game, standing on tiptoe to peer over the shoulders of the crouching footmen, once climbing the back of a rather tall archer for a closer look at the proceedings, only to be shaken off like a dog shakes off water. On that occasion I asked Breca if it would hurt to let the little fellow play, and he told me that I had yet to learn the difference between disdain and respect. Told me that compassion toward a kender was the ruin of fortunes, or some such rural proverb I scorned until later that night, when I had lost a substantial amount of money to the little creature, trying to guess under which of three walnut shells he had placed a piece of dried corn.

Indeed, I was no gambler, but I was drawn by the kender, by the sense of childhood and of play, by the sense that he felt distracted from his true business by the preparations for siege. It reminded me of how things stood with me ten years ago, when I was six and put away childish things in the service of Solamnia, and perhaps those memories lost me even more money at dice, for I challenged the kender at gaming often, trying to decide whether I pitied him or envied him.

The other outlandish folk were more distant, in keeping with the customs of their people. The dwarf was impatient for battle, at the ramparts often, wrapped in metal and furs and a sullen quiet, brandishing his wicked-looking axe and staring out over the expanse of snow for dragons, armies, movement. I had little to say to him, and suspected he preferred it that way.

Nor had I much to say to the elf maiden, exotic, distant, and a little frightening in her shining and most unfeminine armor. Golden hair, green eyes—the legend that their women are more beautiful than ours cannot be proved true or false by one example, one woman, but if it could, no doubt the elves would have sent this one for comparison.

Yet unlike many of the girls of our country, posing, giggling, bearing garlands and gloves for the knight of their fancy, for any boy at the borders of knighthood, this one, this Laurana, was not caught up in her own beauty. Indeed, she seemed to have forgotten or be forgetting such things, rapt in a story of lances and of high battle, the like of which I could not know, with all my imagining, with all my waiting. And forgive me, kind lady who copies my words to an absent brother, but now it seems that flowers and scarves, the tedious attention to hair, to the slope of a dress on the shoulders—it seems that such things are distant now, the meaningless steps to a dance I have left early, no longer able to see my partner. More important now is the memory of the elf maiden, kneeling and glittering perhaps less brightly than I remember but as brightly as I saw her at the time, above the lances she had brought for the defense of the tower, offering to instruct us in their use, had we not been so rigid and scornful and dazzled as to refuse her teaching.

For the lances were the great mystery as we waited, what Breca might have called the wild card in the deck, the painted shard of lead that served as the spot on the die. But not at all like a die so loaded, the lances seemed larger and heavier than they were, lying in the courtyard of the fortress—larger and heavier because of the legends around them. For you remember the *Song of Huma*, that *he took up the dragonlance, he* took up the story, and the story, whatever it was, lay somewhere upon each of the weapons, so at times you might imagine that they gleamed with some light beyond polishing, beyond tricks of reflected sun or moonlight.

But I had grown up among legends, and though I had to admire the workmanship of the lances, had handled several of them in the long days of waiting, like the most Measured of our knights I believed this light, this mystery, was the play of wishes and dreams over an exquisite but finally quite ordinary weapon. And believing this I refused the instructions of elf and female in the use of the lances.

Instead of instructions, I listened to the laughter of gamblers and the songs, songs which, if not invented in secret by Breca, were invented in secret by one much like him:

> Oh where the north wall is crumbling,
> Let us put mortar and brick,
> Let us stack limestone on limestone
> Laid down with a promise and lick,
>
> And wherever limestone will fail us
> And mortar and brick give way,
> Let us stack footman on footman
> Laid down with the promise of pay.

And listened to the politics from on high, to the speculations of Heros and the grumbling of the foot soldiers. For something was clearly afoot, and Heros described it as a bitter dance of moons, Derek's on the wane and Sturm's waxing, power flowing like light away from one man into another.

Heros championed neither of the factions: both were, as he would say, *too variable*. There was Sturm

on the rise, once dishonored, once the companion of
dwarves and kender and elves and the vagabond mage
with the hourglass eyes whom nobody had trusted or
quite mistrusted, and could the road back to honor lie
in the company of such a patchwork crew? Heros did
not have the answer, and without certain answers it
was his nature to disapprove.

Derek, on the other hand, had ceased to be an
option, his armor too bright from polishing too much
and too long, his eyes too bright from something far
more unsettling than wine or the fever of approaching
battle. He had taken to winding a horn in imitation of
Huma, and at all hours of the night the footmen were
called on alert, equipped and assembled to find only
that the alarm had been raised by Lord Derek himself,
alarmed by what he considered the unnatural
closeness—or sometimes distance—of the red moon
and the silver. And the men did not complain loudly,
nor comment too loudly when Lord Derek wore the
horns of a stag on his helmet, as if in recalling the old
divine contest between the hero and the quarry, he
had chosen to play both the hunter and the hunted.

It was one night, not long before his riding forth,
pursuing a disaster of which you have no doubt heard,
that I was awakened once again by the sound of the
horn winding. I armed myself, thinking continually,
*Perhaps this time, perhaps he will not cry wolf for-
ever*, and moved through a courtyard as silent as if
nothing had happened, the footmen crouched around
the fires sleeping or drinking or dicing, or drinking
and dicing themselves to sleep, all as if the night were
soundless and as safe as any other. And of all these,
only Breca watched the battlements where, outlined
in red and silver, a glittering figure all metal and antler
sounded a lonely horn.

I stood beside Breca, who never took his eyes from

the solitary figure as he leaned on the pommel of his two-handed sword, chuckling a dry laugh as desolate as the winter outside the fortress and, glancing sideways at me, murmuring, *That one has a thousand deaths on him. He has been dismounted by the winter and the ice and the waiting and there is not a thing in the Measure to cover this, so they will do nothing.*

And when I ventured that perhaps Lord Derek had lost some faculties, but that the most brilliant of generals often seemed at sea in the times of peace and waiting, Breca asked me where I had read such things, *for you must have read them.*

This one is not only at sea but capsized, he said. *For they all are at sea, Crown, Sword, or Rose, and this one at his best had not enough sense to pour piss from a boot if the directions was on the heel. And this,* he said, pausing to light his pipe, the sword still upright beneath his elbow, point to the ground, *this is the one they will surely pick to lead us.*

And so in the early days of the siege, before Lord Derek unraveled completely and rode off into death and the horrible oblivion of legends, we spent our time watching the battlements and the dwindling food, looking for smoke on the horizon and listening to the sound of the horn by night and the rumor by day that somewhere, forgotten within the bowels of the fortress, lay something the kender had stumbled upon in his curious wanderings, something that could—if time and place and desperation were to meet—alter the course of the siege.

It is tiring to remember this all, Bayard, for already I grow unaccustomed to the old habit of seeing, and though it would seem that the memory of vision would be that much more strongly burned into the thoughts of the newly blind, when you lose the habits of seeing you often lose the memories of sight, for the motions of the eyes and the mind grow rusty and with them the thoughts established before through those motions.

And what is more, the light must be fading, night must be approaching, for the warmth that settles upon the sill of my window is fading now and I smell smoke and burning tallow as I face into the room. Some things there are for which the night should have no ear, and among those are the ride of Lord Derek and the disasters that followed. So again in the morning, if my nurse will only remain patient—patient and undeniably kind—I shall recount the darkest leg of the journey.

THREE

It was rumor that passed among us once more, rumor again of movement and of battle, but this time there seemed more substance to it, for on the battlements and in the chambers the knights were silent, the only storm arising from a conference room high in the tower, where Alfred and Derek and Sturm waged a war of words and of rising voices, an occasional shout or a fragment of speech caught when the wind died and the sound descended to the courtyards and the barracks of the fortress.

We could make nothing of this debate above us, these loud quarrels like the distant cries of predatory birds, but it was different from the nights of the winding horn, the sudden preparations for the false alarms, for now we did nothing but wait—no preparations, no rumors of what was taking place beyond *something is taking place*—and the fortress incredibly silent, as though the horses were lost in thought and the vermin had quit the rafters and the middens by instinct, going Huma knows where into the winter darkness..

I awoke on the second night to the jostling of Heros. He was fully armed, having dressed himself while I slept, as though there was no time to waken a squire (or as I came to see later, as though somehow in arming himself he took part in a strange penance, having last performed the task on the night of vigil before his knighthood ceremonies).

Derek is riding out, he said flatly, averting his eyes as my thoughts rose out of sleep, constructing once again from the bare walls and the damp cold of the chamber just where it was I had awakened, at first thinking that Heros was announcing retreat, surrender, abandonment, then realizing it was none of these and all of these at the same time—that an attack too monstrous to be ill-advised and too foolish to be heroic was set to begin, and that in the courtyards of the fortress the footmen were marshalling.

There was nothing to be said, nothing to be asked except, *And you?*

His eyes still avoided me. *Sturm feels that the defense of the fortress remains the defense of Palanthas. I agree with Sturm.*

But not agreement, I thought. *Nothing more than sheer and deliberate survival, if not a lasting survival then the weeks, the days, or even the hours that staying behind will give us. That is why you have armed yourself without recourse to squire and to ceremony. That is why you are glad that the room is dark, Sir Heros, Solamnic Knight of the Sword.* But there was no blame in this, Bayard, no blame except for the old and honored folly that would make a man ashamed to breathe when his companions breathed no longer, and with that blame what the blame could not banish—a pride in Sir Heros that he could feel the shame, that such folly was both old and honored.

———

From the window of the corridor they looked diminished, frail in their armor and swords and pikes as they assembled, stamped the cold from their feet, and fell into line behind the mounted knights. I could single out Breca in the foremost column, standing a head taller than those around him, and once I believe he glanced up at the window to where I was standing, the flatness of his eyes apparent even from a distance, even through the shadows of the wall and the dark air of the morning. And perhaps because of that darkness there was no expression I could see on his face, but there is an expression I remember, may have imagined in this permanent and greater darkness from which I speak to you.

For if an expression could be featureless, void of fear and of dread and finally of hope, containing if anything only a sort of resignation and resolve, that was Breca's expression and those of his companions, saying (if such a blankness, a nothing can say anything), *This is not as bad as I imagined but worse than I expected*, and nothing more than that when the doomed gates opened—the very gates he had called indefensible a short week before he marched out onto the plains and into the lifting darkness.

And then again it was the waiting, the waiting no chronicler records in accounts of this or of any battle. You have heard, certainly, how the news of Derek's defeat was brought to us, of the bodies draped over the red-eyed horses and of the soft threats of the Dragon Highlord. Of knights so ruled by the Measure that they let the enemy speak, let him taunt, until one among us (the elfmaiden it was), not ruled by an old and wasted chivalry but by something more profound and ancient—an instinct for survival underlined by anger—wounded him with a well-placed green arrow. Of listening to the birds who remained by night as they sang their songs of bereavement, their songs perhaps of Heros and of Sturm.

Again it was the waiting, until they attacked and breached the walls.

And how can I explain to you, Bayard, what it was like when the waiting ended, how the draconians charged from a place beyond vision, growing in size and in number as they covered the miles from their camp unto the foot of the walls, sidling like crabs from the path of our arrows, rushing through the rain of oil and pitch we set down before them, clutching the walls with a fierce suction of the hands and climbing like chameleons, like salamanders (for some of them were pitch-covered, burning as they climbed) up to the crest of the battlements, where the sound of metal on metal, of metal on flesh, rose up around me and banished thought.

And you do not stop to reflect on the drawing of blood in anger. All the preparation in swordsmanship, in tactical combat and even in the vows of bravery and steadfastness adds up to nothing like the Measure tells you, none of these fanciful promises to live your life so that the death of your enemy is made worthy by your living, for who knew how long the living would last after your enemy—or even the last of the enemies—had fallen. But the preparing led only to the surprisingly heavy lunge of the sword and the small resistance of armor and skin and gristle and finally bone against it, when the training tells you, *I suppose this one is dead and where is the next one nearest*, and as though in a corridor of dreams the voice of the dwarf beside you echoing, *Draw forth your sword, son, before he hardens into stone*, and another before you all green scales and arms, who is falling then over the parapet, head and metallic jaw collapsed beneath the swift rising hammer of the dwarf, and the thought clears for a moment again to discover three more of them crouched in a file on the battlements, small red eyes flickering behind the bristle of curved weapons like some horrible boars in a thicket you are supposed to remember but cannot, so you let the thought alone and try the sword again, one of them falling and two of them trampled in a flood of knights which in turn is bearing you like baggage or a fallen comrade down the steps from the battlements so quickly that for a moment you feel you are falling, assuring yourself that this cannot be, for a fall would take place much more slowly, but then in the final fall who was to say how time would collapse or how the mind would suspend the fragment of years, trying to remember everything, but then, on your feet and buoyed by your own heavy running, you see the doors of the tower and within them the elf maiden shining, and you think, *So this is death which is more than I expected but everything I imagined*, but then you are inside the tower with the last of them, the heavy doors closing behind you and the sound of bolt upon bolt upon bolt staying them fast.

No, it is not pretty to write, and be sure it is not pretty to tell. But there is more, and soon I will speak from recollection of sound and rumor only. Soon the story continues without eyes, and the ugliness passes. Bear with me, my dear, my nurturing one, the last hour of the telling.

The magic of the tower was sealed for the last time, and there for the first time I knew what it was that the kender had discovered in a deep chamber. No larger than a dove, than the heart of a child, the orb was glowing with a light and whiteness surpassing the downpour of sun on the snow we had ridden through days on end, we had watched from the walls in our waiting. And it seemed fitting that before the darkness all things should resolve once more into white, as the elf maiden Laurana began to instruct us, quietly and urgently, in the final dance we were too stubborn, to noble to learn when the dance would avail us. The lances, surprisingly light, we placed at arrest, in the noble absurd salute to the thing we knew was coming because we heard from beyond the walls the stuttering thunder of heavy wings, the breathing, and though we could not guess through which wall, which aperture it would drive its ancient and sinuous head, it was coming, we knew.

And the mortar and stones of the northern wall shook and flaked, and Laurana seized the orb (though never again would I see her as I turned northwards, lifting the flange of the lance to my shoulder, its butt secure beneath my arm that was stronger now, having something to do at last after all the cold and the waiting and the loss of Breca and of Heros, it seemed, who was not among us and somehow forgiven by his absence and the meaning of his absence) and a great sweetness fell upon me, whether from the orb itself, as the legends say, or from that moment of repose in the mind when, pushed past all endurance, you can say *at least there is no more of this, nothing left but a brief pain and then peace surpassing*. We proffered the lances: the Solamnic salute, the prayer that our lives henceforth be worthy of the taking of lives, and again I offered the prayer with the others, thinking of Heros, of Breca, that through all the silliness of the prayer their wounds somehow were made cleaner.

And there was confusion, a shrapnel of walls, for a moment those dull reptilian eyes glowing a red that was lifeless in its ancient light, and I thought of Breca's eyes and what the poet says of foxfire, and there was heat unsurpassed like the Cataclysm had come again, then complete and abiding dark.

And from there, dear Bayard, and dear woman whose patience has been long, has been stalwart, it came to me as it came to you, by report and by rumor. How as we brought the lances to arrest, Sturm was upon the battlements, trading his death for our time in an impossible stand, how the lance of the Dragon Highlord rode through him cleanly and finally, how the sun burst. How Laurana spoke to the Dragon Highlord Kitiara over his remains, with the fortress, the countryside, with all of Krynn watching or listening as the future turned on her heart's sounding. All of this having everything and nothing to do with all of us.

And I heard, as they drew me to the window, through the bandages and the pain and the fading smell of my flesh and the flesh of others, Sturm's funeral begin in what must have been sunlight, and of the many words spoken over the body only these last in recollection, vivid and fathomless as the coded song of the birds I am hearing once more through the windows of the hospital, saying:

Free from the smothering clouds of war
As he once rose in infancy,
The long world possible and bright before him,
Lord Huma, deliver him.

Upon the torches of the stars
Was mapped the immaculate glory of childhood;
From that wronged and nestling country,
Lord Huma deliver him.

Lord Huma, deliver us all. And deliver especially you, my brother, for last night my nurse and I spoke briefly, spoke quietly of the world remaining after Sturm, after Breca, after Heros, after the passage of my eyes. And with the gift of the sighted for prophecy, she ran down the lists of light, describing the world made possible at the cost of despair, at the cost of the smell of the corpse fires lingering under the herbs and the metal and the fragrance of flowers and clean bedding, at the cost of the sun diminished to warmth only.

And within those lists lie the armies of the Dragon Highlord driven away, as Mother says, *once again from our land and from those things we are honor bound to defend by the Measure and the Code*, of Takhisis back into the void and somewhere unraveling in a dark I can only dream through my darkness, in a story that remains unimaginable because I cannot see its ending. Of the freedom to do what we want, of the wronged and nestling country made right as we raise our children in prosperity and peace, as we commit the young men not to the study of swords but to a study of lore and of history, a study finally of themselves.

She finds comfort in this. She writes the final page in this comfort. But I shall tell you, Bayard, no doubt frustrated by your brother and by history as you dance with the sword in our home. I shall tell you that when these studies commence, when once again young men begin to study themselves, that your training, your ardor, will not go without issue.

For when the time comes, we shall take up arms again.

ABOUT THE WRITERS

A resident of the island of Manhattan, **HAROLD BAKST** has long been a fan of folk and fairy tales. His novel, *The Strange Voyage of Kian the Mariner*, just such a fable about the weird adventures of an unlikely trio of sea explorers, will be published by TSR in 1987.

Bruce, Rooney, the dogs, the computer, and **NANCY VARIAN BERBERICK** romp around in a 130-odd year-old house, a former funeral home, in Blairstown, New Jersey. Her novel, *The Jewels of Elvish*, will be published by TSR in 1988. Were that not enough, her DRAGONLANCE® novel is also cooking for 1988.

Having red hair has not been the only influence on **TONYA R. CARTER'S** life—she was also born the year that Buzz Murdock departed "Route 66." Her first novel, *Red Sands*, will be published by TSR in 1988.

A native Utahan, **DEZRA DESPAIN** now resides in Indianapolis, Indiana, where she works hard at being Supermom and loving wife, but mostly succeeds in just doing the wash on Saturdays. Currently, she is working on a TSR adventure gamebook set in the world of Krynn.

LAURA HICKMAN lives in a 100-year-old Victorian house in rural Wisconsin with her three children, twelve cookie jars, and her childhood sweetheart, **TRACY HICKMAN**. She has written several adventure modules for TSR. She enjoys having lunch with the Lake Geneva Amazons and writing cuddly science-fiction stories.

RICHARD A. KNAAK has contributed to each of the previous best-selling DRAGONLANCE *Tales*. A native Midwesterner, he is of moderate height and moderate looks with one moderately long eyebrow running across his forehead. Old legends to the contrary, he claims this is not a sign that he is either a warlock or a werewolf. The fact that many of his neighbors carry large amounts of wolfsbane and silver on their persons is mere coincidence. He is writing the first DRAGONLANCE® novel for publication in 1988.

KATE NOVAK grew up in Pittsburgh, where she received a

B.A. in Chemistry from the University of Pittsburgh. After getting married, she gave up laboratories; her husband Jeff keeps her from starving while she pursues her writing career. Her works published by TSR include pick-a-path, adventure gamebooks and game modules. She is a Girl Scout leader and a fussy cat owner.

NICK O'DONOHOE, who also wrote "Love and Ale" and "Dragon-flight" for the DRAGONLANCE® *Tales* series, writes mystery novels featuring private eye Nathan Phillips.

KEVIN D. RANDLE is one of the few people ever born in Cheyenne, Wyoming. After a stint in the Army as a helicopter pilot, he attended the University of Iowa, where he paid his tuition by writing about UFOs for a variety of publications. His three science fantasy novels to date include *Once Upon A Murder*, published by TSR. He also writes adventure novels as one half of Eric Helm and hopes to move to Las Vegas, where it is warm in the winter and he can gamble.

BARBARA and SCOTT SIEGEL are a happily married couple who have authored a total of 30 books in diverse areas. In addition to their books, they are proud to have contributed a short story to each volume of the DRAGONLANCE *Tales* series. Barbara and Scott live in New York City, where they continue to search for Krynn cuisine.

The first books **PAUL B. THOMPSON** ever read were *The Iliad* and *The Arabian Nights' Entertainment*. He never recovered. His first science fiction novel, *Sundipper*, is from St. Martin's Press.

MARGARET WEIS is one half of the creative team that has lovingly nurtured into existence the DRAGONLANCE *Chronicles* trilogy, the *Legends* trilogy, and the *Tales* trilogy for TSR. She looks forward to a period of rest and other writing endeavors, after which, if ever, she and **TRACY HICKMAN** will resume the DRAGONLANCE saga.

MICHAEL WILLIAMS'S work has appeared in all six of the DRAGONLANCE novels and in the two previous collections of *Tales*. Newly married, he and his wife Teri live in Louisville. They also have a summer home on Krynn.